HYSTERICAL LAUGHTER

HYSTERICAL LAUGHTER

Four Ancient Comedies About Women

LYSISTRATA, SAMIA, CASINA, HECYRA

Translation, Introduction, and Notes by
DAVID CHRISTENSON

New York Oxford
OXFORD UNIVERSITY PRESS

Oxford University Press is a department of the University of Oxford.
It furthers the University's objective of excellence in research,
scholarship, and education by publishing worldwide.

Oxford New York
Auckland Cape Town Dar es Salaam Hong Kong Karachi
Kuala Lumpur Madrid Melbourne Mexico City Nairobi
New Delhi Shanghai Taipei Toronto

With offices in
Argentina Austria Brazil Chile Czech Republic France Greece
Guatemala Hungary Italy Japan Poland Portugal Singapore
South Korea Switzerland Thailand Turkey Ukraine Vietnam

For titles covered by Section 112 of the US Higher Education Opportunity Act, please visit www.oup.com/us/he for the latest information about pricing and alternate formats.

Published by Oxford University Press
198 Madison Avenue, New York, NY 10016
http://www.oup.com

Library of Congress Cataloging-in-Publication Data
Hysterical laughter : four ancient comedies about women : Lysistrata, Samia, Casina, Hecyra / translation, introduction, and notes by David Christenson.
pages cm
ISBN 978-0-19-979744-8
1. Greek drama (Comedy)--Translations into English. 2. Latin drama (Comedy)--Translations into English. 3. Women--Drama. I. Christenson, David M. (David Michael) II. Aristophanes. Lysistrata. English. 2014. III. Menander, of Athens. Samia. English. 2014. IV. Plautus, Titus Maccius. Casina. English. 2014. V. Terence. Hecyra. English. 2014.
PA3465.A1 2014b
882'.0108--dc23

2014015770

Contents

Preface *vii*

About the Translator *ix*

Introduction *1*

Greek Old Comedy 4

Greek New Comedy 10

Roman Comedy 14

Women in the Ancient World 20

Note on the Translation 30

Further Reading 31

ARISTOPHANES' *LYSISTRATA* 39

Lysistrata 50

MENANDER'S *SAMIA* 115

Samia (The Woman from Samos) 125

PLAUTUS' *CASINA* 163

Casina 172

TERENCE'S *HECYRA* 223

Hecyra (The Mother-in-Law) 236

Appendix: Olympian Deities 285

Preface

This volume uniquely brings together a rich group of comedies about women and gender by the four most prominent (surviving) comic playwrights of Greek and Roman antiquity. It is intended for use not only in a variety of ancient culture and literature in translation courses, but also should benefit those more generally interested in gender and women's studies, theater and theater history, and cultural studies. The introduction, notes, and essays accompanying each comedy, all of which assume no prior background in classical studies, are designed to guide users toward a greater understanding of these plays, without dogmatic interpretation or discouraging the reader's development of her/his own ideas. My primary goal was to produce lively, highly readable translations of the four comedies that are accurate reflections of their originals.

I owe special thanks to Gonda Van Steen, who is responsible for innumerable improvements to my work. Jay Erskine Caldwell, M.D., and Boris Shoshitaishvili deserve hearty thanks for their useful suggestions on a draft of the Introduction. Several outside readers commissioned by Oxford University Press provided invaluable feedback, for which I am deeply appreciative: Niall W. Slater, Emory University; Charles Platter, University of Georgia; Cristina G. Calhoon, University of Oregon; Marie C. Marianetti, Lehman College CUNY; Mary C. English, Montclair State

University. Mary-Kay Gamel, University of California, Santa Cruz, read the entire manuscript and provided excellent suggestions. All remaining errors are of course my own. I am also extremely grateful to Charles Cavaliere of the Press for his unstinting patience and encouragement throughout this process.

About the Translator

David Christenson earned his Ph.D. in Classical Philology at Harvard University. He is Professor of Classics at the University of Arizona, where he has won various mentoring and teaching awards. This is his third volume of translations of ancient comedies. His scholarly publications include a Latin edition and commentary of Plautus' *Amphitruo* (2000), a forthcoming edition and commentary of Plautus' *Pseudolus,* and a forthcoming book that focuses on the social and metatheatrical aspects of Roman comedy, in addition to articles and chapters on Latin literature. He was awarded a Loeb Classical Library Foundation Fellowship in 2011–12.

Introduction

EACH OF THE FOUR plays in this volume in some way challenges ancient stereotypes about women. In Aristophanes' *Lysistrata* (411 BCE) the eponymous heroine successfully persuades the women of Greece to deny their husbands sex in an effort to end the Peloponnesian War. *Lysistrata* is the first extant comedy to feature female main characters and foregrounds women's civic roles in classical Athens. The play continues to delight modern audiences internationally and has even spawned a women's global peace movement in recent years.[1] Menander's *Samia* or *The Woman from Samos* (*ca.* 315 BCE) strikingly confounds conventional Athenian categories of gender and status. Its titular character, the Samian courtesan Chrysis, defies the social and comic stereotype of the duplicitous and mercenary prostitute. After her lover Demeas misconstrues her relationship with his adopted son Moschion, Chrysis, the outsider, paradoxically is made to uphold the values of the idealized female Athenian citizen.

The central character of Plautus' *Casina* (*ca.* 185 BCE) is Cleostrata, who, in the course of frustrating her elderly husband's raging lust for the 16-year-old slave girl and play's namesake, is transformed into Plautine theater's most powerful figure when she successfully directs a punitive transvestite play-within-the-play. Against the backdrop of a period in which Roman women became more socially visible and were increasingly asserting their

1. The Lysistrata Project: http://www.lysistrataproject.org/.

rights to ownership of property, some regard *Casina* as a milestone in the history of feminist theater. Terence's *Hecyra* or *The Mother-in-Law* (160 BCE) features two anguished mothers/mothers-in-law, Myrrina and Sostrata, whose husbands wrongly accuse them of undermining their children's marriage. The play's complicated love triangle includes a prostitute named Bacchis who works actively to *save* her lover Pamphilus' marriage. Terence treats each of these women with novel sensitivity and depth, and *Hecyra* powerfully dramatizes the injustice of rashly ascribing negative stereotypes to women.

FIGURE 1.1: *Nighttime scene depicting a man aggressively approaching a door, with a woman holding an oil lamp on the other side; on a red-figure* chous *(jug), Attic,* ca. *430–420* BCE *(Metropolitan Museum of Art, Fletcher Fund, 1937, New York): http://www.metmuseum.org/toah/works-of-art/37.11.19*

All four comedies were written by men and performed by male actors representing women. Each play was generated in a culture in which men assumed an exclusively privileged position in public life and dominated women in general, and each seems to end in a way that reestablishes the pre-play world's status quo (Fig. 1.1). Most modern critics understandably hesitate to label these plays "feminist" or apply to them modern democratic ideas of equality between the sexes. Regardless of whether any of the four plays in some way advances a feminist agenda, all to varying degrees reveal how gender roles can be constructed, examined, undermined, deconstructed, or reasserted. Since theater is a mirror of our social lives (and vice versa?), the plays inevitably expose traditional feminine roles in real life as social constructions, and open up ample space for interrogating these roles even through time and across cultures. No less in the ancient world than today, drama at its core is about the construction and assumption of roles and so is always evaluative, critical, and potentially subversive. How socially transformative a theatrical experience proves to be depends on particular historical and cultural factors, and of course the viewpoints of individual theatergoers.

This volume brings together four rich and provocative comedies that illustrate, in entertaining and often surprising ways, the possibilities for theater as an agent of gender awareness or destabilization even in environments most unreceptive of social transformation i.e., the traditionalist and patriarchal societies of ancient Athens and Rome. Collectively, these comedies address such issues as the status of women in traditionally male-controlled arenas like politics and war, women's rights to ownership of property in general and of their own bodies in particular, the piercing omnipresence of the male gaze, and men's perception of woman as a problematic other, along with the clichés and mischaracterizations that result from reducing our social experience to simplistic male–female polarities. Viewed more positively, the four plays dramatize a capacity for intelligence, honesty, self-control, empathy, and cooperation among their main female characters that, while by no means the exclusive province of women, stands in stark contrast to the posturing, selfish blundering and socially destructive misbehavior of their male counterparts. It is remarkable that the core issues these ancient plays raise remain as fresh, relevant, and important today as ever.

GREEK OLD COMEDY

Ancient scholars came to designate the comic performances of fifth-century BCE Athens as "Old Comedy." Our understanding of this style of comedy rests primarily on the 11 extant plays of Aristophanes,[2] since only titles and fragments of the broader comic repertoire of this period survive. The career of Aristophanes (*ca.* 450–385 BCE), the most renowned playwright of Old Comedy, spanned roughly 40 years, but little reliable biographical information about him survives. Socrates, whom Aristophanes satirizes in his *Clouds*, was a slightly older contemporary. Socrates' disciple Plato represents Aristophanes as a colorful character in his *Symposium* (189c2–193d5), where the comic playwright offers an imaginative exegesis of human love (we were originally tri-sexed, spherical beings, but split in half by Zeus for our rebelliousness, we spend our lives searching for our severed half). The political voice that emerges from Aristophanes' comedies is both elitist and enlightened, in that his plays show clear sympathy with the average citizen living under Athenian democracy, while often privileging aristocratic tradition and the leadership of Athens' "beautiful and good" (*kaloi kai agathoi*) class.

Tragedy and comedy of fifth-century Athens were performed at state-sponsored religious festivals in honor of Dionysus, the god of wine and fertility. The greatest of these festivals, the City Dionysia, which instituted competitions in comedy in 486 BCE, was held during the spring in the open-air Theater of Dionysus on the south slope of the Athenian Acropolis. A lesser festival of Dionysus, the Lenaea, where comic competitions were established in roughly 440 BCE, took place in February and was probably the venue in which *Lysistrata* debuted. The cult statue of

2. Why these plays survived is something of a mystery. For the history of the transmission of Aristophanes' text, see Henderson's (Oxford, 1987) edition of *Lysistrata*, Introduction l–lxix, and Sommerstein, A.H., "The History of the Text of Aristophanes," pp. 399–422 in G.W. Dobrov (ed.), *Brill's Companion to the Study of Greek Comedy* (Leiden and Boston, 2010).

Dionysus was brought from his temple to the theater for the festivals, and thus the god literally presided over the performances in his honor. The festivals were grand public and civic occasions as well as ritual celebrations and featured displays of patriotism and power (but also of critical inquiry) during the heyday of Athens' political influence.[3] A special civic duty or "liturgy" supporting the dramatic festivals fell to Athens' wealthiest citizens: a *choregos* was responsible for organizing, training, and financially sponsoring a chorus (along with any necessary extras or musicians) in the months leading up to the festival.[4] As comic choruses consisted of 24 costumed performers, such a liturgy required the outlay of enormous expense. Drama was an extremely competitive enterprise in Athens, with the state funding awards for the best poet and actor in both tragedy and comedy, as decided by a randomized judging system designed to prevent bribery.[5] A victory in a dramatic competition brought considerable glory upon the *choregos*—or, potentially, shame in the case of a poor performance.

The Theater of Dionysus in Athens eventually accommodated as many as 14,000 to 17,000 spectators, whose ranks during the Great Dionysia included representatives of the entire populace: male citizens, women,[6] slaves, and children, as well as resident

3. See further Goldhill, S., "The Great Dionysia and Civic Ideology," pp. 97–129 in J. Winkler and F. Zeitlin (eds.), *Nothing to Do with Dionysos? Athenian Drama in its Social Context* (Princeton, 1990).

4. For speculation on the preparations of actors and chorus for an Aristophanic performance, see Ley, G., "Rehearsing Aristophanes," pp. 291–308 in G.W.M. Harrison and V. Liapis (eds.), *Performance in Greek and Roman Theater* (Leiden, 2013).

5. For details of the organization of Athenian dramatic festivals, see Csapo, E., and Slater, W.J., *The Context of Ancient Drama* (Ann Arbor, 1995): 103–185. For a hypothetical model of precisely how the judging system might have worked, see Marshall, C.W. and van Willigenburg, S., "Judging Athenian Dramatic Competitions." *Journal of Hellenic Studies* 124 (2004): 90–107.

6. For the long-debated issue of women's attendance at Greek dramatic performances, see further Henderson (1991b) and Goldhill, S., "The Audience of Athenian Tragedy," pp. 54–68 in P.E. Easterling (ed.), *The Cambridge Companion to Greek Tragedy* (Cambridge, 1997).

aliens and foreigners. The precise configuration of the theater's space in the fifth century BCE is still disputed, as it seems not to have become a permanent stone structure until the mid-fourth century BCE. During Aristophanes' floruit, the spectators' area probably consisted of blocks of wooden seats that formed three sides of a rectangle on the foothills of the Acropolis and may have accommodated only about 5,000 spectators.[7] These seats flanked a circular area or orchestra (introduced at an uncertain date) with side entrances; this area certainly was used by the chorus and may also have been the individual actors' space. Visual representations of theaters on vases from the late fifth century BCE have suggested a slightly elevated wooden platform as a distinct space for actors, though the existence of such a raised stage is doubted by some. Behind the performance space was a stage-building (*skene*) that had at least one door or set of double doors through which actors could pass and was painted to represent a scene. For *Lysistrata,* the Acropolis presumably was represented on the stage backdrop, though the actors simply could have pointed to the real thing rising above the theater. An *ekkyklema,* a platform with wheels that could be rolled out through the central door(s) of the stage-building, was used to depict scenes imagined to have taken place inside. Stagehands deployed a crane-like device to lift actors up from behind the skene, as in the case of a god (i.e., *deus ex machina*) brought forth to tie up the loose ends of a tragedy. Props seem to have been relatively scarce in fifth-century drama; Myrrhine, however, utilizes several props in her striptease scene with Kinesias at *Lysistrata* 916ff. Our picture of the Athenian theater in Aristophanes' day thus remains regrettably vague.

The chorus plays an essential role in Old Comedy. At the root of the word "comedy" is *komos,* "band of revelers," which suggests the genre's origins may lie in some sort of festive dance

7. See further Goette, H.R., "The Men Who Built Theatres: *Theatropolai, Theatronai,* and *Arkhitektones,* An Archaeological Appendix," pp. 116–121 in P. Wilson (ed.), *The Greek Theatre and Festivals: Documentary Studies* (Oxford, 2007).

performance in honor of Dionysus. The pervasive invective, frank sexuality, and aggressive obscenity of Old Comedy similarly point to fertility rituals, though these features also are found in other types of Greek poetry (e.g., that of Archilochus of Paros) from the seventh century BCE on. Old Comedy thus reflects what appears to be a long tradition of ritual abuse of powerful members of society, and after the creation of Athenian democracy (508/7 BCE) it provided the ordinary citizen with a sanctioned outlet to attack Athens' most prominent politicians, generals, and intellectuals, as well as to advocate better policies for the city. Most attempts to curb such free speech on the comic stage seem to have been unsuccessful; Aristophanes himself faced, and apparently beat, charges of slander by the Athenian demagogue Cleon.[8] But while the city's leading men and sometimes even the Olympian gods (as in Aristophanes' *Birds*) could be ridiculed with impunity on Old Comedy's stage, Aristophanes' extant works maintain an abiding respect for the institution of democracy itself and for Athens' venerable religious traditions. To what extent Old Comedy exerted influence on contemporary Athenian society and politics is much debated, but it is noteworthy that, in 405 BCE, the city gave Aristophanes a special award for one of his choruses' advocacy (*Frogs* 686–705) of restoring citizenship rights to those who had lost them on political grounds. *Lysistrata* and Aristophanes' other plays focusing on women (*Assemblywomen, Women at the Thesmophoria*) further reveal that the stage of Old Comedy provided a productive space for investigating the contrasting roles of men and women within the city-state.

An Aristophanic comedy typically starts with a hero who has conceived a grand scheme, however fantastical in nature. The comic hero naturally faces obstacles to implementing

8. See further Sommerstein, A., "The Alleged Attempts to Prosecute Aristophanes," pp. 145–174 in I. Sluiter and R.M. Rosen (eds.), *Free Speech in Classical Antiquity* (Leiden, 2004).

his/her plan, most often from a hostile chorus that must somehow be won over. Lysistrata faces an additional internal challenge from the young wives themselves, who are much challenged by the abstention from sex she demands of them. This great scheme is eventually realized, and a good part of the comedy is dedicated to demonstrating the mostly positive effects of its implementation, leading up to a celebratory finale. Verisimilitude is not a high priority in Aristophanic comedy, and there is no sustained attempt to create fourth-wall illusionism as in modern realistic drama. Audience members are frequently addressed or referred to, as is the occasion of performance itself. There are drastic and sometimes vague changes of scene, and the passage of time can be fluid and arbitrary. The omnipresence of the chorus and its many songs contribute much to this aura of highly stylized drama, perhaps especially so in the plays featuring animal choruses (e.g., Aristophanes' *Wasps*). The musical scores and precise dance movements of the chorus are, unfortunately, irrecoverable.[9] Grotesque masks,[10] padded costumes, and the (leather) phalluses of male characters—often represented as torturously erect in *Lysistrata*—similarly mark Old Comedy's spectacle.

Readers approaching Aristophanes for the first time may be struck by Old Comedy's apparently loose or even chaotic structure, but the plays are built on clear constituent parts. They begin with a **prologue** (*Lysistrata* 1–253), which serves to introduce the situation and characters and may extend over several scenes. Whereas the mythic figures of Greek tragedy and their associated stories were already known to a classical audience, comedy usually required the invention of fictional characters and plots and so necessitated an exposition of these. No doubt, audiences

9. Cf. Zarifi, Y., "Chorus and Dance in the Ancient World," pp. 227–246 in M. McDonald and J.M. Walton (eds.), *The Cambridge Companion to Greek and Roman Theatre* (Cambridge, 2007).

10. For an overview of the use of masks in ancient comedy, see McCart, G., "Masks in Greek and Roman Theatre," pp. 247–267 in M. McDonald and J.M. Walton (eds.), *The Cambridge Companion to Greek and Roman Theatre* (Cambridge, 2007).

much anticipated the **parodos** (*Lysistrata* 254–386) or—often extended—entry of the chorus, perhaps especially when the plays' titles announced the use of an animal chorus (e.g., Aristophanes' *Frogs*) with appropriate costuming. The audience of *Lysistrata* was treated to the rowdy entrances of two semi-choruses, first the charcoal-bearing old men and then the women carrying pitchers of water on their heads. The **parabasis** is a definitive feature of Old Comedy, which, at a moment when all the characters are offstage, suspends the play's action and allows the chorus to offer insight on topical matters, seemingly in the voice of the playwright. In *Lysistrata,* the gender-divided chorus is not unified until near the end of play, which accounts for the lack of a typical parabasis; Lysistrata's woolworking analogy and call for civic solidarity (567–597), however, serve as a substitute. Aristophanes' plays also usually feature at least one **agon** or debate consisting of a formal speaking contest between two characters that the second speaker wins. *Lysistrata* again is exceptional for lacking a formal agon, as the Administrator is not allowed to formally state his case before he is roundly denounced and banished from the play by Lysistrata (486–613). The play's contentious semi-choruses also assume an agonistic role as they exchange threats and insults. **Episodes** are scenes featuring the actors speaking to each other (in iambic trimeter, the meter closest to everyday speech), but they are interspersed with choral songs and interludes as well. The **exodos**, which strictly refers to the chorus' exit, describes the conclusion and grand finale of the play (*Lysistrata* 1296–1321) and features joyous dancing and singing, as when all parties reconcile at the end of *Lysistrata.*

The example of *Lysistrata* alone suffices to show that not all these formal structural elements are always present in Aristophanes' plays. Because, however, they can sometimes be glimpsed in the fragmentary remains of other fifth-century comic playwrights, they appear to be essential markers of Old Comedy. Generic features aside, Aristophanes' linguistic inventiveness and musical virtuosity cannot be over-emphasized. The extraordinary richness of Aristophanic imagery and metaphor in particular, whether found within crudely sexual and scatological banter or the comedian's more sublime choral lyrics, rings through loudly and clearly, even in translation.

GREEK NEW COMEDY

Ancient Alexandrian scholars schematized the evolution of Athenian comedy into three distinct phases: Old, Middle, and New Comedy. The last of these marks comedies (mostly) produced at festivals in Athens from the last quarter of the fourth century BCE (the death of Alexander the Great in 323 BCE is a useful point of reference) down to at least the second century BCE. The high point of Greek New Comedy extends from *ca.* 325 BCE to *ca.* 250 BCE. Middle Comedy survives only in fragments and through titles of plays and is a convenient catch-all for the period of comedy between the death of Aristophanes and the establishment of the very distinct genre of New Comedy.[11] In this transitional period, comedy gradually became less Athenocentric and more universal, and a stock set of characters (some had roots in Old Comedy) developed, including clever slaves, pimps and prostitutes, parasites, young men in love, grouchy fathers, saucy cooks, and braggart soldiers (cf. Fig. 1.2).

By the time of New Comedy, plays no longer focused on contemporary Athenian politics and Athens' most prominent citizens but were both more cosmopolitan and domestic in their emphasis on the daily trials in the lives of mostly upper-middle and middle-class families of Athens or any Hellenistic city. The fantastical schemes, vigorous invective, obscenity, and musical diversity of Old Comedy completely disappeared. Old Comedy's

11. For an overview of this phase of comedy, see Arnott, G., "Middle Comedy," pp. 279–331 in G.W. Dobrov (ed.), *Brill's Companion to the Study of Greek Comedy* (Leiden and Boston, 2010).

grotesquely padded costumes gave way to the *chiton,* a belted everyday garment that came in different lengths depending on the wearer's age and gender, and which was worn with tights. The exciting twentieth-century discovery of terracotta masks on the island of Lipari off the northern coast of Sicily, some of which date to the third century BCE, demonstrates that masks in New Comedy were more humanlike than those of Old Comedy.[12] Most notably absent are the chorus and its exuberant singing and dancing that Old Comedy had integrated into the action of the play. At the end of an act of a Greek New Comedy, a character typically signals the approach of "drunken revelers." This formulaic announcement, along with regular notations in the surviving texts ("[song] of the chorus"), indicates that in New Comedy the comic chorus had been reduced to performing some sort of interlude between acts in the theater's orchestra. Comedy decidedly had become much quieter and more domestic.

Apart from surviving fragments and titles and extant Roman adaptations of Greek New Comedy, our understanding of the genre is colored by the extant works of Menander (*ca.* 342–290 BCE). Menander, who is credited with writing over 100 plays, was an Athenian citizen and said to be a close associate of Demetrios of Phaleron, the Macedonian-supported leader of an oligarchic regime in Athens from 317 to 307 BCE, at which point democracy was restored. The first performance of *Samia* falls within Demetrios' reign, but like Menander's other extant comedies it shows little trace of the political strife of the time. Despite being highly acclaimed in antiquity, Menander's comedies for reasons that are unclear disappeared in the seventh century CE and do not survive in a medieval manuscript tradition (i.e., via continuous copying by

12. The presence of the masks in Sicily (along with finds of masks elsewhere) indicates that Greek New Comedy was easily transportable, as is also suggested by ancient artistic representations of Menandrian scenes (as for *Samia*: see Introductory Essay 115 and Fig. 1.2) that have been found throughout the Greco-Roman world. See further Wiles (1991).

hand). Instead, a small percentage of Menander's plays were only rediscovered through fortuitous twentieth-century papyrus finds that had been preserved in the dry climate of Egypt; these yielded one complete comedy, *Dyskolos* or *The Grumpy Man* (first published in 1958), and six other substantially preserved plays, including *Samia*. Much less fortunate were popular playwrights of New Comedy such as Diphilus of Sinope (born *ca.* 350 BCE), the author of some 100 lost comedies,

FIGURE 1.2: *Scene from Act III of Menander's* Samia *depicting Chrysis (with baby), Demeas, and the cook; mosaic from The House of Menander, Mytilene, Lesbos, fourth century* CE: *http://en.wikipedia.org/wiki/File:Samia_(Girl_from_Samos)_Mytilene_3cAD.jpg*

including the source play for Plautus' *Casina*, and Apollodorus of Carystus (he produced his first play in 285 BCE), who seems to have been heavily influenced by Menander and was the author of the play Terence adapted for *Hecyra*.

Perhaps reflecting the general shift to more domestic comedy, the backdrop of the Theater of Dionysus in Menander's day now apparently depicted as many as three doors, and a city street in front of the households represented by these doors served as the play's setting and acting space. In contrast to the plays of Aristophanes, the comedies of New Comedy more faithfully observe unities of time and place and consist of five clearly demarcated acts. No heroic or otherwise exuberantly triumphant character stands out among the casts of Menander's plays (as in, e.g., *Lysistrata*). His comedies not infrequently feature stereotypical and implausibly coincidental situations involving, for example, the reunion of children separated at birth with their families, but Menander still manages to portray sensitive and psychologically subtle relationships among a variety of characters.[13] These include the rich and less fortunate, both citizens and non-citizens, free persons and slaves, parents and children (especially fathers and sons), all of whom are associated with individual households within a single neighborhood. Dramatic problems most typically arise in Menander because of his characters' ignorance, misunderstanding, or prejudices (as happens throughout *Samia*); the audience often enjoys knowledge that characters lack and so can appreciate the tensions and ironies inhering in their situations. As serious conflicts with potentially grim consequences often occur, a good part of a Menandrian play may not seem comic. But although households suffer disruptions, family harmony inevitably is restored, most often through a marriage at the play's end, and the prospect of the citizen family's continuation through the generation of legitimate children.

13. For an insightful study of the plots of New Comedy in light of other classical narrative genres, see Lowe, N.J., *The Classical Plot and the Invention of Western Narrative* (Cambridge, 2000): 188–221.

Other characteristics of Menander's plays include the use of prologues formally detached from the play's action and often delivered by omniscient divinities. These occur at the beginnings of plays or are delayed until after an opening scene or two and may feature such thematically appropriate abstractions as "Misapprehension" (*Agnoia* in *Perikeiromene*) and "Chance" (*Tyche* in *The Shield*). Moschion's regrettably mutilated opening monologue substitutes for a divine prologue in *Samia*, and Moschion playfully apologizes for the substantial amount of background material to be navigated there: "I'll go through all the details / Of our family's business now, since I've got time" (19–20). Outside of prologues, some Menandrian characters, such as Demeas in *Samia*, seek to develop special rapport with the audience, whom they directly address as *andres* ("Gentleman;" see Samia, note 55).[14] But despite the unrealistic nature of some of his dramatic techniques and plots, already in antiquity Menander was praised for his skill in capturing human psychology and depicting the complexities of social life; the ancient scholar Aristophanes of Byzantium (*ca.* 257–180 BCE) is said to have exclaimed: "O Menander and Life, which of you imitated the other?" To modern readers accustomed to the tradition of theatrical realism, Menander's plays perhaps initially are much more accessible than Aristophanes', and Menander (along with Plautus and Terence) is rightfully considered to be the "father" of the modern sitcom.[15]

ROMAN COMEDY

Menander died well before the beginnings of Roman theater in 240 BCE, but his comedies and those of other popular New Comedy playwrights, in addition to enjoying revivals in Athens,

14. For audience address in Menander, see further Bain, D., *Actors and Audience: A Study of Asides and Related Conventions in Greek Drama* (Oxford, 1977): 185–207.

15. See further Grote, D., *The End of Comedy: the Sit-Com and the Comedic Tradition* (Hamden, CT, 1983).

continued to be performed throughout the Hellenistic world by itinerant acting companies, such as the "Artists of Dionysus." Much of southern Italy and Sicily, though under Roman control in the third century BCE, had been colonized by Greeks centuries earlier, and the earliest Roman playwrights probably encountered performances of Greek New Comedy there. The hybrid comic genre they created came to be known as the *fabula palliata*, or "play in Greek costume." Roman playwrights did not slavishly translate Greek New Comedy but productively adapted it for the Roman stage and for their own audiences. Native, non-literary forms of Italian drama no doubt also influenced the adaptation of Greek New Comedy in Rome:[16] for example, the earliest extant fragments of Roman drama include musically elaborate songs or *cantica*, which do not correspond to anything in Greek New Comedy (these were used extensively by Plautus). Roman Comedy also did away with the five-act structure and choral interludes of Greek New Comedy, and so its action, like Old Comedy's, consisted of continuous scenes.

Despite the enormous popularity and influence of Plautus (born 254 BCE), nothing certain is known about his life. Most of the 21 Plautine plays that survive (not all are complete) probably premièred between *ca.* 200 and 184 BCE, the year of Plautus' death. Plautus' plays continued to be performed for centuries after his death and survived in manuscript tradition down to the Italian Renaissance, when they enjoyed a great revival of interest. Though an extensive ancient biography of Terence dating back to *ca.* 100 CE survives, few of its details are reliable. Terence's six extant plays were performed between 166 and 160 BCE. After Terence's death in 159 BCE, his plays were regularly revived on the Roman stage. Their survival ultimately was ensured by their central position in the educational curriculum, and they too were copied by hand down to the time of the invention of the printing press.

16. See further, Panayotakis, C., "Comedy, Atellane Farce and Mime," pp. 130–147 in S. Harrison (ed.), *A Companion to Latin Literature* (Malden, MA, 2005).

Productions of Roman plays mostly occurred in connection with state-sponsored religious festivals. Another occasion for drama in Rome were funeral games in honor of distinguished Roman aristocrats (as was the case for the second failed performance of *Hecyra*). In addition to religious rituals and theatrical performances, Roman festivals and games included various sideshows, such as boxing matches and gladiator contests (for these, see the prologues of *Hecyra*). The plays were performed in the Roman forum, in a circus (the venue for Roman chariot racing), or in front of a god's temple. The Roman senate allocated funds for the festivals. In addition, magistrates (*aediles*) charged with administering the festivals contributed to them from their own private funds in order to cultivate political support from the Roman people. Roman theater must have been a grand spectacle, with a broad swath of the sharply hierarchical city's population—upper and lower ranks, women and men, young and old, free and slave, rich and poor, Roman and Italian—assembling in theaters that were temporarily constructed for the festivals and then dismantled.[17]

Consequently, nothing survives of the theaters in which Plautus' and Terence's plays were put on. In the absence of contemporary visual evidence, we rely mostly on the plays themselves to reconstruct a general layout of the early Roman theater. As was the case for Greek New Comedy, the action unfolds on what is supposed to be a street in front of up to three houses, each with a door for the entrances and exits of characters. The audience sat on wooden benches, with the best seats directly in front of what was probably only a slightly raised stage reserved for the senatorial elite from 194 BCE on.[18] The stage had two side

17. No permanent (stone) theater was constructed in Rome until Pompey's in 55 BCE, apparently because the senate and the sponsors of the festivals for political purposes viewed the construction of temporary structures as a means of demonstrating their munificence toward the Roman people: cf. Gruen, E.S., *Culture and National Identity in Republican Rome* (Ithaca, 1992): 209–210.

18. See further Moore, T.J., "Seats and Social Status in the Plautine Theater." *Classical Journal* 90 (1994): 113–123.

wings, one of which led to the forum/center of town, the other to the country and/or harbor. In stark contrast with Greek stone theaters that featured a large orchestra, temporary Roman theaters encouraged interaction between actors and audiences, a situation that Plautus in particular exploited.[19] The actors wore masks, but it is unclear if these were precisely the same types used in Greek New Comedy. Only a few details are known about costumes in Roman comedy. They seem to have been codified to distinguish character-types; for example, an old man (*senex*) wore a white wig and cloak and held a walking stick, older women wore green or light blue, while a young man's cloak was darkly colored (crimson or red).[20]

The relatively scant remains of Greek New Comedy plays prevent us from analyzing precisely how Plautus and Terence adapted their sources. The papyrus discovery in 1968, however, of a small portion of Menander's *Dis Exapaton* or *The Double Deceiver*, the source play for Plautus' surviving *Bacchides*, allows for some direct comparisons. The parallel texts reveal that Plautus has added much musical accompaniment to Menander's scene, obscured an act-division, and altered Menander's dramatic pace by combining what had been separate speeches in different acts; Plautus has also freely removed or added entire speeches. Where Menander is more focused on his characters' psychological motivations, Plautus turns jokes and delineates character in only the broadest strokes. Plautus also changes the names of Menander's characters, and he superimposes an entirely distinct style, replete with alliteration, assonance, puns, and other characteristic marks of Plautus' linguistic exuberance. Plautine comedy thus makes a significant departure from its Greek models.

Plautus also adds a thick layer of Romanization to his Greek sources. While the notional setting of Plautine comedy usually is Athens, Plautus injects clear references to Roman customs, laws,

19. For a reconstruction of an early Roman stage, see Beacham, R.C., *The Roman Theatre and its Audience* (Cambridge, MA, 1992): 56–85.

20. For costumes and masks, see further Manuwald (2011): 68–80.

political institutions and magistrates, the topography of Italy and Rome, and sometimes even current issues, such as those related to marriage in *Casina*. The resulting comic world is a richly provocative collage of things Greek and Roman, which has been dubbed "Plautinopolis."[21] The effect of Plautus' conflation of the two cultures might have allowed his audience some scope for escapism, but they also knew that they were watching characters inhabiting a world very much like their own. In Plautus' and Terence's lifetimes, the Romans' successful entry into international politics (marked by victories over Carthaginian and Greek rivals) had challenged many of the traditional norms and values of Roman society. As a consequence, issues such as the effects of wealth upon morality, social mobility, the integrity of the family, personal and group identity, gender, sexuality, and the otherness of foreigners figure prominently in the extant comic drama of the first half of the second century BCE.

Metacomedy is a pervasive feature of Plautus' plays. Literary self-awareness is a mark of Latin literature from its beginnings, given its derivative status from Greek literature.[22] Plautine comedy displays an especially pronounced tendency to broadcast its status as *theater-in-the-process-of-being-performed*, as characters often allude to the stock roles they are playing, comment on the audience's reception of the play, and directly refer to details of theatrical production. While this play with the dramatic construct is present in Greek Old Comedy, it is less evident in the remains of Greek New Comedy (and in Terence). *Casina* provides an excellent example of a metacomic play-within-the-play. There the heroine Cleostrata and her friend Myrrhina humiliate the former's philandering husband Lysidamus by dressing up Chalinus as the 16-year-old slave after whom he lusts. As the gender-bending faux-wedding they stage is about to spill out

21. The term was coined by Gratwick (1982): 113.

22. See further Braund, S.M., *Latin Literature* (London and New York, 2002): 190–224.

onstage, Myrrhina exclaims: "No playwright has ever devised a better / Plot than this clever production of ours!" (860–861). Similarly, at the end of *Casina,* Cleostrata agrees to forgive Lysidamus because "this play is long and I don't want to make it any longer" (1006). No testimony survives as to how Plautus' plays were received by his contemporaries, but this persistent baring of theatrical underpinnings and how the play's society is constructed might well have induced some in the audience to reflect upon the construction and artificiality of the social roles they played in their own world.[23]

Terence's comedy sometimes suffers unfairly from comparison with that of his predecessor Plautus. Since antiquity, critics have noted a relative lack of verbal exuberance in Terence. It is the case that Terentian language overall is far less imaginative, aggressive, and innovative than Plautus'; Terence's actors also engage in much less direct address to the audience than Plautus' do, there is less obvious Romanization,[24] and Terence uses metacomic devices more sparingly and with greater subtlety. Terence instead gives his characters smoother, more naturalistic discourse, and in this respect he closely follows Menander. Terentian characters, for example, deliver elegant monologues that skillfully capture their thoughts, or they sometimes speak to each other in realistically broken and elliptical dialogue.[25] Terentian drama's aesthetic aims, in contrast to those of Plautine comedy, are more carefully focused on delineating character and exploring the subtleties of human relationships.

The prologues of Terence's comedies mark a new direction in the comic tradition, in that they all refuse to convey plot background and instead treat contemporary theatrical

23. See further Christenson (forthcoming [2014]).

24. Terence's plays nonetheless are grounded in contemporary Roman thought and experience: see Starks, J.H., "*opera in bello, in otio, in negotio*: Terence and Rome in the 160s BCE," pp. 132–155 in Augoustakis and Traill (2013).

25. See further Karakasis, E., *Terence and the Language of Roman Comedy* (Cambridge, 2008).

and literary disputes in which Terence depicts himself as embroiled. As Terence assumes his audience is interested in the esoteric literary matters his prologues typically address, exposition of the plot is reserved for an opening scene. The main charge against which Terence repeatedly defends himself in his prologues is that his methods of composition are somehow "contaminated" because he sometimes takes plot elements or entire scenes from different Greek comedies and combines them into a single Roman adaptation. Terence's defensiveness suggests that, for literary purists at least, this recombining of Greek texts was controversial for a still nascent literature in Latin. The process Terence describes of course reflects Latin literature's derivative status: the development of Latin literature in essence was a mass appropriation of Greek texts, with authors increasingly marshaling together a host of literary texts in the service of creative adaptation. The charge of contamination in fact heralds the beginnings of the intertextual play that gives Latin literature so much of its richness and its uniquely creative stamp.[26] The two surviving prologues of *Hecyra*, however, are focused on the perhaps not unrelated matter of the play's initial failures (see Introductory Essay 223–224). Fortunately, the barrage of criticism Terence characterizes his plays as being subjected to did not impede their survival or his career.

WOMEN IN THE ANCIENT WORLD

The study of women's lives in the ancient Greco-Roman world is fraught with formidable difficulties. Whether the evidence preserved is literary, material, or documentary, it overwhelmingly reflects male perspectives of women and is deeply embedded in the popular biases and ideological assumptions of patriarchal

26. See further Goldberg, S.M., *Constructing Literature in the Roman Republic: Poetry and its Reception* (Cambridge, 2005) and Hinds, S., *Allusion and Intertext: Dynamics of Appropriation in Roman Poetry* (Cambridge, 1998).

social structures. The representation of ancient women in our sources is further skewed in that it focuses on elite classes of women, who constituted only a minute fraction of women in society. It thus is all but impossible to satisfactorily construct even a broad overview of the diverse lives of women from this incomplete and unreliable body of evidence.

Nor is it possible to gain a general sense of women's levels of literacy and what educational opportunities were available to them in the ancient world. We remain unaware of any systematic system of education that included girls, such as state-funded schools in modern democracies. Male guardians usually determined the extent of education females received, and, if it was provided at all, this could range from the basics required for household management to—probably rarely and primarily for the elite—extensive training in the liberal arts. Very few literary works written by women survive, such as those of the seventh/sixth century BCE Greek lyric poet Sappho of Lesbos and the first-century BCE Roman elegiac poet Sulpicia. Several philosophical schools, such as the Epicureans, admitted women, a few of whom are said to have taught and published their works (e.g., the sixth-century BCE Pythagorean Theano and the late antique Neoplatonist Hypatia). We also have a few accounts of Roman imperial women who volunteered to follow their husbands in the Stoic "noble suicide."

GREECE

Myths about women can be telling. The poet Hesiod (eighth/seventh century BCE) paints a begrudging picture of the archetypal Greek woman (*Theogony* 570ff., *Works & Days* 54ff.). As punishment for Prometheus' theft of fire from the gods, Zeus has various gods fashion Pandora, "a beautiful evil" (*kalon kakon, Theogony* 585). Pandora is an elaborate work of art(ifice), whose shining garment, exquisite veil, and elaborate golden wreath conceal her craftiness and cunning within. Moreover, a woman is a useless drain on the household's resources; a seductive woman is merely "after your barn," Hesiod declares at *Works & Days* (373–374). She also generally weakens a man and makes him dependent, since she is necessary for procreation and perpetuation of the family. While all this is a notoriously crotchety Boeotian farmer's take on a cultural myth (other sources from this early period [e.g., Homer] are less obviously misogynistic), stereotypical views of women as unproductive, untrustworthy, and flighty creatures, sharply distinct from men and generally lacking the latter's reputed self-control, persist throughout Greek literature and history.[27]

The oft-cited statement of ideal womanly virtue found in the fifth-century BCE history of Thucydides, while free of Hesiod's malice toward woman, to modern ears represents only a marginally more progressive outlook. On a most solemn civic occasion, the public funeral oration for those who died in the first year of the Peloponnesian War (431 BCE), Thucydides represents the renowned Athenian politician Pericles as saying "the greatest glory of a woman is to not be spoken about by men, whether in praise or blame" (*The Peloponnesian War* 2.45). Outside their homes, women living under Athenian democracy effectively are to be silent and invisible. Such a pronouncement in a prominent fifth-century BCE Athenian text helps locate the remarkable outspokenness and public visibility of Aristophanes' heroine Lysistrata within its contemporary cultural context.

As seems generally to have been the case for women throughout the ancient Mediterranean world, even free female citizens in classical Athens did not share the rights and privileges of their husbands and fathers. Women could not participate in the city's political process or hold political office. In the event of a husband's or father's absence, Athenian women were appointed

27. An especially notorious example is a seventh-century BCE iambic poem attributed to Semonides of Amorgos, a misogynist tirade in which women are equated with various animals in the most unflattering terms (text with translation, commentary, and illustrations in Lloyd-Jones, H., *Females of the Species: Semonides on Women* [London, 1975]).

a male guardian (*kyrios*), who represented them if needed in public life. Athenian women could not own property and were entrusted with only short-term allowances for household provisions. Their husbands maintained control over their dowries, although these notionally were intended for their and their children's support.

Within the Athenian citizen family structure, a woman's primary role was to bear legitimate children (cf. the end of *Samia*) and raise them within the household whose daily management and figurative preservation she oversaw. Despite the availability of household slaves, this responsibility must have placed an enormous burden on Athenian girls, who typically married at 14. They also faced the likelihood of marrying a much older man (usually in his 30s), who might be acculturated to the common notion that his teenage bride was a wild creature in need of taming. Such expectations, coupled with fears about the legitimacy of children, easily led to the seclusion, tight supervision, and even infantilization of Athenian wives.

The extant (esp. literary) evidence for women's lives overwhelmingly comes from Athens, a factor that no doubt presents further distortions of the realities throughout Greece. In the militaristic city-state of Sparta, for example, women underwent extensive physical training and competed in athletics out of the belief that this would better prepare them for the rigors of childbirth and produce stronger offspring for the state. Similarly, in the best interests of their health, Spartan women did not marry until they were 18. Spartan males were sequestered in military barracks from an early age and well into adulthood, and so women seem to have taken control of households in their absence. The physical fitness and independence of mind with which Aristophanes invests the Spartan Lampito in *Lysistrata* may thus reflect realities in classical Sparta.

In addition to their domestic duties, Athenian women engaged extensively in religious activity. They attended and participated in the city's religious festivals, such as the Pananthenaia, an annual summer celebration of Athena (Fig. 1.4). The city's cults of female deities

FIGURE 1.3: Prothesis *(laying out of the dead scene) with female mourners; on a black figure terracotta funerary plaque, Attic,* ca. *520–510* BCE *(Metropolitan Museum of Art, Rogers Fund, 1954, New York): http://www.metmuseum.org/Collections/search-the-collections/254801*

usually required female priestesses, who garnered prestige and possibly some public influence for their important religious services. Lysimache, the priestess of Athena Polias for much of the fifth century BCE, appears to have been an enormously respected figure (cf. *Lysistrata*, Introductory Essay 44). Some civic cults were maintained exclusively of men altogether, such as the Thesmophoria, a fertility festival for married women that commemorated the goddess Demeter's loss of her daughter Persephone. There were still other non-official and usually (in origin) foreign religious cults exclusively for women, such as that of Adonis (cf. *Lysistrata* 387ff. and *Samia* 36ff.). Athenian women played prominent roles in various purification rites, including those associated with weddings and childbirth, and they also cleaned and outfitted the bodies of male relatives for burial (Fig. 1.3; cf. the mock preparation of the Administrator for burial at *Lysistrata* 599ff.).

FIGURE 1.4: Ergastinai *(weavers) in a procession, perhaps part of the Panathenaic Festival; Pentelic marble, east frieze of the Parthenon, Athens,* ca. *445–435* BCE *(Louvre Museum): http://en.wikipedia.org/wiki/File:Egastinai_frieze_Louvre_MR825.jpg*

Depending on their economic and social status, free women fulfilled a great variety of other functions in ancient Greek society. They generally were not as sequestered in their home as used to be supposed, as they at times must have needed to fetch water from wells (cf. *Lysistrata* 327ff.) and carry out other household-related errands. Some women worked in the fields, while others were employed as artisans or sold products, especially food, in the markets. There is evidence that free women were employed as midwives and wet-nurses and sometimes acted as physicians in treating gynecological disorders. Less fortunate women served as sex workers in degrading and dehumanizing circumstances. This broad class of sexual entertainers for men included *hetairai*—the status of Chrysis in *Samia* before she moved in with Demeas[28]—who typically are portrayed as better educated and enjoying more freedom than their less fortunate counterparts in the ancient sex industry.

28. Menander's Chrysis, who is also a resident foreigner or *metic* in Athens, nonetheless is surprisingly well received by the women in Demeas' neighborhood: see further *Samia*, Introductory Essay 123–124.

There is evidence, some documentary, that suggests women's lives may have changed for the better in certain areas of the ancient Greek world during the Hellenistic Period (323–31 BCE), when the successors of Alexander the Great established powerful queens in some places (such as the Ptolemies in Egypt). How this development might have trickled down to the lives of women in general is unclear, but for purposes of this volume, it is assumed that the everyday lives of the vast majority of women living in Athens at the time of Aristophanes and those in Menander's heyday probably were not substantially different.[29]

ROME

Rome had its own myth about the introduction of women. As narrated by the Augustan Age historian Livy (*History of Rome* 1.9–13), the recently created city of Rome lacked women. The fledgling city's neighbors disdainfully rejected King Romulus' offers of an alliance through intermarriage, and so the Romans, reflecting their militaristic character, invited the Sabine people to a festival in order to abduct their unmarried females. In Livy's account, the Sabine "wives" eventually are won over by Romulus and their new husbands. When inevitable war between the Roman and Sabine men breaks out, the women heroically interpose themselves between the battle lines made up of their fathers and husbands (Fig. 1.5). The Sabine women assert that they would rather die than "live as widows or orphans" (Livy 1.13.3) and thereby demonstrate their willingness to sacrifice their bodies at a critical moment of early Roman history. The men drop their arms and unite in everlasting solidarity. The myth tidily illustrates how Roman women are defined in relationship to men and how marriage in a patriarchal society is conceived as a transfer of women from their fathers to their husbands. The Sabine women also prefigure the use of women to secure alliances between

29. An excellent collections of images representing Athenian and other ancient women's lives can be found in Neils (2011).

FIGURE 1.5: *Jacques-Louis David,* The Intervention of the Sabine Women, *1799 (Louvre Museum): http://en.wikipedia.org/wiki/File:The_Intervention_of_the_Sabine_Women.jpg*

families, as frequently happened among the elite and powerful clans who for centuries dominated Roman Republican politics.

For married women (*matronae*) there was also the heroic exemplum of the beautiful and virtuous Lucretia, best known from Livy's dramatic account (1.57–58) set at the birth of the Roman state. A model Roman wife in every respect, Lucretia commits suicide after she is raped by King Tarquinius Superbus' son Sextus. Despite her husband's and father's insistence that she is guiltless, Livy's Lucretia is made to kill herself to prevent any possibility of her creating a bad precedent for (unchaste) women.[30] Lucretia's noble sacrifice of her body to the greater social cause thus leads directly to the expulsion of King Tarquin

30. For the necessity of Lucretia's death owing to the threat she poses to male self-control, see Joshel, S.R., "The Body Female and the Body Politic: Livy's Lucretia and Verginia," pp. 112–130 in Richland (1992).

and the founding of a new body politic, the Roman Republic (traditionally dated to 510 BCE).

Like their Greek counterparts, Roman women were formally excluded from the political process. They too might be placed under the guardianship (*tutela*) of male relatives, but in some circumstances this control could be lifted. Under Roman law women were allowed to inherit property. There were two forms of marriage for Roman women: marriage *cum manu* ("with [the transfer of] power" [i.e., to the husband]) and marriage *sine manu* ("without [the transfer of] power") (Fig. 1.6). In the latter case, a wife remained under the guardianship of her father, who retained ownership of any property she brought with her to the marriage, and she retained her

FIGURE 1.6: *Funerary sculpture of a married Roman couple (Gratidia M.L. Chrite and M. Gratidius Libanus); marble, originally in relief, late first century* BCE *(Vatican Museums): http://ancientrome.ru/art/artworken/img.htm?id=2560*

right to inheritance within the clan into which she was born. The growing preference for this type of marriage in the times of Plautus and Terence no doubt reflected a desire to preserve wealth within a woman's natal family. Dowries were the norm in either form of Roman marriage but had to be returned by husbands to their fathers-in-law in the event of divorce, which seems to have been common among the elite classes, where it often reflected shifting social and political alliances among men (high mortality rates owing to disease and warfare may have made remarriage common in all the free classes). In comedy, as probably also in real life, the dowered wife (*uxor dotata*) is stereotypically portrayed as holding leverage over her husband, who has otherwise invested or spent the dowry, as may be assumed to be the case for Cleostrata in *Casina* (see further *Casina,* Introductory Essay 165–166).

As the legally stated purpose of Roman marriage was the creation of legitimate children, the ideal of the modest and self-effacing Lucretia working at the loom late into the night persists in Roman literature and life. An idealizing tombstone inscription (*Corpus Inscriptionum Latinarum* 1^2.1211, second century BCE) in honor of a certain Claudia reads: "Her parents named her Claudia. She loved her husband with her heart. One of the two sons she bore remains on earth, the other is under it. She was a pleasant conversationalist and walked in an appropriate manner. She maintained the house and worked wool." Roman girls, in contrast to boys, did not have "first names" but took a feminine form of the family name of their father (e.g., any daughter of Marcus Tullius Cicero was named "Tullia" and would be distinguished from her sisters only by their relative ages). As was the case for the legendary Sabines, the identities of Roman women as they transitioned from being daughters to wives and mothers were primarily circumscribed by their relationships to men. Women of the lower classes, by working in shops associated with their husbands' trades, might have created something of a distinct professional identity for themselves, though not necessarily a socially positive one if they worked in places generally considered unsavory (e.g., inns, taverns).

The participation of women in the state religion of Rome was less extensive than it was in classical Athens. Most official cults in Rome were administered by male priests. The Vestal Virgins, who enjoyed a strong civic presence, were a notable exception. These priestesses, who probably came exclusively from the elite classes, at an early age committed themselves to Vesta, the goddess of the hearth, pledging to serve in the goddess' cult for 30 years without marrying. There were some exclusive women's festivals, such as that of the Bona Dea or "Good Goddess," although her nocturnal ceremonies were closely supervised by the highest magistrate present in Rome. Roman women also participated in worship outside the sanction of the state religion, as in the case of imported non-Roman or some Italic deities. The mostly female worship of Bacchus (Dionysus), however, was sharply curtailed by an emergency decree of the Roman senate in 186 BCE (see further *Casina*, Introductory Essay 168).

NOTE ON THE TRANSLATION

In these translations I have attempted to strike a fruitful balance between liveliness and fidelity to the source texts. In the service of the latter, the prose translations here are line for line, without, it is hoped, coming off as too clumsily literal or unclear in English. I purposefully have avoided over-indulgence in current slang and imminently doomed ephemeral references, as I did not want to create overly familiarized representations of these ancient comedies and the cultures in which they were produced. Much of these comedies' foreignness thus is deliberately preserved by not domesticating the names of characters and usually leaving in references to ancient Greek and Roman deities, institutions, places, persons, events, etc. These are explained in the notes at the bottom of the page or in the Appendix on Olympian deities. I thus translate more for the classroom than the stage, but it is my hope that these translations can be adapted for performance without undue effort (cf. *Lysistrata,* note 10). The plays were transmitted without stage directions, and I have included these only to help readers avoid possible confusions. I otherwise mostly leave it to the reader's pleasure to imagine what is taking place onstage. Those deeply offended by uninhibited and pornographic language should avoid my translation of *Lysistrata* and other faithful translations of Aristophanes altogether.

For *Lysistrata,* I have closely consulted the Greek texts of Wilson (Oxford, 2007) and Henderson (Cambridge, MA, 2000) and made extensive use of the commentary of Henderson (Oxford, 1987); for *Samia,* the text of Arnott (Cambridge, MA, 2000) and the commentaries of Bain (Warminster, 1983) and Gomme and Sandbach (Oxford, 1973). For *Casina,* I have most closely consulted the Latin texts of de Melo (Cambridge, MA, 2011) and Lindsay (Oxford, 1910) and made extensive use of the commentary of MacCary and Willcock (Cambridge, 1976); for *Hecyra,* the texts of Barsby (Cambridge, MA, 2001) and Lindsay (Oxford, 1926) and the commentaries of Carney (Pretoria, 1963) and Ireland (Warminster, 1990).

FURTHER READING

ARISTOPHANES AND OLD COMEDY

Bowie, A.M., *Aristophanes: Myth, Ritual and Comedy* (Cambridge, 1993).

Dobrov, G.W. (ed.), *Beyond Aristophanes: Transition and Diversity in Greek Comedy* (New York and Oxford, 1995).

Dover, K.J., *Aristophanic* Comedy (Berkeley and Los Angeles, 1972).

Henderson, J., "A Brief History of Athenian Political Comedy." *Transactions of the American Philological Association* 143 (2013): 249–262.

Henderson, J., *The Maculate Muse* (2nd ed., New York, 1991a).

Henderson, J., "Women and the Athenian Dramatic Festivals." *Transactions of the American Philological Association* 121 (1991b): 133–147.

Konstan, D., *Greek Comedy and Ideology* (New York and Oxford, 1996): 15–90.

Lowe, N. J., *Comedy. Greece & Rome*: New Surveys in the Classics, no. 37 (Cambridge, 2007): 21–62.

MacDowell, D.M., *Aristophanes and Athens* (Oxford, 1995).

Olson, S.D. (ed.), *Ancient Comedy and Reception: Essays in Honor of Jeffrey Henderson* (Berlin and Boston, 2013).

Platter, C., *Aristophanes and the Carnival of Genres* (Baltimore, 2007).

Revermann, M., *Comic Business: Theatricality, Dramatic Technique, and Performance Contexts of Aristophanic Comedy* (Oxford, 2006).

Rusten, J. (ed.), *The Birth of Comedy: Texts, Documents, and Art from Athenian Comic Competitions, 486–280* (Baltimore, 2011).

Silk, M.S., *Aristophanes and the Definition of Comedy* (Oxford, 2000).

Slater, N.W., *Spectator Politics: Metatheatre and Performance in Aristophanes* (Philadelphia, 2002).

Sommerstein, A.H., *Talking about Laughter: and Other Studies in Greek Comedy* (Oxford, 2009).

Sommerstein, A.H. (ed.), *Tragedy, Comedy and the Polis* (Bari, 1993).

Taaffe, L.K., *Aristophanes and Women* (London, 1993).

Taplin, O., *Comic Angels* (Oxford, 1993).

Van Steen, G.A.H., *Venom in Verse: Aristophanes in Modern Greece* (Princeton, 2000).

Zeitlin, F.I., *Playing the Other: Gender and Society in Classical Greek Literature* (Chicago and London, 1996).

MENANDER AND GREEK NEW COMEDY

Brown, P.G.McC., "Love and Marriage in Greek New Comedy." *Classical Quarterly* 43 (1993): 189–205.

Fantham, E., "Sex, Status and Survival in Hellenistic Athens: A Study of Women in New Comedy." *Phoenix* 29 (1975): 44–74.

Goldberg, S.M., *The Making of Menander's Comedy* (Berkeley and London, 1980).

Gutzwiller, K., "The Tragic Mask of Comedy: Metatheatricality in Menander." *Classical Antiquity* 19 (2000): 102–137.

Henry, M., *Menander's Courtesans and the Greek Comic Tradition* (repr. Frankfurt am Main, 1988).
Hunter, R.L., *The New Comedy of Greece and Rome* (Cambridge, 1985).
Ireland, S., "New Comedy," pp. 336–396 in G.W. Dobrov (ed.), *Brill's Companion to the Study of Greek Comedy* (Leiden and Boston, 2010).
Konstan, D., *Greek Comedy and Ideology* (New York and Oxford, 1995): 93–164.
Lape, S., *Reproducing Athens: Menander's Comedy, Democratic Culture, and the Hellenistic City* (Princeton, 2003).
Lowe, N.J., *Comedy. Greece & Rome*: New Surveys in the Classics, no. 37 (Cambridge, 2007): 63–80.
Nervegna, S., *Menander in Antiquity: the Contexts of Reception* (Cambridge, 2013).
Petrides, A.K., and S. Papaioannou (eds.), *New Perspectives on Postclassical Comedy* (Newcastle, 2010).
Rosivach, V.J., *When a Young Man Falls in Love: The Sexual Exploitation of Women in New Comedy* (London and New York, 1998).
Sommerstein, A.H. (ed.), *Menander in Contexts* (Routledge Monographs in Classical Studies 16) (New York, 2014).
Traill, A., *Women and the Comic Plot in Menander* (Cambridge, 2008).
Walton, M.J., and P.D. Arnott (eds.), *Menander and the Making of Comedy* (Westport, CT, and London, 1996).
Wiles, D., *The Masks of Menander: Sign and Meaning in Greek and Roman Performance* (Cambridge, 1991).
Zagagi, N., *The Comedy of Menander* (London, 1991).

PLAUTUS, TERENCE, AND ROMAN COMEDY

Anderson, W.S., *Barbarian Play: Plautus' Roman Comedy* (Toronto, 1993).
Augoustakis, A., and A. Traill (eds.), *A Companion to Terence* (Malden, MA, 2013).
Beare, W., *The Roman Stage* (3rd ed., London, 1964).
Boyle, A.J. (ed.), *Rethinking Terence. Ramus* 33 (Special Volume, 2004).
Chalmers, W.R. "Plautus and his Audience," in D.R. Dudley and T.A. Dorey (eds.), *Roman Drama* (London, 1965): 21–50.
Christenson, D.M., "Metatheatre," in Dinter (Forthcoming [2014]).
Dinter, M., *The Cambridge Companion to Roman Comedy* (Cambridge, Forthcoming [2014]).

Duckworth, G., *The Nature of Roman Comedy* (2nd ed., Norman, OK, 1994).

Dutsch, D.M., *Feminine Discourse in Roman Comedy: On Echoes and Voices* (Oxford, 2008).

Fontaine, M., *Funny Words in Plautus* (Oxford, 2010).

Forehand, W.E., *Terence* (Boston, 1985).

Fraenkel, E., *Plautine Elements in Plautus*, trs. T. Drevikovsky and F. Muecke (Oxford, 2007).

Goldberg, S.M., *Understanding Terence* (Princeton, 1986).

Gratwick, A.S., "Drama," pp. 77–137 in E.J. Kenney and W.V. Clausen (eds.), *The Cambridge History of Classical Literature II: Latin Literature* (Cambridge, 1982).

Konstan, D., *Roman Comedy* (Ithaca, NY, 1983).

Leigh, M., *Comedy and the Rise of Rome* (Oxford, 2004).

Lowe, N.J., *Comedy. Greece & Rome*: New Surveys in the Classics, no. 37 (Cambridge, 2007): 81–132.

Manuwald, G., *Roman Republican Theatre* (Cambridge, 2011).

Marshall, C.W., *The Stagecraft and Performance of Roman Comedy* (Cambridge, 2006).

McCarthy, K., *Slaves, Masters, and the Art of Authority in Plautine Comedy* (Princeton, 2000).

Moore, T.J., *The Theater of Plautus: Playing to the Audience* (Austin, TX, 1998).

Parker, H., "Plautus vs. Terence: Audience and Popularity Re-Examined." *American Journal of Philology* 117 (1996): 585–617.

Sharrock, A., *Reading Roman Comedy: Poetics and Playfulness in Plautus and Terence* (Cambridge, 2009).

Slater, N.W., *Plautus in Performance: the Theatre of the Mind* (Princeton, 1985).

Wiles, D., *The Masks of Menander: Sign and Meaning in Greek and Roman Performance* (Cambridge, 1991).

Wright, J., *Dancing in Chains; the Stylistic Unity of the Comoedia Palliata* (Rome, 1974).

GREEK AND ROMAN WOMEN

Bauman, R., *Women and Politics in Ancient Rome* (New York and London, 1992).

Blundell, S., *Women in Ancient Greece* (Cambridge, MA, 1995).

Connelly, J.B., *Portrait of a Priestess: Women and Ritual in Ancient Greece* (Princeton, 2007).

Cox, C., *Household Interests: Property, Marriage Strategies, and Family Dynamics in Ancient Athens* (Princeton, 1998).

D'Ambra, E., *Roman Women* (Cambridge, 2007).

Dean-Jones, L. *Women's Bodies in Classical Greek Science* (Oxford, 1994).

Dixon, S., *Reading Roman Women: Sources, Genres, and Real Life* (London, 2001).

Dixon, S., *The Roman Family* (Baltimore and London, 1992).

Fantham, E. et al. (eds.), *Women in the Classical World* (New York and Oxford, 1994).

Gardner, J.F., *Women in Roman Law and Society* (London and Sydney, 1986).

Hawley, R., and B. Levick (eds.), *Women in Antiquity: New Assessments* (London and New York, 1995).

Hemelrijk, E.A., *Matrona Docta: Educated Women in the Roman Elite from Cornelia to Julia Domna* (London and New York, 1999).

Joshel, S.R., and S. Murnaghan (eds.), *Women and Slaves in Greco-Roman Culture: Differential Equations* (London and New York, 1998).

Just, R., *Women in Athenian Law and Life* (London, 1989).

Lefkowitz, M.R., and M.B. Fant (eds.), *Women's Life in Greece and Rome: A Source Book in Translation* (3rd ed., Baltimore, 2005).

Lewis, S., *The Athenian Women: an Iconographic Handbook* (London and New York, 2002).

Llewellyn-Jones, L. (ed.), *Women's Dress in the Ancient Greek World* (London, 2002).

Neils, J., *Women in the Ancient World* (London and Los Angeles, 2011).

Pomeroy, S., *Spartan Women* (Oxford, 2002).

Richlin, A., *Pornography and Representation in Greece and Rome* (Oxford and New York, 1992).

Saller, R.P., *Patriarchy, Property and Death in the Roman Family* (Cambridge, 1994).

Schaps, D.M., *Economic Rights of Women in Ancient Greece* (Edinburgh, 1979).

Skinner, M.B., *Sexuality in Greek and Roman Culture* (Malden, MA, 2013).

Treggiari, S., *Roman Marriage* (Oxford, 1991).

Wyke, M., *The Roman Mistress: Ancient and Modern Representations* (Oxford, 2002).

TRANSLATION STUDIES

Baker, M., and G. Saldanha (eds.), *Routledge Encyclopedia of Translation Studies* (2nd ed., London and New York, 2009).

Hardwick, L., *Translating Words, Translating Cultures* (London, 2000).

Lianeri, A., and V. Zajko (eds.), *Translation and the Classics: Identity as Change in the History of Culture* (Oxford, 2008).

Pym, A., *Exploring Translation Theories* (London and New York, 2010).

Robson, J., "Lost in Translation? The Problems of (Aristophanic) Humour," pp. 168–182 in L. Hardwick and C. Stray (eds.), *A Companion to Classical Receptions* (Oxford, 2008).

Venuti, L., *The Translator's Invisibility: A History of Translation* (2nd ed., London and New York, 2008).

Venuti, L., *The Translation Studies Reader* (3rd ed., London and New York, 2012).

Walton, J.M., *Found in Translation: Greek Drama in English* (Cambridge, 2006).

LYSISTRATA

Bierl, A., "Women on the Acropolis and Mental Mapping: Comic Body-Politics in a City in Crisis, or Ritual and Metaphor in Aristophanes' *Lysistrata*," pp. 250–290 in A. Markantonatos and B. Zimmermann (eds.), *Crisis on Stage: Tragedy and Comedy in Late Fifth-century Athens* (Walter de Gruyter Trends in Classics Supplementary Volumes 13) (Berlin and Boston, 2011).

Faraone, C.A., "Salvation and Female Heroics in the Parodos of Aristophanes' *Lysistrata*." *Journal of Hellenic Studies* 117 (1997): 38–59.

Foley, H.P., "The 'Female Intruder' Reconsidered: Women in Aristophanes' *Lysistrata* and *Ecclesiazusae*." *Classical Philology* 77 (1982): 1–21.

Fox, M.-J., "The Idea of Women in Peacekeeping: *Lysistrata* and *Antigone*." *International Peacekeeping* 8 (2007): 9–22.

Harriott, R., "*Lysistrata*: Action and Theme." *Themes in Drama* 7 (1985): 11–22.

Martin, R.P., "Fire on the Mountain: *Lysistrata* and the Lemnian Women." *Classical Antiquity* 6 (1987): 77–105.

Olson, S.D., "Lysistrata's Conspiracy and the Politics of 412 B.C.," pp. 69–81 in C.W. Marshall and G. Kovacs (eds.), *No Laughing Matter. Studies in Athenian Comedy* (London, 2012).

Sommerstein, A.H., *Talking about Laughter: and Other Studies in Greek Comedy* (Oxford, 2009): 222–236.

Stroup, S., "Designing Women: Aristophanes' *Lysistrata* and the 'Hetairization' of the Greek Wife." *Arethusa* 37 (2004): 37–73.

Vaio, J., "The Manipulation of Theme and Action in Aristophanes' *Lysistrata*." *Greek, Roman, and Byzantine Studies* 14 (1973): 369–380.

Westlake, H.D., "The *Lysistrata* and the War." *Phoenix* 34 (1980): 38–54.

SAMIA

Arnott, W.G., "Stage Business in Menander's *Samia*," pp. 113–124 in S. Gödde and T. Heinze (eds.), *Skenika: Beiträge zum antiken Theater und seine Rezeption. Festschrift zum 65. Geburtstag von Horst-Dieter Blume* (Darmstadt, 2000).

Goldberg, S.M., *The Making of Menander's Comedy* (Berkeley and Los Angeles, 1980): 92–108.

Groton, A.H., "Anger in Menander's *Samia*." *American Journal of Philology* 108 (1987): 437–443.

Heap, A.M., "The Baby as Hero? The Role of the Infant in Menander." *Bulletin of the Institute of Classical Studies* 46 (2002–3): 77–129.

Keuls, E., "The *Samia* of Menander. An Interpretation of its Plot and Theme." *Zeitschrift für Papyrologie und Epigraphik* 10 (1973): 1–20.

Lape, S., "Gender in Menander's Comedy," pp. 51–78 in A.K. Petrides and S. Papaioannou (eds.), *New Perspectives on Postclassical Comedy* (Newcastle, 2010).

Traill, A., *Women and the Comic Plot in Menander* (Cambridge, 2008): 86–92, 156–169.

West, S., "Notes on the *Samia*." *Zeitschrift für Papyrologie und Epigraphik* 88 (1991): 11–23.

CASINA

Andrews, N.E., "Tragic Re-Presentation and the Semantics of Space in Plautus' *Casina*." *Mnemosyne* 57 (2004): 445–464.

Cody, J.M., "The 'Senex Amator' in Plautus' *Casina*." *Hermes* 104 (1976): 453–476.

Connors, C. "Scents and Sensibility in Plautus' *Casina*." *Classical Quarterly* 47 (1997): 305–309.

Dees, R.L., "Aspects of the Roman Law of Marriage in Plautus' *Casina*." *Iura* 39 (1991): 107–120.

Forehand, W.E., "Plautus' 'Casina': an Explication." *Arethusa* 6 (1973): 233–256.

Franko, G.F., "Imagery and Names in Plautus' Casina." *Classical Journal* 95 (1999): 1–17.

Gold, B., "Vested Interests in Plautus' *Casina*: Cross-Dressing in Roman Comedy." *Helios* 25 (1998): 17–29.

Krauss, A.N., *Untaming the Shrew: Marriage, Morality and Plautine Comedy* (Ph.D. dissertation, University of Texas at Austin, 2004): 89–108.

O'Bryhim, S., "The Originality of Plautus' *Casina*." *American Journal of Philology* 110 (1989): 81–103.

Rei., A., "Villains, Wives, and Slaves in the Comedies of Plautus," in S.R. Joshel and S. Murnaghan (eds.), *Women and Slaves in Greco-Roman Culture: Differential Equations* (London and New York, 1998) 92–108.

Williams, B., "Games People Play: Metatheatre as Performance Criticism in Plautus' *Casina*." *Ramus* 22 (1993): 33–59.

HECYRA

Anderson, W.S., "Resistance to Recognition and 'Privileged Recognition' in Terence." *Classical Journal* 96 (2002): 1–8.

Augoustakis, A., and A. Traill (eds.), *A Companion to Terence* (Malden, MA, 2013).

James, S., "From Boys to Men: Rape and Developing Masculinity in Terence's *Hecyra* and *Eunuchus*." *Helios* (1998): 31–48.

James, S., "Gender and Sexuality in Terence," pp. 175–194 in Augoustakis and Traill (2013).

Knorr, O., "*Hecyra*," pp. 295–317 in Augoustakis and Traill (2013).

Konstan, D. "Terence's *Hecyra*." *Far-Western Forum* 1 (1974): 23–34.

Lada-Richards, I., "Authorial Voice and Theatrical Self-Definition in Terence and Beyond: The *Hecyra* Prologues in Ancient and Modern Contexts." *Greece & Rome* 51 (2004): 55–82.

McGarrity, T., "Reputation Vs. Reality in Terence's *Hecyra*." *Classical Journal* 76 (1980): 149–156.

Penwill, J.L., "The Unlovely Lover of Terence's *Hecyra*." *Ramus* 33 (2004): 130–149.

Slater, N.W., "The Fictions of Patriarchy in Terence's *Hecyra*." *Classical World* 81 (1988): 249–260.

Aristophanes' LYSISTRATA

Lysistrata premièred in 411 BCE, probably at the Lenaean festival early that year (cf. Introduction 4–5). Athens was still feeling the effects of disastrous losses of men and ships in the Sicilian Expedition (415–413 BCE), which had also led various Athenian allies to defect in the still-ongoing Peloponnesian War.[1] The Athenians had begun to rebuild their navy in 412, and Athens was now under the control of a board of 10 elderly Probouloi (the Administrator is one of them), who had been granted exceptional powers to expedite military operations. Although Athens had recovered sufficiently to restore the war to stalemate status, the Athenians had suffered significant territorial losses, the city was now surrounded by Spartan forces, and a secret oligarchic plot that would succeed later in 411 ("The Four Hundred") was afoot. Athens was in no strategic position to negotiate for an armistice, but after 20 years of warfare interrupted only by the Peace of Nikias

1. For the historical context, see further Sommerstein, A.H., "Aristophanes and the Events of 411." *Journal of Hellenic Studies* 97 (1977): 112–126.

(421–414 BCE), many of the city's war-fatigued citizens must have been longing for peace when *Lysistrata* was first performed.

Lysistrata presents a typically Aristophanic fantastical and rebellious scheme. One early morning in Athens, Lysistrata, an Athenian citizen of indeterminate age and marital status (see note 89), convenes a broad coalition of women—young and old, Athenian and non-Athenian, and representatives of all classes of free persons. After much opening comic business based on stereotypes of women's bibulousness, lack of sexual control, bawdiness, and so forth, the younger women swear an oath to launch a sex strike[2] that will force their warrior husbands to negotiate for peace (209ff.). The Spartan Lampito is dispatched to manage the strike in Sparta, and Lysistrata and the others join the old women who have already seized the Athenian Acropolis (Athena's cult center and the location of the state treasury), which serves as the setting for the play. An angry chorus of 12 old men arrives (254ff.), equipped with fire and wood to smoke out (or roast) the women, and they are soon met by a no less feisty chorus of 12 women carrying pitchers of water on their heads (319ff.).

The gender-divided semi-choruses trade insults, and the women douse the men with water (381ff.). Then enters the Administrator, who has come to remove funds from the treasury to further finance the war (421–422). In the confrontation between the Administrator and Lysistrata, the latter argues that the city's normally silenced women have a personal stake in the war and should therefore be allowed to offer advice about it:

> So our advice wasn't needed when you'd messed everything up?
> But then we heard you publicly saying right in the streets,

2. I use this convenient metaphor *passim* (cf. the objections of Morales, H., "Aristophanes' *Lysistrata*, the Liberian 'Sex Strike,' and the Politics of Reception." *Greece and Rome* 2nd Series 60 [2013]: 281–295), even though, for the women, sex obviously is not a commodity they (refuse to) produce for their husbands/quasi-employers. While the women might more accurately be described as withholding sex as a form of activism, "strike" perhaps can bear a more general meaning here (e.g., "protest against a perceived injustice").

> "There isn't a man left in this land." And someone else answering, "No, not a single one, by Zeus!"
> After hearing that, we immediately decided to gather together as women
> Committed to saving Greece. We saw no reason to wait any longer.
> We have useful advice to share with you, if you'll take your turn at listening;
> So if you shut up as we did, we can set you straight on things. (522–528)

Lysistrata gets the best of the thoroughly detestable Administrator, who then is outfitted as a woman and sent off for his (figurative) burial (599ff.). The dueling semi-choruses of men and women trade more insults, until Lysistrata reappears (706) to report that the requisite sexual abstinence is weighing heavily on some of her co-conspirators, who are devising pretexts to leave the Acropolis. Lysistrata manages to rally her troops with a comic oracle that stresses the need for female solidarity (767ff.).

A new plot development unfolds when Myrrhine's phallically challenged and domestically frazzled husband Kinesias arrives, along with a household slave holding the couple's infant child (845ff.). At Lysistrata's prompting, Myrrhine proceeds to tease Kinesias without yielding to his desires (869–951); in the end she succeeds in obtaining his pledge to vote for peace, a process we are to imagine is being repeated throughout Greece. A similarly discomfited messenger from Sparta soon arrives (980) to announce the strike's success in Sparta, and he and Kinesias agree to summon ambassadors from both cities in order to negotiate a peace (1007–1012). The choruses of men and women face off once more, but this time, after the women's chorus leader removes a gnat from her counterpart's eye, they unite in song and dance (1043–1071). This development heralds the play's final movement toward full reconciliation and peace.

Erect delegates arrive from both sides. Lysistrata, who has been offstage since line 864, returns and brings forth the personification of Reconciliation (*Diallage*), apparently an actor wearing a "naked suit," a kind of body stocking stuffed to represent a voluptuous female body (1108ff.). Lysistrata chastises both Athenians and Spartans for denying their religious and cultural commonalities and advocates a spirit of panhellenism instead (1128ff.). Both parties then map out their territorial desires on Reconciliation (1162ff.), with a focus on what they consider to be her erogenous zones, and thus show their willingness to make concessions in order to effect a peace. As all retreat to the Acropolis for a feast, a brief choral interlude follows. The ambassadors return to happily report that the banquet has further sealed peace negotiations. A Spartan ambassador dances solo and sings a song recalling how Athenians and Spartans united to defeat the Persians in the great international wars earlier in the fifth century (1247–1272). Lysistrata[3] and the other women emerge from the Acropolis for the play's finale, in which the married couples dance as an Athenian ambassador calls upon various gods to witness the peace (1279–1290). His song is followed closely by a thoroughly Spartan song of his counterpart (1296–1321). The play closes with a call to celebrate "the all-victorious Goddess of the Bronze House" (i.e., Athena, as she is worshipped as a protective goddess in Sparta).

Lysistrata understandably has been viewed as a feminist play by some, though such a designation calls for considerable qualification. Aristophanes' *Lysistrata, Women at the Thesmophoria,* and *Assemblywomen* often have been lumped together as "women on top" plays: the women do encroach on traditionally "masculine" territory (politics, sex, war), but their cooption of male prerogative never threatens to be lasting. *Lysistrata* features an unambiguously strong-willed and astute heroine as its titular character, albeit a construct of male playwriting and acting. At times, the

3. Probably: see note 195 below.

play nonetheless seems to focalize ancient Athenian women's points of view: as mothers, their civic duty is to produce sons who may perish on the battlefield (589–590, 651); as wives, they miss their campaigning husbands (99ff., 523ff.), if only in comically sexual terms (591–592); and Lysistrata with pathos notes that the shortage of young men caused by the war is creating a growing class of women unlikely to ever marry (592–597).[4] Lysistrata instructs the younger women on how to deal with their husbands' likely use of force ("There's no pleasure in it for them when they force you," 164); what counts as domestic violence today was commonplace in classical Athens. Near the end of the play, Lysistrata tells Reconciliation not to be aggressive with the delegates in "That brutish way our husbands used to treat us" (1117; i.e., before the women gained the upper hand through their protest?). In a lively exchange with the bellicose Administrator in which they dress him up as a woman (520–538), Lysistrata and her colleagues even manage to invert the traditional saw "war is men's work."[5]

Male stereotypes are lavished on the women, especially in the first half of the play, by both male and, more often, female characters: women are bibulous (195ff.); wildly hypersexual (22ff., 107ff., 124ff., 677ff., 715ff.); foolish, flighty, irresponsible, and habitually late (4, 13–15, 42ff.); and even morally depraved (11–12, 252–253, 283–284, 368–369, 387ff., 468). As a comic playwright engaged in a civic competition, Aristophanes should perhaps not be faulted for resorting to these expected clichés. More remarkable is his creation of a female figure to transcend stereotypes. Lysistrata is indeed the first female heroine—that is, a human as opposed to mythical figure like the heroines of tragedy—to appear as a developed character in extant Greek drama. In her rebelliousness,

4. Athenian girls typically married at fourteen: cf. Introduction 23.

5. The women's use of clothing here to assert the counter-claim that "war is women's work" (538) anticipates the modern "coat-rack" theory of gender (i.e., that gender is a kind of social integument that is laid out on our bodies): see Nicholson, L., "Interpreting Gender." *Signs* 20 (1994): 79–105.

perspicacity, assertiveness, and adherence to admirable panhellenic ideals, she stands out among all the play's characters, both male and female, and she rises prominently above the others' pettiness and venality. Her name has suggested to some an identification with Lysimache, the actual priestess of Athena Polias ("Athena the City-Goddess") in 411 BCE,[6] but an even more compelling identification can be made between Lysistrata and the goddess Athena herself, given the Aristophanic heroine's dedication to saving Athens and all of Greece (41, 525–526; cf. 341–343). This identification of the towering heroine with the great city goddess is powerfully evoked if in fact Lysistrata proudly presides over the play's closing scene (see note 195 below).

In contrast to Aristophanes' much later *Assemblywomen* (392 BCE), in which the women coopt the Athenian assembly to organize a new polis built on principles of economic and sexual communism, the women of *Lysistrata* are interested in securing peace, not recasting social institutions at large. Nor obviously is their goal anything like the achievement of absolute equality between men and women—that is, in a modern democratic sense of equal rights, equal opportunities, and the like. Lysistrata mainly pleads for the right of women to be heard on issues of importance, such as the war, that affect all of society:

> All of you listen up now:
> I am a woman and I have a brain:
> I'm quite bright to begin with,
> And since I've listened to a lot of my father's
> And my elders' discussions, I'm not poorly educated.
> (1123–1127)

The play requires no permanent swap of men's (political, military) and women's (domestic, religious) spheres, but only an adjustment

6. See further Connelly, J.B., *Portrait of a Priestess: Women and Ritual in Ancient Greece* (Princeton, 2007): 62–64.

of men's appreciation of the women's value to the city. This is especially the case in the religious sphere, where the women's role in helping to secure Athens' safety is repeatedly emphasized:

> Citizens of Athens, we'll start with
> Some useful ideas for the city.
> I do this out of gratitude for being nurtured by Athens' glorious prosperity.
> At exactly seven years old, I was an Arrhephoros.
> And then, when I was ten, I served as a Grinder for the Foundress,
> And at Brauron I took off my saffron-dress and became a Bear.
> And once, as a lovely young girl, I was a Kanephoros
> And wore a dried-fig necklace. (638–647)

In these few lines, the chorus of women powerfully evoke some of the city's most revered cult practices, especially the Great Panathenaic festival, in which females of all ages play essential roles in ensuring fertility, and thus the city-state's general welfare:

> Aristophanes seems to take special care in investing both Lysistrata and the older women with an unusual kind of authority, a female heroism if you will, that stems from their repeated association with both the day-to-day household economy and the important civic rituals and cults, upon which the safety of the city ultimately depends. (Faraone 1997: 39)

All joking aside, this suggests that the real power that the women exercise lies in the performance of their most traditional roles, again a situation that does not necessarily square with most modern notions of gender equality.

The women's cause is also helped along by the fact that the bulk of the play presents the male characters in an extremely negative light. The chorus of fire-bearing old men manifests an irrational, over-the-top reaction to the women's occupation of the Acropolis (254ff.). They then are put in their place by the leader of the women's chorus:

> That's why offering useful advice is my way of paying back
> my debt to the city.
> I shouldn't be denied a say for being born a woman,
> Especially when my proposals are better than what we've
> currently got.
> I've made my contribution: I supply the city with men.
> The same can't be said of *you*, you decrepit old geezers,
> Since you've wasted our paternal inheritance from the
> Persian Wars
> And don't produce enough revenues to make up for the loss.
> No, it's because of you we're in imminent danger of bankruptcy.
> Any grunts in your defense? If you annoy me the slightest bit,
> I'm going to smack you in the jaw with my rawhide boot!
> (648–657)

Early on, the old men are aligned with the play's villain, the Administrator. This cantankerous old man represents what must have been an increasingly unpopular class of war-profiteers (488ff.). He appears in the play only to access the treasury and to retrieve funds in order to build more ships for the war (421–422).

Lysistrata features surprising conflations of space traditionally demarcated as male or female. To launch their plan, the women must abandon their usual spheres of influence—home, family, and household management—because, in Lysistrata's words, the current crisis calls them to an even higher purpose (15ff.). Kinesias later supplies us with a comically chaotic picture of a household deprived of its usual manager (877ff.). The women occupy the Acropolis to cut off funding for the Athenian war machine, but their control of the city goddess' sacred space takes on a much larger symbolic meaning. Immediately upon entering, the chorus of old men claims that the women "have seized *my* Acropolis" (263; cf. 482), and the Administrator joins them in asking "what their motive was in locking down *our* Acropolis" (488). Staking out exclusive ownership of the Acropolis is tantamount to claiming the entire city. But as noted above, Athenian women play a crucial role in various civic cults of Athena, the most important ones being centered on the Acropolis, to which the play's conspiring older women are able to gain easy access by "pretending to do a sacrifice" (179). The takeover of the Acropolis's space, therefore, is much less a transgressive act than merely the women's attempt to reclaim a share of what was traditionally theirs. In the blind rush to continue the war and now increasingly dependent on the city's financial reserves, the city's leaders, rather, have intruded upon the women's legitimate claim to this space and its role in the city's welfare as the shared property of all citizens.

To shock the audience into this realization, the Acropolis is not only turned into the women's theater of operations but also into a farcical bedroom, complete with bed, pillow, blanket, and unguents, when Myrrhine teases Kinesias there and comically assumes control of their sex life (911ff.). Private and public spheres effectively are reversed and subverted before the audience's eyes. By extrapolation, the idea that women, as skilled household managers, are ideally equipped to manage the city's affairs is the basis for Lysistrata's political vision of solidarity among all free Greek citizens and residents:

> Suppose the city's a great big shorn fleece.
> First you dunk it in a bath to get rid of all the sheep pooh.
> Lay it out on a bed
> And pound out the rabble-rousers and extract the burrs.
> As for the sticky ones who are always glomming onto
> public office:
> Card them out thoroughly and give their heads a good
> plucking.

Then card the remaining wool into a basket of solidarity, with everyone
Harmoniously mixed in together. Include resident aliens, friendly foreigners,
And even those in hock to the public treasury—toss them all in too!
And absolutely do not forget about all the colonies we founded:
Consider them to be flocks of wool laid out separately
From one another. And then take each and every flock of them,
Bring them here, roll them all together into a mass
And create a giant ball of wool. Finally, take it and weave a new cloak for the people. (574–586)

The success of the final banquet on the Acropolis that includes both men and women, along with the dancing of couples that follows (1225ff.), signifies that Lysistrata's plans have triumphed and implies that Athenian men have come to a renewed appreciation of their wives' civic relevance. The closing song in praise of Sparta's version of Athena likewise suggests that a new equilibrium between the sexes has prevailed in Sparta, and by extension in all of Greece.

In the end, *Lysistrata* stops well short of proposing a radically new *polis.* While (re-)asserting women's voices in a society whose political institutions legally excluded them, the central message of *Lysistrata* is simply peace, however unrealistic its prospect might actually have been in 411.[7] Lysistrata and the women exhibit no desire for real political power or for a permanent subversion of the status quo in public life. The crude groping of Reconciliation near the play's end suggests that sexual politics have not been altered significantly in private life and that men probably will continue to

7. See further Sommerstein (2009).

manifest harmful aggression and a lack of restraint in the public sphere. Still, the solidarity exhibited by the women of Athens, in contrast to the factionalism, corruption, and destructive bickering that characterized actual Athenian democracy, presents an enviable model of collaboration for social well-being. Most memorable of all is the cerebral, strategizing, self-controlled, and empowering figure of Lysistrata herself.

LYSISTRATA

CAST OF CHARACTERS (WITH SPEAKING PARTS)

LYSISTRATA: an Athenian woman

KALONIKE: friend of Lysistrata

MYRRHINE: an Athenian woman, wife of Kinesias

LAMPITO: a married Spartan woman

LEADER OF MEN'S CHORUS

CHORUS OF OLD MEN

LEADER OF WOMEN'S CHORUS

CHORUS OF OLD WOMEN

ADMINISTRATOR: an Athenian special magistrate

OLD LADIES #1, #2, and #3: allies of Lysistrata

WOMEN #1, #2, #3, and #4: co-conspirators of Lysistrata

KINESIAS: husband of Myrrhine

BABY: infant child of Kinesias and Myrrhine

SPARTAN MESSENGER

UNITED CHORUS OF OLD MEN AND WOMEN

UNITED CHORUS LEADER

SPARTAN AMBASSADOR

ATHENIAN AMBASSADORS #1 and #2

SCENE 1

(Setting: The stage building represents the Acropolis, with its central doors serving as the Propylaia, the gated entrance to the Acropolis. Lysistrata anxiously paces before this setting until she speaks below.[8]*)*

8. For a detailed reconstruction of the play's staging, see Ewans, M., *Aristophanes: Lysistrata, The Women's Festival, and Frogs* (Norman, OK, 2010): 227–250.

LYSISTRATA[9] You know, if they'd been invited to a Bacchic rave,[10]
Or to Pan's[11] place or to Genetyllis' at Kolias,[12]
You wouldn't be able to get anywhere because of all their tambourines.[13]
But as it as, not a single woman's here,
Except for my neighbor who's coming this way now— 5
Hi, Kalonike. KALONIKE[14] Hello, Lysistrata.
Why the frown? Don't scowl like that, dear!
Those knitted brows don't flatter you any.

LYSISTRATA Honestly, Kalonike, I'm so angry I could just explode!
I'm so aggravated about us women. 10
To the men's way of thinking, we're virtually
Sociopaths— KALONIKE Right. We are, aren't we, by Zeus?[15]

LYSISTRATA They were told to meet here
To discuss a very important matter!
They don't show up, and decided to sleep in instead.
KALONIKE Now, now sweetie, 15

9. Her name means "Disbander of Armies" in Greek.

10. For the god Dionysus/Bacchus, see Appendix. Lysistrata here refers to religious festivals in honor of Dionysus for women only. In comedy, these are stereotypically portrayed as opportunities for women, once freed from their households and male supervision, to engage in bibulous and licentious behavior.
In keeping with the aims of this translation (see Introduction 30–31), I have retained these very specific opening references ("Bacchic rave," "Pan's place," "Genetyllis' at Kolias"). Ewans' (note 8 above) translation demonstrates how these phrases can easily be generalized for a modern performance by his renderings "an orgy," "a sleep-out," "a celebration of the love goddess," respectively.

11. Pan is a lusty rustic deity, at whose grottoes women gathered for festive occasions (cf. 911ff.).

12. Genetyllis is a goddess of childbirth (with erotic associations). The precise location of Kolias is unknown, but it was the site of a temple and women's festival of Aphrodite (see Appendix), referred to here for their erotic connotations. For the stereotyping of women as sexually insatiable, see Introductory Essay 43.

13. I.e., *tympana*, associated with the worship of Dionysus in particular and ecstatic celebrations in general.

14. Her name means "Beautiful Victory."

15. For the Olympian god Zeus, see Appendix.

They'll show. Getting out of the house isn't that easy for us wives:
We're always having to bend over backwards for our husbands,
Or having to wake up the maid, or having to put
The baby to bed, or bathing and feeding it.

20 LYSISTRATA Yes, but there are some things they should consider
More important than all that. KALONIKE So what's up,
Lysistrata darling?
Whatever in the world have you called all of us together for?
What's this business all about? Just how big is it?
LYSISTRATA Oh, it's big. KALONIKE And hard too?

LYSISTRATA Yes it's hard, absolutely! KALONIKE Then why
haven't we all shown up in a flash?

LYSISTRATA I didn't mean *that*. They obviously would have
25 shown up already for that!
But this's something I've been examining
And bouncing around for many sleepless nights.

KALONIKE Must be teeny-weeny after all that nighttime bouncing.

LYSISTRATA Teeny-weeny enough that the salvation
30 Of all Greece[16] rests in the laps of us women.

KALONIKE In the laps of us women? Hardly a safe place for that!

LYSISTRATA Rest assured, Athens' future lies with us.
Whether the Peloponnesians[17] are exterminated—

KALONIKE I'm 100% percent behind that, to be sure!

35 LYSISTRATA And every last Boeotian[18] is completely wiped out—

KALONIKE No, not every last one of them! You've got to spare
the eels.[19]

16. The idea of a unified nation of Greece was only an abstract idea ("panhellenism") in the classical period, as the political unit was instead the city-state (e.g., Athens, Sparta, Corinth).

17. Sparta and her allies on the Peloponnese are Athens' chief enemies in the current war (cf. Introductory Essay 39–40).

18. Boeotia was a region of central Greece whose chief city was Thebes. The Boeotians joined the Peloponnesians in the war against Athens.

19. Eels from Lake Kopias in Boeotia were a delicacy; the war has interrupted their exportation to Athens (cf. 702ff.).

LYSISTRATA I won't—knock on wood—utter one bad word
About the Athenians. Anyway, you know what I'd say.
But if the women all meet together here—
The Boeotians, the Peloponnesians, 40
And us—together we can save Greece!

KALONIKE But what brainy or heroic deeds are we women
Capable of? We just sit around all prettied up,
Wearing our saffron dresses,[20] plastered in make-up,
With our Kimberic[21] lingerie and six-inch heels. 45

LYSISTRATA That's exactly it! These very things will be our salvation—
The saffron dresses, and our perfume, and our pumps,
And the rouge, and our sheer lingerie!

KALONIKE What on earth do you mean? LYSISTRATA Not one man of those left
Will raise his spear against anyone else— 50

KALONIKE By the Two Goddesses,[22] I'm dying my dress saffron right now!

LYSISTRATA Nor take up his shield— KALONIKE Mmm—I'm slipping into my Kimberic see-through!

LYSISTRATA Nor even a knife. KALONIKE That's it! I'm getting some pumps!

LYSISTRATA So shouldn't the women have shown up here already?

KALONIKE "*Shown up here*"? They should have *flown* here ages ago! 55

LYSISTRATA They're true-blue Athenians, dear: you know
Our national motto, "always late when it counts the most."
Not one single woman from the Paralia,[23]
Or even anyone from Salamis![24] KALONIKE The women of Salamis?
They've been busy riding their men's masts since daybreak. 60

20. An expensive, yellow-dyed women's garment usually worn at festivals or other special occasions.

21. Imported from a locale in Asia Minor associated with exotic clothing.

22. Demeter and her daughter Persephone (see Appendix).

23. A district (i.e., deme) of greater Athens, which is collectively known as Attica.

24. An island in the Saronic Gulf off the coast of Athens. Cf. note 81 below.

LYSISTRATA And the ones I expected to show up
Here first, the ladies of Acharnai[25]—
They haven't come at all! KALONIKE Well, Theogenes' wife[26] at least
Has come here and hoisted her sail.
65 Hey, look! Some of them are actually coming now!

LYSISTRATA Oh, and some others are coming over there!
KALONIKE Phew!
Where are they from? LYSISTRATA Stenchville.[27]
KALONIKE By Zeus!
So that's why they're raising such a stink.

MYRRHINE[28] We're not late, are we, Lysistrata?
What do you say? Ouch—silence! LYSISTRATA I don't
70 approve of
Anyone's showing up late for something this important.

MYRRHINE Hey, it was hard to find my girdle in the dark.
But now that we're here, tell us what's so damn urgent.

LYSISTRATA Let's wait a little while longer
75 For the women from Boeotia and the Peloponnese
To arrive. MYRRHINE Agreed, that makes better sense.
Hey, there's Lampito coming right now!

LYSISTRATA Hello, Lampito, my darling Spartan friend!

MYRRHINE How gorgeous you are, sweetie!
80 What a complexion, and that tight body of yours!

25. A deme of Athens that had suffered severe losses in the war.

26. The identification of Theagenes (a very common name) is uncertain, but the description of his wife's "hoisting her sail" characterizes her as stereotypically bibulous (cf. note 10 above).

27. Anagyrous was a deme in a swampy area named for a malodorous plant growing there.

28. A common Greek name meaning "Myrtle" that also was slang for female genitalia.

You could manhandle a bull![29] LAMPITO[30] Very much
yes I think, by Twin Gods.[31]
I am exerciser and I jump at my butt.[32]

KALONIKE And that is one fine titty-rack you've got!

LAMPITO Why you feel me up like animal for sacrifice?

LYSISTRATA Where's this other young woman from? 85

LAMPITO By Twin Gods, she ambassador for you from
Boeotia. MYRRHINE My goodness, she's just like
Boeotia,
What with all that lovely pubic land down there![33]
KALONIKE And I swear by Zeus,
That bush[34] of hers is so neatly trimmed!

LYSISTRATA And who's the other girl? LAMPITO Mighty
fine lady, by Twin Gods, 90
She from Corinth.[35] KALONIKE Mighty fine, by Zeus,
Is right—both in front and in back!

29. Women in the military state of Sparta exercised in the gymnasium and participated in sports, reflecting a Spartan belief in "eugenics" (strong mothers produce strong warriors). Cf. Introduction 23.

30. A common Spartan name that means "Shining," reflecting an ancient stereotype of the beautiful and fit Spartan woman (see further Introduction 23). In the play, Lampito and the other Spartans speak a distorted version of their local dialect of Greek (Laconian), which was distinct from the Athenians' own—to them normative—Attic dialect. For all the Spartans in *Lysistrata*, I have used a form of broken English (as, for example, that in popular comic representations of Russians or a caricature such as Sacha Baron Cohen's Borat) that features linguistic slips commonly made in the course of second language acquisition (e.g., improper use of articles, confusion of words, unidiomatic syntax). In keeping with the aims of this translation (see Introduction 30–31), I have purposely avoided an overly domesticated rendering in, for example, a regional dialect of American English. For Aristophanes' use of non-Attic Greek, see Colvin, S., *Dialect in Aristophanes and the Politics of Language in Ancient Greek Literature* (Oxford, 1999).

31. Castor and Pollux, brothers of Helen and known as the Dioscuri, were important warrior deities in Spartan cult. Cf. note 211 below.

32. The *bibasis* was a competitive form of dance/exercise practiced by Spartan women, in which they vigorously flung their heels up to their buttocks.

33. Boeotia is known for its fertile plains (cf. note 18 above).

34. Literally, the Pennyroyal plant. Depilation of female body hair was commonplace in the ancient Greek world (cf. note 144 below).

35. An influential Greek city-state near the neck of land that joins Athens and mainland Greece to the Peloponnese.

LAMPITO But who's convener of this troop
Full of women here? **LYSISTRATA** That would be me.

LAMPITO Tell to us what you mean to say. **KALONIKE** Yes,
95 dear lady,
What is this serious business you have for us?

LYSISTRATA I'll tell you soon, but first I want to ask you all
This one tiny little question. **KALONIKE** What's that?

LYSISTRATA Don't you really miss the fathers of your children
100 When they're away on active duty? I'm pretty sure
Each and every one of you has a husband off somewhere.

KALONIKE Yes, dear. Mine's been away for five months
In Thrace—he's assigned to guard our general Eukrates
there.[36]

MYRRHINE And mine's been in Pylos[37] for seven whole
months.

105 **LAMPITO** Mine he sometime come home from regiment,
But then he strap up shield and away he fly again.

KALONIKE And you can't find so much as a trace of a lover
these days.
On top of that, ever since the Milesians[38] betrayed us,
I haven't set my eyes upon even a six-inch dildo,
110 Which could've provided me some small comfort in wartime.

LYSISTRATA If I could come up with a way to end
The war, would you join up with my cause?
KALONIKE By the Two Goddesses,
I sure would, even if you made me sell
This dress of mine for drinking money today!

36. A common name, and so any identification with a particular Eukrates is uncertain. The joke here turns on the expectation of a specific place name in Thrace, a region of northern Greece considered to be barbaric by the Greeks (cf. notes 98 and 137 below), rather than the naming of one of the Athenians' own commanders.

37. A western coastal city on the Peloponnese occupied by the Athenians during much of the war, and still held by them in 411 BCE. Cf. 1163.

38. Miletus, a great city of Asia Minor, broke from its alliance with the Athenians the year before the debut of *Lysistrata*. Miletus was a major producer of dildos, and so this is another example of a deprivation brought about by the war (cf. note 19 above).

MYRRHINE I'm in, and I'd hack myself in two like a halibut 115
To donate half of me for the cause.

LAMPITO And I climb to top of Mount Taygetus[39]
To take glimpse of peace from there.

LYSISTRATA Then it's time to reveal my plan to you all:
Ladies, the only way we can force 120
Our men to pursue peace
Is for us to relinquish— KALONIKE What? Tell us!
LYSISTRATA You're on board then?

KALONIKE Yes we are, even if we must sacrifice our lives.

LYSISTRATA Okay, then: *we must renounce dick*!
Hey, why are you all turning away and walking off? 125
What's with all the pursed lips and head-shaking?
What's happened to that shiny complexion of yours? Why the tears?
Are you with me or not? What's the hold up here?

KALONIKE I'm out. The war can just keep crawling on.

MYRRHINE I'm out too, by Zeus. The war will just have to drag on. 130

LYSISTRATA Is that so, my "little halibut"? I believe you just now
Said you'd cut yourself in two for the cause.

KALONIKE Anything, anything else—whatever you want! I'd even
Walk across fire. Anything except *giving up dick*!
Lysistrata, darling, there's just nothing else like it. 135

LYSISTRATA What about you? WOMAN #1 I'd also go with walking across fire.

LYSISTRATA Oh what an ass-fucked bunch all us women are!
No wonder we're the subjects of tragedies!
What are we except Poseidon and a rowboat![40]

39. The highest mountain of Laconia, the region around Sparta.

40. An allusion to a lost play of the fifth-century BCE Athenian tragedian Sophocles, in which a woman named Tyro is seduced by the god Poseidon (for whom, see Appendix) disguised as her lover. She gives birth to two sons, Pelias and Neleus, who are exposed in a small boat but rescued by shepherds and ultimately reunited with their mother.

140 But my lovely Spartan friend: if you alone are
With me, we can still save the day.
Do I have your vote? LAMPITO By Twin Gods, is very hard
For ladies to sleep by self without the cock.
Still, you win. We very, very much need peace.

LYSISTRATA Oh, you darling! You're the only *real woman* in the
145 bunch!

KALONIKE But if we actually did renounce what you were talking about—
And may the gods forbid it!—would there really be a greater chance
Of peace because of it? LYSISTRATA Absolutely! I swear,
If we sat around the house plastered in make-up,
150 And walked by them half-naked in our
See-through slips, with our pubes spelling out a delta,
And our husbands had hard-ons and wanted to fuck,
And we didn't go near them but kept out of their reach,
I'm quite sure they'd be in a big hurry to make peace!

155 LAMPITO Yes, just like Menelaos.[41] He get glimpse of Helen's
Bare-naked cantaloupes and he toss his sword away, yes!

KALONIKE But what if our husbands reject us, my dear?

LYSISTRATA "Skin the skinned dog," as Pherekrates[42] said.

KALONIKE Toys aren't as good as the real thing.
160 And what if they grab us and yank us into
The bedroom by force? LYSISTRATA Hold on to the door for dear life!

41. An allusion to the myth that the Greek hero Menelaos, having planned to kill his adulterous wife Helen after the Trojan war, was unable to do so after being awed by her beauty; she is similarly described as baring her breasts to him in the fifth-century BCE Athenian tragedian Euripides' *Andromache* (629ff.).

42. Pherekrates was a comic playwright, roughly contemporary with Aristophanes. In the context here, the phrase "Skin the skinned dog" clearly means "use a dildo," but the original sense and context of Pherekrates' saying remain obscure.

KALONIKE And what if they start beating us?
LYSISTRATA You'll have to submit, but do it with spite.
There's no pleasure in it for them when they force you.
And we'll find other ways to make their lives miserable.
They'll give up soon enough. No husband will 165
Ever get his rocks off if he doesn't work with his wife.

KALONIKE If the two of you are agreed, we're in too.

LAMPITO We will make our husbands to keep
Peace the right way, no cheating.
But what about your Athenian riffraff? 170
Who gonna keep them from getting stupid?

LYSISTRATA No worries, we'll take care of things on our side.

LAMPITO I don't like, so long as your triremes got sails
And your goddess got no end of money.[43]

LYSISTRATA Now all that's been nicely taken care of, 175
Since we're going to occupy the Acropolis today.
That job is the responsibility of the older ladies.[44]
While we're ironing things out here, they'll go up there
Pretending to do a sacrifice, and then they'll take the Acropolis.

LAMPITO That seem very nice. All you say sound very nice. 180

LYSISTRATA Then why don't we swear an oath over it all
This instant, Lampito, to make things binding?

LAMPITO Show us oath and we swear.

LYSISTRATA Excellent. Where's that Scythian police-woman?[45]
Hey you, focus!
Set your shield down in front of us, upside down. 185

43. Lampito refers to the Athenian treasuries on the Acropolis, thought to be under the guardianship of Athena.

44. Women beyond childbearing years probably enjoyed more freedom of movement in classical Athens than their younger counterparts, as male concerns about the legitimacy of children did not apply to them (cf. Introduction 21–26). Lysistrata's plan exploits this situation, along with the fact that women regularly tended to religious cults on the Acropolis.

45. A comic play on the Athenians' use of male Scythian (i.e., foreigners living northeast of Greece) archers as a kind of police force in the city. At 387, the Administrator enters with an escort of four Scythian policemen.

And somebody give me the severed parts.
KALONIKE What sort
Of oath are we going to swear, Lysistrata?
LYSISTRATA What sort?
Exactly the one Aeschylus is said to have had people swear
When they sacrificed the animal above a shield.[46]
KALONIKE No, Lysistrata!
190 Not an oath about peace above a shield!
LYSISTRATA Well then what sort of oath do you want?
KALONIKE We could get a
White stallion somewhere and cut a slice off of him.[47]
LYSISTRATA A white stallion? Really? KALONIKE So how are we going to swear
The oath? LYSISTRATA If you'll listen, dammit, I'll tell you.
195 We set a big black wine bowl right side up,
We sacrifice a magnum's worth of Thasian wine,[48]
And we swear not to add any water to the wine bowl.[49]
LAMPITO Ooh la la, I like oath more than words can talk.
LYSISTRATA Somebody go in and get a wine bowl and a magnum.
200 MYRRHINE My dear lady-friends, that's quite a hunk of pottery!
KALONIKE Just taking a hold of it could make a girl happy!
LYSISTRATA Let go of it and take a hold of the boar.
Lady of Persuasion[50] and Wine Bowl of Friends,
Favorably accept this women's sacrifice.

46. The reference is to a scene in the Athenian tragedian Aeschylus' *Seven Against Thebes* 42–48.
47. Presumably a sexual joke ("white stallion" = penis?) rather than a serious suggestion.
48. The Aegean island of Thasos produced premium wine. The use of wine, rather than the blood of a sacrificed animal, is appropriate in sanctifying peace agreements.
49. It was considered barbaric to drink undiluted wine in antiquity; for the women's reputed bibulousness, see note 10 above.
50. Peitho ("Persuasion") is a goddess who is closely associated with Aphrodite in Athenian cult.

KALONIKE The blood's the proper color and is spurting forth correctly. 205

LAMPITO And it got a real nice smell, by Castor![51]

MYRRHINE Ladies, let me swear the oath first!

KALONIKE Not happening, by Aphrodite,[52] unless you draw the first lot.

LYSISTRATA Take hold of the wine bowl now, all of you—you too, Lampito!
Now one of you, on behalf of everybody, repeat exactly what I say. 210
All of you will then swear to abide by the terms.
No one, either my lover or my husband—

KALONIKE No one, either my lover or my husband—

LYSISTRATA Will get near me with a hard-on. *Louder*!

KALONIKE Will get near me with a hard-on. Oh, no, 215
My knees are buckling, Lysistrata!

LYSISTRATA I shall lead a cockless life at home—

KALONIKE I shall lead a cockless life at home—

LYSISTRATA Wearing a saffron dress and make-up—

KALONIKE Wearing a saffron dress and make-up— 220

LYSISTRATA So my husband will get extremely hot for me—

KALONIKE So my husband will get extremely hot for me—

LYSISTRATA Never will I voluntarily give my husband what he wants—

KALONIKE Never will I voluntarily give my husband what he wants—

LYSISTRATA But if takes me by force against my will— 225

KALONIKE But if takes me by force against my will—

LYSISTRATA I shall yield spitefully and just lie there like a corpse.

KALONIKE I shall yield spitefully and just lie there like a corpse.

51. For Castor, see note 31 above.

52. For Aphrodite, see Appendix.

LYSISTRATA I shall not lift my pumps up toward the ceiling.

230 KALONIKE I shall not lift my pumps up toward the ceiling.

LYSISTRATA I shall not do "the lioness on a cheese-grater."[53]

KALONIKE I shall not do "the lioness on a cheese-grater."

LYSISTRATA Should I keep these vows, may I drink from the wine-bowl.

KALONIKE Should I keep these vows, may I drink from the wine-bowl.

LYSISTRATA Should I violate them, may the wine-bowl be filled
235 with water.

KALONIKE Should I violate them, may the wine-bowl be filled with water.

LYSISTRATA Does each and every one of you formally agree to these conditions? ALL We do, by Zeus!

LYSISTRATA Then I shall consecrate this wine bowl. (*drinks*)
KALONIKE Just your portion now, dear!
We need to share with each other right from the start here.
(*noise erupts from the stage building*)

LAMPITO What all the hubbub? LYSISTRATA It's what I
240 was talking about before:
The women have just taken Athena's Acropolis!
So Lampito: go ahead and take off,
And manage things as you see fit on your side,
But you'll need to leave these women here as our hostages.
(*Lampito exits*)
245 We should go join up with the other women
On the Acropolis and lock the gates there.

KALONIKE But what about the men? Won't they immediately march
Against us to take it back? LYSISTRATA No need to worry about them.
They lack the verbal- and fire-power

53. A sexual position (cf. "doggy-style"). The crouching lioness with her hindquarters raised in readiness for attack was a common motif in Greek art and on everyday objects such as cheese-graters.

To open up these gates:[54] 250
Only we can do that, and only on our conditions.

KALONIKE That, by Aphrodite is the absolute truth! If it weren't,
We women wouldn't be considered invincible monsters!

(The women pass through the Propylaia [i.e., the central door of the stage building] and enter the Acropolis, the setting for the rest of the play. A semi-chorus of 12 Athenian old men enters the orchestra; each member lugs firewood, an unlit torch, and a pitcher of live charcoal.)

LEADER OF MEN'S CHORUS Forward, Draces,[55] aching shoulder or not,
Lug that load of green olive logs! 255

CHORUS OF OLD MEN Ah, a long life holds many surprises! 256–7
Whoever would have imagined, Strymodorus, we'd have to hear 258–9
That women, that sheer flock of evil 260
We pastured in our homes,
Have control of the Sacred Image[56]
And have seized *my* Acropolis,
And have even dared to fasten the gates
With bars and bolts! 265

LEADER OF MEN'S CHORUS Push on to the Acropolis, Philurgos, as fast as you can,
To encircle them with these logs here, and I mean
Every last woman who incited or partook in this conspiracy!
It's unanimous: we'll build a single pyre and with our very own hands
See they're all charred—starting with Lycon's wife.[57] 270

CHORUS OF OLD MEN By Demeter, I won't be these ladies' laughingstock, as long

54. The Propylaia, the entrance to the Acropolis.

55. Here and elsewhere the chorus addresses some of its members (e.g., Philurgos, 267). The particular names are typical of old men.

56. An ancient statue of Athena made of olivewood.

57. Lycon was a prominent citizen who is mocked elsewhere in comedy, as also is his wife Rhodia (for her alleged promiscuity).

As I'm breathing at least! Kleomenes[58] himself, the first usurper of this place,
275/6 Got away unscathed. Puffed up with Spartan pluck as he was,
He departed minus his weapons (now mine!),
And wearing only shrunken and tattered rags,
And hungry, grimy, unshaven,
280 Unwashed for six years.

LEADER OF MEN'S CHORUS That's how I besieged that fool like a wild beast:
We kept guard at the gates, seventeen rows deep.
But these women here, hateful as they are to all the gods and Euripides[59]—
Could I possibly stand by and tolerate their chutzpah?
If I did, go right ahead and destroy my monument
285 at Marathon![60]

CHORUS OF OLD MEN Now all that's left is that
Tilted trek up to the
Acropolis I so eagerly seek.
How are we, like asses, to haul this
290 Load up without a single mule?
These two logs have made a slope of my shoulders,
But march on I must,
Keeping my fire bright
Without snuffing out the light
I'll need at the end of this road.
294a Gak, gak,
295 Aw, aw, aw the smoke!

58. A Spartan king who briefly seized the Acropolis in 508 BCE at the prompting of Athenian oligarchs. A truce was struck, and he retreated to Sparta, thus marking an important step toward the establishment of Athenian democracy. The old men of the chorus performing in 411 BCE could not have witnessed these events, but their political sympathies are revealed here.

59. The tragic playwright Euripides (cf. note 41 above) was mercilessly mocked by Aristophanes as a misogynist, owing to the various powerful and daring heroines of his plays (e.g., Medea, Phaedra, Electra).

60. Commemorating the Athenian-led defeat of the Persians at the Battle of Marathon in 490 BCE (again, the men of the chorus could not have actually fought in the battle: cf. note 58 above).

Holy Herakles,[61] how horribly
The smoke leapt up from my bucket
To bite out my eyes like a rabid bitch!
By all means, this fire's
The pure Lemnian[62] variety: 300
Only *that* would have so viciously nipped at my poor eyes!
Press on to the Acropolis
To save our goddess!
Her time of need, Laches,
Could never be so dire as *now*!
Gak, gak, 305
Aw, aw, aw the smoke! 305a

LEADER OF MEN'S CHORUS Thanks to the gods, the fire's alive and well.
First we'll put our pair of logs here,
And place our torches in our buckets.
With those ablaze, we'll rush the gates like rams:
If the women don't unbar the gates at our command, 310
The gates will burn and they'll be smoked out.
So let's set our load down. Gak, the smoke! Whooh,
Any of the generals at Samos[63] care to lend us a hand with this wood?
At least these logs have stopped pinching my back.
Your task, bucket, is to stir up your coals, 315
So I'll be the first to bear a blazing torch.
Goddess Nike,[64] join our side, so together we can build
A monument to female insolence interrupted on our citadel.

(A semi-chorus of 12 Athenian old women enters the orchestra; each member is carrying a pitcher of water on her head.)

61. For Herakles, see Appendix.

62. Owing to its volcanic activity, the north Aegean island of Lemnos was proverbial for brilliant fire. In myth, the foul-smelling women of Lemnos murdered their fleeing husbands.

63. Since the year before the first production of *Lysistrata*, the large Aegean island of Samos just off the coast of Asia Minor served as the Athenian navy's headquarters.

64. Nike ("Victory") is identified with Athena on the Acropolis, where her temple (largely intact today) was part of Pericles' recent building program and so was closely associated with democracy.

Leader of Woman's Chorus Women, I think I spot a flash in all the smoke—

320 It could be fire, so let's move it out!

Chorus of Old Women Faster, faster, Nikodike,[65]
Before Kalyke and Kritylla
Become torches, fanned on all sides
By vexing winds
325 And by old men bent on murder!
Oh no, oh no, has aid come too late?
I somehow just now filled my pitcher in the dawn's early light
At the well amid a clanging
And clattering of pots,[66]
330–1 As I jostled with maids
And slave-girls with tattoos,[67]
And struggled to lift it on to my head.
I'm here to help my fellow citizens,
335 Besieged with fire and bearing water.
I hear crazy old men
Are prowling about with mountains
Of firewood on the citadel like bath-stokers,
Belching out the most abusive words
340 About how those female monsters must be roasted into charcoal.
Goddess, preserve these women from the flames,
So they can save both Greece and their fellow citizens
From the madness of war!
For this very cause, Golden-crowned
345 Athena Polias,[68] they seized your sanctuary.
I call upon you to be our ally,

65. As the men in the preceding semi-chorus (cf. note 55 above), the women address some of their members by name.

66. Like wool-working (cf. 493ff.), fetching water was a traditional female occupation, even for free women (cf. Introduction 21–26).

67. Runaway slaves were branded as such with tattoos.

68. The women invoke the city goddess of Athens (= the "Goddess" in 341 and "Tritogeneia" in 347) by an ancient title bearing venerable associations that long predate democratic Athens.

Tritogeneia, bearing aid and water,
If any of them dares
To set fire to that shrine of yours.

SCENE 2

LEADER OF WOMAN'S CHORUS Whoa, whoa! What's this now? Disgusting men! 350
These are acts no decent or god-fearing men would ever dare!

(*The two half-choruses face each other.*)

LEADER OF MEN'S CHORUS This is a problem we never imagined we'd see:
Look at this new swarm of women at the gates coming to help!

LEADER OF WOMAN'S CHORUS You're scared of us, are you? You think there's a lot of us now?
Why, you've only seen the teeniest fraction of us women so far. 355

LEADER OF MEN'S CHORUS We're not going to tolerate their blather, are we, Phaedrias?
Shouldn't someone crack a log over their heads?

LEADER OF WOMAN'S CHORUS Let's set our pitchers down on the ground too,
So they'll be out of our way if one of them comes at us.

LEADER OF MEN'S CHORUS By Zeus, if someone had smacked me in the jaw a few times 360
(Just like happened to Boupolos[69]), we wouldn't have to listen to them now!

LEADER OF WOMAN'S CHORUS Here you go: take your best shot. I'll just stand here and take it.
But please note that this will be the last time any bitch yanks your balls off!

LEADER OF MEN'S CHORUS Shut up or I'll tan your ugly-ass old hide!

69. Bupolos was a sculptor who was verbally attacked and driven to suicide by the sixth-century BCE poet Hipponax.

Leader of Woman's Chorus If you so much as come near
365 Statyllis and lay a finger on her—

Leader of Men's Chorus And what if I give you a knuckle-sandwich? Got a smart answer for that?

Leader of Woman's Chorus I'll rip out your lungs and entrails and then viciously chew them up.

Leader of Men's Chorus What poet has ever said it better than Euripides:[70]
"Could there exist a creature more shameless than a woman?"

Leader of Woman's Chorus Let's pick up our water pitchers,
370 Rhodippe.

Leader of Men's Chorus What are you here for with that water, you god-forsaken bitch!

Leader of Women's Chorus And what are you here for with that fire, worm-food? Gonna torch yourself?

Leader of Men's Chorus Clearly, I'm here to build a pyre and roast your friends.

Leader of Women's Chorus Clearly, I'm here to drench that pyre of yours with *this*.

Leader of Men's Chorus Drench my pyre? **Leader of Wom-**
375 **en's Chorus** As you'll soon see in person.

Leader of Men's Chorus I'm thinking I should broil you with this here torch of mine.

Leader of Women's Chorus Any chance you've got some soap? I'd love to give you a nice bath.

Leader of Men's Chorus *You* bathe *me*, you old hag?
Leader of Women's Chorus A pre-nuptial bath, my dear.

Leader of Men's Chorus Such arrogance!
Leader of Women's Chorus Well, I'm not a slave.

70. See notes 41 and 59 above (369 may be a quote from a lost play of Euripides).

LEADER OF MEN'S CHORUS I'll shut that yapper of yours up soon enough. LEADER OF WOMEN'S CHORUS Still think you're judge and jury?[71] 380

LEADER OF MEN'S CHORUS Set her hair on fire! LEADER OF WOMEN'S CHORUS Just the job for Acheloos[72] here! (*douses them*)

LEADER OF MEN'S CHORUS No! Shit! LEADER OF WOMEN'S CHORUS Not too warm was it?

LEADER OF MEN'S CHORUS Yeah right, too warm—now, stop it! Hey, what are you doing?

LEADER OF WOMEN'S CHORUS I'm watering you, so you'll grow up to be big and strong.

LEADER OF MEN'S CHORUS My growth spurt's long over, and now I'm just trembling. 385

LEADER OF WOMEN'S CHORUS Since you've got all that fire, why not heat yourself up some?

SCENE 3

(*The Administrator enters with two slaves wielding crowbars and four Scythian policemen.*)

ADMINISTRATOR[73] Yet another flare-up of female decadence,
Complete with tambourines, nonstop "Sabizioses,"[74]
And this Adonis cult[75] on the rooftops![76]
It came down just like this in the Assembly once: 390

71. Jurors in democratic Athens received a small fee for jury service; impecunious old men seem to have relied on jury service for income. Cf. 620ff.

72. The longest river in Greece, quasi-proverbial for water in general.

73. The Administrator is one the 10 Probouloi invested with extraordinary powers to govern Athens in its current state of emergency (cf. Introductory Essay 39).

74. An eastern god whose ecstatic cult had recently been introduced into Greece.

75. Another eastern god (cf. note 74 above), in myth the short-lived consort of Aphrodite. In Athens, his cult was celebrated by women (privately and outside traditional civic religion), who ritually mourned his death on rooftops.

76. The usual setting for celebrations of Adonis (cf. *Samia*, note 18).

Demostratos[77] (may he be forever screwed!) was advising us
To send the expedition to Sicily as his wife's dancing
And yelling "Poor Adonis." He proceeded to move
That we enlist recruits from Zakynthos,[78]
395 As his wife, now quite drunk on the rooftop,
Says, "Mourn for Adonis!"[79] But he just kept pushing his motions,
Filthy, godforsaken member of the Wing-nut family that he is.
This is just the sort of unbridled behavior you can expect from women!

Leader of Men's Chorus You don't know the half of it! Care to hear how depraved they are?
On top of every other imaginable outrage, they dumped their
400 pitchers
On us! Now we've got to squeeze-dry
Our clothes just like we do when we pee in them.

Administrator I swear by Salty Poseidon,[80] we men do reap what we sow!
Seeing as we're facilitators of our wives'
405 Wickedness and teach them how to be decadent,
Is it any wonder such plots as these are popping up among them?
Are *we* not guilty of going to the craftsmen's district and saying,
"Goldsmith, regarding that necklace you made my wife:
She was, as they say, *getting down* the other night
410 And the connecting-rod slid right out of the hole.

77. An advocate of the disastrous Athenian naval expedition launched against Syracuse in Sicily in 415 BCE: see further Introductory Essay 39–40.

78. An island west of mainland Greece, an ally of Athens throughout the Peloponnesian War.

79. For the thesis that the women in *Lysistrata* are metaphorically conducting an Adonis celebration on the Acropolis, see Reitzammer, L., "Aristophanes' *Adôniazousai*." *Classical Antiquity* 27 (2008): 282–333.

80. For the god Poseidon, see Appendix.

I'm just about to sail over to Salamis,[81]
So if you've got some time this evening, please do
Go see her and jam that rod right back into the hole."
Or one of us goes to the sandal-maker, who happens to be
A young stripling with a full-grown tree trunk between
his legs, 415
And says, "I've got a job for you: a tight thong's
Been pinching the rim of my wife's foot.
It's a tender area, but could you stop by our place
Around noon and stretch things out for me down there?"
These antics have gotten us to where we are. 420
And here I am, an Administrator who has procured
Timber for boat-oars and have come now to get funds for that—
Here *I* am, locked outside the gates by these women!
No point in just standing around: get me some crowbars,
(*to one of his slaves*)
So I can put an end to their insolence once and for all. 425
What's with the mouth-breathing, loser? Why are you
gawking?
Did I tell you to go looking for a *bar* or for *crowbars*?
Now let's slide the crowbars under the gates:
You pry from there, and I'll pry at the same time from here.
(*Lysistrata enters from the stage building.*)

LYSISTRATA Stop that right now, 430
I'm coming out on my own. Why the crowbars?
We don't need muscle, we need smarts and common sense.

ADMINISTRATOR Really, you filthy thing? Where's a policeman?
Grab her and tie her hands behind her back!

LYSISTRATA I swear by Artemis,[82] if this "public servant" 435
Lays a single finger on me, you'll have to listen to him cry!

ADMINISTRATOR Scared, are you? (*to second policeman*) Help
him grab her
By the waist and tie her up this instant!

81. Cf. 59–60. Mention of Salaminian-style oarsmanship may also suggest a sexual position, that of "women on top."

82. For the goddess, see Appendix.

Old Lady #1 I swear by Pandrosos,[83] if you so much as
440 Touch her, I will beat the living shit out of you!

Administrator Beat the living shit out of me, will you? I need another policeman.
(*to third policeman*) Tie up our trash-talking friend here first!

Old Lady #2 I swear by the Bringer of Light,[84] if you lay
A single finger on her, you'll be wearing an eye-patch in no time!

Administrator What's all this now? I need a cop. Grab her
445 (*to fourth policeman*).
This'll be the end of at least one of your forays.

Old Lady #3 I swear by Tauropolos,[85] if you come close to her,
I'll tear out your hair and make *it* scream!

Administrator Damn! Now I'm screwed: that's the last of my cops!
450 But women must never have the upper hand
Over us men! Scythians, take up your positions and
Engage them! **Lysistrata** By the Two Goddesses, you'll soon see
We have four companies of our own inside,
Each made up of combat-ready warrior-women!

455 **Administrator** Scythians, twist their arms behind their backs!

Lysistrata Allied guard of women, come forward, and on the double!
All ye soup-and-vegetable-selling offspring of the market,
Dive-owning sellers of garlic and bread,
Tear at them! Pommel them! Smite away!
Assault them with the raunchiest words in your arsenal!
460 (*The Scythians exit at the advance of the women-warriors.*)
Whoa! Disengage! No plundering now!

83. Daughter of the legendary Athenian King Cecrops; she was worshipped on the Acropolis as a hero.

84. Phosphorus, epithet of both Artemis and Hekate. Hekate is an old and complex deity, associated with (among other things) magic, the moon, and crossroads. Athenian worshippers offered her cakes with small (lit) torches on top.

85. Epithet of Artemis.

ADMINISTRATOR Pitiful! My police-bodyguard's been crushed!

LYSISTRATA What were you expecting? That you'd be fighting
Against some slave girls? Or were you assuming women don't have
Enough spunk for war? ADMINISTRATOR By Apollo, I know you're 465
Full of spunk—when you're drinking in bars!

LEADER OF MEN'S CHORUS Why squander all these words, Administrator of this land?
Why even bother wrangling with these creatures?
You're aware of the bath they just gave us,
Fully clothed as we were and without any soap! 470

LEADER OF WOMEN'S CHORUS You, sir, must not engage in random acts of violence against
Your neighbors. Do it again and you're looking at a pair of black eyes.
I'd prefer to be sitting around at home like a proper young lady,
Causing no trouble whatsoever, not bothering so much as a flea,
But if someone provokes me by raiding my nest, I'm all wasp. 475

CHORUS OF OLD MEN O Zeus, tell us what we are to do with these beasts! 476–7
We simply cannot take any more of this,
So let's investigate what's happened here together:
What possible motive drove them 480
To seize Kranaos'[86] citadel,
And *our* Acropolis, a lofty and hallowed area
Not open to all.

LEADER OF MEN'S CHORUS Question her with extreme prejudice and scrutinize her every word!
It's our disgrace if acts of this nature go unprosecuted! 485

ADMINISTRATOR Very well, then. Now the first thing I want to hear from them, damn it all,
Is just what their motive was in locking down *our* Acropolis.

86. Legendary Athenian king.

LYSISTRATA It was to keep the treasury safe from *you and your war.*

ADMINISTRATOR You think we're at war because of the money in there? LYSISTRATA Yes, and that's led

To the whole mess here. And the desire to steal it caused Pisander[87]

490

And the other career politicians to always be stirring up trouble. They can

Stir up as much trouble as they want, but now they can't get the money.

ADMINISTRATOR What are you going to do?

LYSISTRATA You have to ask? We're going to manage the treasury.

ADMINISTRATOR *You*? Manage the treasury?

LYSISTRATA What's so weird about that?

495

Don't you put us all in charge of household finances?

ADMINISTRATOR That's not the same thing!

LYSISTRATA Why not? ADMINISTRATOR Because these are military finances!

LYSISTRATA But why's there a war in the first place?

ADMINISTRATOR National security—so we can protect ourselves!

LYSISTRATA We'll protect you. ADMINISTRATOR *You*?

LYSISTRATA Yup. We sure will. ADMINISTRATOR That's absurd!

LYSISTRATA We'll be your saviors, whether you like it or not.

ADMINISTRATOR Disgusting! LYSISTRATA Infuriated now, are you?

Well, that won't stop us. ADMINISTRATOR By Demeter, this simply isn't right!

500

LYSISTRATA We're saving you nonetheless, friend.

ADMINISTRATOR But I don't wanna be saved.

LYSISTRATA All the more reason to do it.

87. A contemporary political figure depicted as corrupt by Aristophanes, he was instrumental in establishing "The Four Hundred," an oligarchical council that temporarily seized power in Athens later in 411 BCE.

ADMINISTRATOR Since when do you care about war and peace?
LYSISTRATA Allow me to explain. ADMINISTRATOR Chop-
chop, or you're in for a lot of pain. LYSISTRATA Listen up,
And how about keeping those fists of yours down?
ADMINISTRATOR I really can't—
Managing my anger is quite a challenge.
OLD LADY #1 Then you're in for some serious pain! 505
ADMINISTRATOR Keep cawing away at yourself, you old hag.
I want to hear from this one. LYSISTRATA Certainly.
Up until now, we—as respectable women should do—
Quietly put up with whatever you men did.
And just because you didn't let us make a peep doesn't mean
we liked it.
We knew full well what you were up to, and though we were
cooped up in the house, 510
We'd often hear about some important political business you'd
messed up.
Though we were hurting inside, we'd put on a smile and ask,
"Any decision about an amendment to the peace treaty
At the assembly today?"[88] "How's that your business?," my
husband[89] would say.
"How about shutting up?" And I shut up.
OLD LADY #1 I never would have! 515
ADMINISTRATOR And you'd be worse for wear if you hadn't.
LYSISTRATA Precisely why I shut up.
Later, we'd hear about some even greater blunder of yours
and we'd ask,
"Why are you managing affairs of state like such a moron,
my husband?"

88. In 418 BCE, the Athenian Assembly had altered the text of a peace treaty (= the Peace of Nikias, 421 BCE) to indicate that the Spartans had broken the treaty.

89. Apart from the mention of her husband here, the Athena-like Lysistrata elsewhere—in contrast to the other women—does not appear to be married (is she to be thought of as a war widow?).

Instantly I'd get that icy stare, and he'd tell me I'd better get back to my knitting,
If I didn't want a serious head-cracking. "War is men's work,"[90]
520 he'd say.

Administrator He got that right, damn it!

Lysistrata How's that, my unfortunate friend?

So our advice wasn't needed when you'd messed everything up?
But then we heard you publicly saying right in the streets,
"There isn't a man left in this land." And someone else answering, "No, not a single one, by Zeus!"
After hearing that, we immediately decided to gather together
525 as women
Committed to saving Greece. We saw no reason to wait any longer.
We have useful advice to share with you, if you'll take your turn at listening.
So if you shut up as we did, we can set you straight on things.

Administrator *You* set *us* straight? This is absurd and intolerable!

Lysistrata Shut up!

Administrator *Me* shut up for *you*, you detestable beast
530 with a veil
On your head! I'll kill myself before that happens!

Lysistrata If it's just the veil
That's holding you back, take mine here and keep it.
Now put it on your head—
And shut up!

535 **Old Lady #1** And take this sewing basket here too.

Lysistrata Now pull up your skirt, chew some beans,
And start sowing:
"War is women's work."[91]

90. A quotation of Homer, *Iliad* 6.492, where the Trojan warrior Hector dismisses his wife Andromache's concerns for him as he departs for battle, and instructs her to return to her wool-making. Cf. Introductory Essay 42–43.

91. Cf. note 90 above.

Leader of Women's Chorus Jump up and away from your pitchers, women, so we too
Can take our turn in bringing help to our friends. 540

Chorus of Old Women Never will I tire of dancing, 541–2
Never will my knees give in to weariness and fatigue!
For virtue's sake, I'll take on any task
With women such as these: 545
They've got gifts, charm, pluck,
Smarts, patriotic spirit,
And common sense!

Leader of Women's Chorus Most manly of grannies and thorny mommies,
Stay the course, and let anger guide you forth: the wind's behind you. 550

Lysistrata So long as sweet Eros[92] and Cyprian[93] Aphrodite
Inspire desire in our thighs and breasts,
And engender prolonged passion and raised clubs in our husbands,
We'll one day be called Lysimaches[94] among the Greeks.

Administrator For doing what? **Lysistrata** First of all, we'll put a stop to the crazies 555
Shopping in the market in full armor. **Old Lady #1** By Paphian[95] Aphrodite!

Lysistrata These days, you'll find them strutting around the market in arms—
In the pottery and vegetable stalls alike, as if they're Korybants![96]

92. Eros is a personified god of desire/love.

93. I.e., "of Cyprus" (the large eastern Mediterranean island), a traditional epithet of Aphrodite, suggesting her possible eastern origins.

94. For the idea that Lysistrata in name and bearing recalls Lysimache, the (historical) priestess of Athena Polias whose name similarly means "Disbander of Battle," see Introductory Essay 43–44.

95. Paphos is a city-state on the island of Cyprus (see note 93 above), the site of a major sanctuary and cult of Aphrodite.

96. Mythic figures associated with ecstatic dancing in armor and madness.

Administrator By Zeus, men must be men!

Lysistrata But what's more ridiculous

Than some dude with a Gorgon-emblazoned[97] shield buying sardines? 560

Old Lady #1 Damn straight! I actually saw a cavalry captain with longhair ride into

The market on horseback and have an old lady slop gruel into his helmet!

Another guy, a Thracian who was rattling his shield and spear like he was Tereus,[98]

Terrified the fig-seller and then inhaled all her figs!

Administrator The cities are all tied up in a big ball of confusion: how can you possibly 565

Unravel this mess? **Lysistrata** It's very simple.

Administrator Oh, really? Do show me how.

Lysistrata Think of a ball of wool that's all tangled. You take a hold of it like this,

And using your spindles you gently draw out the strands, one this way, one that.

That's exactly how we'll untangle this war, if we're given a chance:

We'll send ambassadors—one this way, one that—to unravel it all. 570

Administrator How moronic! You really think you can put a stop to this horrible predicament

We're in with yarn and spindles? **Lysistrata** Absolutely. And if you weren't such a moron,

You'd manage all our city's affairs on the model of our wool-working.

97. The frightening Gorgon monster was a common motif on shields, ridiculously incongruous here in the case of the shopping warrior, who neatly satirizes bellicose Athenian patriots.

98. A savage mythical king of Thrace: see notes 36 above and 137 below.

ADMINISTRATOR I'd love to see how. LYSISTRATA Suppose the city's a great big shorn fleece.
First you dunk it in a bath to get rid of all the sheep pooh. Lay it out on a bed 575
And pound out the rabble-rousers and extract the burrs.
As for the sticky ones who are always glomming onto public office:
Card them out thoroughly and give their heads a good plucking.
Then card the remaining wool into a basket of solidarity, with everyone
Harmoniously mixed in together. Include resident aliens, friendly foreigners, 580
And even those in hock to the public treasury—toss them all in too!
And absolutely do not forget about all the colonies we founded:
Consider them to be flocks of wool laid out separately
From one another. And then take each and every flock of them,
Bring them here, roll them all together into a mass 585
And create a giant ball of wool. Finally, take it and weave a new cloak for the people.

ADMINISTRATOR Horrible the way these women blather on about pounding, balls of wool, etc.,
When they take no part in the war. LYSISTRATA I beg to differ, dirtbag!
We do more than our share here! First of all, we gave birth to sons
And then sent them off to war—
ADMINISTRATOR Shush! Don't dredge up past sorrows.[99] 590

99. Perhaps with reference to the recently failed Sicilian Expedition (see Introductory Essay 39 and notes 159 and 174 below), but the war had been dragging on for many years and most audience members probably had lost loved ones in any of various conflicts.

LYSISTRATA Secondly, when we deserve to be having some fun in our prime,
All these campaigns mean we're sleeping alone. And putting aside our situation,
What about the young girls growing old in their rooms? It's sad.

ADMINISTRATOR And men don't get old too?

LYSISTRATA Now that's not the same thing at all.
A grizzled and gray man can find a young bride the instant he's
595 back from war.
A woman's prime is short-lived: if she doesn't make use of it,
No one wants to marry her and she sits at home hoping for good omens.[100]

ADMINISTRATOR But any man who's boner-capable—

LYSISTRATA Oh, why don't you just go off and die?
600 Here's a plot of land. You buy the coffin.
And I'll make you a nice honey-cake,[101]
And here, take this for a wreath.

OLD LADY #1 And here, take these ribbons.

OLD LADY #2 And this crown is all yours.

605 LYSISTRATA That should do it. Anything else? Off to the boat.
Charon's[102] calling for you,
And here you are making him late.

ADMINISTRATOR It's absolutely outrageous for me to be subjected to this!
So help me Zeus, I'm marching straight over to my fellow Administrators
610 To show them in person what you've done to me. (*exits*)

LYSISTRATA You're not going to complain to them about our little funeral, are you?

100. I.e., omens portending marriage.

101. The cake is to placate Cerberus, the three-headed guardian of the traditional underworld. The women here comically prepare the elderly Administrator for burial, as was the duty of Athenian women in real life (cf. Introduction 23–24).

102. The ferryman who takes the souls of the dead across the River Styx.

But enough of that: two days from now, at the crack of dawn
You'll get your third day rites from us.

(*The women, including Lysistrata, exit through the central door of the stage-building, which represents the Propylaia, the gated entrance to the Acropolis.*)

LEADER OF MEN'S CHORUS It's time for every free man to be awake now!
We must strip down, men, and face the current crisis. (*they remove their cloaks*) 615

CHORUS OF OLD MEN I seem to have caught the scent
Of something much bigger than meets the eye here.
The most prominent smell is that of Hippias'[103] tyranny. 618–9
I'm also quite afraid that certain Spartan men 620
Have sneakily banded together at Cleisthenes'[104] house
To incite our godforsaken women to seize our money
And my sustenance—my jury pay![105] 625

LEADER OF MEN'S CHORUS Outrageous, isn't it? That they should admonish us citizens now
And, despite their being women, blather on about the weapons of war!
And the idea that they'd try to reconcile us with the men of Sparta,
Who are about as trustworthy as a starved wolf!
Men, all they've woven here is a plot against us, and one that aspires to tyranny. 630
They won't make me their subject. I'll be on guard,
And "I'll bear my sword in a branch of myrtle."[106]

103. The last of the Athenian tyrants (Peisistratidai), expelled in 510 BCE. Cf. note 107 below.

104. Frequently mocked as effeminate in Aristophanes. For the stereotypical view of a Spartan preference for anal sex, cf. notes 175 and 185 below.

105. See note 71 above.

106. A quotation from a popular song praising the tyrant-slayers (see note 107 below).

I'll do my shopping in the market in full arms, right next to Aristogeiton.[107]
I'll stand next to him like this (*strikes a pose*). Which reminds me:
635 I should belt this godforsaken old bag right in the jaw.

LEADER OF WOMEN'S CHORUS Go ahead: even your mom won't recognize you when you get home.
All right ladies: let's put our sweaters down on the ground and start.

CHORUS OF OLD WOMEN Citizens of Athens, we'll start with
Some useful ideas for the city.
I do this out of gratitude for being nurtured by Athens'
640–1 glorious prosperity.
At exactly seven years old, I was an Arrhephoros.[108]
And then, when I was ten, I served as a Grinder for the Foundress,[109]
And at Brauron I took off my saffron-dress and became
644–5 a Bear.[110]
And once, as a lovely young girl, I was a Kanephoros[111]
And wore a dried-fig necklace.[112]

107. In 514 BCE, Aristogeiton and his friend Harmodius killed the Athenian tyrant Hipparchus, brother of Hippias (see note 103 above), but failed to kill the latter and were executed.

108. Each year, two girls (Arrhephoroi) from elite families lived on the Acropolis in the service of Athena Polias (see note 94 above), where they wove Athena's robe (*peplos*) for the great Panathenaic Festival in Athens. For the evidence of a girl's progression through such religious roles in real life, see Connelly, J.B., *Portrait of a Priestess: Women and Ritual in Ancient Greece* (Princeton, 2007): 27–55.

109. An important service involving the grinding of corn for sacred cakes in honor of Athena.

110. At Brauron in eastern Attica, girls from aristocratic Athenian families participated in rites and running races in honor of Artemis, in which they somehow became "bears," perhaps as part of their ritual transition to marriageability, which was figured as the "taming" of young girls (cf. Introduction 23). For the cult at Brauron, see further Sourvinou-Inwood, C., *Studies in Girls' Transitions: Aspects of the Arkteia and Age Representation in Attic Iconography* (Athens, 1988).

111. I.e., "a basket-carrier." Young girls carried baskets as part of various festivals; perhaps the Panathenaic Festival (cf. note 108 above) is meant here.

112. Figs are symbols of fertility.

LEADER OF WOMEN'S CHORUS That's why offering useful advice is
my way of paying back my debt to the city.
I shouldn't be denied a say for being born a woman,
Especially when my proposals are better than what we've
currently got. 650
I've made my contribution: I supply the city with men.
The same can't be said of *you*, you decrepit old geezers,
Since you've wasted our paternal inheritance from the
Persian Wars[113]
And don't produce enough revenues to make up for the loss.
No, it's because of you we're in imminent danger of
bankruptcy. 655
Any grunts in your defense? If you annoy me the slightest bit,
I'm going to smack you in the jaw with my rawhide boot!

LEADER OF MEN'S CHORUS Is this not the very height of insolence?
And to me it looks as if things will only get worse. 659–60
Every man equipped with balls must make a stand!
Off with our shirts: a man shouldn't be wrapped up like a pastry.
A man should smell like a man from the get go![114]

CHORUS OF OLD MEN Come on, Whitefeet,[115]
All of us who went to war against Leipsydrion[116] 665–6
When we still had it.
Now, yes now's the time to be young again, to sprout
New wings all over, and to shuffle off this geriatric coil! 670

113. The spoils of the wars against the Persians (concluded in 479 BCE) had greatly enriched the Athenian coffers.

114. The men have already (615) removed their outer garments, as also the women (637). They now apparently strip down naked, and remain so until the women help dress them again (1021). It is unclear if the actors playing the women similarly disrobe at 687–90 or merely threaten to do so; for the thesis that the women bare all, see Sommerstein (2009): 237–253.

115. The meaning of this is unclear (it may simply be a way of referring to foot-soldiers).

116. Location (on Mt. Panes in northern Attica) of a battle against the tyrant Hippias (cf. note 107 above) following his brother's assassination in 514 BCE, the memory of which was preserved in patriotic song.

Leader of Men's Chorus If any of us lets these women have the slightest grip,
There'll be no end to their hands' hard work.
They'll even go so far as to build ships,
675 So they can engage in naval battle against us, as Artemisia[117] did.
And if they take up horsemanship, all bets are off for our cavalry.
A woman is a creature fond of mounting and riding:
The faster you go, the tighter she clings. Consider the Amazons
On horseback warring with men, as painted by Mikon.[118]
680 The necks of them all need to be grabbed,
Locked and slung in the stocks!

Chorus of Old Women If, by the Two Goddesses, you provoke me enough,
683–4 I'll release my inner sow, and before you
685–6 Can call your goons for help you'll be skinned alive!

Leader of Women's Chorus Ladies! Let's take off our skirts, and
687–8 fast (two can play at this game!),
689–90 So they can get a good whiff of how we women are bitin' mad![119]

Women's Chorus Just one of you have a go at me now:
You'll never enjoy a taste of garlic
Or black beans again![120]
One nasty word from you and you'll have more rage than you can handle.
I'll be the midwife the beetle was to the eagle[121] (that's *you* in
695 this story!).

117. A queen from Halicarnassus (a Greek city in Asia Minor) who served as a naval commander on the Persian side at the Battle of Salamis in 480 BCE.

118. Fifth-century BCE Athenian painter and sculptor whose mural depicted the mythical Amazons invading Athens and its king Theseus. This story took on ideological significance after the Persian Wars as a mythic prefiguration of war between (reputed) civilization and barbarism, but here reflects male hysteria about gynecocracy.

119. Do the women match the men in stripping here? See note 114 above.

120. While the eating of raw garlic was pervasive in ancient Greece, jurors (see note 71 above) were characterized as bean-chewers (cf. modern chewing gum).

121. In one of Aesop's *Fables*, the beetle takes vengeance against the eagle by destroying its eggs (there probably is a joke here on eggs as testicles).

LEADER OF WOMEN'S CHORUS As long as I've got my friends Lampito and Ismene, who's
Theban upper-crust, you won't intimidate me.
You're powerless, even if you do take a vote seven times.
Why? Because all your neighbors hate you, loser.
Yesterday I held a block-party in honor of Hekate[122] 700
For all the girls, and invited my friend from next door,
A helpful girl I'm especially fond of—a Boeotian eel.[123]
But they refused to let her come because of your decrees.
The only way you'll ever stop passing those is to have
Someone grab your leg, lug you away, and break your neck! 705

SCENE 4

(*Lysistrata enters from the Acropolis.*)
O Lady of our allied enterprise,
Why do you trek from your castle so grimly countenanced?[124]

LYSISTRATA It's the deeds of wicked women and the female psyche
That make me lose heart and pace back and forth like this.

LEADER OF WOMEN'S CHORUS Tell us what, tell us what! 710

LYSISTRATA It's truth, the truth it is.

LEADER OF WOMEN'S CHORUS What spells such doom? Enlighten your friends!

LYSISTRATA It is grievous to say, and still more grievous not to say.

LEADER OF WOMEN'S CHORUS Keep me not clueless about the woe that has struck us.

LYSISTRATA That tale is briefest to tell: *we really need a fuck*![125] 715

LEADER OF WOMEN'S CHORUS Ah, Zeus!

122. A polymorphous goddess associated with witchcraft, the moon, crossroads, and the underworld. She was popular among women and her altars and statues often stood in front of private homes. Cf. note 84 above.

123. See note 19 above.

124. 706ff. here mimic the high diction of tragedy and brilliantly culminate in Lysistrata's bathetic announcement at 715.

125. While the sex-strike has hit the "strikers" hard, Lysistrata remains—asexually and Athena-like (cf. Introductory Essay 43–44)—dedicated to the cause.

LYSISTRATA Why invoke Zeus?[126] It is what it is.
And realistically, I can no longer keep them off
Their husbands: they're all leaving their posts.
720 The first one I caught was beating around the bushes
Right over by Pan's Grotto.[127]
A second deserter was sliding down a cable
She was clutching. And just yesterday I had to drag
Another one down by her hair from a sparrow:[128]
725 She was planning to fly over to Orsilochos'[129] house!
They're pulling out every possible excuse
To go back home. Here's one of them now.
Hey you, what's the rush?

LEADER OF WOMEN'S CHORUS I need to go home.
It's about my Milesian[130] wool:
The moths are devouring it right down back there.
730 LYSISTRATA Moths, right!
Get back in here! WOMAN #1 Oh, I'll be right back, I swear!
I just need to spread it out on the bed.

LYSISTRATA Whoa, whoa! You're staying put here and you won't be doing any bed-spreading!

WOMAN #1 So I'm just supposed to let my wool get wrecked?
LYSISTRATA Yes, if need be.

735 WOMAN #2 Oh no, oh no, not my lovely flax!
I left it at home with the stalk unbeaten.
LYSISTRATA Here's another one
Going off to beat her stalk of flax.
Now get right back here! WOMAN #2 Please, I promise
I'll pound that stalk and then be back super-fast.

126. More paratragic language (cf. note 124 above).

127. See note 11 above.

128. Sparrows have long and various associations with sexuality (e.g., they draw Aphrodite's chariot in a famous poem of the seventh/sixth century BCE lyric poet Sappho).

129. The identification of Orsilochos is uncertain (a well-known adulterer or pimp?).

130. Another fine export of Miletus (see note 38 above) that would be hard to acquire during the war.

LYSISTRATA No, no, no! NO pounding! If you set a precedent, 740
All the women will want to go to pound-town.

WOMAN #3 Holy Eileithyia,[131] delay this birth
Until I'm free of this holy turf!

LYSISTRATA What are you babbling about now?

WOMAN #3 I'm on the verge of having a baby!

LYSISTRATA But you weren't even pregnant yesterday!

WOMAN #3 Well I am now today. 745
Please, Lysistrata, let me go home right this minute,
So I can be with my midwife. LYSISTRATA That's quite a story.
What's this hard thing here? (*touches her stomach*)

WOMAN #3 A little baby boy!

LYSISTRATA By Aphrodite, you clearly have some hollowed-out
Metal object there. Let me see. 750
You silly thing! There's no baby in there! That's the
Holy Helmet[132] you're carrying. OLD LADY #3 I swear, I really am pregnant!

LYSISTRATA And so what was this for? WOMAN #3 In case the delivery started
While I was still on the Acropolis: I'd get into the helmet
And make it my nest the way pigeons do. 755

LYSISTRATA Nonsense! That's just an excuse. It's clear what you're up to.
You *must* stay for your helmet's Amphidromia.[133]

WOMAN #3 But I haven't been able to sleep a wink here on the Acropolis
From the instant I saw the Guardian Snake.[134]

131. A very old goddess of childbirth.

132. Presumably the helmet from Athena's cult statue in the Parthenon, her main temple on the Acropolis.

133. A ceremony in which an infant is formally welcomed into the household at five days of age.

134. A snake was thought to guard the Acropolis and was pacified by being fed honeycakes.

760 **Woman #4** Ah, I'm suffering from sleep-deprivation too:
It's the owls[135]—their hooh-hooing's killing me!

Lysistrata Enough with the fantasies, you crazy ladies!
It's reasonable for you to miss your husbands, but surely you realize
They miss you. There's no doubt the nights
765 Are very tough for them. Practice patience, my friends.
You won't have to keep this up for very much longer.
There's an oracle[136] that says victory is ours
As long as we don't factionalize. Here, check it out.

Woman #3 You tell us what it says. **Lysistrata** Hush up and I will.
770 "When the swallows[137] band close together
In flight from the hoopoes and renounce the penis,
Evils will cease, and High-Thundering Zeus will turn
The world upside down." **Woman #3** So we'll be lying on top?

Lysistrata "But if the swallows form factions and fly off from
775 The holy temple, there no longer can be any doubt
This bird's the most disgusting creature with wings."

Woman #3 That oracle left little to the imagination, by Zeus! Gods help us!

Lysistrata Times are tough, but let's not give up.
Betraying the oracle would be
An utter disgrace, my dears. Let's go inside. (*Lysistrata and the*
780 *four women exit into the stage building.*)

Chorus of Old Men I'll tell you a tale I heard
When I was just a boy.

135. The owl was closely associated with Athena and appeared on Athenian coins.

136. Oracles (prophecies) and oracular shrines, while ubiquitous in the ancient world, often were regarded with skepticism by educated individuals. Lysistrata is cynically exploiting the women's belief in them here.

137. This recalls a gruesome myth in which King Tereus of Thrace (cf. note 98 above), once married to the Athenian princess Procne, lusts for her sister (Philomela) and secretly rapes and mutilates her. The sisters exact their revenge by feeding Tereus his son Itys and then morph into the swallow and the nightingale, to be forever pursued by Tereus, now a hoopoe.

Once upon a time, there was young man called Melanion.[138] 784–5
Wanting nothing to do with marriage, he took to the hills 786–7
And lived like a hermit. 788
He had a fine dog, 791
And wove his own nets 789
So he could hunt rabbits. 790
Such was his hatred, he never returned home again. 792
As much as Melanion detested women, 793–4
We, sensible men that we are, 795
Hate them no less.

LEADER OF MEN'S CHORUS How's about I give you a kiss, hag—

LEADER OF WOMEN'S CHORUS You'd have to give up onions first!

CHORUS OF OLD MEN And then raise my leg and kick you!

LEADER OF WOMEN'S CHORUS That's some bush you've got there.[139] 800

LEADER OF MEN'S CHORUS For sure. Myronides[140]
Kept a rough patch down there
And turned a hairy cheek to all his enemies.
Likewise for Phormion.

WOMEN'S CHORUS Now I'll tell you a tale
À la your friend Melanion. 807
There was a notorious vagabond by name of Timon,[141] 808–9
Whose face could be glimpsed skulking in thorny shrubs 810–11
(He belonged to the Furies'[142] brood).

138. Melanion is better known in myth for his pursuit of Atalanta (with the aid of the golden apple). His dedication to virginity and hunting here, as also his misogyny, recall the figure of Hippolytus, the namesake of an extant play (428 BCE) by Euripides. Cf. note 141 below.

139. For the men's nudity, see note 114 above.

140. Myronides, like Phormion in 804, was a popular fifth-century BCE general.

141. Timon, whether a historical or mythic figure, came to be the archetypal hater of mankind and of human society in general. The women's assertion that he only hated men (819–820) is an *ad hoc* comic distortion to match the men's claim (see note 138 above) that Melanion was a misogynist. See further Hawkins, T., "Seducing a Misanthrope: Timon the Philogynist in Aristophanes' *Lysistrata*." *Greek, Roman, and Byzantine Studies* 42 (2001): 143–162.

142. The grim and relentless spirits of vengeance.

Such was his hatred that he withdrew
To a deserted spot,
815 Where he fervently cursed the wickedness of men.
In this way he joined up with our crusade
To despise wicked men of your ilk until the end of time.
819–20 But to women he was most warm-hearted.

LEADER OF WOMEN'S CHORUS Would you like me to give you a knuckle sandwich?

LEADER OF MEN'S CHORUS No, please—you're scarin' me!

LEADER OF WOMEN'S CHORUS How about a good kick instead?

LEADER OF MEN'S CHORUS We'd get a full view of your snatch.[143]

LEADER OF WOMEN'S CHORUS At least you won't catch a glimpse
825 of any crotch-locks:
I may be elderly,
But I practice controlled
Burning in that area.[144]

SCENE 5

LYSISTRATA Hey, hey, ladies! Come on over here
Quickly!

830 WOMAN Tell me what's up! What's with all the shouting?

LYSISTRATA It's a man! I see a crazy-looking man coming
Who's being violently pulled along by Aphrodite's power!
O Guardian Goddess of Cyprus, Cythera[145] and Paphos,
Stay the hard course thou doth travel![146]

WOMAN Where is the man, whoever he is?

835 LYSISTRATA He's by Chloe's[147] shrine.

WOMAN Holy Zeus, there is he! Who in the world is it?

143. Cf. note 114 above.

144. I.e., she singes her pubic hair with a lamp (cf. modern "waxing"). Cf. note 34 above.

145. Cythera is an island off Cape Malea on the Peloponnese, a cult center of Aphrodite (and said to be her birthplace). For Cyprus and Paphos, see notes 93 and 95 above.

146. A parody of religious language, especially in the obvious double-entendre "hard."

147. Referring to a shrine to Demeter Chloe (= "Of Grass/Greenery") near the Propylaia.

LYSISTRATA Take a look. Does any of you recognize
him? MYRRHINE (*on the roof of the stage building*)
I most
Certainly do! It's my husband Kinesias!

LYSISTRATA So now your task is to burn and torment him,
To tease his dick, and to make a show of affection (or not!), 840
To follow his every wish—except for what our wine-bowl
knows we must not do![148]

MYRRHINE No need to worry. I've got this under control.
LYSISTRATA And I'll stay,
To join you in befuddling him here,
And slowly roasting him. The rest of you, shoo!

(*Myrrhine and the rest of the women exit. Kinesias enters with his slave Manes, who holds Myrrhine's and Kinesias' baby.*)

KINESIAS[149] Ah, ah, damn it all! Such convulsions, 845
Such tension—it's as if I'm being stretched to capacity
on the rack!

LYSISTRATA Who's that there inside our lines?
KINESIAS Me. LYSISTRATA Are you a man?

KINESIAS Yes, *obviously* I am! LYSISTRATA Then you need
to disappear instantly.

KINESIAS And who do you suppose you are to be throwing
me out? LYSISTRATA The daytime guard.

KINESIAS By the gods, go get Myrrhine for me! 850

LYSISTRATA How about that! I'm supposed to go get Myrrhine?
And who are you?

KINESIAS I'm her husband—Kinesias of Paionidai![150]

LYSISTRATA Hello, my darling! Your name is not unknown to us,
And we've often heard it mentioned

148. Cf. 209ff.

149. His names means "Fucker" (reflecting an obscene sense of the verb *kinein*, "to move").

150. The name of Kinesias' deme suggests the obscene sense of the Greek verb *paiein* (i.e., "pound," "bang"). To (over-)emphasize the obscenity here, one could call him "Fuckhead of Pound-town." Cf. note 149 above.

855 Because "Kinesias" is always passing over your wife's lips.
Every time she handles an apple or egg, she says
"Ooh, I'm swallowing this one for Kinesias!"
Kinesias By the gods!

Lysistrata By Aphrodite, indeed! And whenever we fall to talking
About men, your wife instantly pipes up with
860 "Compared with my man Kinesias, all the others are just boys."

Kinesias C'mon now, go get her! **Lysistrata** Well? What's in it for me?

Kinesias By Zeus, there's this (*makes an obscene gesture*), if you want it.
How about this? (*offers his money-purse*) Whatever I've got on me is yours.

Lysistrata I'll go down and get her for you. (*exits into the stage building*) **Kinesias** Make it snappy!
865 There hasn't been an ounce of joy in my life
Since the moment she left the house.
It's agony me for me to go in there,
And everything seems so empty. I try to eat,
But food gives me no pleasure. All I have left is . . . THIS BONER!

(*Myrrhine appears on the roof of the stage building.*)

Myrrhine (*calling back inside*) I love him, I really do love him,
870 but he
Doesn't want my love! Don't make me go out to him.

Kinesias Myrrhine sweetie-pookins, why are you doing this to me?
Come down here. **Myrrhine** I absolutely am not coming down!

Kinesias You still won't come down when I ask nicely, Myrrhine?

Myrrhine You might be asking for me, but you don't really
875 need me.

Kinesias I don't need you? All this pressure is killing me.

Myrrhine I'm out of here. **Kinesias** No, please at least listen to your baby here.
You there, call for mommy.

Baby Mama, mama, mama.

Kinesias So what is wrong with you? Don't you feel sorry for your baby? 880
He hasn't been washed or fed in six days![151]

Myrrhine Of course I pity him. It's his father who's neglectful.

Kinesias Come down here, you vixen—for the baby.

Myrrhine What's more important than being a mother? I've got to go down there. **Kinesias** (*to the audience*) I can't help it.
She somehow looks quite a bit younger to me, 885
And there's something more enticing in her eyes.
And when she lashes out or looks down her nose at me,
It turns me on and I'm ready to explode with passion!

(*Myrrhine enters from the stage building.*)

Myrrhine Aw, my darling sweet little baby with such an awful father!
Now let mommy give you a kiss, you sweet thing! 890

Kinesias Why are you behaving so badly? Acting up with
Those other women, giving me such grief,
And hurting yourself too? **Myrrhine** Get your hands off me!

Kinesias And you've made a complete mess of all our stuff at home,
Both yours and mine! **Myrrhine** I really don't care much about that. 895

Kinesias And you don't care much if the hens are dragging away
Your finest wool? **Myrrhine** Absolutely not at all.

Kinesias And what about Aphrodite's sacred rituals?[152] You haven't
Celebrated them for the longest time. Please come home!

151. The passage of time can be loose in Old Comedy: cf. Introduction 7–10.

152. I.e., sex.

Myrrhine Nope, that's just not happening unless you all reach
900 an agreement
To put a stop to the war. **Kinesias** Okay then: if that's what people decide,
That's exactly what we'll do. **Myrrhine** Okay then: if that's what people decide,
I'll come back home. But for now I'm sworn to stay.

Kinesias Then at least lie down here with me—it's been such a long time.

905 **Myrrhine** Absolutely not! But that doesn't mean I don't love you.

Kinesias You do love me? Then why not lie down with me, Myrrie-poo?

Myrrhine That's ridiculous! Right in front of the baby?

Kinesias Well, certainly not! Manes, take the kid home!
(*Manes exits with the baby*)
There, the baby is out of our way.
Now lie down, please. **Myrrhine** Now just where, my
910 dear, could one possibly
Do that around here? **Kinesias** Where? The Grotto of Pan[153] will work.

Myrrhine But how would I go back to the Acropolis in a purified state?[154]

Kinesias No problem at all. You can clean up in the Klepsydra.[155]

Myrrhine Then you want me to break my oath, dear?

915 **Kinesias** Oath, smoath—I'll take the heat for that.

Myrrhine Okay, I'll go get us a portable bed.
Kinesias No need for that.
The ground will do just fine. **Myrrhine** By Apollo,[156] no!

153. See note 11 above.

154. It was necessary to bathe after sex to restore one's ritual purity (i.e., so as to be able to enter sacred space such as that on the Acropolis).

155. A spring on the Acropolis.

156. For Apollo, see Appendix.

I'm not going to let a man in your condition lie directly on the ground. (*exits*)

Kinesias Isn't is obvious how deeply my wife loves me?

Myrrhine Here we are. Now lie down there while I slip out of these clothes. 920

Hold on, we need a thingamabob . . . oh yeah, I mean a mattress. I'll get one.

Kinesias A mattress? Please no, not on my account.

Myrrhine By Artemis,

We're not doing it on the cords! That's disgusting!

Kinesias But how about a kiss first?

Myrrhine There you go. **Kinesias** Ooh-la-la, now get back here with it in a flash! (*Myrrhine exits*)

Myrrhine Ta-dah, a mattress! Lie down and I'll get undressed. 925

Hold on, we need one of those thingees . . . oh yeah, a pillow. You've got to have a pillow.

Kinesias But I don't need one! **Myrrhine** But I sure do. (*exits*)

Kinesias So what's this make my cock here? A hungry Herakles[157] at the dinner table?

Myrrhine Up, up, up with you! Now, is that everything?

Kinesias Yes, it has to be! Now come here, my little jewel. 930

Myrrhine I've just about got my bra unhooked. Now don't forget:

Don't you dare deceive me about the peace agreement!

Kinesias As Zeus is my witness, may I die if that happens!

Myrrhine Hey! You don't have a blanket.

Kinesias Really, it's not a blanket I need! What I *really* want is a FUCK.

Myrrhine No worries, you'll get that, just as soon as I'm back. (*exits*) 935

Kinesias This person and her bedspreads are wearing me down!

157. For Herakles, see Appendix. The joke here turns on Herakles' superhuman appetite.

Myrrhine Up, up, you. **Kinesias** Is *this* up enough for you?

Myrrhine How about some cologne?[158] **Kinesias** By Apollo, no, not for me!

Myrrhine Regardless, *by Aphrodite,* I'm putting some on.

940 **Kinesias** O Lord Zeus, please make the stuff spill out!

Myrrhine Put out your hand: take some and rub it on yourself.

Kinesias Phew! By Apollo, that does not smell good!
And it reeks of more delay and less sex.

Myrrhine Look what I did! I brought the Rhodian[159] fragrance!

Kinesias That's okay. Leave it be, you strange creature!

945 **Myrrhine** Oh, nonsense! (*exits*)

Kinesias May the inventor of perfume burn eternally in hell!

Myrrhine Here, take this bottle. **Kinesias** But I already have a bottle.[160]
Just lie down, you beast, and do not bring me
Another single thing! **Myrrhine** Sure, will do, by Artemis!

950 I'm taking my sandals off now. But don't forget, darling:
You *will* be voting for a peace treaty. (*exits and returns to Acropolis*)
Kinesias It'll get due consideration.
My wife's worn me down to the bone and wrecked me!
On top of that, she got me all pumped up and then let the air out of my balloon!
The horror! I've been deprived of the lovliest lady!

955 I've been screwed and now have nobody to screw!
Who'll take care of this poor orphan?

158. Perfume is a standard accompaniment of sex in the ancient world.

159. I.e., from the large Aegean island of Rhodes. Rhodes defected from Athens after the Sicilian Expedition (see note 99 above), and Athenian bitterness over that may be behind the unpleasant characterization of the cologne here.

160. The vessel for perfume (*alabastron*) is phallic in shape.

Where's that hustler, Fox-Dog?[161] (*surveys the audience*)
I need to hire one of his private nurses.

CHORUS OF MEN Ah, poor beguiled wretch, your soul
Is aggrieved in tragic suffering. 960
And I do pity you—alas!
What human organ could endure it?
What scrotum, what soul,
What testicles, what dong
Could survive the torture 965
Of being deprived of a morning fuck?

KINESIAS O Zeus! The horrible pressure!

CHORUS OF MEN Just look at what she's done to you!
What an abominable monster!

KINESIAS No, no, she's sweet as candy! 970

CHORUS OF MEN Sweet? She's poison, utter poison!

KINESIAS Okay, she's poison then! O Zeus, Zeus,
Please roll her up and fling her round
Like a tumbleweed caught up
In one of your blasting whirlwinds! 975
Take her aloft and then let her go,
So she'll plummet back to earth,
And stick a quick and perfect landing
On this pommel horse of mine!

SCENE 6

(*A messenger from Sparta enters, trying to conceal his erection under his cloak.*)

161. The nickname of Philostratus, an Athenian pimp. The call for the pimp here perhaps underscores one of the more unrealistic premises of the play—that is, the men could simply seek sexual release with prostitutes or with either their slaves or boys (given the prevalence of pederasty in ancient Athens). As the play's focus is on (re)asserting the importance of women citizens in Athens (cf. Introductory Essay 44–49), we apparently are expected to suspend our disbelief on this point.

980 **Spartan Messenger** Where is Oldmannery[162] of Athen-City
Or big Government Cheeses[163]? I got news for them.

Kinesias What are you supposed to be? A human or a human dick?

Spartan Messenger By Twin Gods,[164] I am messenger, young buck.
I come from Sparta about peace talk.

985 **Kinesias** And so that's why you've got a spear hidden on you there?

Spartan Messenger No, by Zeus, no spear!

Kinesias What are you hiding from me?
What are your covering up with your cloak there?
Case of crotch-swell from the trip here?

Spartan Messenger You crazy man,
By Castor! **Kinesias** C'mon, that's a boner, you wily dodger!

Spartan Messenger I swear by Zeus, it certainly no boner. Stop
990 blubber-talk!

Kinesias So just what is that? **Spartan Messenger** A rod, Spartan stiffy-staff for walking.

Kinesias Yeah, sure, and *this* is a Spartan walking rod too.
Hey, I think I know what's going on, so you can level with me:
How are things going for you all in Sparta?

995 **Spartan Messenger** All Sparta rise up in confusion and allies
Have boners too. Is need for pussy.

Kinesias Who's responsible for this disaster?
Is it Pan?[165]

Spartan Messenger Not Pan. I think Lampito start it
And then other women in all Sparta

162. The Spartan mistakenly assumes Athens has a Council of Elders (*Gerousia*), as that in Sparta. For the Spartans' dialect, see note 30 above.

163. The ambassador correctly refers to the Athenian *prytaneis* (i.e., representative boards who oversaw Athenian political assemblies).

164. See note 31 above.

165. For the perennially erect god Pan, see note 11 above.

Line up together like in race 1000
And say "ready, set go—*no pussy for you*!"

KINESIAS How are you doing then? SPARTAN MESSENGER It hard. We bent way over
Like men keeping lamp lit in wind over the Sparta town.
Women not let us touch their
Sweet cherries 'til we as group together 1005
Make peace treaty to rest of Greeks.

KINESIAS Now I get it: this whole affair
Is a joint conspiracy involving all the women of Greece.
Advise your fellow citizens to send ambassadors here
With full diplomatic powers to strike an agreement with us. 1010
I'll advise our Council to select our own
Ambassadors by formally presenting this cock of mine to them.

SPARTAN MESSENGER I fly away now. You say very, very good advice.

(*The Spartan Messenger and Kinesias exit.*)

LEADER OF MEN'S CHORUS No beast is tougher to tangle with than a woman.
No fire, no leopard is as dogged as she is. 1015

LEADER OF WOMEN'S CHORUS You've learned that hard lesson, but you still do battle with me.
Naughty boy! Why can't we be best friends forever?

LEADER OF MEN'S CHORUS Because I have no plan to stop hating women.

LEADER OF WOMEN'S CHORUS Stop doing that on your own time, but in the meantime I can't
Stand seeing you so exposed. Just look for yourself how ridiculous you are! 1020
I'm coming over there to put your shirt back on you.

LEADER OF MEN'S CHORUS By Zeus, that's a pretty nice thing you've done.
You know, it wasn't very nice of me to take it off so angrily in the first place.

Leader of Women's Chorus There, you look much less ridiculous—and like a real man now.[166]

1025 And if you weren't such a prick to me, I'd have already snatched
That beast that's still in your eye and removed it.

Leader of Men's Chorus That's what was hurting me. Take this ring of mine
And pick it out. Then show it to me once it's out—
By Zeus, it's been gnawing at my eye for quite a while now.

Leader of Women's Chorus I'll do it even though you've been
1030 such a grump of a man.
O Zeus! That is some monster gnat living in there!
Look for yourself: it appears to be Tricorysian![167]

Leader of Men's Chorus Damn, what a relief! That bug's been digging wells in my eye forever,
And now that it's gone, I've got a bunch of tears streaming out.

Leader of Women's Chorus Even though you've been such a
1035 naughty boy, I'll wipe them away
And give you a kiss. **Leader of Men's Chorus** No kisses!
Leader of Women's Chorus That's really not your choice.

Leader of Men's Chorus Oh, screw you! You're born manipulators!
That old saying has it exactly right about you all:
"Can't live with or without you marauders."[168]
1040 But now it's time to make peace, and from now on
I'll do you no ill and expect the same from you.

Leader of Women's Chorus Let's all take our places together and commence our song.

166. The Greek idealization of the naked male form as seen (esp.) in athletes and artistic representations of gods did not extend to old men's bodies. Cf. note 114 above and see further Bonfante, L., "Nudity as a Costume in Classical Art." *American Journal of Archaeology* 93 (1989): 543–570.

167. Tricorythus was a swampy area near Marathon where insects no doubt were bountiful.

168. An old misogynistic paradox: cf. Hesiod, *Theogony* 600–612 and *Works & Days* 57–58, and Introduction 21–22.

(The two semi-choruses unite and address the audience together.)

United Chorus of Old Men and Women We're not here, gentlemen,
To utter so much as a single slander
Against a fellow citizen.[169] 1045
It's just the opposite:
We've only good things to say
And do, as we've already got
More than our share of evils.
Instead, let's have every man and woman 1050
Speak up if they're
In need of a little cash—
Oh, let's say around two or three minae.[170]
We've got it inside, along with sacks for lugging it.
If peace ever comes about, 1055
All loans will promptly be forgiven—
That is, if any loans were actually ever given!

Leader of Men's Chorus We're wining and dining
Some Karystians[171] guests tonight,
Their crème de la crème! 1060
I've planned a soup,
And an ex-piglet of mine
Has been nicely grilled
Into succulent slices.
So come on over today! Be sure to rise early 1065
And take a nice bath,
Both you and the kids! Walk right in,
Don't bother to ring.
Proceed inside,
Make yourself at home (as if you really were)— 1070
Seeing that the door will be locked!

169. Choral songs in Old Comedy in fact often did this.

170. A significant sum, perhaps the equivalent of as many as 150 days' wages of a skilled laborer in the classical period.

171. Karystos was a loyal ally of Athens in the war. Cf. 1181ff.

SCENE 7

(*The Spartan delegation enters, along with their slaves, its members trying to conceal their erections under their cloaks.*)

UNITED CHORUS LEADER Hey, here come the Spartan ambassadors, dragging their beards,
And what looks like a pigpen over their thighs.
Gentlemen of Sparta! Greetings first,
1075 And then please tell us how you're doing.

SPARTAN AMBASSADOR I don't need give lecture 'bout that:
You take good look how we doing.

CHORUS LEADER Arrgh! Matters are much more pressing,
And the inflammation has gotten even worse!

SPARTAN AMBASSADOR Not speakable—who could say the
1080 words? But peacemaker
Should come, make peace for us how he want.

(*The Athenian delegation enters, along with their slaves, its members trying to conceal their erections under their cloaks.*)

CHORUS LEADER Ah, look: here are some of our homegrown heroes
Making belly-tents out of their cloaks the way
Wrestlers do.[172] Could be a bad case of abdominal swelling
1085 Or an old injury has popped up again.

SPARTAN AMBASSADOR Can anyone say where is Lysistrata?
We men are here—see man parts?

CHORUS LEADER The symptomology of both groups is consistent:
I take it the pressure overcomes you in the morning?

ATHENIAN AMBASSADOR #1 In the name of Zeus, our bones are
1090 wearing thin from this!
If we don't have a settlement soon,
Our only remaining option is fucking Cleisthenes![173]

172. Greek wrestlers competed in the nude, and so the point of comparison here is the forward incline of their upper bodies as they seek to gain a hold on their opponent, the objective being to throw him to the ground.

173. See note 104 above.

Chorus Leader If you've got any brains, you'll tuck those things under your cloaks.
Otherwise, some Wang-whacker[174] may catch sight of you.

Athenian Ambassador #1 You've certainly got that right!
Spartan Ambassador By Twin Gods, 1095
Is so! We got to put cloaks on again.

Athenian Ambassador #1 Hello, Spartans! We sure have fallen on hard times.

Spartan Ambassador O friend, our times is very hard too:
The men here (*pointing to audience*) maybe saw us playing on ourselves.

Athenian Ambassador #1 Let's focus now, Spartans, and get right down to business: 1100
What is the reason for your visit here? **Spartan Ambassador** We are ambassadors,
Here to make settlement.

Athenian Ambassador #1 Excellent, so are we.
So we should invite Lysistrata—
She's the only person capable of reconciling us.

Spartan Ambassador Yes, by the Twin Gods, invite Mr. Lysistrata[175] too if want. 1105

Athenian Ambassador #1 Oh, it seems she needs no invitation from us:
She probably heard us. Here she comes right now.

(*Lysistrata enters from the stage building.*)

Leader of United Chorus Greetings, manliest of all women! Now we need you to be
Harsh or gentle, upper crust or low class, snooty or sweet,

174. An allusion to the mutilation of the herms—guardian statues of the god Hermes (see Appendix) with prominent phalluses found throughout Athens—in 415 BCE just before the launch of the Sicilian Expedition (see notes 99 and 159 above). The Chorus Leader suggests that some of the perpetrators of this sacrilegious act, superstitiously blamed (in part) for the expedition's failure, are still in the city.

175. Either a joke about the Spartans' alleged penchant for anal sex (cf. note 104 above) or a jab at a contemporary (effeminate) Lysistratos.

All this in one woman. You've cast all Greece's leaders under
1100 your spell;
All their disputes have been handed over to you to fix.

LYSISTRATA It's easy work if you catch them when they're eager
For peace and not sniffing each other out.

We'll soon find out. Hey, Reconciliation, where are you?

(*The personification of Reconciliation enters; the actor*[176] *playing her wears a "naked suit."*)

(*to Reconciliation*) Take hold of the Spartans' hands first and
1115 bring them here,

And don't be rough or pushy about it—you know,
That brutish way our husbands used to treat us.
Handle him the way wives do their husbands at home:
If he refuses to give you his hand, drag him along by his dong.
1120 Go get the Athenians too.
Drag them here by any bodily part they offer you.
You Spartan gentlemen stand close to me here.
Athenians, over there. All of you listen up now:
I am a woman and I have a brain:
1125 I'm quite bright to begin with,
And since I've listened to a lot of my father's
And my elders' discussions, I'm not poorly educated.[177]
Now that I have your attention, I'm going to ream out
The both of you, just as you deserve. The two
of you sprinkle
Holy altars from a single vessel, as if you were
1130 blood relatives.
You do this at Olympia, Thermopylai, Delphi, and

176. For the proposal that Reconciliation was played by a woman, see Zweig, B., "The Mute Nude Female Characters in Aristophanes' Plays," pp. 73–89 in A. Richlin (ed.), *Pornography and Representation in Greece and Rome* (New York, 1992). If the actor, like all members of the cast with speaking parts, was male, what might have been the effects of having *him* sexually groped in the manner Reconciliation is here?

177. On education for women in the classical period, see Introduction 20–21.

I could name a lot of other places if I needed to.[178]
And when we've got armies of barbarian enemies,[179]
You're bent on destroying Greek cities and citizens.
So much for my first point. 1135

ATHENIAN AMBASSADOR #1 My turtle's gonna die if it can't put its head back in its shell soon!

LYSISTRATA Turning to you now, Spartans:
Do you remember when Perikleidas the Spartan
Came here once and sat down at our altars,
And as a pale suppliant of Athens wearing a crimson cloak 1140
Begged for reinforcements?[180] At that time, you were being
Rattled by the Messenians and shaken by Poseidon.[181]
And Cimon arrived with four thousand soldiers
And saved all of Sparta.
This is what they did for you: and you in turn 1145
Want to overrun the land that came to your rescue?

ATHENIAN AMBASSADOR #1 By Zeus, Lysistrata, they're the wrongdoers here!

SPARTAN AMBASSADOR We do wrong yes, but words cannot say beauty of her ass!

LYSISTRATA You think I'm going to let you Athenians off the hook?
Do *you* remember when the Spartans in turn 1150

178. Lysistrata names three panhellenic (see note 16 above) festivals where Greeks of various city-states gathered to celebrate shared religious and cultural practices. She refers to the famous games in Zeus' honor at Olympia (near Pisa on the Peloponnese), the major festival of Apollo at Delphi, his chief oracular site, and the lesser-known Pylaia of Demeter at Thermopylai (cf. note 193 below).

179. Especially the Persians.

180. Taking advantage of the chaos following a major earthquake in 464 BCE, Sparta's helots (i.e., its enslaved population) and the neighboring Messenians revolted.

181. The god (aka "The Earth-Shaker") was believed to be responsible for earthquakes. The Athenian general Cimon was sent to Sparta with a large force, but the Spartans ultimately rejected the Athenians' help, and relations between the two city-states deteriorated as a result. Lysistrata here distorts events in the Athenians' favor. Cf. note 183 below.

Came armed and annihilated a whole bunch of Thessalians,[182]
Along with Hippias' associates and allies?[183]
You were dressed like slaves,
And they were the only ones there to help.
1155 They were your liberators that day:
They restored Athens' cloak of freedom.

Spartan Ambassador I never seen a woman finer.

Athenian Ambassador #1 And I've never seen a nicer cunt!

Lysistrata Why then, after so many fine mutual favors,
1160 Are you still at war and doing nothing to stop the depravity?
Why not reconcile instead? What's stopping you?

(*Both parties proceed to map out their desires on Reconciliation's body; see further Introductory Essay 42–49.*)

Spartan Ambassador We willing for it, if you give us back this
Round bottomland. **Lysistrata** Which one, friend?
Spartan Ambassador Pylos,[184] the gate here.
We want for long time and been trying to squeeze way in.[185]

Athenian Ambassador #1 By Poseidon, you are not going to do
1165 that!

Lysistrata Let them have it, sir. **Athenian Ambassador #1** Then how can we still stick it to them?

Lysistrata Ask them for some other region in return.

Athenian Ambassador #1 Let me take a closer look here—
okay, first give us the

182. Thessaly, a northern region of Greece, provided cavalry for the tyrant Hippias (see notes 103 and 107 above).

183. As in her account of Cimon and the "liberation" of the Spartans (see note 181 above), Lysistrata exaggerates in portraying the Athenians as being enslaved to Hippias.

184. A strategic city on the western coast of the Peloponnese controlled by the Athenians (cf. note 37 above); *pylos* = "gate" in Greek.

185. The Spartans' alleged inclination toward anal sex is again hinted at.

Pubic Triangle,[186] and the Gulf of Poontang[187]
Just behind it—and how about The Legs[188] here? 1170

SPARTAN AMBASSADOR By Twin Gods, you can't have it all, Mister!

LYSISTRATA Let go of it: stop arguing about a pair of legs!

ATHENIAN AMBASSADOR #1 I'm going to strip down naked to do some plowing.

SPARTAN AMBASSADOR By the Twin Gods, I gonna get up early to plow poop-furrow.

LYSISTRATA There'll be time for that after you're reconciled. 1175
And if you've officially decided on peace,
Go back and confer with your allies.

ATHENIAN AMBASSADOR #1 Confer with our allies, ma'am? Have you noticed these boners of ours?
Won't each and every one of them reach the same resolution we have:
We all need to FUCK!

SPARTAN AMBASSADOR All our allies very much want this, 1180
By Twin Gods! ATHENIAN AMBASSADOR #1 And, by Zeus, the Karystians[189] certainly will too!

LYSISTRATA Very well then. For now, be sure to preserve your precious bodily fluids
So we women can entertain you on the Acropolis
With all the goodies we have in our boxes.
There you must give each other your pledges of trust. 1185

186. The Greek puns on the place name Echinous and the word for "sea-urchin" (suggesting pubic hair).

187. The Malian Gulf here = Reconciliation's vagina.

188. "The Legs" here refer to the long walls of Megara, a city-state located between Corinth and Athens, and a former Athenian ally currently on the Spartans' side in the war.

189. See note 171 above.

And then each of you can take his wife
And go home. **ATHENIAN AMBASSADOR #1** Let's go right now!

SPARTAN AMBASSADOR Lead way fast! **ATHENIAN AMBASSADOR #1** Yes, absolutely, as fast as you possibly can!

(*Lysistrata, Reconciliation, and the delegations exit; the slaves sit down around the central door of the stage building.*)

CHORUS Elaborate throws,
1190 And fancy mantles and saffron robes
And gold jewelry, everything I have,
I'll gladly bestow on all
Your sons, and whoever's daughter serves
As Kanephoros.[190]

1195–6 I invite all of you to take
What you want from my things at home.
Nothing's been sealed so tight
As to keep you from breaking in
1200 And carrying off its contents.
Take a good look, but there's nothing to see
Unless your eyes are much better than mine.
Out of bread and got slaves and a brood
Of small kids to feed?
1205–6 Feel free to take some fine little
Grains of wheat from my house:
A generous measure of these
Will grow into a handsome young loaf.
1210 The poor may also come
To my house with sacks and bags:
My slave will load them down
With handfuls of wheat.
That said, I must warn you not to approach my door:
1215 Unless you'd like to meet my watchdog!

190. See note 111 above.

SCENE 8

(*Athenian Ambassador #1 appears from within, pounding on the Propylaia and threatening the slaves spread out before it. He wields a lit torch.*)

ATHENIAN AMBASSADOR #1 Open up the door, you! You shouldn't have been there in the first place![191]
Why are all of you sitting there? How's about I light you
On fire with this torch? (*to audience*) How played is that?
I'm simply not going to do it. But if we really have to,
We'll somehow get ourselves through it to please you. 1220

ATHENIAN AMBASSADOR #2 (*enters from the gates*) We'd be happy to help you go through all that trouble: (*to slaves*)
Get lost or you'll be sadly missing your hair soon!

ATHENIAN AMBASSADOR #1 Yeah, get lost, so when the Spartans come out after their dinner,
They can easily make their way through here.

ATHENIAN AMBASSADOR #2 That's the best party I've ever been to! 1225
The Spartans were such a delight, and it turns out
We Athenians are quite the witty conversationalists when we're drunk.

ATHENIAN AMBASSADOR #1 Fair enough, seeing that we lose our wits when we're sober.
If I can convince my fellow Athenians of this,
We'll henceforth and forever more do our diplomacy drunk. 1230
As things are now, every time we go to Sparta sober,
We instantly find a way to mess things up.
What usually happens is that we don't listen to what they're saying,
And we each assume all sorts of things they don't actually say,
And so we come back here with different accounts of the same events. 1235
But just now everything went smoothly. If somebody

191. The gratuitous threats to the mute slaves onstage here are a reminder of the harsh realities of slavery in a society where it was naturalized.

Sang *Telamon* when he was supposed to sing *Kleitagora*,[192]
We said "bravo!" and swore it was awesome.
But look: those slaves are back again.
Get lost, you human whipping posts! (*the slaves flee and*
1240 *perhaps exit*)

ATHENIAN AMBASSADOR #2 Hey, now they're coming out of there!

(*The Spartan delegation enters from the Acropolis, accompanied by a piper.*)

SPARTAN AMBASSADOR Take pipes, my friend,
So I can dance and sing
Beautiful song to Athenians and us.

1245 ATHENIAN AMBASSADOR #1 By the gods, grab hold of those pipes!
I really love watching you Spartans dance!

SPARTAN AMBASSADOR Memory, inspire for this young man
Your own Muse,
Who knows about us and the Athenians,
1250 How they at Artemisium[193]
Sailed, godlike,
Against the Persian fleet
And prevailed,
While Leonidas led us
1255 Like crazy boars, I think,
Sharpening the tusk, and lot
Of foam flowed around our jaws,
1258–9 And lot flow down legs too.
1260 The Persian men as many as
The grains of sand.
Maiden goddess,
Wild Killer of Beasts,[194] come here

192. The *Telamon* and *Kleitagora* were two very distinct popular songs (the blundering choice is overlooked here in the festivities).

193. Site of a critical naval battle (480 BCE) in the Persian Wars, which took place simultaneously with the Spartan general Leonidas' attempt to hold off the Persians with a force of just 300 at the pass of Thermopylai (cf. note 178 above) in northern Greece.

194. Artemis, prominently worshipped at both Athens and Sparta.

For peace treaty.
Keep us friends for long time. 1265
And now let friendship always be smooth 1266–7
Because of pact, and let us not be wily 1268–9
Foxes to each other anymore. 1270
Come to here, come
O Maiden Huntress!

(*Lysistrata*[195] *and both the Athenian and Spartan women enter.*)

ATHENIAN AMBASSADOR #1 Since everything else has turned out so well,
You Spartans should now take your wives[196] back home;
You Athenians do the same. Let each man stand beside his wife, 1275
And each wife beside her husband, in celebration of
This happy ending, by taking up a dance for the gods.
And may we together aim to never go astray like this again.
Bring on the dance, bring on the Graces,[197]
And call forth Artemis 1280
Along with her twin, the Kindly Healer;[198]
The Nysian[199] too,
Who among his maenads[200] flashes his eyes ecstatic. 1283–4
And call upon Zeus ablaze with lightning, together with 1285
His blessed wife and queen.[201]
And include the divine spirits,[202] to serve
As vigilant witnesses

195. Lysistrata's appearance (as a mute character) here is conjectural, as elsewhere in the play her entrances are explicitly announced. If she does appear, she perhaps does not dance as the others, but stands majestically apart in an Athena-esque pose. Cf. Introductory Essay 42.

196. I.e., the hostages taken at 244.

197. The Charites, who personify grace and charm and enjoy continuous music and dancing.

198. Apollo.

199. Dionysus.

200. In myth, the ecstatic female followers of Dionysus: cf. note 10 above.

201. Hera: see Appendix.

202. The *daimones*, non-anthropomorphic supernatural powers in the Greek pantheon.

Of this generous Peace[203]
1290 That the goddess Cypris[204] forged.

CHORUS Alalai, hail Paian,
Rise up, iai!
Dance for victory, iai!
Evoi, evoi, evoi, evoi!

ATHENIAN AMBASSADOR #1 Produce a song, my Spartan friend,
1295 a novel one to match our own.

SPARTAN AMBASSADOR Abandon anew lovely Mt. Taygetos,[205]
O Spartan Muse! Come, to graciously
Hymn for us the god of Amyklai,[206]
Athena of the Bronze House[207]
1300 And the noble sons of Tyndareos,[208]
Who sport along the Eurotas.[209]
Step it up now,
Yes, jump ever so slightly!
Let's launch a hymn for Sparta,
1305 Where dances for gods
And the pounding of feet are cherished,
And where along the Eurotas
Young girls sway like fillies
Raising dust
1310 In a flurry of feet.
Their hair's flung 'round
1312–3 Like maenads playfully wielding their thyrsoi.[210]

203. Hesychia, a personification of peace.

204. Aphrodite: cf. notes 93 and 95 above.

205. See note 39 above.

206. An important site of the worship of Apollo near Sparta.

207. Spartan cult of Athena, where she served as the citadel's protective goddess, much like Athena Polias (cf. notes 94 and 108 above) at Athens.

208. Castor and Pollux: see note 31 above.

209. A river passing through Sparta; Apollo's sanctuary at Amyklai was located on its banks.

210. A wand wreathed with ivy and topped with a pine cone, carried by reveling maenads (see note 200 above).

Leda's daughter[211] leads the way,
The pure and pleasing leader of the dance. 1315
Now come bind your hair back with your hands, 1316–7
Prance on your feet like a deer, and speed the dance with your
shouts. 1318–9
Sing now of the all-victorious Goddess of the Bronze
House![212] (*all exit*) 1320–1

211. Helen, in myth the daughter of Leda (the wife of Tyndareos) and Zeus (appearing to Leda disguised as a swan), worshipped as a kind of tree goddess in Sparta. She also is the sister of the Dioscuri (see notes 31 and 208 above).

212. See note 208 above.

Menander's SAMIA

We possess what we have of *Samia* owing only to papyrus finds of the twentieth century. The Cairo papyrus published in 1907 preserves lines 216–416 and 547–686; another papyrus (P. Bodmer XXV) that provides significant sections of the play's beginning and end was published in 1969. Owing to these and a few other more fragmentary finds, Acts III, IV, and V of *Samia* are nearly complete. Sizeable parts of Acts I and II are missing or mutilated and are so noted in the translation. The entire play is estimated to be *ca.* 900 lines total. Ancient evidence of *Samia* is also preserved in a fourth-century CE mosaic found at Mytilene on the island of Lesbos (Fig. 1.3). The mosaic depicts the extremely intense scene from Act III in which the angry Demeas, wielding a raised stick (cf. 440), evicts Chrysis from his house. The latter is sympathetically represented with baby in hand as the cook looks on. The nurse, who appears in the scene (373) of Menander's play, is absent on the mosaic. As the first

Athenian performance of *Samia* was sometime around 315 BCE, Menander's comedy apparently enjoyed lengthy currency.

The plot of *Samia* at first suggests a straightforward enough New Comedy. Prior to the play, Moschion, a young man adopted by a wealthy Athenian bachelor named Demeas, (apparently) raped his next-door neighbor Plangon during a festival in honor of Adonis being celebrated at her father's house.[1] As a result, she became pregnant and has given birth just prior to the play. Nikeratos, Plangon's father, has been away on an extended business trip to Pontus with Demeas. In the absence of both fathers, Moschion has confessed to the rape—a rarity in New Comedy—to Plangon's mother and has agreed to marry Plangon, for whom he expresses genuine affection (cf. 165, 728–729). At the news of his father's return, however, Moschion, ashamed of his behavior (47–49), suddenly becomes fearful (65ff.) and launches a plan to pretend the baby is Chrysis', Demeas' live-in mistress and formerly a courtesan on the island of Samos. Chrysis, who recently lost her own baby, has already been nursing Plangon's (78; cf. notes 22 and 54). Unbeknownst to Moschion, during their travels Demeas and Nikeratos have agreed that their children should be married. With the need to identify Plangon's rapist removed, and with father and son both keen for the marriage with Plangon, Nikeratos, once apprised of his daughter's rape, needs only to be placated for the perceived affront to his honor, which in turn should result in the previously arranged marriage. But that would have made for a much less interesting play.

The conspiracy struck by Moschion and Chrysis regarding the baby's paternity shifts the plot in an entirely different direction. The

1. A nocturnal festival is a typical setting for rape in New Comedy, although modern categorical distinctions between consensual sex, seduction, and rape are not always clearly drawn in the comedies: see notes 8, 19 and 20 below and, for example, Harris, E.M., *Democracy and the Rule of Law in Classical Athens* (Cambridge, 2006): 297–332 and James, S., "Reconsidering Rape in Menander's Comedy and Athenian Life: Modern Comparative Evidence," pp. 24–39 in A.H. Sommerstein (ed.), *Menander in Contexts* (Routledge Monographs in Classical Studies 16) (New York, 2014).

first complication arises when Demeas is led to believe that Chrysis has had his baby:[2]

DEMEAS It seems that, unbeknownst to me, my mistress has become
My wife!

MOSCHION Your wife? I'm not following you.

DEMEAS It seems that I become a father to a son in secret.
To hell with her! She can take him and
Get right out of my house! MOSCHION Oh, not that!
DEMEAS What do you mean, "not that!"?
Do you really expect me to raise a bastard son
In my own house? That doesn't square with my way of thinking!

MOSCHION In the name of the gods, if you're a human being,
Who among us is legitimate, and who's a bastard?
DEMEAS You aren't serious,
Are you?

MOSCHION I'm absolutely serious, as Dionysus is my witness!
I don't think ancestry makes any difference;
If you look at the issue fairly, a good person
Is legitimate, a bad person is both a bastard
And a slave . . . (130–143)

The text unfortunately breaks off here, and when it resumes, Demeas and Moschion have moved on to the topic of the marriage. It thus is uncertain whether or not Moschion at this point convinced his father to raise what he believes to be his illegitimate child, or if the matter of paternity was for now brushed aside. Nonetheless, Moschion, himself a product of adoption at an early

2. According to Athenian law dating back to Pericles (451 BCE), only a child of two citizens can be regarded as legitimate. A male child of Demeas and Chrysis, a free person but resident foreigner, thus could not participate in civic politics or inherit property.

age (7ff.), here significantly raises the issue of whether individual character is more important than legal status.

Nikeratos shortly agrees to proceed with the wedding this same day. Demeas goes into his house to help with arrangements on his side but returns at the beginning of Act III to report some startling news: inside, he has overheard Moschion's former wet-nurse refer to the baby as Moschion's. He then chanced upon Chrysis nursing the infant and has concluded that she must be its mother. Given his confidence in Moschion's good character, he at first is reluctant to believe that his son has had an affair with his mistress, but he then bullies Parmenon into admitting that the child's father is Moschion (315ff.) without allowing the slave to explain Chrysis' role in the matter.

Demeas still talks himself into exonerating his son of wrongdoing and mistakenly concludes that Moschion's readiness to marry Plangon is only a smokescreen to separate himself from a predatory Chrysis, against whom he now channels all his anger:

> He wasn't so eager
> Because of love, as I thought was the case then, but he wanted to
> Get away from the house and at last escape this Helen of mine.
> She's to blame for what has happened.
> She obviously got her claws on him when he was drunk
> And not in control of himself. Fortified wine and youth
> Can create a lot of foolishness when they've got
> A co-conspirator close at hand.
> It seems utterly incredible to me that
> Someone who is so well behaved and reasonable
> To others would treat *me* in this way,
> Not even if he's ten times adopted and not my son by birth!
> It's not his birth, but his character I look at.
> The woman's a slut, a menace! But what of it?
> She won't be around for long. Now, Demeas, you

Must be a man! Forget that you missed her, stop wanting her,
Hide the trouble that's happened as best
As you can for your son's sake. And as for the lovely
Samian lady:[3]
Throw her out of your house, headfirst
And straight to hell! You have the excuse that she
Kept the child. Nothing else needs to be made known.
Bite your lip, be tough, brave, and strong! (335–356)

While Demeas' anger over the presumed affair of his son and mistress is understandable, and his resolution to suppress his feelings for Chrysis and proceed with his son's wedding seems natural enough (cf. 447–448), the audience knows that his hasty and stereotypical characterization of Chrysis as a seductress is grossly unwarranted. He rushes into his house, only to return onstage shortly, now violently driving out Chrysis and the baby (369ff., as depicted on the Mytilene mosaic). Without revealing his suspicion about the affair—and so giving Chrysis a chance to explain—Demeas angrily lambasts Chrysis for her alleged ingratitude over his extricating her from her former life as a *hetaira*. Obviously suppressing his deep emotion, he seeks to end their relationship by a cold settling up of accounts:

You've got all your things. In addition,
You can have some slave girls and some gold. Get out of
My house! (381–383)

3. Only here and at 265, where Demeas also angrily addresses himself regarding his mistress' alleged treachery, is Chrysis pejoratively referred to as "the Samian woman" (Moschion calmly refers to her as his father's "Samian girlfriend"—if the conjectural supplement of the papyrus is correct at 36—before revealing her personal name at line 56 of his prologue). As she otherwise is addressed or referred to as "Chrysis" throughout the play, this suggests that Menander's choice of title not only focalizes Demeas' misdirected anger toward her but perhaps also hints at the broader unfairness in reducing Chrysis to the status of foreigner/Samian courtesan. For the general conventions in referring to women in comedy, see Sommerstein, A.H., "The Naming of Women in Greek and Roman Comedy," pp. 43–69 in A.H. Sommerstein, *Talking about Laughter: and Other Studies in Greek Comedy* (Oxford, 2009).

He further engages in gratuitously vitriolic fantasy about how miserable her life will be after she loses the protection and financial security she enjoys as his mistress:

> You're such hot stuff! You'll see
> Exactly what you are once you're in town.
> Unlike what you're used to, the girls there run off
> To dinner parties for ten drachmas
> And drink fortified wine until they die.
> If they don't jump at that kind of invitation,
> They starve. You'll learn this the same as everyone else,
> I'm sure, and you'll realize who you are and how you went wrong. (390–397)

We are afforded a glimpse of Demeas' inner feelings here and get a clear sense that Chrysis has been much more than a hired sex worker to him. Nikeratos fortuitously appears and takes Chrysis and the baby to safety within his house. At this point, Nikeratos believes that the baby is Chrysis' and Demeas', since the women of his household have told him so, and he also knows Chrysis is nursing it (410–411). Nikeratos, evidently accepting of the idea of his neighbor's raising an illegitimate child, assumes that Demeas is only temporarily being unreasonable.

When Moschion begins to plea on behalf of Chrysis (452ff.), Demeas concludes that his son was not the innocent partner in an affair, as he had assumed. Nikeratos joins his neighbor in his misdirected outrage and farcically compares Moschion to some of myth's most notorious intra-familial sex criminals (i.e., Tereus, Oedipus, and Thyestes [495–496]) and even wildly asserts that if he had such a son, he would prosecute him for murder (510–514). After Nikeratos exits, Moschion discloses the truth to Demeas—that Chrysis is generously helping him protect his secret about the rape (528–529). No sooner is this revealed than

Nikeratos angrily reappears to report that he has just seen Plangon nursing the child inside, at which point Moschion runs offstage. Comically frenetic chaos ensues. Demeas reports hearing Nikeratos' threat to incinerate the baby inside the house (553–555). Nikeratos rushes in and out of his house twice; the first time he reports that Chrysis has sworn his wife and daughter to a conspiracy of silence and that Chrysis is refusing to give up the baby. The second time (568ff.), in a reprise of the Mytilene mosaic scene, a stick-wielding Nikeratos chases Chrysis and baby from his house. This time Demeas protects Chrysis and the baby by sending them into his house and then sets about defusing his outlandishly livid neighbor. To accomplish this, he engages in clever repartee that draws on the god Zeus' stealthy impregnation of Danaë as an amusing parallel to Nikeratos' own situation (588ff.). Demeas eventually placates Nikeratos, and the two fathers agree to proceed with the wedding, which is to commence at the end of the play, just after Moschion and Demeas resolve their lingering conflict.[4] When Demeas from outside his house instructs Chrysis to direct the final preparations for the wedding (730) inside, it is clear that both the status quo in their relationship and normalcy within the household have been restored.

Samia thus provides a fascinating glimpse into the personal lives of two Athenian families. No female member of Nikeratos' household speaks in the play, but Menander nonetheless creates an evocative picture of energetic life inside the house. Demeas first alerts us to this when he asserts that Nikeratos will be hard put to persuade his wife to expedite the wedding (200). And later, apparently at the insistence of his wife, Nikeratos announces his plan to take Demeas to task for his eviction of Chrysis (421)

4. For this much-discussed scene (616ff.), in which Moschion pretends that he will run off to become a mercenary because of Demeas' slighting of his character, see Konstan, D., "Menander and Cultural Studies," pp. 31–50 in A.K. Petrides and S. Papaioannou (eds.), *New Perspectives on Postclassical Comedy* (Newcastle, 2010), who interprets Moschion's confrontation of his father as a necessary stage in his transition to adulthood.

when he reports the strong reaction to this development within his household:

> In the middle of the wedding preparations
> A terrible omen occurred. A woman's been kicked out,
> And has come to our house with a baby!
> There are lots of tears, and the women are quite upset.
> (423–426)

Although their precise motivations are never made explicit, Nikeratos' wife and daughter are complicit in the plan to pass the baby off as Chrysis', and they resist telling Nikeratos about the rape and Plangon's having given birth themselves (558–560). His unnamed wife's silence leads the bilious Nikeratos to twice declare that he will murder her (560–561, 580–581). Plangon is the only female member of Nikeratos' household to appear onstage (i.e., for the wedding at 725ff.), though she remains silent there, symbolically significant as she and her baby are for the continued welfare of both households.

When Demeas helps out with the wedding preparations he finds himself in what seems to be predominantly defined as the female space of his house:

> I happened to go into the pantry. I was looking things over
> There and selecting out more supplies,
> And didn't come out right away. While I was in there,
> A woman came down from upstairs
> Into the room across from the pantry,
> Which happens to be a weaving room—
> You pass through it to go upstairs or to
> The pantry. (229–236)

In this striking vignette that smacks of everyday life, Menander has Moschion's former wet-nurse calm the neglected infant through typical baby talk (242ff.) and imaginatively draws the audience into these intimate recesses of Demeas' household as well.[5] Demeas' house, in contrast to Nikeratos', has a female spokesperson in the non-citizen Chrysis, who moves freely from house to house during the play. In her opening appearance there is an initial suggestion that she may live up to the stereotype of the manipulative comic prostitute, when she assures Moschion that she can manage Demeas' anger:

> Oh, he'll get over it eventually,
> Seeing that he's terribly in love—just like
> You are, my young friend. That can make
> Even the angriest man come to terms peacefully in an
> instant. (80–83)

Despite Demeas' later echoing of this stereotype (cf. pp. 119–120 above), the former *hetaira* proves to be anything but a sexual mercenary. From the start, we see Chrysis showing maternal concern for Plangon's baby (84–85; cf. Demeas' characterization of her as a mother at 265–279), and, as we have seen, in two lively scenes she appears onstage shielding herself and the baby from the irate stick-wielding old men. Both visually and in light of her empathetic nature, Chrysis remains a highly sympathetic character throughout; some audience members probably took issue with Demeas' harsh characterization of her as replaceable merchandise ("Another girl will be pleased with what I have, Chrysis," 385).

We witness Demeas treating Chrysis as his *de facto* wife when she is twice (413–415, 730) put in charge of the preparations for the wedding, and the slaves regard her as the mistress (258) of the house, corresponding to Demeas' role as its master (256). Nikeratos' wife, instead of being suspicious of the ex-concubine

5. The role of Demeas calls for a virtuoso actor, as is especially seen in his representation of various women's direct speech (226–227, 242–248, 252–260) in this Act III monologue.

next door, has become Chrysis' close friend, and the two women frequently visit each other's houses (36–38). Chrysis in fact hosted the Adonis festival at which Moschion rapes Plangon, whose guests include other, presumably free women (40–41). As noted above (p. 122), Nikeratos' wife and daughter collude and sympathize with the vulnerable Chrysis, despite Nikeratos' demands. The play thus paints a clear picture of a woman who manages Demeas' household like a wife, demonstrates her ability to be a mother, and is accepted socially by the married and free women within her immediate community. What disqualifies Chrysis from becoming Demeas' wife is Athenian law and its insistence on marriage being "For the procreation of legitimate children" (727), i.e., the offspring of Athenian citizens.

The tension between legitimacy/citizenship and character was highlighted early in the play by the adopted Moschion (pp. 117–118 above). It similarly applies to the case of Chrysis, who not only is positively presented as a sympathetic character throughout but also is instrumental in legitimizing the marriage of Moschion and Plangon in that she preserves their baby from the dangers alternately posed to it by each head of the two households: "the play . . . uses a child temporarily branded as a bastard to interrogate the social meaning of both kinship and gender."[6] Demeas generally admits to having misjudged matters (702–705) but never apologizes to Chrysis, perhaps yet another realistic touch. Still, *Samia* portrays Demeas and Chrysis as reconciled in the end and suggests that their relationship will continue as before; Demeas' initial complaint that his mistress has become his wife (130) may ironically be true. To be sure, Menander has aptly and subtly dramatized the social, legal, and emotional complexities of these two fourth-century BCE Athenian families and provided, if only indirectly, a refreshing look at women's interior lives that transcends male stereotypes and prescribed social boundaries.

6. Lape (2010): 68.

SAMIA (THE WOMAN FROM SAMOS)

CAST OF CHARACTERS (WITH SPEAKING PARTS)

MOSCHION: a young man, adopted son of Demeas

CHRYSIS: a Samian courtesan, now living with Demeas

PARMENON: a slave of Demeas

DEMEAS: a wealthy and elderly bachelor

NIKERATOS: a relatively poor old man, neighbor of Demeas and father of Plangon

COOK: unnamed cook hired for the wedding feast

(*Setting: A street in Athens in front of the houses of Demeas and Nikeratos, which are accessible through two doors in the stage backdrop.*)

ACT I

[*The opening* ca. *10 lines of the play are mutilated or lost altogether. Here Moschion must have entered from Demeas' house and informed the audience of his father's name and his adoption before the text picks up below. For the preservation of the play on damaged papyrus, see Introductory Essay 115.*]

MOSCHION[7]

. . . why I must upset myself . . . 2

. . . it's painful, since I made a mistake.[8]

. . . I think this will be . . .

7. His name means "Young Calf" in Greek and so suggests immaturity.

8. If Moschion even refers to impregnating Plangon here, it is not clear that he is admitting to culpability in a rape. See further note 19 below and Parmenon's (unchallenged) assertion that Moschion has "wronged" Plangon at 68.

5 . . . reasonably to make clear to you[9]
In detail what my father's character is.
I remember well how he spoiled me as a little boy,
Just after he adopted me. But enough of that—
I wasn't old enough yet to appreciate his kindness.
10 Next, I was registered[10] the same as everyone else,
"Just another face in the crowd," as they say.
And I swear I've actually become more miserable
Because we're rich. I stood out for my philanthropy
When I financed a chorus.[11] He provided me with hunting dogs
15 And horses.[12] I distinguished myself as a cavalry officer.[13]
I was able to help my friends in need with modest assistance.
Thanks to him, I was a decent person. I paid him back
For everything in an appropriate way: I was well behaved.
It just so happened then—I'll go through all the details
20 Of our family's business now, since I've got time—
That he became infatuated with a courtesan
From Samos,[14] as is natural enough.
He kept their relationship hidden, since he was ashamed. But despite his wishes,

9. You (plural) here = the audience.

10. At the age of 18, an Athenian male underwent formal examination before his father's demesmen (for Attic demes [= districts], see *Lysistrata*, note 23) to determine his fitness for citizenship.

11. An indication of how wealthy Demeas is. Financing the training of a chorus for a dramatic performance at a public festival in Athens was an important (Introduction 5) and very expensive civic responsibility of wealthy individuals up until 315 BCE; if the play debuted (cf. Introductory Essay 115–116) after this change, Moschion is nostalgically referring to a lapsed institution.

12. Further indications of the family's wealth and elite status.

13. I.e., for his tribe (= *phyle*); Athenian citizens were divided into 10 tribes for political and military purposes.

14. An Aegean island on the coast of Asia Minor, famous for its expensive and elegant courtesans in antiquity.

I found out about it, and came to the conclusion
That his younger rivals would become a nuisance 25
If he didn't become the courtesan's protector.[15]
He was embarrassed about this, perhaps because of me,
But I told him to take her in . . . 28

[*In the lost* ca. 20 *lines here, Moschion probably told the audience that Demeas took the courtesan from Samos into his house and that she was pregnant when Demeas left on a business trip to Pontus. He also must have begun to provide information about Nikeratos and his family next door.*]

. . . the girl's mother[16] became friends with my father's 36
Samian girlfriend. They spent most of their time at her
house,
Though they sometimes were at ours. I happened
To rush down from our farm one day, and I found
Them all gathered for the Adonis festival[17] here at our
house, 40
Along with some other women. As often happens,
The festival turned out to be a lot of fun, and I became
A virtual spectator, since the women's partying
Was keeping me awake anyway.
They carried some gardens up onto the roof,[18] 45
Danced, and soon spread their all-night party out
everywhere.

15. This suggests that she was a free person (cf. 577) and not a slave, but as a foreigner (and so a non-citizen) living in Athens, she will benefit from Demeas' role as her protector. For the role of *hetairai* ("companions"/"courtesans") in Greek society and comedy, see Introduction 25.

16. I.e., the wife of Nikeratos and mother of Plangon (= "the girl" here).

17. For the women's festival in honor of the eastern deity Adonis, see *Lysistrata,* notes 74 and 75. For festivals as the conventional setting for rape in New Comedy, see Introductory Essay 116.

18. The typical setting for festivals of Adonis; the plants (with fast-growing seeds) were part of the ritual lament for the god (cf. *Lysistrata* 389).

I'm hesitant to tell you the rest. Perhaps I'm ashamed
When there's no point in being so—but I'm still ashamed.[19]
The girl got pregnant. Having said that, I've also told
50 You what happened before. I didn't deny
The responsibility was mine, but I went
To the girl's mother on my own. I promised to marry her[20]
Once my father returned, and I swore an oath to that.
The baby was born just recently. I acknowledged it.[21]
55 Then there was a most fortunate happenstance:
56 Chrysis—that's what she goes by—had a baby . . .[22]

[In the lacuna of ca. 25 lines here, Moschion probably explained that Chrysis' baby had died and that she has been nursing Plangon's (and his) child. At the end of his monologue he exited for the harbor, where he had already sent Parmenon, to see if there was news of his father's return. Chrysis must then have entered from Demeas' house—only the very end of her monologue is preserved at 59–60 below.]

59 **Chrysis**[23] They're coming our way here now . . .
60 I'll wait and listen in on what they're saying.

Moschion You saw my father with your very own eyes,
Parmenon?

Parmenon[24] You're not deaf, are you? Yes!

Moschion And our neighbor?[25]

19. It is not entirely clear why Moschion is ashamed and says that he "made a mistake" in 3 (cf. 68). His sense of shame and wrongdoing regarding Plangon may primarily have to do with his behavior's possibly leading to a marriage not arranged by his father. For the differences between ancient and modern perspectives of rape, see Omitowoju, R., *Rape and the Politics of Consent in Classical Athens* (Cambridge, 2002), with discussion of the situation in *Samia* at pp. 197–203. Cf. *Hecyra*, Introductory Essay 229–230.

20. The usual legally and socially acceptable solution—unpalatable as it seems to us—to the rape of a free, unmarried girl: cf. Introductory Essay 116.

21. I.e., the baby has been taken into his father Demeas' house.

22. The papyrus is mutilated and "had a baby" is only a conjecture here.

23. Her name means "Gold," appropriately for a Samian courtesan (see note 14 above).

24. A typical comic slave's name (= "Trusty (sidekick)" in Greek): cf. *Hecyra*, note 18.

25. Nikeratos, who accompanied Demeas on his trip to Pontus.

PARMENON They're both back here. MOSCHION Excellent!
PARMENON So you need to be
A man and immediately start a conversation about
Your marriage. MOSCHION But how? I've lost all my courage 65
Now that the reality of it is right around the corner.
PARMENON What do you mean?

MOSCHION I'm ashamed to face my father.
PARMENON You pantywaist!
But how's it happen that you have no fear of the girl
You've wronged[26] and her mother? CHRYSIS (*stepping forth to address Parmenon*) Why all the shouting, you awful person?

PARMENON So Chrysis is here too. You're actually wondering why 70
I'm shouting? That's silly! I want the wedding to happen now,
And I want this guy here to stop crying
At this door, and I want him to remember exactly
What he swore he'd do personally: make the sacrifice,[27] put on a garland,[28]
Prepare the wedding cake[29]—are those enough reasons 75
For me to be shouting? MOSCHION I'll do it all. I don't need
To be told. CHRYSIS I'm quite sure you will.
MOSCHION What about the baby?
Do we let *her*[30] keep nursing it as she is,
And claim she's the one who gave birth to it?
CHRYSIS Certainly! Why not?

26. Cf. notes 8 and 19 above.

27. The bridegroom's responsibility before the wedding ceremony: cf. note 40 below.

28. Worn by the bridegroom throughout the wedding festivities.

29. A sesame and honey wedding cake, to be portioned out to guests by the bridegroom (cf. 125 and 190) during the festivities.

30. Chrysis, at whom Moschion points here.

Moschion My father will go ballistic. **Chrysis** Oh, he'll
80 get over it eventually,
Seeing that he's terribly in love—just like
You are, my young friend. That can make
Even the angriest man come to terms peacefully in an
instant.[31]
And I think I'd sooner put up with just about anything
85 Than having a wet-nurse in some government housing[32] . . .

[Ca. *20–25 lines are missing here. Chrysis and Parmenon must have exited into Demeas' house and left Moschion alone onstage. The fragmentary remains of the end of his monologue begin at 90 below.*]

90 **Moschion** . . . I'm most wretched of all.
91 I'm going to hang myself immediately . . .
Only a speaker . . . than a friend
I'm . . . in these current cases.
94 Why don't I go off to some deserted place
And practice? This is no small battle I've got ahead. (*exits for*
95 *the country*)

(*Demeas and Nikeratos enter from the direction of the harbor, in the middle of a conversation.*)

Demeas[33] You do notice the changed environment,
How different it is here from that horrible place?
Pontus![34] Fat old men, never-ending fish,
A kind of nausea in everything. Byzantium![35]

31. Chrysis' assertion here that infatuated men can easily be manipulated suggests that she is a conventionally mercenary prostitute (cf. *Hecyra*, Introductory Essay 233–234), an expectation that is soon frustrated (see further Introductory Essay 123–124).

32. Unwanted babies would be exposed or given to (often poor) foster families, as Chrysis assumes might happen.

33. A common name for old men in comedy, of uncertain etymology.

34. The northwestern shores of the Black Sea, famously abundant in fish, but at the edge of civilization for Greeks. Demeas and Nikeratos presumably were conducting business there.

35. I.e., modern Istanbul, known in antiquity for its absinthe plant (= "Wormwood" at 100). Byzantium would be a likely stop for travellers to or from Pontus.

Wormwood, everything is bitter! But here, I swear by
Apollo,[36] 100
There is perfection even for the poor! Dear, dear Athens,
May you receive all the blessings you deserve,
So that those of us who love the city may be
Happiest in every possible way![37] Move on inside!
(*to slave accompanying them*) Hey you, human statue—why
are you standing there gawking at me? 105

Nikeratos What amazed me the most about that place,
Demeas, was that sometimes you couldn't see
The sun for the longest time. It'd seem
Like a kind of thick fog completely shadowed it over.

Demeas There wasn't anything remarkable to see there, 110
So the sun shone upon the locals as little as possible.

Nikeratos By Dionysus,[38] you've got that right!

Demeas Let's leave
That stuff for others to worry about. Now as for
What we were talking about—
What do you think we should do? **Nikeratos** You mean
about
Your son's wedding? **Demeas** Absolutely.

Nikeratos As I've always said, 115
Let's set a day and move forward—and hope
For the best. **Demeas** That's what's best?

Nikeratos I think so. **Demeas** Me too—
And I thought so before you did. **Nikeratos** Call me
when you leave . . . 118

[Ca. *10 lines are missing, in which Demeas and Nikeratos must exit for their houses; one of them would have announced the conventional (in Greek New Comedy) approach of a drunken band of partyers (i.e., the chorus approaching for its first entr'acte performance).*]

36. For the god Apollo, see Appendix.

37. For a discussion of possible contemporary political dimensions in this passage, see Fountoulakis, A., "Going beyond the Athenian *Polis*: A Reappraisal of Menander, *Samia* 96–118." *Quaderni urbinati di cultura classica* 93 (2009): 97–117.

38. For the god, see Appendix.

CHORAL INTERLUDE[39]

ACT II

[The beginning of Act II is mutilated, but Demeas must have entered from his house and delivered a short monologue (perhaps not noticing Moschion's arrival via the side wing leading to the country) to express his anger over Chrysis' apparently having had his baby and not exposed it. The papyrus picks up with Moschion's own address to the audience.]

120 MOSCHION . . . I'm back here
And I didn't practice a single thing I wanted to.
Once I was outside the city and all alone,
I imagined that I sacrificed, invited my friends,
Sent the women off to bathe,[40] and walked around
125 Giving out pieces of the cake.[41] At times I hummed
The wedding song.[42] I was an idiot!
And when I'd had enough of that—Hey,
There's my father! He probably heard me. Hi, dad.

DEMEAS Hello to you too, son. MOSCHION Why the angry face? DEMEAS Why?
130 It seems that unbeknownst to me my mistress has become
My wife![43] MOSCHION Your wife? I'm not following you.

DEMEAS It seems that I became a father to a son in secret.
To hell with her! She can take him and
Get right out of my house! MOSCHION Oh, not that!
DEMEAS What do you mean, "not that!"?
135 Do you really expect me to raise a bastard son
In my own house? That doesn't square with my way of thinking!

39. For the song of the chorus between acts in Greek New Comedy, see Introduction 11.

40. As part of purification ritual in preparation for the wedding.

41. Moschion was daydreaming about the wedding: see note 29 above.

42. The song in the evening procession in which the bride was taken from her home to the bridegroom's house (cf. notes 46 and 119 below).

43. For Chrysis' legal status as a *hetaira*, and her ineligibility for marriage with an Athenian citizen, see Introductory Essay 116–117.

Moschion In the name of the gods, if you're a human being,
Who among us is legitimate, and who's a bastard?
Demeas You aren't serious,
Are you? **Moschion** I'm absolutely serious, as Dionysus is my witness!
I don't think ancestry makes any difference; 140
If you look at the issue fairly, a good person
Is legitimate, a bad person is both a bastard
And a slave . . . 143

[Ca. *20 lines are lost or mutilated here. Moschion and Demeas presumably continued to argue about Chrysis and the baby, but at some point turned to the issue of Moschion's marriage to Plangon.*]

Demeas . . . if they[44] agree, you'll marry her. 150

Moschion Seeing as you've heard nothing about the matter,
Can't you see I'm serious? Won't you help out?

Demeas See you're serious? *Heard nothing*? I know exactly
What you're talking about, Moschion. I'm running over
To our neighbor's here to tell him to arrange 155
The wedding. Everything we're responsible for will be ready.
Moschion Excellent!
I'll go inside now, wash myself,[45]
Pour a libation, light incense, and get
The girl.[46] **Demeas** Don't go yet. Wait until I find out
If our neighbor here will give us his consent to it all. 160

Moschion He won't argue with you. It's not right for me to be present for that,
And I'd just be a nuisance, so I'm out of here. (*exits*)

44. Nikeratos and his family.

45. The bridegroom, as also the bride, ultimately must ritually purify himself with sacred water from an Athenian spring (Kallirhoe): cf. note 118 below.

46. Referring to the culminating evening bridal procession to his house: see note 42 above.

Demeas Chance, it seems to me, is some sort of divinity,
In that it presides over many things we do not see.
165 I had no idea my son here was in love . . .

[*25–30 lines are entirely lost here, in which Demeas continued his monologue. Another* ca. *25 badly mutilated lines survive, from which it is only clear that Nikeratos came out of his house, and eventually agreed to hold the wedding of Moschion and Plangon that same day. Nikeratos then apparently started for his house, but decided to linger onstage. The text becomes readable again after Demeas has called Parmenon out of his house.*]

189 **Demeas** . . . Parmenon! Hey, Parmenon, my boy!
190 Go get some garlands, a sacrificial animal,[47] sesame[48]—
Just buy out the entire market and
Come back here! **Parmenon** You can count on me,
Demeas. **Demeas** And do it quickly—I mean *now*!
Bring back a cook too.[49] **Parmenon** A cook too? After I've bought
195 The rest of the stuff? **Demeas** Yes! **Parmenon** I'll get the cash and I'll be off. (*goes inside*)

Demeas You haven't left yet, Nikeratos? **Nikeratos** I'm going in to tell
My wife to get everything ready inside.
I'll be right behind Parmenon. **Parmenon** (*returns from Demeas' house*) I'm completely in the dark here,
Except for these orders I've been given. I'm off now.

200 **Demeas** He'll have trouble persuading his wife.
But we've got no time for arguing
And delaying. (*to Parmenon*) Still lingering, boy? Run off now!

47. A sheep for the blood sacrifice to be held in connection with the wedding feast (cf. note 27 above and note 50 below).

48. For the garland and sesame cake, see notes 28, 29 and 41 above.

49. The rental of a cook is standard in preparation for festivities of various types in New Comedy.

[Ca. *10 lines are missing. Nikeratos presumably followed Parmenon off to the market, and Demeas delivered a short monologue before exiting into his house. When the text picks up below, Demeas has returned to the stage and begun a long monologue.*]

CHORAL INTERLUDE

ACT III

DEMEAS . . . a fair voyage, 206
An unexpected storm suddenly comes up. 207
It crashes right on top of those who a little while ago
Were speeding along in calm weather, and rears them back.
I experienced this just now: I started to prepare 210
The wedding, and to sacrifice to the gods,
And everything was proceeding just the way I wanted—
But right now I'm not sure if I'm still seeing straight
After I took an unbelievable knockout punch out of the blue!
Dazed as I am, I'm coming forward to you now. 215
Can you believe it? I'll let you decide whether I'm sane
Or crazy, and have entirely misconstrued the facts,
And am actually bringing a huge disaster upon myself.
The instant I went in—being extremely eager to make
The wedding preparations—I explained clearly 220
The tasks at hand and told them to get to work on them,
Especially the cleaning, the baking, and preparing the ritual basket.[50]
Everything was proceeding nicely, although the fast pace
Of the work created some confusion among them,
As happens. The baby had been flung out of the way 225
And was crying on a couch. The women were all shouting

50. A basket holding the essentials for a sacrifice, especially barley to be sprinkled on the victim's head and a sacrificial knife.

"Flour, water, olive oil, charcoal, and right now!"
As I was helping out myself and handing them some of these things,
I happened to go into the pantry. I was looking things over
230 There and selecting out more supplies,
And didn't come out right away. While I was there,
A woman came down from upstairs
Into the room across from the pantry,
Which happens to be a weaving room[51]—
235 You pass through it to go upstairs or to
The pantry. This same woman was Moschion's
Wet-nurse, now up there in years. She'd been
My slave, but now she's free. When she saw
The baby crying and being neglected, and didn't realize
240 I was inside, she goes up to it,
And assumes the coast is clear for baby-talk.
She starts saying the usual things: "You darling baby!"
And "My precious one! Where's your mama?"
She kissed it and carried it all around until it stopped crying.
245 She then says to herself, "Dear me,
Not too long ago I nursed Moschion,
When he was just like you, and I loved him dearly.
248 Now his own child's been born . . ."

[Ca. 5 *lines are missing or mutilated; Demeas is still speaking.*]

251 . . . And a slave girl
252 Came rushing in from outside and she said, "Dear me!
Give the baby a bath! What's going on? It's the
Little one's father's wedding day and you can't take care of him?"
255 The girl immediately says, "Hey, not so loud!
Master's in the house." "Please, no—where is he?"
"In the pantry," and raising her voice a bit says,
"Mistress is calling for you, nurse." And then she quietly adds,
"Go off quickly now! Luckily he hasn't heard anything."

51. For the importance of weaving in the household, see Introduction 22–23 and *Casina*, note 28.

The nurse then said, "Oh my, what a chatterbox I am!" 260
And she went off to somewhere else.
Then I stepped forward very calmly,
The same way I did just now,
Just as if I hadn't heard or noticed a thing.
Outside[52] I spot the Samian woman[53] by herself, 265
Along with the child, which she was breastfeeding.[54]
So it's obvious this child's hers,
But as for who the father is, whether it's me
Or—gentlemen,[55] I can't tell you,
I can't conjecture, but I simply present to you 270
What I heard, without any anger (well, not yet anyway).
I swear by the gods, I know my boy
As someone who has always been well behaved
And as respectful to me as anyone possibly could be.
But at the same time, when I consider that 275
The person saying it once was Moschion's nurse and thought
She was speaking in private, and then I recall
How Chrysis loves it and insists on
Raising it against my will, I'm completely beside myself!
But on a more positive note, there's Parmenon 280
Coming back from the market. I should let
Him take the group he's brought back inside.

52. Most likely in the (typical) central courtyard of an Athenian house.

53. For Demeas' perjorative description of Chrysis as "the Samian women" in self-address, cf. 352 and Introductory Essay 119, note 3.

54. I interpret *didousan titthion* (lit. "offering [it] her little nipple") as indicating nursing here, although the expression is imprecise; for the conjectural nature of Chrysis' pregnancy, see note 22 above. See further Dedoussi, C., "The Future of Plangon's Child in Menander's *Samia.*" *Liverpool Classical Monthly* 13 (1988): 39–42 and Scafuro, A.C., "When a Gesture Was Misinterpreted: *didonai titthion* in Menander's *Samia,*" pp. 113–135 in G.W. Bakewell and J.P. Sickinger (eds.), *Gestures: Essays in Ancient History, Literature, and Philosophy Presented to Alan L. Boegehold* (Oxford, 2003).

55. Here, as at 329, 447, 683 and 734, Demeas addresses the audience as *andres,* "gentlemen," but we should not assume from this that women were prohibited from attending Greek theatrical productions: cf. Introduction 5, note 6.

PARMENON (*entering via the wing leading to the city center, and speaking to the cook*) I swear by the gods, cook, I don't know why
You carry knives around with you! Your blather
285 Can finely chop anything into pieces!

COOK Lousy amateur! PARMENON Me? COOK Yes you, in my opinion, absolutely!
I'm asking how many tables you want to set,
How many women there will be,
When dinner will be served, if we need to hire
290 A waiter, if you have enough cookware inside,
If the kitchen's roofed over,
If everything else is ready— PARMENON In case you haven't noticed,
My friend, now you're chopping me into little pieces,
And not in amateur fashion! COOK Screw you!
PARMENON Right back
295 At you! But go on inside. DEMEAS Parmenon!

PARMENON Is somebody calling me? DEMEAS Yes.
PARMENON Hello, master.

DEMEAS Set down that basket inside and come back here.
PARMENON Will do. (*exits*)

DEMEAS I'm pretty sure that nothing of this sort gets by him. If anyone
Deserves to be called a busybody, it's him. But there's the
300 door—
He's coming out. PARMENON (*returning, and shouting instructions back to the house*) Give the cook everything
He asks for, Chrysis, and keep the old nurse[56]
Out of the wine jugs,[57] by the gods! What do you have
For me to do, master? DEMEAS What do I have for you?
Come here, a little farther

56. Probably the same nurse at 236ff.

57. For women's stereotypical bibulousness in comedy, see *Lysistrata*, Introductory Essay 43 and note 10.

Away from the door. PARMENON There.
DEMEAS Listen up now, Parmenon. 305
I swear by the twelve gods,[58] I don't want
To whip you—for many reasons. PARMENON Whip me? What've
I done? DEMEAS You're helping to keep something from me. I'm well aware of it. PARMENON I am?
I swear by Dionysus, by Apollo over here,[59]
By Zeus the Savior,[60] I swear by Asclepius[61]— 310

DEMEAS Stop! No more oaths! I'm not just tossing out a guess.

PARMENON May the gods never— DEMEAS Hey, you! Look me in the eye! PARMENON Okay, I am.

DEMEAS Whose baby is it? PARMENON Um, ah—
DEMEAS I asked you,
Whose baby is it? PARMENON Chrysis'.
DEMEAS And the father is?

PARMENON You, she says. DEMEAS That's it now! You're lying to me! PARMENON Me? 315

DEMEAS Yes, I know every last detail, and I'm aware
That it's Moschion's, and that you're a co-conspirator,
And that she's nursing it for him now!

PARMENON Says who? DEMEAS Everybody! Just answer this one thing:
Is it all true? PARMENON It is, master, but as for keeping quiet— 320

DEMEAS What do you mean "keeping quiet"? One of you slaves get me
A whip for this scumbag! PARMENON By the gods, no!

58. For the Olympian deities, see Appendix.

59. He refers to an altar of Apollo at the front door of the house.

60. For Zeus, see Appendix.

61. God of healing.

DEMEAS I swear by the Sun,[62] I'll brand[63] you!
PARMENON Brand me?
DEMEAS Yes, right now! PARMENON I'm done for! (*runs off*) DEMEAS Where are you going, you whipping-post?
325 Grab him! O citadel of Kekrops' land,[64]
O Air stretched out above, O[65]—why are you shouting, Demeas?
Why shout, you fool? Get control of yourself, buck up!
Moschion has done you no wrong. That statement
May seem preposterous, gentlemen,[66] but it's the truth.
330 If he had done this on purpose or was goaded on
By desire or simply because he hated me,
He'd still be in that same bold frame of mind,
And still be at war with me. But as things are now,
He's exonerated himself by warmly embracing
335 The marriage plan I suggested. He wasn't so eager
Because of love, as I thought was the case then,[67] but he wanted to
Get away from the house and at last escape this Helen[68] of mine.
She's to blame for what has happened.
She obviously got her claws on him when he was drunk
340 And not in control of himself. Fortified wine and youth
Can create a lot of foolishness when they've got
A co-conspirator[69] close at hand.

62. Helios, the personification of the sun, sometimes identified with Apollo.

63. For the branding (or tattooing) of runaway slaves' foreheads, see *Lysistrata*, note 67 and *Casina*, note 47.

64. A legendary king of Athens (the citadel = the Acropolis).

65. A quotation from a lost play (*Oedipus*) of the fifth-century BCE Athenian tragedian Euripides.

66. For Demeas' unusual (in Menander) interaction with the audience, see note 55 above.

67. See 165.

68. The famous adulteress of the Trojan War: cf. *Lysistrata*, notes 41 and 211.

69. I.e., Chrysis, who (as a *hetaira*) Demeas stereotypically assumes must have seduced Moschion: see further Introductory Essay 118–120.

It seems utterly incredible to me that
Someone who is so well behaved and reasonable
To others[70] would treat *me* in this way, 345
Not even if he's ten times adopted and not my son by birth!
It's not his birth, but his character I look at.
The woman's a slut,[71] a menace! But what of it?
She won't be around for long. Now, Demeas,
You must be a man! Forget that you missed her, stop wanting her, 350
Hide the trouble that's happened as best
As you can for your son's sake. And as for the lovely Samian lady:[72]
Throw her out of your house, headfirst
And straight to hell! You have the excuse that
She kept the child. Nothing else needs to be made known. 355
Bite your lip, be tough, brave, and strong!

Cook (*suddenly enters from Demeas' house*) He should be here, right before the front door.
Parmenon! Hey, boy! This guy's run out on me
Without helping me the least bit! **Demeas** Out of my way,
Move it! (*rushes into his house*) **Cook** By Herakles,[73] what's all this about? 360
Some crazy old man just rushed inside!
What in the world's going on? Guess it's nothing to do with me.
Damn, he's nuts in my opinion!
He certainly did shout up a storm. It'd be just great,
If he smashes all the plates I've set out 365
Into tiny little bits! There goes

70. Literally, "to people outside our family."

71. In his anger Demeas here literally calls her "a ground-pounder" (i.e., a common streetwalker, a more degraded form of prostitution than that of the *hetaira*).

72. See Introductory Essay 119, note 3.

73. For the god, see Appendix.

The door. Damn it all, Parmenon,
For even bringing me to this place! I'll move a little ways off here.

DEMEAS (*pushing the nurse, Chrysis, and the baby out of his house*)[74] Didn't you hear me? Get out! CHRYSIS Oh no! But where?

DEMEAS To hell, and I mean now! CHRYSIS Poor me!
370 DEMEAS Yes, poor you!
Your tears are deeply moving. I'm sure
I'll put a stop to your— CHRYSIS To my what?
DEMEAS Oh, nothing. But
You have the child and the nurse. Get lost now!
CHRYSIS Is this because I kept the baby?
DEMEAS Because of that and— CHRYSIS And *what*?
DEMEAS Because of just that. COOK (*aside*) *That's* the
375 trouble. Now I get it.
DEMEAS You just couldn't handle your luxurious life.
CHRYSIS I couldn't?
Whatever do you mean? DEMEAS You did actually come here to me
In a cotton dress, Chrysis—you do remember?—in a very
Plain one. CHRYSIS Yes, *and*? DEMEAS I was your one and only
When times were tough for you. CHRYSIS And who is
380 that now? DEMEAS Don't give me any lip!
You've got all your things. In addition,
You can have some slave girls and some gold.[75] Get out of
My house! COOK (*aside*) That's quite a display of anger!
I should go over to them.

74. The scene to follow is depicted on a mosaic from Mytilene (see Introductory Essay 115); there Demeas threatens Chrysis with a raised stick (cf. 440). It also (probably) is represented on a mosaic in the Casa dei Dioscuri in Pompeii: see Figure 10b in Nervegna, S., *Menander in Antiquity: The Contexts of Reception* (Cambridge, 2013): 142.

75. Demeas thus reduces their relationship to a transaction: see Introductory Essay 118–119.

Hey, buddy— **Demeas** Are *you* talking to me?
Cook You don't have to lash out at me.

Demeas Another girl will be pleased with what I have, Chrysis—yes, 385
And she'll give thanks to the gods! **Cook** (*aside*) How's that? **Demeas** You've got
A son, you have it all. **Cook** (*aside*) He's not lashing out yet.
But still— **Demeas** Hey, guy! I'll smash your head to bits, if you
Utter a single word to me. **Cook** Fair enough—but, hey,
I'm going in now. (*exits*) **Demeas** You're such hot stuff! You'll see 390
Exactly what you are once you're in town.
Unlike what you're used to, the girls[76] there run off
To dinner parties for ten drachmas[77]
And drink fortified wine until they die.[78]
If they don't jump at that kind of invitation, 395
They starve. You'll learn this the same as everyone else,
I'm sure, and you'll realize who you are and how you went wrong.
Stay there! (*exits*) **Chrysis** Oh my! What terrible luck!

Nikeratos (*returning from the market with a sheep*) After it's sacrificed, this sheep will supply all
The standard offerings for the gods and goddesses. 400
It's got blood, a decent gall bladder, excellent bones,
An enlarged spleen, everything the Olympians need.[79]
I'll chop up the skin and send it to my friends

76. Demeas assumes that she will return to her life as a *hetaira* (cf. note 15 above).

77. The equivalent of five days' wages for a skilled worker in the classical period (cf. *Lysistrata*, note 170) but a mere pittance to the super-wealthy Demeas.

78. I.e., wine that has not been mixed with water, the drinking of which was a mark of "wildness" (cf. *Lysistrata*, note 49 and *Casina*, note 62); Demeas asserts that alcohol abuse comes with territory.

79. The inedible parts of the victim were offered up to the gods in sacrifice; the human participants consume the meat and edible innards.

For a sampling—it's all I'll have left.[80]

405 But, my goodness, what's this all about? Chrysis is standing
Out here in front of the house crying! It's her,
All right. What's happened? **Chrysis** Your good friend
Has thrown me out, that's what! **Nikeratos** Oh, no!
Who? Demeas? **Chrysis** Yes. **Nikeratos** But
why? **Chrysis** Because of the baby.

410 **Nikeratos** I personally heard from the women that you kept
The child and were nursing it. Astonishing!
But he's a nice guy. **Chrysis** He didn't get angry
At first, but only later on—just now. He told me
To get everything in the house ready for the wedding,
415 And when I was busy with that, he came at me like
A crazy person and locked me outside the house.
Nikeratos Demeas's insane.
Pontus is not a healthy place.[81]
Come inside here with me and to my wife.
Cheer up! No need to worry. He'll stop the craziness
Once he has a chance to think over what he's done. (*they exit*
420 *into Nikeratos' house*)

CHORAL INTERLUDE

ACT IV

Nikeratos (*enters from his house, yelling back at his wife inside*) You will wear me out for good, wife! Now I'll go take him on.
By the gods, I wouldn't have wanted this to happen
For any amount of money! In the middle of the wedding preparations

80. Whereas Greeks normally did provide their guests with leftovers, the poor and stingy Nikeratos has other ideas.

81. See notes 25 and 35 above.

A terrible omen occurred. A woman's been kicked out of her house,
And has come to ours with a baby! 425
There are lots of tears, and the women are quite upset.
Demeas's a filthy brute! I swear he'll pay for
Being such a clod! **Moschion** (*enters from the wing leading to the city center*) Is the sun ever going to set? What can I say?
Night's forgotten what it is she does. What a long day! Should I
Go bathe a third time?[82] There's nothing else for me to do.
Nikeratos Moschion, 430
Hello! **Moschion** Are we going to do the wedding now? Parmenon
Said we were when I ran into him just now in the market. Any reason
I can't get your daughter now?[83] **Nikeratos** Are you unaware of what's going on here?
Moschion No, what? **Nikeratos** Really? A strange and terrible thing's happened.
Moschion Oh no, what? I'm clueless here.
Nikeratos It's Chrysis, my young friend. 435
Your father drove her right out of the house just now!
Moschion That can't be! **Nikeratos** It's for real.
Moschion But why? **Nikeratos** Because of the child.
Moschion So where's she now? **Nikeratos** Inside our house. **Moschion** Such awful news!
I'm astounded! **Nikeratos** If it seems so awful to you—
Demeas (*suddenly enters from his house, shouting back inside*)
If I get a hold of a stick, I'll pound those tears out of you 440
Right now! What's with this nonsense? Go help
The cook! Damn it, there certainly is something worth

82. Cf. note 40 above.

83. I.e., to take her home to complete the wedding ceremonies (cf. notes 42 and 46 above).

Crying about so much! Your fine prize has departed
From our house. The facts are clear—Dear Apollo,
445 Hail![84] Grant that the wedding we are about to conduct
May bring good fortune to us all! You see, gentlemen,[85]
I shall swallow my anger and proceed with the wedding.
Lord, see that my true feelings are kept hidden from all,
And force me to sing the wedding-hymn.
450 In my present state, I won't sing my best—but so what?

NIKERATOS You first, Moschion. Go right on up to him.

MOSCHION Father, why are you acting like this?

DEMEAS Like what, Moschion?

MOSCHION Do you have to ask? Just tell me: why did Chrysis get up and go?

DEMEAS (*aside*) Clearly, someone here's acting as a go-between. Not good. (*to Moschion*)
455 This isn't your business, it's entirely mine. Why the nonsense?
(*aside*) This is not good at all. He's plotting against me too.

MOSCHION What?

DEMEAS (*aside*)
That's clear enough. Why otherwise come on her behalf? He really ought
To be pleased at what's happened. MOSCHION What do you think
Our friends will say when they find out about this?

DEMEAS Let me
Worry about my friends, Moschion. MOSCHION I'd be
460 wrong to let you do this.

DEMEAS You think you can stop me? MOSCHION Yes.

DEMEAS (*aside*) See? This is too much!
This is even worse than everything before!

MOSCHION It's not right
To give free rein to your anger. NIKERATOS He's right, Demeas.

84. For the altar of Apollo in front of the house, see note 59 above.

85. See note 55 above.

MOSCHION Nikeratos, go inside and tell her to run right back here.

DEMEAS Moschion, leave it alone. For the third time: leave it to me, *to me*, 465
Moschion. I know all about it. MOSCHION All about what? DEMEAS That's enough now!

MOSCHION But I need to— DEMEAS Need to what? Am I no longer master of
My own household? MOSCHION Just do me this favor. DEMEAS A favor?
Why don't you ask me to abandon my own house
And to leave the two of you here together? Let me 470
Attend to the wedding. You *will* let me—if you've got any sense. MOSCHION I will, yes,
But I want Chrysis to be present too. DEMEAS Chrysis?

MOSCHION Yes, I really do, and mostly for your sake. DEMEAS (*aside*) *Now* it's for certain
And couldn't be clearer. I call you to witness, Loxias,[86] someone's
Conspiring with my enemies! Oh no! I'm going to explode! 475

MOSCHION What do you mean? DEMEAS Do you really want to know? MOSCHION Absolutely! DEMEAS Over here. MOSCHION Tell me.

DEMEAS I'll do just that. The baby is yours. Yes, I know. I heard it from Parmenon,
Who's in on all your secrets. So stop
Playing games with me. MOSCHION If the baby's mine, then how is Chrysis hurting you?

DEMEAS Who is hurting me *then*? You? MOSCHION But how's she to blame? DEMEAS What? 480
Do the two of you feel no guilt? MOSCHION Why are you shouting? DEMEAS You filthy human being!
You dare ask? You do accept the blame, don't you?

86. An epithet of Apollo ("The Ambiguous One"), perhaps owing to his riddling oracles (cf. *Lysistrata*, note 136). Demeas again addresses the statue of Apollo (see note 84 above).

And yet you're brazen enough to look me in the eye and say this?
How can you completely reject me like this?
Moschion Reject you?
What do you mean? **Demeas** *What do I mean*? You dare
485 ask? **Moschion** The thing I did
Isn't so terrible—I'd assume millions of men have done
This very same thing, father. **Demeas** Great Zeus, such audacity! Before
These gentlemen,[87] I ask you: who's the mother
Of the baby? Tell Nikeratos if you don't think this
490 Is so terrible. **Moschion** It certainly will be terrible
If I have to be the one to tell him. He'll go ballistic when he hears it all.

Nikeratos You're the worst of the worst! I'm finally starting to understand
What's happened, what an abominable thing this is!

Moschion That's the end of me! **Demeas** Do you get it now, Nikeratos?

Nikeratos Do I ever! Oh, the wicked deed! O, the beds of
495 Tereus,[88]
Oedipus,[89] Thyestes[90] and all the others whose
Stories we're told[91]—you've topped them all!
Moschion I have?

Nikeratos Were you so bold as to actually do this? And so cold? Demeas,
You should summon up the wrath of Amyntor[92] and
Blind him right here on the spot!

87. See note 55 above.

88. Tereus raped his sister-in-law Philomela: see further *Lysistrata*, note 137.

89. Oedipus unknowingly married his mother Jocasta (cf. the fifth-century BCE Athenian tragedian Sophocles' *Oedipus Rex*).

90. Thyestes spitefully committed adultery with his brother Atreus' wife Aerope.

91. I.e., mostly in Athenian (tragic) drama.

92. In myth, Phoenix, son of Amyntor, was blinded by his father for having sex with the latter's mistress. In some versions of the story he was tricked by her and falsely accused by his father (as Moschion here).

Demeas (*to Moschion*) You're the reason everything's known to him. 500

Nikeratos Have you no boundaries? Is there any bed you wouldn't violate?

And I'm supposed to give you my daughter to be your wife?

I'd rather—knock on wood and with all due respect to Nemesis[93]—

See her married to a Diomnestus![94] We'd all agree

That would be a disaster! **Demeas** (*to Moschion*) I knew you wronged me, but I restrained 505

My anger.

Nikeratos You're acting like a slave,[95] Demeas.

If he'd violated my bed, that'd be the last time

He or his sex-pal committed that offense! The whore

Would be up for sale first thing in the morning, and my son

Would simultaneously be disinherited. There would be standing room only 510

In every barbershop, in every public walkway,[96] so that the entire population

Could gossip about me from sunrise on, saying how Nikeratos

Is a real man, justified in prosecuting his son for murder. **Moschion** What murder?

Nikeratos I consider it murder if someone rejects authority and does this.

Moschion (*aside*) By the gods, this mess is making me dehydrated and frozen stiff! 515

93. Goddess of retribution, called upon here to avert any evil that might follow the statement he is about to make about his daughter.

94. The identification of Diomnestus is uncertain, but he presumably is a contemporary adulterer in Athens.

95. I.e., a dishonorable coward, as slaves were assumed to be in the ideology of ancient slavery.

96. Colonnades, like barbershops, were notorious locales for men's gossip.

NIKERATOS And on top of everything else, I welcomed the perpetrator
Of these evils into my home! DEMEAS Throw her out, Nikeratos,
By all means! Consider yourself as wronged as I am, as true friends do.

NIKERATOS If I so much as see her, I'll explode! You have the nerve to look
Me in the eye, you Thracian savage?[97] Step aside! (*exits*)

520 MOSCHION Honestly, father, listen to me!

DEMEAS I'll not hear a thing. MOSCHION Not even if everything you suspect happened
Didn't happen? I'm finally beginning to understand what's happening. DEMEAS Everything?

MOSCHION Chrysis is not the mother of the child she's currently nursing.
She's claiming it's hers as a favor to me. DEMEAS What are you saying?

MOSCHION The truth! DEMEAS But why is she doing you
525 this favor?

MOSCHION Much as I don't want to, I'll tell you, so once you know the truth
I'll escape a felony by admitting to a misdemeanor.

DEMEAS I'm dying to hear what you have to say. MOSCHION Nikeratos' daughter
Is the mother and I'm the father. That's what I wanted to keep secret.

DEMEAS How do you mean? MOSCHION That's the reality of it. DEMEAS Careful—don't even think of
530 tricking me!

MOSCHION When you can check the facts? What would I be angling at by doing that?

97. For reputed Thracian "wildness," see note 88 above and *Lysistrata*, note 36.

Demeas Nothing—but there's the door. **Nikeratos** (*rushes frantically from his house and addresses the audience*) Poor, poor me!
What a sight I just saw! Through my door I hasten forth,
A madman stabbed in the heart by unforeseen woe![98]

Demeas (*aside*) What in the world is he jabbering about?
Nikeratos It's my daughter! I just now 535
Found her breastfeeding the baby inside!
Demeas (*aside*) So that's what it was.

Moschion Are you listening, father? **Demeas** You've done me no wrong at all, Moschion.
My suspicion made me do wrong to you.
Nikeratos Demeas, just the man I want.

Moschion I should be off. **Demeas** Buck up!
Moschion Just seeing him kills me. (*runs off*)

Demeas What's the problem? **Nikeratos** I just now found my daughter 540
Breastfeeding the baby in the house!

Demeas Maybe she was pretending to? **Nikeratos** She wasn't pretending! The instant
She saw me coming in she fainted. **Demeas** Maybe she thought—

Nikeratos You're going to wear me down for good with your "maybes"! **Demeas** This is
My fault. **Nikeratos** Come again. **Demeas** In my opinion your story's not believable. 545

Nikeratos But I really saw it! **Demeas** Now you're blathering. **Nikeratos** I didn't make this up!
But I'll go back—(*exits*) **Demeas** You know what? Just a minute, friend—Oh, he's gone.
Everything's turned on its head now. That should do it. Damn!
Once he finds out the truth, he'll be raging and shouting.

98. Nikeratos here uses lofty language associated with tragedy.

550 He's a harsh character, a filthy brute with a stubborn way.
Shame on me for having such suspicions! Damn!
By Hephaestus,[99] I do deserve to die! Wow! (*hears shouting inside*)
That was some sound! I was right! He's calling for fire,
He's telling them to torch the baby! I'll have to watch
My grandson being roasted! He's crashing at the door again!
555 The guy's
Like a whirlwind, or a hurricane! **Nikeratos** Demeas, this Chrysis of yours
Is conspiring against me and doing horrible things!
Demeas How so?

Nikeratos She's persuaded my wife to admit to nothing at all,
And my daughter too! She's taken the baby by force,
560 And says she won't give it back. Don't be surprised
If I murder her. **Demeas** Murder your wife?

Nikeratos Yes, she's in on it all too. (*exits*) **Demeas** No, Nikeratos!

Nikeratos I wanted you to have advance warning.
Demeas He's out of his mind!
He's rushed off inside. How's a person to deal with these problems?
565 By the gods, I've certainly never found myself swept up
In such chaos as this before! The best course now is to explain clearly
What's happened. But, damn it, there's the door again.

Chrysis (*enters frantically, with the baby, and being chased by Nikeratos, who carries a stick*) Oh, poor me! What can I do? Where can I flee?[100] He's going to take
My baby! **Demeas** Chrysis, over here!
Chrysis Who's there? **Demeas** Run inside!

99. For the god, see Appendix.

100. Tragic-sounding (i.e., aporetic) language.

Nikeratos Hey you! Where are you off to? **Demeas** As
Apollo is my witness, I think I'm in for some 570
Single combat today! What are you after? Who are you
chasing? **Nikeratos** Demeas!
Get out of my way! Just let me get hold of the baby
And then I'll listen to the women's story. **Demeas** Absolutely not!

Nikeratos You're going to hit me? **Demeas** I sure am. (*to Chrysis*) Get inside! Right now!

Nikeratos I most certainly will hit you! **Demeas** Run,
Chrysis! He's stronger than me! 575

Nikeratos You started it[101]—I have witnesses to testify to that!

Demeas And what about you? You're hunting down a free
woman
With a raised stick! **Nikeratos** You're making a false
accusation. **Demeas** As are you.

Nikeratos Bring the child out to me. **Demeas** Ridiculous! It's mine. **Nikeratos** It's not yours!

Demeas It's mine! **Nikeratos** Oh, my fellow citizens!
Demeas Shout all you want. **Nikeratos** I'm going in 580
To kill my wife. What else can I do? **Demeas** That nasty
plan again!
I won't allow it. Hey, where are you going? Wait!
Nikeratos Don't so much as lay a finger on me!

Demeas Get a hold of yourself! **Nikeratos** You're
obviously abusing me, Demeas,
And you're in it together with them all. **Demeas** Then
question me,
And stop harassing your wife. **Nikeratos** Your son has
taken me 585
For a ride. **Demeas** Nonsense! He'll marry your
daughter.

101. Under Athenian law, the lander of the first blow was considered guilty of assault.

It's not the way you think. But take a little stroll
With me here. NIKERATOS *You want me to stroll with you?*
DEMEAS Yes, and get a grip on yourself.
Listen up, Nikeratos. Surely you've heard our tragedians[102]
Recounting how Zeus morphed into a shower of gold that
590 poured
Itself through a house's roof and raped a girl locked up inside?[103]
NIKERATOS Yeah—so what? DEMEAS Let's try to be open
to all possibilities. Think about it:
Is there any part of your roof that's leaking?
NIKERATOS Most of it is. But what's that
Got to do with what you're talking about? DEMEAS Zeus
sometimes morphs into gold,
595 Sometimes water. Get it? This is his work. It didn't take us long
To figure that out. NIKERATOS You're mocking me.
DEMEAS Absolutely not, I swear!
You certainly are just as good as Acrisius[104] was.
And if his daughter was good enough for Zeus, then your
daughter— NIKERATOS Oh, no! No!
Moschion tricked me! DEMEAS No need to be afraid—
he'll marry her.
600 There's no doubt that what's happened has a god's hand in it.
I can name you thousands now walking among us who are
The gods' descendants. Do you really think our situation is
strange?
First, there's Chairephon,[105] who's wined and dined at no charge:
Surely you consider him divine? NIKERATOS I guess. I'm
at a loss—

102. Both Euripides and Sophocles (and probably various other Athenian tragic poets) wrote plays about Danaë (see note 103 below). Demeas playfully invokes myth here to calm Nikeratos down.

103. Referring to the myth in which Zeus, disguised as a shower of gold, penetrates a tower in order to rape and impregnate Danaë, who had been locked there by her father Acrisius. The latter feared an oracle that she would give birth to a hero who would kill him (i.e., Perseus).

104. See note 103 above.

105. A (real-life) example of a parasite—that is, in comedy someone who sponges off wealthy patrons in exchange for small favors.

I'm not going to argue with you pointlessly.
Demeas Now you're making sense, Nikeratos. 605
Take Androcles.[106] Such a long life: he runs, he jumps, has a huge
Stake in everything. He walks around all swarthy. You wouldn't catch him dead
Looking pale, even if someone slit his throat. How's he not a god?
But pray that everything here turns out well. Burn some incense,
Pour out a libation. My son will come for your daughter in no time. 610

Nikeratos It has to happen this way— **Demeas** You're making sense again.

Nikeratos But if I'd caught him at that moment—
Demeas Stop it! Don't upset yourself. Focus
On preparing things inside. **Nikeratos** I will.
Demeas As will I in my house. **Nikeratos** Off you go.

Demeas You are one sharp fellow. And thanks to all the gods,
I now know not a single suspicion of mine was true. (*they exit into their respective houses*) 615

CHORAL INTERLUDE

ACT V

Moschion (*enters via the wing leading to the city center*) I was delighted just now when I was cleared of
The false charge I faced, and I realized
My luck in all this had turned out to be pretty good.
But now that I've had a chance to calm down

106. The reference is uncertain, but Androcles apparently is mentioned here as a type of successful (and corrupt?) athlete turned celebrity.

620 And think things over, I'm absolutely
Beside myself, and so irritated
About the terrible things my father assumed I'd done.
If the situation with the girl was fine
And there weren't obstacles in my way, like my pledge to her,
My desire, our lengthy relationship—all of which have taken
625 away my freedom—
He'd never make a charge like this against me again,
At least in person, as I'd be long gone
From the city, far out of his sight in Bactria[107] or
Caria,[108] or somewhere else, living my life as a mercenary
there.
630 But because of you, dearest Plangon, I don't dare do
Anything that courageous. And Love,
Currently the ruler of all my thoughts, won't allow it anyway.
And yet I shouldn't let this just go altogether,
Like some wimpy coward. I want to scare him—
635 Just for pretend—by claiming that
I'm taking off. This will make him more cautious
About behaving so stupidly toward me in the future,
When he sees this is no trivial matter as far as I'm concerned.
But here's the person I most wanted
640 To see, at just the right time and place.

PARMENON (*returns from the wing by which he had run off at 324*) Damn it all, I've made myself out to be
Such a foolish and contemptible person by my actions!
Though I did nothing wrong, I got scared and ran away
From master. But what had I done to justify my behavior?
645 Let's go through it all carefully, point by point:
1. My young master violated a girl
Who was free: Parmenon's in no way responsible for that.
2. She got pregnant: Parmenon's not responsible.

107. A region that includes northern Afghanistan, at the time of the play in process of being Hellenized, largely through Greek mercenaries.

108. A region of southwestern Asia Minor, frequently a site of military conflict.

3. The baby was then brought into our house:
He was the one who brought it in, not me. 650
4. Someone in our household said she gave birth to the child:
What wrongdoing is Parmenon guilty of there?
None. So why did you run away like that,
You cowardly loser? Ridiculous! 5. He threatened that
He'd brand me. Note to self: it doesn't make a fingernail's 655
Difference whether the punishment is justified or not—
It's not pleasant in either scenario. **Moschion** Hey, you!
Parmenon Hi.

Moschion Stop all this nonsense right now and go
Inside! **Parmenon** What for? **Moschion** To bring me out military garb
And a sword.[109] **Parmenon** A sword for *you*?
Moschion And on the double! 660

Parmenon What for? **Moschion** Go and do what I've told you, and without stopping
To chat. **Parmenon** But what's this all about?
Moschion If I could get a hold of
A whip— **Parmenon** No need for that, I'm off. (*exits*)
Moschion Then why are you
Still here? My father will be out here soon. (*to audience*) Obviously,
He'll beg me not to go. And for a time 665
He'll beg me in vain, as it should be. And then,
At just the right moment, I'll give in to him. I only have to seem
Convincing—but damn it, that's something I can't actually be!
This is the truth. There's the door: he's coming out.

Parmenon (*enters from the house*) Your information about what's going on inside the house here 670
Is woefully outdated. You lack the facts and haven't heard anything,
But there's no reason to get worked up or lose all hope.

109. This equipment will suggest that he is about to set out as a mercenary: see notes 107 and 108 above.

MOSCHION Where's the equipment I asked for?
PARMENON They've started your wedding: wine's flowing,
Incense's smoking, a sacrifice's happening, offerings are burning in Hephaestus' fire!
MOSCHION Hey! Where's the equipment?
PARMENON They've been waiting for you
675 forever—yes, you!
Why haven't you got the girl already?[110] Lucky you,
You're trouble-free! Buck up! What do you need?
MOSCHION Giving me advice,
You dirtball? (*strikes him*) PARMENON Oh, Moschion—why this treatment? MOSCHION Run in
And bring out what I told you to, pronto! (*strikes him*)
PARMENON You've split open my lip![111]
MOSCHION Are you still blathering— PARMENON I'm out
680 of here, geeze! Turns out my good news
Is bad! MOSCHION Still here? PARMENON But the wedding really is starting. MOSCHION That again?
Bring me out some other news! (*Parmenon exits*) Now he'll come out here.
But suppose he doesn't beg me to stay, gentlemen,[112] but goes ballistic
And gives me the go ahead to leave, which I didn't really think of before?
What then? Maybe he won't do that, but if he does—
685 anything's possible.
Damn, I'll look foolish, if I do a one-eighty!
PARMENON There! Here's the cloak and the sword—take them!

110. See note 42 above.

111. For the idea that Moschion's (distasteful to us) beating of Parmenon here is part of his transition to becoming an adult-citizen in a slave-owning society, see Konstan, D., "Menander's Slaves: The Banality of Violence," pp. 144–158 in B. Akrigg and R. Tordoff (eds.), *Slaves and Slavery in Ancient Greek Comic Drama* (Cambridge, 2013).

112. For audience-address in *Samia*, see note 55 above.

MOSCHION Give 'em here. Did anyone inside see you?
PARMENON Nope. MOSCHION Not a
Single soul? PARMENON Right, nobody.
MOSCHION You're kidding? May Zeus damn you!
PARMENON You should be on your way—you're babbling.
DEMEAS (*enters from his house*) Tell me, where is he? 690
And what in the world's this? PARMENON Go off now.
Fast! DEMEAS What's with the outfit?
What's the problem? Are you going somewhere? Give me a
straight answer, Moschion.
PARMENON As you can see, he's leaving and is on the road.
I should also
Say my goodbyes to people inside. I'll go do that. (*exits*)
DEMEAS Moschion,
Your anger only makes me love you more, and I understand 695
If you're saddened by my falsely accusing you.
But for all that, consider who you're mad at: *me*,
I'm your father. I took you in way back when you were a child
And I raised you. If your life has in any way been good,
I'm the person responsible for that. That's the reason 700
You should tolerate anything I do, even if it hurts you,
Seeing as you're my son. I accused you unjustly:
I was misinformed, mistaken, misled, and mental,
But look how I focused on your interests even if that meant
Wronging others. Whatever suspicions I had I kept to myself, 705
And didn't make them public for our enemies to rejoice over.
But here you are publicizing my mistake now, and you're
gathering
Witnesses to my stupidity. I expect better from you,
Moschion. Don't make a monument to the one day
In my life that I slipped up and forget everything good I'd
done before. 710
I could say a lot more, but I'll stop now. There's no glory in
Grudging obedience, but plenty for a son who eagerly obeys
his father.

Nikeratos (*enters from his house*) Stop bothering me! Everything's ready: baths, sacrifice, ceremony.
If the guy ever shows, he can take my daughter away with him.
But what is this? **Demeas** By Zeus, I have no idea.
715 **Nikeratos** You must have some idea:
A military cloak? I'd assume he intends to take off.
Demeas And so he says.
Nikeratos So he says? Who's going to let that happen? He's a confessed rapist,
Caught red-handed![113] I'll have you arrested, young man, right this instant![114]
Moschion Please do arrest me. **Nikeratos** Still disrespecting me? Put down the sword,
Right now! **Demeas** Put it down, Moschion. By the
720 gods,
Don't provoke him! **Moschion** I'll let it go, then. You've won me over with your
Appeals and prayers. **Nikeratos** With my prayers? Get over here! **Moschion** You're going to arrest me?
Demeas No, no! Bring the bride out here.
Nikeratos Really?
Demeas Absolutely! (*Nikeratos runs into his house*)
Moschion If you'd done this in the first place, you wouldn't have
Had to go to the trouble of preaching to me just now.
Nikeratos (*returning with Plangon*[115]) Move along now,
725 daughter.
Before these witnesses, I hand this girl over to you to have,
For the procreation of legitimate children,[116] and as dowry all my possessions—

113. The word *moikhos* (literally, "adulterer") was also used of someone who raped or seduced a woman of free status living in a male citizen's house. Nikeratos rashly overstates the case here in claiming Moschion was caught in the act.

114. For the (uncertain) legal situation surrounding the rape, see notes 8 and 19 above.

115. Her name means "Doll" (made of wax).

116. Athenian marriage formula, as occurs elsewhere in Greek New Comedy.

When I die, which, I pray, will be never.[117]

Moschion I hereby pledge to take her,

Hold her, and love her. **Demeas** We need only get the purifying water.

Chrysis, send along the women, the water-bearer,[118] and the piper.[119] 730

Someone bring out a torch and garlands here, So we all can escort them to their home. **Moschion** This guy's got them. (*pointing to a slave coming from Demeas' house*) **Demeas** Garland your

Head and dress appropriately! **Moschion** No problem. **Demeas** Beautiful boys,

Young men, old men, gentlemen,[120] one and all,

As a mark of your goodwill, give Dionysus[121] the hearty applause he loves! 735

And may the immortal patron of these finest festivals,

The goddess Nike,[122] always bless my plays!

117. The expected dowry is not to be handed over now, probably both because Nikeratos is poor and because of the rape.

118. To fetch sacred water from an Athenian spring (Kallirhoe) for the bridegroom's ritual purification (cf. note 45 above).

119. The piper, a female slave, is part of the procession to the bridegroom's house (cf. note 42 above).

120. See note 55 above.

121. For the god (the patron deity of theater in Athens), see Appendix.

122. For the goddess Nike ("Victory"), see *Lysistrata*, note 64. Here Demeas' mention of Nike is part of a conventional ending calling for the play's victory in the dramatic contest.

Plautus' CASINA

Casina is Plautus' adaptation of the lost *Klerumenoi* or *The Lot Drawers* by the Greek New Comedy playwright Diphilus (born *ca.* 350 BCE). A reference in the play to Bacchic rites no longer being practiced (see note 92) suggests that it premièred after the Roman senate's emergency decree outlawing the worship of the god Bacchus in 186 BCE, but before Plautus' death in 184 BCE. While the cast of characters in *Casina* is typical of New Comedy, its plot features an unusual twist. Lysidamus, the elderly head of the household (= the *paterfamilias* for Romans), lusts after the play's namesake, a 16-year-old slave who never appears in the play. Casina's name suggests *casia,* the Greek word for cinnamon, and for the men who have locked in on her scent in *Casina* she remains an impalpable and unattainable object of desire. Lysidamus' son Euthynicus is also infatuated with Casina, though Plautus also has removed him (64–66) from his adaptation of Diphilus. Since Casina is a slave, she cannot marry a free citizen, but Lysidamus' wife Cleostrata hopes to make Casina sexually available for

Euthynicus by having her married off to Chalinus, a household slave and close associate of her son.[1] Lysidamus aims to reserve sexual access to Casina for himself by arranging for his country slave Olympio to marry her. The competition for Casina is decided by a drawing of lots (Scene 7), which Lysidamus' surrogate Olympio wins. Erotic contests between father and son occur elsewhere in New Comedy (e.g., in Plautus' *Asinaria* and *Mercator*), but by removing the typically lovesick *adulescens* from the play and having his mother take up his cause, Plautus has created an entirely different emphasis: *Casina* is a power struggle between husband and wife for the control of a female slave's body.

Comic decorum demands that a *senex amator* (i.e., an old man in love) fail in his age-inappropriate pursuit. Love decidedly is for the young in ancient comedy, and so Euthynicus, not Lysidamus, is destined to have Casina. The audience is given a hint of the ultimate outcome when the prologist notes that Cleostrata "gave the girl as much attention/As she would her very own daughter" (45–46)—in other words, Casina was raised as if she were a free person and so is eligible for marriage with Euthynicus. Sure enough, by a remarkable but typical coincidence of New Comedy, Casina, who, the prologist tells us (37ff.), was exposed at birth and rescued by a slave of Lysidamus', will prove to be the freeborn daughter of the next-door neighbors. In Diphilus' play, the revelation of the girl's free birth must have occurred in a climatic recognition scene that led into marriage preparations. In keeping with the play's shift of emphasis to spousal discord and competition for power, Plautus relegates all that pertains to this marriage to a brief epilogue (1012–1018).

In her opening song, Cleostrata gives clear signs that she will be a formidable opponent for her husband when she

1. Legally unsanctioned quasi-marriages between slaves apparently were common in the Greco-Roman world: cf. note 14 below.

promises to "torture" Lysidamus with hunger and thirst (154); food and its (non-)consumption serve as running metaphors for male desire in *Casina*. In the thematically significant scene that follows, Cleostrata's conversation with her neighbor Myrrhina about marriage (170ff.), there are immediate suggestions that Cleostrata may assume the empowering role of comic heroine to defeat her husband. First, for perhaps some segment of Plautus' audience, the conversation between the two wives may have invited typological comparisons with the opening of *Lysistrata*, owing to the similarity of the characters' names (Lysistrata/ Cleostrata, Myrrhine/Myrrhina). In both scenes, the stronger character is visibly angry and reveals that the source of her discontent is male misbehavior. There is a sharp contrast between Lysistrata's public and political concerns and Cleostrata's singularly domestic dispute, but both characters subsequently proceed to vanquish and humiliate their male adversaries by devising clever schemes that require the solidarity of each play's other female characters. In both *Lysistrata* and *Casina*, the status quo in gender relations is restored at play's end, but only after we witness the remarkable intelligence of two heroines who in vastly differing circumstances publicly expose and correct the egregious misbehavior of men.

Much of Cleostrata's and Myrrhina's conversation focuses on the status of women within Roman marriage, about which the two express sharply opposed views on the issue of ownership of property as this pertains to Casina:

MYRRHINA . . . But how is it she's yours?
A decent wife's not supposed to have private property
Behind her husband's back. If she does, it's damaged goods—
You know, stolen from her husband or earned on her back!
In my opinion, all that's yours is your husband's.

CLEOSTRATA You're disagreeing with your best friend about
this? MYRRHINA Shh,

Silly person, and listen up:
Don't oppose your husband.
Let him lech, let him do whatever he wants, as long as he provides for you at home.

CLEOSTRATA Are you nuts? You're acting against your best interests.

MYRRHINA No, silly!
The one thing you never want to hear your husband to say is—

CLEOSTRATA What?

MYRRHINA "Out of the house, woman!" (198–212)

Myrrhina here assumes the attitude of a traditionalist—she engages in wool-working onstage as she speaks (164–169)—in advocating an old form of Roman marriage (*cum manu*), in which a father's absolute power over his daughter is transferred to her husband In the period after the Second Punic War (concluded in 201 BCE), marriages in which a father retained his power over his daughter (*sine manu*) increasingly were replacing the more traditional *cum manu* arrangement (cf. Introduction 28–29). Cleostrata's assertion that she can rightfully own property apart from her husband's strongly suggests that she is not under Lysidamus' power. Cleostrata may also have come to their marriage with a large dowry, which could pose a looming financial liability for a husband in the event of a divorce. These factors may explain why, as becomes increasingly clear in the play, Cleostrata seems to have the upper hand over Lysidamus in general, as he himself quips: "Not much we can do, since my wife's in charge even though I'm not dead" (409).

The topic of women's ownership of property was very current for Plautus' audience. As the result of catastrophic losses of men during the Second Punic War, many Roman women had inherited property. In response to this development, a law had been passed (*lex Oppia*) in 215 BCE to limit women's expenditures on luxury goods. Matters came to a head in 195 BCE, when Roman women publicly demonstrated in support of repealing the *lex Oppia*. Despite resistance from traditionalists such as Cato the Elder (234–149 BCE), the women succeeded in securing a repeal of the sumptuary law. The controversies were unlikely to have subsided by the debut of *Casina*, and Cleostrata's and Myrrhina's exchange here thus probably goes to the heart of contemporary debates on marriage.

In its comic context, Cleostrata's cause is bolstered by the thoroughly repulsive nature of her husband and his behavior. On the level of smell, he is the polar opposite of Casina, the alluring "Cinnamon-Girl," in that we are made to imagine him as reeking of a noxious combination of cologne (236–240), wine (245–246), and halitosis (727–728). Moreover, Lysidamus is a most poor specimen of a *paterfamilias*. His manifest lack of sexual control extends beyond the 16-year-old Casina, as we also witness him engaging in verbal sex-play with his farm manager Olympio (452ff.; cf. 724–725). And his nervous reaction to Cleostrata's claim (242ff.) that he has just come from a brothel, as also his wrinkled clothing (246), suggests that her charge is accurate. While married men in Rome apparently employed prostitutes without incurring shame, such assignations were problematic once they became frequent and expensive.[2] In light of Lysidamus' advising Olympio to spare no expense for his projected "love-banquet" with Casina (490–501), Cleostrata's charge that he is behaving irresponsibly and jeopardizing his finances ("Oh go ahead and do whatever you want: drink, eat, squander all your money" [248]) should not

2. They were of course much preferred to sexual relations with married women or freeborn virgins. A scholiast on the Augustan Age poet Horace cites an anecdote in which Cato the Elder, after witnessing a friend exiting the same brothel on multiple occasions, says to the man: "I praised you because I thought you were a visitor here, not a resident."

be dismissed as the stereotypical nagging of a shrewish comic wife. Lysidamus' amorous obsessions have also compromised his public life, as we see when he returns from the forum to flippantly report that his fixation on Casina has caused him to lose a legal case he pled on a relative's behalf:

> What possibly could be stupider
> Than for a man in love to go to the forum
> On the very day his lover awaits him?
> That's exactly how stupid I was, when I squandered the day
> In court to help a foolish relative of mine.
> It gives me great pleasure to say he lost his case—
> That'll teach him to drag me into court as his advocate on a day like today! (563–569)

As Lysidamus' scheme unravels, he gradually surrenders whatever means of control he had over his household. When he hears Pardalisca's fictional report that Casina is running amuck inside the house, he pleads with his female slave to beg his wife to defuse the situation—and even offers Pardalisca a bribe to do so (704–712). His dependence on his foreman Olympio in the conspiracy to enjoy Casina compels Lysidamus to absurdly concede that he is his slave's slave (737). After his homoerotic tussle with Chalinus disguised as Casina, Lysidamus is forced to publicly admit his disgrace, and, fearful of his wife as he is, he goes so far as to equate himself with a runaway slave:

> Anyone of you care to fill in for me here?
> There's no hope for my shoulders inside that house!
> Apart from playing the bad slave and hitting the road,
> I'm fresh out of ideas. (951–955)

Lysidamus eventually faces up to Cleostrata in his disheveled state (Scene 23), minus the cloak and walking stick he loses in his struggle with the "bride" Chalinus. In a desperate attempt to explain away his predicament to his wife, Lysidamus blames the loss of his apparel on Bacchants, the female worshippers of the god Bacchus. Myrrhina notes (980–981) the impossibility of this claim, especially in light of the fact that at the time of the play's debut, the Roman senate had recently prohibited Bacchic rites (p. 163 above). Conservative moralists condemned the cult of Bacchus as a locus of immorality, the transgression of traditional gender roles, and the general fomenting of social chaos. Sensationalistic reports of the Bacchants' control over male worshippers circulated, and it was even claimed that the women forced these men to have sex with each other. Cleostrata's and Myrrhina's use of Chalinus to humiliate Lysidamus through violent quasi-homoerotic acts echoes the allegations of sexually transgressive acts alleged to have been perpetrated by women in the cult. Lysidamus' obviously false allegations here about Bacchants perhaps satirize lingering male hysteria about the cult.

Casina features a striking transformation of Lysidamus' household space, as Cleostrata and her co-conspirators Myrrhina and Pardalisca strip Lysidamus' domicile of all of its familiar male prerogative: "power and control in this comedy ultimately emanate from the domestic realm."[3] Cleostrata's rise to comic heroine is primarily theatrical, in that she assumes the role of director of a play-within-the-play. In the first stage of her plan, Cleostrata takes advantage of Chalinus' eavesdropping on her husband and Olympio (Scene 9) to frustrate Lysidamus' plan to free up Alcesimus' house for the tryst with Casina by successfully setting the two patriarchs off against each other (Scenes 11, 13). As a harbinger of events to come, Lysidamus is treated to Pardalisca's fictional account (621ff.) of a Casina armed with two swords and murderously raging throughout the house in search of Olympio and his master. Delivered as a parody of a tragic messenger's

3. Andrews (2004): 452.

speech, Pardalisca's narrative anticipates the figurative castration of the sexually aggressive master and slave at the hands of Chalinus. We then learn from Pardalisca (Scene 16) that Cleostrata and Myrrhina have devised a faux-wedding and honeymoon, for which they are now costuming Chalinus to play the role of Casina inside the house (769–770).

Before their final degradation, we witness an overly excited Lysidamus and Olympio gloatingly singing the marriage chant "Hymen, O Hymen, O Hymenaeus" (800, 808). Pardalisca delivers the "bride" to the eager pair in a song that ominously parodies Roman marriage ideals:

> He-Casina has given off a stench from far, far away!
> Gently lift your feet above the threshold, tender bride;
> Safely commence this journey—
> *And stomp upon your husband always*!
> May all power be yours to crush and defeat him,
> Your voice, your command perched on high to beat him!
> His job is to fill your closets, yours to empty his pockets!
> Strive to deceive him, by night and by day! (814–824)

This time, Lysidamus' house has been coopted for an all-too-real theatrical performance. The sexual farce commences inside, and the women emerge from the house to await the entrance of the physically violated Lysidamus and Olympio:

> What fine entertainment we've enjoyed inside!
> And now we're out here on the street to watch the wedding festival.
> Oh my, I've never laughed so much in my life
> And don't think I'll ever laugh like that again! (855–858)

The household is about to be turned inside out, as the shocking and humiliating events Lysidamus and his farm's foreman have experienced inside will be publicly exposed on the street that serves as the play's setting. The audience's identification with the women seems complete here, as Cleostrata, Myrrhina, and Pardalisca take up the role of a model (internal) audience. Myrrhina shortly after makes explicit the connection between their scheme and theater (860–861): she and Cleostrata are present not just as spectators, but also as playwrights and directors at the debut of their own show. After Lysidamus suffers his much-deserved public humiliation, Cleostrata leaves no doubt that she is the play's controlling force when, in a final metacomic (and typically Plautine) flourish, she decides to forgive her husband on the ground that *Casina* already is a long enough play (1005–1006).

In the end, Cleostrata has Chalinus return the walking stick and cloak that Lysidamus had lost during their sexual wrangling, a gesture that marks his restoration as head of the household (1009). The closing joke of the epilogue (1015–1018) similarly acknowledges that husbands like Lysidamus will keep trying to escape their wives' notice in pursuing extramarital sexual affairs. In this particular case, however, Cleostrata and her neighbor have succeeded in justifiably frustrating one old man's inappropriate desires. In terms of the play's metaphor of cuisine, Lysidamus has been starved out, and in a clever celebratory take on male stereotypes of female gluttonousness (cf. Introduction 21–22 and *Lysistrata*, note 10), Pardalisca characterizes the triumphant wives as "a pair of gourmandesses:/They could down a whole boatload of chow!" (777–778). It is also significant that Plautus has pointedly framed the relationship of husband and wife in the light of contemporary controversies about women's property rights, and so also power relations within Roman marriage. Though *Casina* cannot without qualification be dubbed a feminist comedy, it is reasonable to assume that the play inspired some audience members to leave the theater still debating the politics of marriage.

CASINA

CAST OF CHARACTERS (WITH SPEAKING PARTS)

OLYMPIO: slave of Lysidamus and foreman of his farm in the country

CHALINUS: slave of Lysidamus and sidekick of Lysidamus' son Euthynicus

CLEOSTRATA: wife of Lysidamus

PARDALISCA: Cleostrata's personal slave/maid

MYRRHINA: wife of Alcesimus and friend of Cleostrata

LYSIDAMUS: head of the household

ALCESIMUS: neighbor and friend of Lysidamus

CITRIO: a cook hired to prepare the faux-wedding feast

(*Setting: A street in Athens in front of the houses of Alcesimus and Lysidamus, which are accessible through two doors in the stage backdrop.*)

PROLOGUE

Greetings, you top-notch group of spectators!
You're right to respect Fides,[4] and she returns the favor!
If you're down with that, show me you're reasonable folks
By giving me a nice round of applause.
5 People who appreciate a vintage wine are smart,[5]
As are connoisseurs of vintage plays.
And since you like aged words and workmanship,
You should also like aged plays.

4. The personification of Trust, one of many such abstractions worshipped in Roman religion. She had a prominent temple on the Capitoline Hill in Rome.

5. 5–22 were composed for a revival of the play sometime after Plautus' death in. 184 BCE.

And aren't the new plays they put on today
Even more worthless than the new coinage? 10
Now there's a rumor circulating
That you're eager for some Plautine plays.
Good news: we're here to present one of *his* vintage comedies!
The oldsters among us here loved this play,
Though I'm well aware the youngsters don't know it. 15
But we're here to make sure that situation changes.
The play was a hit the instant it hit the theater,
Back in the time of our very best playwrights.
They all may have taken a one-way trip down south,[6]
But their plays please us so much we almost forget they're gone. 20
Now I want all of you to listen carefully to what I have to say,
And to give our acting company your closest attention.
Got debts? Cast all your worries aside,
There's no need to fear the debt collectors today![7]
It's festival time, and we should have a festive time with the
bankers. 25
What calm! Absolute peace and quiet throughout the forum![8]
Those bankers know what they're doing: they accept no payments
From you now, and make no payments to you after the festival!
Now empty out your ears and pay close attention:
It's time to learn the name of this play: 30
In Greek this comedy's called *Klerumenoi,*[9]
In Latin it's *Sortientes*. Diphilus[10] is the Greek author.

6. I.e., to the underworld, where the shades of the dead were thought to congregate.

7. Plays were performed during Roman festivals, when all financial and legal business normally was suspended (see Introduction 16).

8. The business center of Rome.

9. "The Lot-Drawers" in Greek (= *Sortientes* in Latin). The Greek play took its name from the scene (= Scene 7 of *Casina*) in which lots were drawn for the right to marry Casina.

10. Popular Greek New Comedy playwright, born ca. 350 BCE, who provided the source play for several surviving Roman comedies.

Plautus, the comedian with the name that barks,[11]
Got hold of it and reworked it all over again in Latin.
35 An old man lives here. He's married and has a son
Who lives with his father in this very same house.
The old man's got a slave who's laid up sick now,
Or laid up in bed to be more precise.
At the crack of dawn sixteen years ago
40 That same slave saw a woman
Abandoning a baby girl. He went right up to her
And asked if he could have the baby.
He talked her into it and took the baby straight home,
And he begged his mistress to look after it and raise it.
45 His mistress agreed and gave the girl as much attention
As she would her very own daughter.[12]
After the girl was old enough
To attract the attention of men, the old man
Fell madly for her and so did his son.
50 Now father and son are marshaling their troops against each other.
Neither one knows the other's exact strategy.
The father's drafted his farm's foreman to ask
For the girl's hand in marriage. If that's successful,
The dirty old fellow hopes to spend a night away from home
55 Behind his wife's back. Meanwhile the son's
Commissioned his wingman to marry the girl.
That way *he* can keep the girl he's so in love with in his camp.
The old man's wife has gotten wind of the geezer's infatuation,
And is taking up her son's cause.
60 Once the old man realized his son was in love,
And saw him as an obstacle to his plan,

11. The Latin adjective *plautus* ("flat") was used to describe the floppy ears of a dog.

12. I.e., the girl was raised as if she were a free person, not the slave that she technically is.

He sent the young man abroad.
But the mother—she's clever—will be her son's ally-in-absentia.
Oh, in case you're wondering, the son won't show up today:
Nope, not in this comedy. Plautus had other ideas: 65
He wrecked a bridge along the young man's way home.[13]
Now I suspect some of you are mumbling among yourselves,
"*What the hell*? A slave wedding?[14] Impossible!
Since when do slaves propose or get married?
It's unprecedented! It doesn't happen anywhere in the whole
world!" 70
I happen to know otherwise: they do it in Greece[15] and in
Carthage,[16]
And in Apulia[17] right here in our own backyard!
Why, there it's even the custom to make more fuss
About slave weddings than those of free folks.
Anyone willing to bet me a bottle 75
Of sweet wine on this? I'm in, as long as
The umpire is a Greek, a Carthaginian, or an Apulian.[18]
What about it? No takers? Huh, I guess no one's thirsty.
Now, to get back to the abandoned girl,

13. Plautus' removal of Euthynicus (1014), who presumably appeared in the source play by Diphilus (note 10 above), reorientates *Casina* as a competition between husband and wife: see Introductory Essay 163–164.

14. Roman slaves were legal non-entities and so could not marry; they did, however, often live together in families, a practice known as *contubernium* ("the sharing of a hut").

15. Extra-legal connubial arrangements among slaves similar to those made in Rome (see note 14 above) also seem to have occurred in Greece.

16. No evidence survives to determine whether or not slave marriages were legally binding in Carthage, Rome's hated North African rival in the Punic Wars. The same is true for Apulia (see note 17 below).

17. Apulia (modern Puglia) is a region of southeastern Italy that was heavily influenced by Greeks and Greek culture from an early date.

18. Roman sources stereotypically portray their enemies, such as the Carthaginians and Greeks, as untrustworthy. The joke here rests on the assumption that a judge from these places would be easily corruptible.

80 The one the slaves are dying to marry so badly:
She'll be discovered to be a freeborn Athenian
And a chaste young girl.[19] There most certainly
Won't be any sexing of her in this comedy!
But you can be sure as soon as the play's over,
85 Anybody who slips "her" the money
Can go straight to the honeymoon,[20] no ceremony required!
Well, that's the gist of it all. Be well, good luck, and keep winning
Victories via your true valor, as you always have before!

SCENE 1

(*Olympio enters from Lysidamus' house with Chalinus close behind him.*)

Olympio[21] Oh, so I'm not supposed to take care of my business
90 By myself and however I please without your permission?
Damn it, why are you following me? Chalinus[22] Oh, I'll
Follow right behind you wherever you go, just like a shadow,
And you can go to hell for all I care:
I'll be right there dogging you. Take that as a clue
95 As to whether or not you and your bag of tricks can steal away
Casina to be your wife behind my back.

Olympio Mind your own business! Chalinus Have you no shame?
Why is a worthless rube like you creeping around in the city?

19. These factors will make her eligible for legitimate marriage: see further Introductory Essay 163–164.

20. An allusion to the fact that Roman actors were mostly slaves and so more likely to prostitute themselves. They were also exclusively male, which lends a homoerotic twist to the joke here (cf. the transvestite "marriage" in the play at 798ff., and Introductory Essay 168–169).

21. The farm-foreman's name incongruously suggests Olympia (the great cult center of Zeus and site of the ancient Olympics) or Mt. Olympus (mythical home of the gods) in Greece.

22. His name means "Horse-Bridle" in Greek.

OLYMPIO Because I feel like it. CHALINUS Shouldn't you be doing your duty out there on the farm?
Why stick your nose in city business here 100
When you've got so much work to do out there in the country?
You're just here to steal my bride, aren't you? Get your hide back to the farm!
There's piles of *doodie* for you to deal with there!

OLYMPIO I know exactly what my duty is, Chalinus.
I've got someone very capable tending the farm, 105
And once I get what I came to town for—you know,
Marrying that girl you're so hot for, your fellow slave
(Yummy little Casina,[23] my lovely and tender little Casina!),
And escorting her back to the country
And straight into my bed—then *I'll be doing my duty.* 110

CHALINUS *You're* going to marry her? I don't think so!
Over my dead body! She'll never be yours!

OLYMPIO She's *my* booty. You might as well go hang yourself!

CHALINUS Oh, she's *your* booty now, you bag of crap?

OLYMPIO You'll see. CHALINUS Screw you!
OLYMPIO You can be sure 115
I'll never run out of ways to torture you at my wedding.

CHALINUS What've you got in mind? OLYMPIO What do I have in mind, you ask?
For starters, you'll carry the wedding torch for my bride.
Then it's back to being your worthless old self.
Next, once you're back there on the farm, 120
You'll be provided with one pitcher, one path,
One well, one bucket, and eight vats.
These will always be full or you'll be full of scars.
Lugging all that water will make you so bent over and tanned
That we'll make saddle straps for horses out of you! 125

23. Her name is related to *casia*, Greek for "cinnamon." Casina, who never appears in the play, remains a tantalizing and unattainable object of desire to the males in the play: see further Introductory Essay 163–164.

And when you'd like a bite to eat,
You can feast yourself on cattle fodder,
Or eat dirt like a worm. My plan is to make sure you're hungrier
Than Hunger[24] itself out there in the sticks!
130 And once you're exhausted and starving,
Accommodations will be made for you to get the sleep you deserve.

CHALINUS What do you mean? OLYMPIO Tightly tied to the bedroom window frame,
You'll be tied up in fits while you listen to me kissing her,
And she says, "My dear little Olympio, love of my life,
135 Sweetie pie, honeykins, my one and only joy,
Let me kiss those little eyes of yours, my darling.
Let me love you to death, my precious little private party,
My teeny-weeny love-bird, my lovey-dovey, my bunny-rabbit!"
While you listen to her telling me all this, scumbag,
140 You'll wriggle about like a mouse trapped in the wall.
Don't so much as even think about answering me:
I'm going in. I'm sick of your babbling. CHALINUS Right behind you.
I'll be there to watch every little thing you do.

SCENE 2 (SONG)

(Cleostrata and Pardalisca enter together from Lysidamus' house, already in song.)

CLEOSTRATA[25] Lock down the pantry and bring me the keys!
145 I'm going next door here to my neighbor's.
Come get me if my husband wants me.

PARDALISCA[26] The old man's already demanded that his lunch be served.

24. A play on Roman religion's tendency to personify abstractions (cf. note 4 above).

25. Her name means "Renowned-Army" and recalls the heroine of *Lysistrata*: see Introductory Essay 164–165.

26. A diminutive form of (Greek) *pardalis*, "panther."

CLEOSTRATA Shh!
Off with you now! He'll get no lunch from me
And there'll be no cooking today! 150
He's taken a stand against my son and me,
All in the service of his lust,
That *total disgrace to the human race*!
I'll torture lover-boy with hunger, torture him with thirst,
Along with sharp and sharper treatment. 155
Oh, I'll make sure he chokes on my bitterest words!
I'll see he leads just the sort of life he deserves—
In hell's waiting room!
That chaser of disgrace!
That barn-load of human waste! 160
I'm going off to complain to my neighbor.
Oh, look! Her door's opening and she's coming out.
Maybe this isn't the best time for me to visit.

SCENE 3 (SONG)

(*Myrrhina enters from her house, still addressing her slaves inside.*)

MYRRHINA[27] Follow me next door here, girls.
Hey, anybody listening there? 165
I'll be over here,
If my husband or anyone else wants me.
When I'm working by myself at home, sleep numbs my
hands. 168–9
Didn't I tell you to bring my knitting?[28]

CLEOSTRATA Hi, Myrrhina![29] 170–1

MYRRHINA Oh, hi! Why the knitted brow? 172–3

CLEOSTRATA Oh you know how it is for a woman in a bad
marriage:[30] 174–5

27. For the meaning of her name, see *Lysistrata*, note 28.

28. Myrrhina pointedly is engaged in wool-working, the most traditional female activity in the ancient world (cf. Introduction 22–23).

29. For the typologically similar opening scene of *Lysistrata*, see Introductory Essay 165.

30. For the contrasting types of Roman marriage referred to in this scene, see Introduction 28–29 and Introductory Essay 165–167.

176–7 There's more than enough grief at home and elsewhere.
I was just coming to see you.

Myrrhina Same here.
What's troubling you so much now?
180–1 When you're upset, I'm upset.

Cleostrata Yes, I know. There's no better neighbor than you.
You're everything I want myself to be.

Myrrhina I'm very fond of you too.
185 Now, please tell me what's the matter.

Cleostrata I'm being treated in the worst possible way in my own home!

Myrrhina Oh my, what is it? Tell me again, please—
I really haven't wrapped my head around what's wrong!

Cleostrata It's my husband. He treats me in the worst way,
190 And there's no way for me to exercise my rights!

Myrrhina Strange if true. It's the men who usually
Demand more rights from their wives!

Cleostrata He actually wants my maid—and against my wishes!
She's the one I raised at my own expense.[31]
195 He says he wants her for his foreman,
But I know he's hot for her himself. **Myrrhina** Shh!
Please, no! **Cleostrata** No, it's okay for us to speak. We're alone.

Myrrhina So we are. But how is it she's yours?
A decent wife's not supposed to have private property
200 Behind her husband's back. If she does, it's damaged goods—
You know, stolen from her husband or earned on her back!
In my opinion, all that's yours is your husband's.[32]

31. This indicates that Cleostrata is married *sine manu* (cf. note 30 above).

32. Myrrhina refers to the oldest and most conservative form of Roman marriage (= *cum manu*), in which a father's absolute power over his daughter is transferred to her husband. In this arrangement, a wife's property became her husband's.

CLEOSTRATA You're disagreeing with your best friend about this? MYRRHINA Shh,
Silly person, and listen up:
Don't oppose your husband. 205
Let him lech, let him do whatever he wants, as long as he provides for you at home. 206–7

CLEOSTRATA Are you nuts? You're acting against your best interests.

MYRRHINA No, silly! 208–9
The one thing you never want to hear your husband say is—

CLEOSTRATA What?

MYRRHINA 'Out of the house, woman!'[33] 210–12

CLEOSTRATA Shh! Quiet! MYRRHINA What's up?
CLEOSTRATA Look! MYRRHINA Who is it?
CLEOSTRATA It's my husband,
Coming this way! Please, go back in your house now!
MYRRHINA Okay, I'm off!

CLEOSTRATA We'll talk later when we have a chance. 215
Goodbye for now! MYRRHINA Goodbye!

SCENE 4 (SONG THROUGH 251)

(*Lysidamus enters from the forum wing of the stage.*)

LYSIDAMUS[34] There's nothing brighter, nothing mightier than love!
What could have more taste and more grace?
It's a total mystery to me that cooks who love their spices
Leave out this single finest spice of all: 220
Just a dash of love and a dish is a winner!
Without a sprinkle of love there's no flavor, no savor!

33. A formula of divorce, which normally was a simple speech-act such as this in ancient Rome. See further, Rosenmeyer, P.A., "Enacting the Law: Plautus' Use of the Divorce Formula on Stage." *Phoenix* 49 (1995): 201–217.

34. It is not clear what this name means or if the old man was even so named by Plautus; for the hypothesis that his name should be "Casinus," see O'Bryhim (1989).

Love converts bile to honey, and makes an old grump a charming fellow.
I draw this lesson directly from my own experience: now that I've fallen for Casina,
225 I'm all aglow, and I'm the spitting image of Spiffiness herself![35]
I keep the perfumers busy, and I wear the most pleasant scents
To please her—*and I do*—but my wife tortures me with each breath she takes.
Look at her standing there so dour and sour! Time to sweet talk the old bag.
How goes it my dearest and only delight?

CLEOSTRATA Get lost! And keep your hands off me!

LYSIDAMUS My dear Juno,[36] you shouldn't be so cross with your
230 Jove![37]
Where are you going? **CLEOSTRATA** Let go of me!

LYSIDAMUS Wait! **CLEOSTRATA** I'm not waiting!

LYSIDAMUS Then I'll follow you!

CLEOSTRATA Are you crazy? **LYSIDAMUS** Yes, crazy for you!

CLEOSTRATA Keep the craziness to yourself!

LYSIDAMUS You can't resist. **CLEOSTRATA** Oh, You're killing me!

LYSIDAMUS (*attempting not to be heard*)
I only wish! **CLEOSTRATA** Now that's something I can actually believe!

LYSIDAMUS Look at me, sweetie. **CLEOSTRATA** Oh I'm
235 your sweetie now?
Do I smell cologne somewhere?

35. For Roman personifications—this one of *Munditia* (lit. "Cleanliness") is comic—see notes 4 and 24 above.

36. For the goddess Juno, see Appendix.

37. For the god Jupiter/Jove, see Appendix.

LYSIDAMUS (*aside*) Caught red-handed! I'd better wipe my head off with my cloak.
I wish Mercury[38] would zap that perfumer who sold me this stuff!

CLEOSTRATA You utterly worthless old coot! I can barely keep from calling you what you deserve!
An old slug like you, promenading through town and reeking of cologne![39] 240

LYSIDAMUS I was only helping a friend buy some cologne. CLEOSTRATA Not the least hesitation about lying!
Have you no shame at all? LYSIDAMUS I've got as much as you want me to have. CLEOSTRATA Which whorehouse did you visit?

LYSIDAMUS Me? In a whorehouse? CLEOSTRATA I know more than you think. LYSIDAMUS Really? So what do you know?

CLEOSTRATA That out of all the worthless old slugs in the world there's not a single one more worthless than you!
Where've you been? Which whorehouse? What'd you have to drink? 245
You're stinking drunk! Look how your cloak is all wrinkled![40] LYSIDAMUS The gods can zap
Us both if I drank so much as a single drop of wine today!

CLEOSTRATA Oh go ahead and do whatever you want: drink, eat, squander all your money!

LYSIDAMUS That's enough now, wife! Control yourself! You're making my ears ring! 249–50
Save yourself a little something to nag about tomorrow.
Any chance you can control your temper and do something

38. For the god Mercury, see Appendix.

39. A man wearing scented hair-oil in ancient comedy usually has been engaging in extramarital sex (or is about to do so).

40. His wrinkled cloak is another sign that he has been engaging in extramarital sex (cf. note 39 above), though it never is confirmed that Lysidamus has been frequenting brothels (cf. Introductory Essay 167–168).

Your husband wants for once instead of always fighting him?
Cleostrata Such as? **Lysidamus** Glad you asked.
It's about that maid of yours,[41] Casina. She should marry our foreman.
He's a good slave, and he can provide her well with wood, hot
255 water, food,
Clothing, and a proper place to raise their children.
Much better that she marries him than that shady wingman of my son's.
He hasn't saved so much as a penny of his own money.

Cleostrata I'm really shocked that a man your age doesn't remember how to behave properly.

Lysidamus What do you mean? **Cleostrata** If you did
260 the decent and proper thing,
You'd let me be the one concerned with the maid: that's my job.

Lysidamus But how in the hell could you give her to that no-good Chalinus? **Cleostrata** Because
We both should be looking out for our only son.
Lysidamus So he's an only son?
He's just as much my only son as I'm his only father.
265 He should be the one giving in to my wishes, not vice versa!

Cleostrata You're really asking for trouble, mister! Something stinks here! **Lysidamus** (*aside*) She's picked up my scent!
You mean *me*? **Cleostrata** Yes, you! What's with the stuttering? Why are you so hot and bothered about that match?

Lysidamus I just think she deserves to marry a good slave, not a worthless one.

Cleostrata What if I talk Olympio into giving her up to Chalinus
As a favor to me? **Lysidamus** But what if I talk Chalinus
270 into giving her up to
Olympio? I think I can do that.

41. For Cleostrata's ownership of Casina, see note 31 above.

CLEOSTRATA Fair enough. Want me to call Chalinus out here for you?
You can ask him, I'll ask Olympio. LYSIDAMUS Let's do it.

CLEOSTRATA He'll be here soon. Now we'll find out who can be the most persuasive.

LYSIDAMUS If only Hercules[42] and the rest of the gods would destroy that woman! 275
Poor me! Here I'm being tortured by love and she makes it her business
To oppose me! She must have gotten wind of my plans,
And that's why she's putting all her resources behind Chalinus.
He's someone I wish all the gods and goddesses would blast!

SCENE 5

(*Chalinus enters from Lysidamus' house.*)

CHALINUS Your wife said
You wanted to see me. LYSIDAMUS I most certainly do.
CHALINUS Well? 280

LYSIDAMUS First of all, show some respect when you talk to me:
It's stupid to scowl at your betters!
Now, I've long considered you a good and decent sort of person. CHALINUS Great.
If that's the case, why don't you free me? LYSIDAMUS I'd really like to. 284–5
But what I really, really want is your wanting to do me a favor.

CHALINUS Tell me what you want. LYSIDAMUS Listen up carefully:
I promised the foreman he could marry Casina.

CHALINUS But your wife and son promised her to me!
LYSIDAMUS Right.
But would you rather be a free bachelor 290
Or an enslaved husband? The same goes for your children.
It's your choice, take your pick.

42. For the god Hercules, see Appendix.

CHALINUS Hmmm, let's see: if I'm free, I'd have to support myself. Now you do.
My mind's made up about Casina: she's mine and mine alone.

295 LYSIDAMUS Then go inside and call my wife out here this instant!
And bring back a water urn and some lots with you.
CHALINUS Okey-dokey.

LYSIDAMUS I'll fend off that attack of yours one way or another now!
If I can't persuade you, there's always the lots:
That's how I'll exact my vengeance on you and your supporters. CHALINUS Except that
I'm going to win. LYSIDAMUS The only thing you'll be
300 winning is a whipping.

CHALINUS Go ahead and plot any scheme you want. She's going to marry me.

LYSIDAMUS Now get out of my sight. CHALINUS Can't bear the sight of me? I'm not going to disappear.

LYSIDAMUS Poor, poor me! Could the cards be more stacked against me?
I'm worried my wife's already talked Olympio out of
305 Marrying Casina. If she has, take a gander at one ex-old man!
If she hasn't, there's a morsel of hope for me in the lots.
But if things don't shake out my way, I'll transform my sword into a pillow—
And toss myself right on top of it. But look! Perfect, here comes Olympio.

SCENE 6

(*Olympio enters from Lysidamus' house, shouting back at Cleostrata.*)

OLYMPIO Lady, you might just as soon toss me into a hot oven
310 And bake me into a burned biscotto
As get me to do you what you want!

LYSIDAMUS Saved! Judging from what he says, there's hope.

OLYMPIO Lady, you can threaten me all you want with talk about my freedom.

Even if you and your son are against me,
And no matter how much the two of you try to stop it, 315
I can become free for just about nothing.

LYSIDAMUS What's that, Olympio? Who're you arguing with?

OLYMPIO Same woman you always are. LYSIDAMUS Oh, my wife.

OLYMPIO You consider her your wife? You're more like a hunter and his dog,
The way you spend night and day with that bitch! 320

LYSIDAMUS So what's she up to? What's she saying to you?
OLYMPIO She's begging
And pleading with me not to marry Casina.
LYSIDAMUS Yes—and?

OLYMPIO I said I wouldn't let Jupiter have her,
Even if he begged me. LYSIDAMUS The gods will bless you for that!

OLYMPIO She's boiling mad now, and about to blow! 325

LYSIDAMUS I'd like to see her split right down the middle!

OLYMPIO That already should have happened if you'd done your husbandly duty.[43]
Come on, this love-affair of yours is obnoxious!
Your wife's my enemy, your son's my enemy,
The whole damn household's my enemy!
LYSIDAMUS Oh, so what. 330
As long as your one and only Jupiter is on your side here,
You shouldn't give a rat's ass for those lesser deities.

OLYMPIO What a pile of crap! As if you didn't know well enough
How the human Jupiters can suddenly die off!
Tell me this, "Jupiter": when you die 335
And the lesser gods inherit your kingdom,
Who'll be there to protect my back, head, and legs?

43. The sexual euphemism here is typical of Plautus, who, in contrast to Aristophanes, almost never meets any modern definition of obscenity.

LYSIDAMUS You'll be much better off than you think
If we win and I get to sleep with Casina.

340 OLYMPIO How's that going to happen, seeing as
Your wife's dead set against me marrying her?
LYSIDAMUS Here's the plan:
I toss the lots into the urn and draw
One for you and one for Chalinus . . . on second thought,
We'll have to draw our swords and fight it out.

345 OLYMPIO And what if the drawing turns out the other way?

LYSIDAMUS Bite your tongue! I trust in the gods and all our hope lies with them.

OLYMPIO Well I wouldn't pay so much as a penny for that thought.
It may be that all mortals trust in the gods,
But I've seen a good number of the faithful deceived by them!

LYSIDAMUS Shh! Be quiet a minute! OLYMPIO Why?
350 LYSIDAMUS Chalinus is coming
Out with the urn and the lots.
Time to close ranks and battle it out.

SCENE 7

(Cleostrata and Chalinus, who holds the urn and lots, enter from Lysidamus' house.)

CLEOSTRATA What does my husband want me to do, Chalinus?

CHALINUS What he wants is to see your pyre set up outside the city[44]—with you on it.

CLEOSTRATA I'm quite sure he does. CHALINUS I think
355 you can clip the "quite" off that "sure"!

LYSIDAMUS (*to Olympio*) I've got more experts around here than I thought: this one's a regular soothsayer.
Why don't we bring the battle standards closer and charge?
Follow me! And just what are you two up to?
CHALINUS I've got everything you ordered:

44. Burials were not allowed within the city walls.

Wife, lots, urn, and yours truly. **Olympio** And one of yours truly is truly one too many of you!

Chalinus It must seem that way to you: I'm the prick in your side, 360

And I'm ripping your tiny heart out! Look at you sweating, you human punching bag!

Lysidamus Shut up, Chalinus! **Chalinus** Stick it to him! **Olympio** No, to *him*—he likes the receiving end[45] of that.

Lysidamus Put the urn here and give me the lots! Now pay attention, everyone!

I was thinking, my dear wife, that you'd let Casina

Marry me. And I do still think that way now too. 365

Cleostrata Casina marry you? **Lysidamus** Yes, me—oops, I really didn't mean that!

I meant "me" when I said "him," and wanting her all for myself as . . .

Damn! I've got it all wrong again! **Cleostrata** You sure do—both your words and your behavior!

Lysidamus "Him," no "me" . . . I'm back on the right track now.

Cleostrata You're still making a lot of mistakes. **Lysidamus** You know, that happens when you really want something. 370

But Olympio and I, recognizing your right in this, ask that you— **Cleostrata** Yes?

Lysidamus I'll tell you, honey-pie. Now in regard to Casina: could you do

Our foreman a favor? **Cleostrata** No, and I won't even consider it!

Lysidamus In that case, I'll draw lots for both sides. **Cleostrata** Anybody stopping you?

45. For (extensive) sexual euphemism in Plautus, cf. note 43 above.

LYSIDAMUS In my informed judgment, that would be the best
375 and fairest procedure.
If it goes our way, we'll celebrate;
If otherwise, we'll keep a level head about everything. Take a lot
And see what's written on it. OLYMPIO "One."
CHALINUS Not fair! You gave it to him first.

LYSIDAMUS Take this one, will you? CHALINUS Give me it! Wait, something just occurred to me:
What if there's another lot underwater?
380 LYSIDAMUS Dirtbag!

So you think I'm just like you? CLEOSTRATA Now calm down: there isn't a lot in there.

CHALINUS I pray the gods will give me— OLYMPIO A ferocious beating!
Judging by your kind of piety, that's what you deserve.
But wait a minute. That lot of yours there isn't made out of wood, is it?

CHALINUS Why's that matter? OLYMPIO Because I'm
385 afraid it'll float on top of the water.

LYSIDAMUS Bravo! Careful now: throw them both in here.

Wife, stir up the lots. OLYMPIO Don't trust your wife!
LYSIDAMUS Calm down!

OLYMPIO She'll jinx us if she touches the lots!
LYSIDAMUS Quiet!

OLYMPIO I am quiet. Dear gods, I pray—
CHALINUS You'll bring a yoke and chain—

OLYMPIO That the lot falls out in my favor—
390 CHALINUS And hang him up by the feet!

OLYMPIO And that you blow your eyes out of your head right through your nose!

CHALINUS What are you afraid of? There's a noose all ready for you.

OLYMPIO You are so dead! LYSIDAMUS Both of you pay attention, now! OLYMPIO I'm listening.
LYSIDAMUS Now then, Cleostrata,

So there won't be any suspicions about me cheating,
It's in your hands: you draw the lots. **Olympio** You're killing me! **Chalinus** No loss there. 395

Cleostrata Very well then. **Chalinus** Dear gods—I pray your lot's escaped from the urn!

Olympio Just because *you're* a runaway slave doesn't mean everyone else is one too.
And I hope yours is all dissolved, just as they say
Happened to Hercules' descendants way back when.[46]

Chalinus You'll soon be so warmed up from my whips that you'll dissolve! 400

Lysidamus Olympio, pay attention now! **Olympio** I would if this man of letters[47] would let me!

Lysidamus May all the good luck be mine! **Olympio** Yes, and mine, too!

Chalinus No, mine! **Olympio** No, no, mine! **Chalinus** No, it's all mine! **Cleostrata** My guy'll win, and your life will be pitiful.

Lysidamus Punch the bum in the face, Olympio. Well? How about it?

Olympio Punch or slap? **Lysidamus** Your call. **Olympio** Take *that*! 405

Cleostrata What'd you hit him for? **Olympio** Jupiter's orders.

Cleostrata (*to Chalinus*) Hit him right back in the jaw! **Olympio** Hey, Jupiter: he's pounding me to bits!

Lysidamus Why'd you hit this guy? **Chalinus** Juno's orders.

46. The descendants of Hercules (see Appendix) drew lots to divide up regions of the Peloponnese among themselves. One of them secured Messenia by arranging for his rival's lot to be made of (dissolvable) sun-dried rather than kiln-fired clay.

47. Olympio refers to letters branded on Chalinus, presumably to mark an attempt to run away from the household (cf. *Samia*, note 63), with a pun on his preceding learned allusion to Hercules' descendants.

LYSIDAMUS Not much we can do, since my wife's in charge even though I'm not dead.[48]

CLEOSTRATA Chalinus has every right to speak up just as much
410 as Olympio does. OLYMPIO Why'd
He have to go and ruin my prayers? LYSIDAMUS Be on the lookout out for another beating, Chalinus!

CHALINUS *Now* you tell me—after I've been beaten to a pulp! LYSIDAMUS Come on now, wife,
Draw the lots! You two pay close attention. I'm so afraid, I've lost my bearings!
My heart's palpitating, dancing, pounding,
And absolutely thumping its way right out of my chest!
415 CLEOSTRATA I've got a lot. LYSIDAMUS Pull it out.

CHALINUS Are you done for now? OLYMPIO Let's see! It's mine! CHALINUS This is extreme torture!

CLEOSTRATA You lose, Chalinus. LYSIDAMUS The gods were on our side, Olympio!
Yahoo! OLYMPIO All thanks to my piety, and that of my distinguished ancestors![49]

LYSIDAMUS Go inside, wife, and make preparations for the wedding. CLEOSTRATA As you wish.

LYSIDAMUS You know it's quite a trip from here to the country
420 villa. CLEOSTRATA Yes—and?

LYSIDAMUS Hard as it must be for you, go inside and take care of everything. CLEOSTRATA Okay.

LYSIDAMUS Let's both go in too, to move things along faster. OLYMPIO I'm not stopping you.

LYSIDAMUS I don't want to say anything else in his presence.

48. For Cleostrata's general domination of her husband, see Introductory Essay 164–171.

49. Bluster in the mouth of a slave, who, according to a fiction of Roman law, was denied parents, let alone "distinguished ancestors."

SCENE 8

(*Chalinus is left alone onstage.*)

CHALINUS It'd be a waste of effort to hang myself now—
A waste of energy and rope, that is. 425
I'd only be giving aid and comfort to my enemies.
And what's the point when I'm already as good as dead now anyway?
That lot did me in, and now the foreman's marrying Casina.
What bothers me most is not his winning
So much as all the old man's efforts 430
To get her married to him rather than me.
The wretched geezer was so jumpy and nervous,
And the way he whooped it up when the foreman won!
Hey, the door's opening. I'll slide in over here.
If it isn't my dear old buddies coming out. 435
I'll set up a little ambush for them over here.

SCENE 9

(*Olympio and Lysidamus enter from the latter's house and Chalinus proceeds to eavesdrop.*)

OLYMPIO Just let him come to the farm! I'll send the guy back to town
Tied to a cart like a charcoal salesman.[50]

LYSIDAMUS Yes, go for it! OLYMPIO I'll see everything's arranged.

LYSIDAMUS If Chalinus was home, I'd send him 440
Out shopping for food with you as a way of rubbing
Our enemy's nose in a little extra misery.

CHALINUS (*aside*) I'll make like a crab and creep along the wall here
To secretly eavesdrop on their conversation.
One of them's torturing me, the other disgusts me: 445

50. Heavily weighed down by his wares, which hung in buckets from a wooden fork placed over his shoulders.

Look at that loser all dressed up in white![51]
That human storehouse of torture tools![52] I'd postpone my own death
To push him on down to hell in front of me!

OLYMPIO Now haven't I served you well? Thanks to me
450 You've got what you're so damned hot for!
She'll be yours this very day without your wife knowing a thing.
LYSIDAMUS Quiet!
And as the gods are my witness, I don't know if I can keep my lips off you!
I could just kiss you so hard, my sweetie-pie!

CHALINUS (*aside*) Huh? "Kiss you so hard?" "My sweetie-pie?"
455 Sounds like he wants to burrow up into his foreman's bladder![53]

OLYMPIO You do kind of love me, don't you?
LYSIDAMUS Oh, more than I love myself.
Mind if I hug you? CHALINUS (*aside*) Huh? Hug him?
OLYMPIO Why not.

LYSIDAMUS Holding you is like sliding my tongue over sweet honey.

OLYMPIO Whoa Off my leg there, horn-dog!

460 CHALINUS (*aside*) Oh, so *that's* how he got promoted to foreman!
Which reminds me: one night a while back I was escorting the geezer
Back home and he tried to make me his butler—by way of my back door![54]

OLYMPIO Now haven't I been super-submissive and a source of pleasure to you today?

LYSIDAMUS I'll treat you better than I will myself for the rest of my life!

51. I.e., as a Roman bridegroom.

52. An example of a typically imaginative (and grotesque) Plautine phrase (i.e., *stimulorum loculi* [literally, "lockbox(es) of prods/goads"]), notoriously difficult to translate.

53. Cf. note 43 above.

54. Cf. the use of "gates" for the anus in *Lysistrata* (notes 184 and 185).

CHALINUS (*aside*) Damn! These two will be wrestling with each together in no time! 465
The old guy always had a thing for the ones with beards!

LYSIDAMUS Oh the kisses I'll pour down on Casina today—
So, so many joys and my wife won't know a thing!
CHALINUS (*aside*) Ah hah!
Now I'm back in the game!
So *he's* madly in love with Casina. Got ya both! 470

LYSIDAMUS I'm chomping at the bit to squeeze and kiss her right now!

OLYMPIO Whoa let her get married first. Damn! What's your rush? LYSIDAMUS I'm in love.

OLYMPIO I don't think our entire plan can be pulled off today.
LYSIDAMUS Oh yes it can—
If you've got any hope of becoming a free man tomorrow.

CHALINUS (*aside*) Now they've really got my attention! 475
Here's a chance to kill two birds with one stone.

LYSIDAMUS A love-nest is ready at my friend's house next door.
He knows all about my little affair,
And said he'd provide the perfect venue for it.

OLYMPIO What about his wife? Won't she be there?
LYSIDAMUS Everything's neatly arranged. 480
My wife's going to call her over for the wedding—
To be with her, to help her out, and spend the night.
I told her to do it and she said she would.
So my neighbor will be out of the house and his wife will be sleeping here.
You'll take your wife off to the farm—the "farm" being right next door here— 485
So Casina and I can enjoy our honeymoon.
And tomorrow before dawn you'll take her to the real farm.
Clever, eh? OLYMPIO Masterful!
CHALINUS (*aside*) Keep on plotting away:
You'll live to regret your clever little scheme!

LYSIDAMUS Know what to do now? OLYMPIO Tell me.
490 LYSIDAMUS Take this money,
And run off and buy some food, but not plebeian stuff:
I insist on the finest delicacies . . . because she's so delicate
herself.[55] OLYMPIO Okay.

LYSIDAMUS Buy some cuttlefish, calamari, and limpets—
The finest fish you can find. CHALINUS (*aside*) Or the
fishiest fish, wise-guy!

LYSIDAMUS And sole. CHALINUS (*aside*) Just the sole? But
495 I'd prefer a whole sandal
To smash your face in with, you worthless old geezer!

OLYMPIO Want any catfish? LYSIDAMUS No, I've got more
than enough of that already—
You know, that catty wife of mine who never shuts up!

OLYMPIO Once I get to the fish market I'll decide
What looks best. LYSIDAMUS Fine, now scoot on out of
500 here!
Don't worry about the price, and don't scrimp on quantity.
Now I've got to meet my neighbor over here
To make sure he does his part for my cause.
OLYMPIO Should I go now? LYSIDAMUS Yes!

(*Olympio exits via the forum wing, and Lysidamus enters his neighbor's house; Chalinus is left alone onstage.*)

CHALINUS If you bribed me with my freedom three times over,
You couldn't stop me from inflicting a load of hurt on those
505 two today!
I'm going to tell my mistress every last detail.
I've caught my enemies red-handed!
If my mistress is willing to play her part,
The game is ours, and I'll be one fine victor.
510 Luck is on our side! Losers will soon be winners.
I'll going inside to add a little spice of my own

55. For the correspondence between food and sex, as this pertains especially to Casina ("Cinnamon Girl") in the play, see Introductory Essay 171.

To what that cook's got simmering.
What he thinks is ready for him won't be served,
And as for what I've got cooked up for him—there's no way he's ready for that!

SCENE 10

(*Lysidamus and Alcesimus enter from the latter's house.*)

LYSIDAMUS We'll soon find out whether you're friend or foe, Alcesimus. 515
Now's the time for the ultimate test.
And as for lecturing me about my love-life: put it all in storage.
"With your gray hair!" "The age difference!"
To say nothing of "A married man!" Put it *all* in storage.

ALCESIMUS[56] I've never seen a man more disgustingly in love! 520

LYSIDAMUS Make sure the house is empty.

ALCESIMUS Yes, damn it, I told you I'd send
All the male slaves and every last maid over to your house.

LYSIDAMUS You smart, smart man!
But make sure they follow the blackbird's song, you know:
"With food and provisions press on like you're marching to Sutrium."[57]

ALCESIMUS I'll remember. LYSIDAMUS This city doesn't need to pass a decree to declare you one smart guy. 525
I'm off to the forum. Take care. I'll be back soon.

ALCESIMUS Have a nice walk.

LYSIDAMUS Oh, and teach your house the alphabet.

ALCESIMUS The alphabet? LYSIDAMUS Yes, especially "M" and "T"!

56. His name may mean "Helper" in Greek.

57. A reference to a Roman army's march (fourth-century BCE) to the Etruscan town of Sutrium that had become proverbial for a forced march in which soldiers brought their own food supplies (the role of the blackbird is uncertain). Here the proverb is mock-grandiosely applied to the stream of slaves flowing from Alcesimus' house to the neighbors' in the service of Lysidamus' (doomed) erotic expedition.

ALCESIMUS Yes, "empty house." My oh my, you're just too witty for your own good.

LYSIDAMUS Hey, why bother being in love if you can't also be suave and sophisticated?
Now don't make me have to come looking for you.

530 ALCESIMUS I'll be right here at home.

SCENE 11

(*Cleostrata enters from Lysidamus' house.*)

CLEOSTRATA So that's why my husband kept insisting
That I run over and invite my neighbor here!
It was so he could free up an empty nest for himself to get a taste of Casina!
Now that's exactly why I won't be inviting her at all.
535 Those impotent old goats just lost their big opportunity.
But look who's coming: the "pillar of the community," the "sentinel of the senate"!
It's none other than my distinguished neighbor, the procurer of my husband's love nest.
He's not worth the salt he's made of!

ALCESIMUS Odd my wife hasn't been invited next door yet.
She's all dressed up and has been waiting a long time for an
540 invitation.
But look: here comes the invite. Hi, Cleostrata.

CLEOSTRATA Hello to you, Alcesimus.
Where's your wife? ALCESIMUS She's inside waiting for an invitation from you.
Your husband asked me to send her over to help out with the preparations there.
Want me to call her? CLEOSTRATA No, let her be. I'm sure she's busy. ALCESIMUS No, she's not.

CLEOSTRATA Never mind. I don't want to bother her.
545 I'll see her later.

ALCESIMUS Aren't you preparing for a wedding over there?

CLEOSTRATA I've got it all under control.

ALCESIMUS Don't you need some help? CLEOSTRATA I've got plenty of that at home. I'll visit
Her after the wedding. Goodbye. Give her my regards. (*starts walking to her house*)

ALCESIMUS (*to the audience*) What am I supposed to do now? I've made a complete disgrace of myself,
All because of that worthless and toothless old goat! 550
He dragged me into this and made me promise my wife's help,
As if she were some sort of plate-licker![58] That contemptible human being,
Promising me his wife would invite her over! And now she doesn't even need her!
I wouldn't be surprised if our neighbor lady got wind of the whole plot.
Hmmm . . . but when I think about it, I suppose 555
She'd have made a federal case out of it if she was on to us.
I'll go in and put that old barge of mine back in mothballs. (*exits*)

CLEOSTRATA (*to the audience*) Now he's beautifully befuddled! The way these old fools fret!
If only that worthless and decrepit husband of mine would show up
For a dose of the same medicine I made his friend swallow! 560
I'd love to set the two of them at each other's throat.
Look, here he comes now. What a distinguished expression! As if he were respectable!

SCENE 12

(*Lysidamus enters from the forum wing.*)

LYSIDAMUS (*to the audience*) What possibly could be stupider
Than for a man in love to go to the forum
On the very day his lover awaits him? 565
That's exactly how stupid I was when I squandered the day

58. I.e., as if she were a slave or a hanger-on at a party.

In court to help a foolish relative of mine.
It gives me great pleasure to say he lost his case—
That'll teach him to drag me into court as his advocate on a day like today!
570 The way I see it, if you need a lawyer,
You'd better ask him first
If he's got his wits about him.
If he says no, just send the witless fellow—such as myself—home!
But look, there's the wife out in front of the house. Ouch!
575 She'd have to be deaf not to have heard all this.

CLEOSTRATA (*aside*) Oh I heard all right, and with great cost to you!

LYSIDAMUS I'll go over to her. How are you, my little joy?

CLEOSTRATA I was just waiting for you. LYSIDAMUS Everything all set now?
Did you bring our neighbor over here
To help you? CLEOSTRATA I invited her like you
580 told me,
But your best buddy next door
Got into some argument with his wife
And refused to let her come over to help me.

LYSIDAMUS That's all your fault! You should have turned on the charm!

CLEOSTRATA Charm is what whores turn on for other women's
585 husbands,
My dear, and is not part of a proper wife's duties.
You can go get her yourself. There are things inside
That require my immediate attention, my dear hubby.
LYSIDAMUS Get right on them then.
CLEOSTRATA All right.
(*aside*) He's in a terrible fright!
I'll make sure that old horn-dog is completely
590 miserable today!

SCENE 13

(*Alcesimus enters from his house.*)

ALCESIMUS Let's see if lover-boy is back from the forum.
The nerve of that crazy old coot making a fool out of me and my wife!
But there he is, right in front of his house. Hey, I was just coming to see you.

LYSIDAMUS Right back at you! You're so worthless! What do you have to say for yourself?
What did I tell you to do, what did I *beg* you to do?
ALCESIMUS What's that? 595

LYSIDAMUS Nice job of clearing your house out for me!
Oh, and thanks for bringing your wife over to our place!
And thanks to you, I'm screwed, and so is my big opportunity!

ALCESIMUS Go screw yourself! You told me your wife
Would invite my wife over to your house. 600

LYSIDAMUS Yes, and she says she invited her, but you said
She couldn't come. ALCESIMUS Is that so? She told me
Herself that she didn't need her to help.

LYSIDAMUS Is that so? She just told me herself to invite her.

ALCESIMUS Is that so? Ask me if I care. LYSIDAMUS Is that so? Oh, you're killing me! ALCESIMUS Is that so? Good! 605
I'll just hang around for a while. I want to—

LYSIDAMUS Is that so? ALCESIMUS —cause you some trouble! LYSIDAMUS Is that so? I'll gladly return the favor!
But you'll never have the last "Is that so?" today!

ALCESIMUS Is that so? May the gods damn you once and for all!

LYSIDAMUS Are you going to send your wife to my house or not? 610

ALCESIMUS You can escort her to hell yourself, along with
Your whole gang, your wife and your girlfriend included!
Get lost and let me handle this—I'll tell my wife
To come over to your place through the garden. (*exits*)

615 LYSIDAMUS (*to the audience*) Now that's being a true friend.
Whatever in the world could have jinxed my affair?
Whatever could I have done to offend Venus[59] so much,
And to create so many delays for a lover like me?
Hey!

620 What's all that shouting coming out of our house?

SCENE 14 (SONG)

(*Pardalisca rushes frantically from Lysidamus' house.*)

PARDALISCA[60] I'm dead, I'm done, I'm totally dead!
My heart's paralyzed from panic, my poor limbs are trembling!
I don't know where to seek help, shelter, safety, or support!
I haven't so much as a clue where to look.

625 Such strange events I've seen inside the house—
Boldness, brazenness never seen before!
Beware, Cleostrata, flee from her now,
So her rage doesn't destroy you for good!
She's out of her mind! Snatch the sword away from her!

LYSIDAMUS What's scared her to death and made her run out

630 here like this?
Pardalisca!

PARDALISCA Alas for me! What sound takes up residence
in my ears?[61]

LYSIDAMUS Look back here at me. PARDALISCA Oh,
master— LYSIDAMUS What's wrong?
PARDALISCA I'm done for!

59. For the goddess Venus, see Appendix.

60. Her song parodies similarly dramatic entrances by distraught female characters in tragedy. For Plautine comedy's engagement with tragedy, see Sheets, G.A., "Plautus and Early Tragedy." *Illinois Classical Studies* 8 (1983): 195–209.

61. A parody of tragic language.

LYSIDAMUS Done for? PARDALISCA Yes, and so are you!
LYSIDAMUS Me? How?

PARDALISCA Woe to you! LYSIDAMUS No, that's "woe to *you*." PARDALISCA Catch me before I fall!

LYSIDAMUS Whatever it is, tell me this instant!
PARDALISCA Please hold my breast, 635–6
And fan me with your cloak! LYSIDAMUS Now this has got me nervous! 637–8
Unless she's buried her nose too deeply in Bacchus' undiluted bouquet.[62] 639–40

PARDALISCA Touch my face, hold me! (*seductively*)
LYSIDAMUS Oh, go to hell!
And take your face, breast, and last breath along with you!
If you don't tell me right now what's going on,
I'll take this stick and bash your brains out, you snake!
You've been yanking my chain all this time, bitch! 645

PARDALISCA Oh, master! LYSIDAMUS Yes, my slave?
PARDALISCA You are far too cruel! LYSIDAMUS You have no idea about that! 646–7
Out with whatever's going on, and keep it short!
What was all the commotion about in there?
PARDALISCA Listen and I'll tell you.
It was horrible, simply horrible what just happened in our house! 650
Your maid has behaved in a manner so
Unbecoming of a young lady raised in Athens!

LYSIDAMUS What'd she do? PARDALISCA Fear's foot has tripped up my tongue.[63]

62. For the god Bacchus, see Appendix. Ancient wine had a relatively high alcohol content, and it was considered uncivilized to drink it without adding water (cf. *Lysistrata*, note 49). The traditionalist *paterfamilias* took great pains to prevent women under his power from consuming alcohol in his household.

63. Paratragic (cf. note 61 above).

LYSIDAMUS Is there any way you can tell me what's up?
PARDALISCA Yes.
655 Your maid, the one you want the foreman to marry,
Inside just now she— LYSIDAMUS What's she doing in there?

PARDALISCA She's chosen the worst possible female role-model,
She's threatening her husband, his life—

LYSIDAMUS What? PARDALISCA Ahhh!
LYSIDAMUS What is it? PARDALISCA Yes, his life, she wants to take his life!

And the sword— LYSIDAMUS What?
PARDALISCA The sword— LYSIDAMUS What about
660 the sword?

PARDALISCA It's in her hands. LYSIDAMUS Oh no, what for?

PARDALISCA She's prowling all about the house.
No one dares to get near her, they're all cowering
Under chests and beds amid all the commotion.

665 LYSIDAMUS That's it. I'm as good as dead!
What sickness has overcome her so quickly?

PARDALISCA Insanity. LYSIDAMUS Who could be more screwed than I am?

PARDALISCA If you only knew what's she's saying—

LYSIDAMUS I have to know! What'd she say?
PARDALISCA Just listen!
670 She swore by every last god and goddess
She'd murder the man who shares her bed tonight!

LYSIDAMUS Murder ME?

PARDALISCA What? None of this has anything to do with you.
LYSIDAMUS Damn!

PARDALISCA You've got no business with her, right?
673–4 LYSIDAMUS I meant to say "murder my foreman."

PARDALISCA (*aside*) Now he's wandering way off the
675 beaten path!

Lysidamus She isn't threatening me, is she?
Pardalisca Her anger's
Directed at you more than anyone else.
Lysidamus Why? **Pardalisca** Because you're the one having her married to Olympio.
She says neither you nor her husband will see the next day. 678–9
I was sent here to tell you
To be on guard against her. **Lysidamus** Oh me oh my,
I'm dead now! **Pardalisca** (*aside*) As you should be! 682–3

Lysidamus (*aside*) Has there ever been an old lover as
Unlucky as me!

Pardalisca (*aside*) I'm just playing with him for kicks! 685
Everything I told him happened was pure fiction!
My mistress and the woman next door are running the show,
And I'm only here to have some fun with him!
Lysidamus Hey there, Pardalisca!

Pardalisca Yes? **Lysidamus** There's something—
Pardalisca What? **Lysidamus** —I want to ask you.

Pardalisca You're holding me up. **Lysidamus** And you're bringing me way down! 690
Does Casina still have a sword?

Pardalisca No, not exactly—she has two swords!
Lysidamus Why two? **Pardalisca** One to kill you first,
And the other one is for the foreman.

Lysidamus (*aside*) Who among the living is as dead as I am!
It's time for me to put on some body armor. 695
What about my wife? Why didn't she take them away from her?

Pardalisca Nobody dares to get close to her.
Lysidamus How about trying a little persuasion?
Pardalisca Your wife tried,
But Casina says there's no way she's putting them down
Until she's assured she isn't marrying the foreman.

LYSIDAMUS She'll marry him today, and just because she
700 doesn't want to!
There's no reason I won't finish what I started,
And have her marry me—
I meant marry the foreman! PARDALISCA You keep
making that mistake.

LYSIDAMUS Fear keeps tripping up my words.
705 But please tell my wife that I'm *begging*
Her to beg Casina to put down the sword so I can come back
inside!

PARDALISCA I'll tell her.

LYSIDAMUS Don't just tell her—*beg her.*[64] PARDALISCA Yes,
I'll beg her too. LYSIDAMUS And use all your patented
charms.
Listen up: if you pull this off, there's a new pair of sandals in it
for you,
708–12 A gold ring for your finger, and lots of other goodies.

PARDALISCA I'll give it my best.

LYSIDAMUS Make sure you succeed!

715 PARDALISCA I'm off right now,
If you're done. (*exits*)

LYSIDAMUS Move along and do as I say.
Look, it's my partner-in-crime, back from shopping!
And he's leading a parade!

SCENE 15 (SONG)

(*Olympio returns from the forum with Citrio the cook, his assistants, and groceries.*)

OLYMPIO Hey, sticky-fingers, keep those pricks of yours in line!
720 CITRIO Why'd you call them pricks?

64. In reality the *paterfamilias* could exact absolute power over members of his household, and so Lysidamus' solicitousness here in asking his slave to ask his wife to get control of Casina is absurdly comic, but also demonstrates the extent of Cleostrata's control of the household: see further Introductory Essay 168–171.

Olympio Because they latch on to everything like prickly bushes. And if you pull back,
They rip you to pieces! When they're hired, they bankrupt their bosses! 721–2

Citrio Come on now! **Olympio** It's my master! I'll make myself all high and mighty and meet him!

Lysidamus Greetings, my good man. **Olympio** That I am. **Lysidamus** What's up? **Olympio** You're horny. I'm hungry and thirsty. 724–5

Lysidamus Quite an elaborate entrance you made there! **Olympio** Ah, indeed, on this day . . .

Lysidamus Just hold on, however great you may think you are— **Olympio** Pee-yew! That's some stench coming from your mouth![65]

Lysidamus What's the matter? **Olympio** Phew—that! **Lysidamus** Stand still. **Olympio** You're so annoying!

Lysidamus I can be painfully annoying to you,
And I will be if you don't stand still. **Olympio** Great Zeus![66] 730
Keep away from me, unless
You want me to hurl right now!

Lysidamus Wait. **Olympio** What now? Who *is* this man?

Lysidamus Your master. **Olympio** What master? **Lysidamus** The one whose slave you are. **Olympio** Me, a slave?

Lysidamus Yes, and mine. **Olympio** I'm not a free man then? 735–6
Think, think again— **Lysidamus** Now just stand still! **Olympio** Stop it!

65. The old man's halitosis sharply contrasts with the sweet and aromatic scent associated with the young Casina (see note 23 above and line 1018 in the epilogue).

66. Lysidamus and Olympio here intersperse broken Greek phrases with their Latin. This apparently was commonly done in (real-life) colloquial Latin, but there is also metacomic play here in that Athenian characters are made to pepper their Latin with what should be their native Greek (cf. Introduction 17–19).

LYSIDAMUS Okay, I'm your slave. OLYMPIO Perfect!
LYSIDAMUS At your service, my dearest Olympikins,
My father, my protector[67]— OLYMPIO There! Now you're making sense.

740 LYSIDAMUS Yes, I'm all yours.

OLYMPIO What do I need with a slave as worthless as you?

LYSIDAMUS What now? When do I get my refreshments?

OLYMPIO When dinner is cooked.

LYSIDAMUS Then move inside with this crew!

745 OLYMPIO Inside now, hurry now, double-time, all of you!
746–7 I'll be in soon enough myself. Let's make it a scrumptious feast,
All elegant and spiffy. I've got no stomach for barbarian[68] slop![69]
Still there? LYSIDAMUS You go. I'm staying out here.
749–50 OLYMPIO What's holding you back?

LYSIDAMUS She said Casina's got a sword,
And she plans to kill us both with it in there!

OLYMPIO Whatever! Let her have her sword.
They're talking trash! I know these women well,
754a And they're all bad apples.
Come into the house with me now. LYSIDAMUS I smell
755 trouble!
You go in first and see what's happening in there

OLYMPIO My life is just as valuable as yours.
Come along with me! LYSIDAMUS If you insist—in we go.

67. An absurd inversion of master/slave power relations.

68. From the nominally Greek perspective of Roman comedy, "barbarian" (*barbaricus*) humorously refers to Romans and Italians.

69. Spinach, exemplary of simple fare. The joke turns on both a Roman belief in a Greek feeling of cultural superiority (here in cuisine) and the Romans' own idealization of themselves as practical and frugal in comparison with Greeks.

SCENE 16

(*Pardalisca enters and reports what is going on inside Lysidamus' house.*)

PARDALISCA I swear, there's never been a festival
At Olympia[70] or Nemea[71] so full of fun as this farce 760
Being performed inside at the expense
Of our old master and our foreman Olympio!
They're sprinting all over the house.
The old man is crashing around the kitchen, harassing the cooks:
"How about *today*? If you're going to serve it, serve it now! 765
Hurry up! Dinner should already be done."
Meanwhile, the foreman is walking around with a garland[72] on his head,
All decked out in white, and spiffed-out sharp.
The two ladies are in the bedroom getting the son's wingman
Into his costume, so he can give his hand in marriage to our foreman! 770
And it's all so cleverly concealed, as if they didn't have any idea
How this plot's going to end! And the cooks are playing their part perfectly,
Tipping over pots, dousing out the fire under the ladies' direction,
And all to starve out the old geezer! The ladies
Hope to drive the old man out of the house without that dinner, 775
So they can stretch out their stomachs all by themselves.
Those women are a pair of gourmandesses:
They could down a whole boatload of chow![73]
But look, the door's opening!

70. For Olympia, see note 21 above.

71. Nemea, a sanctuary of Zeus on the northeast Peloponnese, hosted one of the four major panhellenic religious and athletic festivals.

72. I.e., as part of his wedding apparel.

73. For the central themes of satiety and consumption, see Introductory Essay 171.

SCENE 17

(*Lysidamus exits from his house and meets Pardalisca outside.*)

LYSIDAMUS (*to Cleostrata inside*) I'll have dinner at the farm, my
780 dear,
But you two should dine here once supper's ready.
I'll escort the newlyweds out to the farm.
There are a lot of shady characters out there,
And I don't want any of them grabbing her. Have a nice time,
785 And do send the two of them right out.
We need to get there before dark. I'll be back tomorrow—
And tomorrow, my dear, I'll hold a party here.

PARDALISCA (*aside*) Everything's going according to plan: the ladies are kicking the old guy
Out of the house without dinner! LYSIDAMUS What are you doing here?

PARDALISCA I'm on a mission for my mistress.
790 LYSIDAMUS Seriously? PARDALISCA Seriously.

LYSIDAMUS You're spying, aren't you? PARDALISCA Nope. LYSIDAMUS Move along, damn it!
Here you are dawdling *outside* while everyone else is bustling around *inside*! PARDALISCA I'm going in.

LYSIDAMUS Yes, please do, you queen bitch!
Is she gone? Now I can say what I want:
By golly, a horny man may be plenty hungry, but it's not food
795 he needs!
But look, here comes the foreman with a garland and a torch:[74]
My comrade, my colleague, my co-husband!

SCENE 18

(*Olympio enters from Lysidamus' house.*)

OLYMPIO Go on now, flute-player! When they bring the new bride out here,

74. In Roman wedding ceremony, the bride was led to her husband's house by torchlight procession.

Fill this whole street with the sweet sound of my wedding song,
Hymen, O Hymen, O Hymenaeus![75] 800

Lysidamus How goes it, my savior? **Olympio** I'm starved and there's no salvation in that!

Lysidamus And I'm madly in love! **Olympio** And I don't care at all. You're full of love, all right!
My empty guts have been grumbling all day!

Lysidamus Now just what is keeping those slowpokes in there so long?
It's on purpose: the more I hurry them, the faster I get nowhere! 805

Olympio Let's strike up the old wedding song again. That'll bring them out.

Lysidamus And I'll accompany you, since we're co-bridegrooms.

Lysidamus and Olympio Hymen, O Hymen, O Hymenaeus!

Lysidamus Poor, poor miserable me! I may split my gut open from singing
That wedding song before I get a chance to split apart[76] what I really want. 810

Olympio Geeze! If you were a stallion, there'd be no chance of taming you!

Lysidamus How's that? **Olympio** You're way too hard to handle. **Lysidamus** But you've never even taken me for a ride.

Olympio Uggh! May the gods put the kibosh on that! But the door's creaking. They're coming out.

Lysidamus The gods do want to save me!

75. A Greek wedding refrain. Hymen or Hymenaeus came to be thought of as a personified god of weddings.

76. For the sexual meaning, cf. 326 above.

SCENE 19 (SONG)

(The "bride" Chalinus, Pardalisca, Cleostrata, and Myrrhina enter from Lysidamus' house.)

PARDALISCA (*to the women*) He-Casina[77] has given off a stench from far, far away!

815 Gently lift your feet above the threshold, tender bride;
Safely commence this journey—
And stomp upon your husband always![78]

819–20 May all power be yours to crush and defeat him,

821–2 Your voice, your command perched on high to beat him!
His job is to fill your closets, yours to empty his pockets!
Strive to deceive him, by night and by day!

825 OLYMPIO The slightest slip-up and she'll be sorry!

LYSIDAMUS Be quiet! OLYMPIO No!
LYSIDAMUS What's your problem? OLYMPIO A nasty woman's giving nasty advice!

LYSIDAMUS You'll undo everything I've done for me!
Can't you see that's what they want?

PARDALISCA Come on, Olympio,

830 Take your wife from us, just as you want to.

OLYMPIO Give my wife to me right now—if you're ever going to give her to me.

LYSIDAMUS Go inside then! CLEOSTRATA Please be gentle with this gentle virgin. OLYMPIO Yeah, sure.
Goodbye. LYSIDAMUS Move along now.
CLEOSTRATA Goodbye then. (*the women exit*)

LYSIDAMUS Is my wife gone yet? OLYMPIO No worries—

835 she's inside. LYSIDAMUS Woohoo!
A free man at last now!
My little sweetheart, my honey-bun, my teensy little breath of fresh-air. OLYMPIO Hey,

77. The masculine form, Casinus, of Casina.

78. Pardalisca parodies wedding ritual here by turning the Roman ideal of a wife's subservience and obedience to her husband on its head. See further Introductory Essay 170–171.

A word to the wise: She's mine! **Lysidamus** Yes, but I get the first fruits.

Olympio Hold this torch. **Lysidamus** No, I'd rather hold *her*. (*hugs the bride*) 840

Mighty Venus,[79] that was some gift you granted me when
You let me hold her! **Olympio** (*embraces the bride*) Oh,
Your sweet little body, so soft,
My teeny-weeny wifey-poo. Ow! What the—

Lysidamus What's the matter? **Olympio** She just stomped on my foot 845

Like an elephant! **Lysidamus** Quiet, you!
Her breasts are softer than a cloud.

Olympio What a pretty little nipple—Ouch!

Lysidamus What's wrong? **Olympio** She just slammed me in the chest. And it was a battering ram, not an elbow!

Lysidamus Why are you so rough when you touch her? 850

Make love to her, not war—follow my lead.
Ouch! **Olympio** What's the matter?
Lysidamus Damn, she's strong!
She almost knocked me out with that elbow!
Olympio Now that you mention knocking her up—

Lysidamus Let's just go in the house. **Olympio** Come along now, my pretty little pretty!

SCENE 20 (SONG)

(*Myrrhina, Pardalisca, and Cleostrata enter from Lysidamus' house.*)

Myrrhina What fine entertainment we've enjoyed inside! 855

And now we're out here on the street to watch the wedding festival.
Oh my, I've never laughed so much in my life
And don't think I'll ever laugh like that again!

Pardalisca I'm dying to know what the new He-bride is doing with his new husband!

79. For the goddess Venus, see Appendix.

860 MYRRHINA No playwright has ever devised a better
Plot than this clever production of ours![80]

CLEOSTRATA I can't wait to see the old man come out with his brains beaten in!
Surely he's earned the undisputed title of WORLD'S MOST WORTHLESS OLD MAN:
Not even his pimp of a neighbor
865 Who set up his love-shack
Can challenge him for that.
Get in line here, Pardalisca,
To mock each man as he comes out.

PARDALISCA My pleasure, as always.

CLEOSTRATA Watch them from here and tell us everything they
870–1 do in there!
Right behind me here now, dear. MYRRHINA Right, so then you can speak
Out as boldly as you feel like. CLEOSTRATA Quiet!
The door creaked.

SCENE 21 (SONG)

(*Olympio rushes out from Lysidamus' house.*)

OLYMPIO I've got nowhere to run, nowhere to hide, and no-
875 where to hide my disgraceful hide!
This shameful marriage of ours! My master and I have really done it
This time! I don't know if I'm more ashamed or more afraid,
But I do know the two of us are idiots! This kind of stupidity is all new to me:
I'm ashamed to admit I've never been so ashamed before now. Listen up and I'll relate
What happened to me. It's worth your trouble to listen to the
880 whole mess I made inside!
I led my new bride inside and took her straight

80. For the women's empowering and metacomic role as playwrights, see Introductory Essay 169–171.

To the back room. It was as dark as a well in there.
The old man was off somewhere, so I says to her, "lie down!"
I get her all situated, I prop her up and talk super sweet to her,
Because I wanted to beat the old man to the first fruits. 885
I had to start slow since I was constantly looking out for him.
So I ask her for a little kiss and a little foreplay.
But she just pushes my hand away
And doesn't even let me kiss her!
So I start to move things along, as I'm dying for a whiff of Casina. 890–1
I decide this is *my* duty, not the old man's, and so I bolt the door to keep him from breaking up the party. 892–3

CLEOSTRATA (*to Pardalisca*) Okay, go up to him now.

PARDALISCA Now where's that new little bride of yours?

OLYMPIO Damn, I'm dead! She knows everything!

PARDALISCA You'd better come clean 895
With all the details. What's going on in there? What's Casina up to?
So is she obeying your every wish like a good wife should? 896

OLYMPIO I'm too ashamed to say. PARDALISCA Come on—details!
Just as you started. OLYMPIO No, I'm too ashamed! 897–8

PARDALISCA Suck it up! 899–900
So what happened after you got into bed?

OLYMPIO It's disgraceful! PARDALISCA It'll be a good lesson for everyone here to hear.

OLYMPIO It's all so . . . [81] PARDALISCA Stop stalling. Continue. OLYMPIO When . . . I reached down there . . .

PARDALISCA Yes? OLYMPIO Uggh! 904–5

PARDALISCA Yes? OLYMPIO It was horrible!

PARDALISCA What was it? OLYMPIO It was huge . . .
I was afraid she had a sword. I started to look for it . . .
. . . and as I'm groping around for the sword, I get hold of a handle.
But it was no sword: the shaft would have been a *lot* colder. 910

81. The text of 903–908 is mutilated.

PARDALISCA Keep going! OLYMPIO I really can't, I'm so ashamed. PARDALISCA Was it a radish?
OLYMPIO No. PARDALISCA A cucumber possibly?

OLYMPIO No, it definitely wasn't any variety of vegetable at all!
But whatever is was, it'd never suffered any kind of damage.
All I can say is, it was thriving and full-grown—

PARDALISCA So then what happened? More details!

915–6 OLYMPIO Then I says to her, "Please, Casina,

917–8 My little wifey-poo, please don't treat your husband like this.
It's not right to do me this way

920 After all I had to do to get you."
She doesn't say a peep and wraps her dress tightly around that thing
Only you women have got. When I see that pass is blocked,
I request to enter by another route. I try to turn her over[82]
With my arms . . . still not a peep out of her . . .

925 I start to move up for a . . .
And then she . . .

MYRRHINA What a delightful story!

OLYMPIO And for a kiss and . . .
A bristly beard pricks my lips!
I jumped right up on my knees, and she bashes my chest with

930 both of her feet!
I tumble headfirst out of bed, and she jumps down and starts pounding my face!
I got up and ran without saying a word and wearing what you're looking at,
And thinking I should let the old man have a taste of that same medicine.[83] PARDALISCA Fantastic!

82. The text of 923–928 is mutilated.

83. While the physical mistreatment described as being suffered by Olympio and Lysidamus is humorously hyperbolic and well deserved in their case, it also indirectly points to the violence a slave like Casina might have experienced at the hands of her rapists.

But where's your little cloak? **Olympio** I left it inside.
Pardalisca Well now, is that enough trickery for the two of you? **Olympio** Yup, 935
We both deserved it. Look, the doors creaked. She better not still be after me!

SCENE 22 (SONG)

(*Lysidamus runs out of his house, obviously ruffled and missing his walking staff.*)

Lysidamus Oh, the disgrace! I'm burning up with shame,
And I've got no idea what to do in this mess,
Nor how I can even look my wife in the face—
I'm so dead! 940
All my disgrace is out in public, all of poor me
Is totally dead!
. . . my wife's got me by the throat, caught red-handed,[84]
. . . with no possible way to clear my name.
. . . poor, poor cloak-less me, 945
. . . thanks to my not-so-secret nuptials!
. . . the way I see it,
. . . it's best for me
. . . to go face my wife inside,
And to offer her up my sorry hide for punishment. 950
Anyone of you care to fill in for me here?
There's no hope for my shoulders inside that house! 952–3
Apart from playing the bad slave[85] and hitting the road,
I'm fresh out of ideas. 955
Think that's all nonsense?
Truth of it is, I'll be beaten:
I may deserve it but that doesn't mean I like it!
I think maybe I'll take off this way—

84. The text of 943–949 is mutilated.

85. An indication of how drastically the household's social hierarchy has been inverted (cf. note 67 above and Introductory Essay 168–170).

Chalinus (*heard from offstage*)
960 Hey, stop right there, lover!

Lysidamus I'm dead! Someone's calling me. Better pretend
961–2 I didn't hear—

SCENE 23

(*Chalinus, who has Lysidamus' walking-stick and cloak, joins the group onstage.*)

Chalinus Yoo-hoo! Where are you, my Greek-loving[86] friend?
If you're planning on a little foreplay with me, now's a good time.
Oh, please do come back to bed. I swear by Hercules,[87] *you're*
965 *a dead man*!
I've found a very solid judge to settle things out of court. (*brandishes the walking-stick*)

Lysidamus (*aside*) I am a dead man! This guy and his club[88] are going to un-man my man parts!
Hmmm. That way dead-ends with a groin-wreck. I'd better go this way.

Cleostrata Well hello, lover-boy. **Lysidamus** (*aside*) Oh no, face to face with the wife!
970 I'm stuck between a rock and a hard place with nowhere to run
Wolves on one side, dogs on the other—and the wolf's got a club!
Damn! Guess I'd better change the ancient proverb
And go this way: the path of the bitch will be better, right?

Myrrhina How's it going, bigamist? **Cleostrata** What's with this get-up, my dear husband?

86. The Latin here says "practicing the customs of Massilia" [= modern Marseilles]. This region was colonized by Greeks at an early date and gained a reputation for decadence. The men there were stereotyped as ready to submit to (pathic) homoerotic acts.

87. As men, but not women, swear by Hercules (cf. Appendix) in Roman comedy, Chalinus speaks in his male persona here, whereas his words to this point may have been delivered in falsetto (cf. 977–978).

88. Lysidamus in his fearfulness here (as in 971) refers to his own walking-stick (*scipio*) as a club. Cf. note 89 below.

What've you done with your walking-stick and your cloak?[89] 975

Myrrhina I do believe our adulterous friend lost them while he was shtupping Casina!

Lysidamus I'm so dead. **Chalinus** Aren't we going back to bed? *I'm Casina.*[90] **Lysidamus** Go to hell!

Chalinus Don't you love me? **Cleostrata** Answer me now: what happened to your cloak?

Lysidamus As Hercules is my witness, my dear, some Bacchants[91]— **Cleostrata** Bacchants? **Lysidamus** Yes, Bacchants, my dear wife—Yes, Bacchants for sure— **Myrrhina** That's nonsense and he knows it!

There aren't any Bacchic rites now![92]

Lysidamus Yes, I forgot. 980

Still, the Bacchants— **Cleostrata** What about the Bacchants? **Lysidamus** Well if that can't be so—

Cleostrata You're absolutely terrified! **Lysidamus** Me? Nonsense! **Cleostrata** But you're awfully pale! 982

(*Apart from a few letters in the manuscripts, 983–990 are almost entirely lost; Lysidamus continues to defend himself, however ineffectively.*)

Olympio It's all because of *his* shamelessness that I was made into such a horrible joke! 991

Lysidamus Why don't you shut up? **Olympio** No I won't shut up! You're the one

That begged and begged me to get married to Casina,

89. The walking-stick (cf. note 88 above) is a distinctive feature of the standard costume of the old man (*senex*) in comedy and emblematizes his power as *paterfamilias*. Lysidamus' loss of his cloak in the homoerotic tussle with Chalinus indicates that he now in effect appears onstage in his underwear. Cf. note 97 below.

90. It is easy to imagine Chalinus using falsetto here: cf. note 87 above.

91. Female worshippers (= maenads) of Bacchus, for whom, see Appendix.

92. The Roman senate outlawed the worship of Bacchus in 186 BCE as a threat to public order and morality. Apropos of what has just taken place between Lysidamus and Chalinus inside, opponents of Bacchic worship alleged that its female worshippers dominated men in the cult and forced them to engage in sex acts with each other. The reference to the senate's emergency resolution here dates the play to sometime shortly after this event. See further Introductory Essay 163.

And all because of your lust! **Lysidamus** I did that?

994–5 **Olympio** Nooooh, it was Hector of Troy![93]

Lysidamus Yeah? Well, he would have pounded you hard. Did I really do what you say?

Cleostrata You even ask? **Lysidamus** If I did those things, then, damn it, I did wrong!

Cleostrata Go back in the house. I'll be sure to remind you about it if your memory fails.

Lysidamus Not necessary at all, really! I'll just take your word for it.

But, my dear wife, do forgive your husband now. You ask her
1000 too, Myrrhina!
If ever again I lust for Casina, or just start lusting for her,
Or, all lusting for her set aside, I do anything like this in the future,
You have every right to hang me up and whip me to shreds. Okay, my dear wife?[94]

Myrrhina So help me Castor,[95] I think you should forgive him, Cleostrata. **Cleostrata** All right, I'll do it.

But the only reason I'm going to grant him forgiveness this
1005 time
Is that this play is long—so let's not make it any longer.[96]

Lysidamus You're not mad? **Cleostrata** No, I'm not mad. **Lysidamus** I have your word on that? **Cleostrata** Yes.

Lysidamus Is there anyone in the world who has a more charming wife than I do?

93. Legendary Trojan hero and rival of Achilles in Homer's *Iliad*. Olympio is being extremely sarcastic.

94. That Lysidamus pledges to undergo a torture usually reserved for slaves further emphasizes his subservience to his wife here. Cf. Introductory Essay 168–171.

95. Only women swear by the god Castor (for whom, see *Lysistrata*, note 31) in Roman comedy.

96. As this sort of decision is one only a director or playwright makes, Cleostrata's metatheatrical jest here signals her complete control over the play: see further Introduction 18–19.

CLEOSTRATA All right, give him back his walking-stick and cloak.[97] CHALINUS Take 'em, if you want to.
But, damn it, I am one woefully wronged bride: 1010
I married two men, and neither of 'em did me his marital duty!

EPILOGUE

Spectators, it's my job to tell you what will happen inside:[98]
This Casina will be found out to be the daughter of the next-door neighbor here,
And she'll marry our young master, Euthynicus.[99]
Now the proper thing for you all to do is to give us the props we deserve. 1015
If you do, you'll win the whore you've always wanted without your wife knowing.[100]
But those of you who don't applaud with everything you've got
Will find a he-goat soaked in sewage, and not that dream whore, in your bed!

97. The return of these items marks the restoration of Lysidamus as *paterfamilias* (cf. note 89 above and Introductory Essay 171).

98. It is uncertain who delivers the epilogue; Chalinus, who last spoke, perhaps is the best candidate.

99. The process of revealing Casina's true identity probably constituted an entire recognition scene in the Greek source-play by Diphilus that has been suppressed by Plautus.

100. The epilogist's jesting here suggests a return to more conventionally Roman marital relations between husbands and wives in the post-play world. Cf. Introductory Essay 171.

Terence's
HECYRA

Hecyra generally is considered to be Terence's least successful play, in that he had to put it on a third time after two earlier failures. As the prologue for the second performance has it (Prologue I, 4–5), competing festival entertainments distracted the audience and ruined the play's première (cf. Prologue II, 33–36). According to the second surviving prologue (39–42), delivered on the occasion of the play's third performance, confusion, this time reputedly created by rumors of gladiator displays, similarly led to that play's disbandment. Whatever the veracity of the particulars, the multiple prologues and performances of *Hecyra* suggest that the play, at least initially, was not universally well received by contemporary audiences. Perhaps, as Terence might want us to believe, *Hecyra* was too highbrow for many festivalgoers, especially those who were "utterly dazed and dazzled/By a tightrope walker" (4–5). More to the point, audiences might have found *Hecyra* to be an unusually challenging play that presented many difficulties for first-time spectators. We have no way of determining whether or not Terence changed the play in response to its initially negative reception, but the version we possess was performed in 160 BCE, perhaps at the *Ludi Romani*, an annual festival occurring in September.[1]

Many modern critics have found the plot of *Hecyra* to be unduly complicated, its dramatic pace laborious, and its unusually extensive (for New Comedy) employment of suspense awkward. A plot summary illustrates the difficulties. As we learn fully in the play's second scene, Pamphilus, a young man still under his father Laches' power, has been compelled by the latter to marry Philumena, the girl next door (114–124). The play's opening conversation (Scene 1) between two prostitutes, Philotis and Syra, who work in the neighborhood brothel, revealed that prior to the marriage Pamphilus had maintained a long-term and seemingly committed relationship with their colleague Bacchis. Pamphilus' gossipy slave Parmeno joins the two prostitutes (Scene 2) and informs us that Pamphilus at first refused to consummate the marriage and continued to see Bacchis; we later learn (393–394) that the couple was sexless for the first two months of the marriage and has been married for seven months in all at the play's start. According to Parmeno, Pamphilus grew impatient with Bacchis' changed behavior following his marriage and simultaneously came to feel affection for his forbearing and obliging wife (158–170). Sometime after the couple began conjugal relations, Pamphilus was called away to the island of Imbros to deal with a family inheritance, the details of which are delayed to 459ff. Pamphilus is expected to return home soon, but during his absence Philumena, who has been living in her in-laws' home,

1. For the proposal that the depiction of *Hecyra* as a failure is merely a rhetorical/literary strategy and that all Terence's prologues "can be read between the lines as mirroring the plays they present but apparently sideline," see Gowers, E., "The Plot Thickens: Hidden Outlines in Terence's Prologues." *Ramus* 33 (2004): 150–166. For detailed analysis of the multiple prologues of *Hecyra*, see further Lada-Richards (2004).

appears to have had a sudden falling out with Pamphilus' mother Sostrata (177–189), and Philumena has returned to her parents' home, where she is said to be ill. These two scenes (58–197) that substitute for an expository prologue have thus told us surprisingly little and only raised various questions.

Laches, who has been living at his country home, has gotten wind of the alleged quarrel between mother- and daughter-in-law (presumably through reports by household slaves such as the unreliable Parmeno) and returns to the city. Laches blames his wife, Sostrata, for the rift between the two woman (Scenes 3 and 4), rashly invoking stereotypical views of mothers-in-law as the root cause for all such disharmony. Sostrata then declares her innocence to the audience in a monologue (Scene 5). When Pamphilus at last enters (Scene 6), he has been apprised of the reputed conflict between his mother and his wife, but his conversation with Parmeno is soon interrupted by the uproar of female voices (314–318) within the house of Phidippus, Philumena's father. Believing his wife to be seriously ill Pamphilus runs into the house, only to discover the real reason for the clamor (and for his wife's departure from his parents' home): Philumena was pregnant and has just given birth!

The stunned Pamphilus emerges from Phidippus' house and meets his mother (Scene 7), whom he quickly brushes off. Left alone onstage (Scene 8), he nervously informs the audience of the circumstances surrounding the childbirth that has just taken place inside, including Philumena's mother Myrrina's revelation (382–401) that her daughter had been raped before her marriage, and that she plans to expose her unwanted grandchild, who is presumed to be illegitimate (she is aware of the couple's sexual history). It is not until Scene 17 (817ff.), just before the end of the play, that we learn from Bacchis that "the degenerate" (383) who raped Philumena is none other than Pamphilus himself, who did not recognize his victim during the nighttime assault.

The rape occurred nine months ago, and so the baby Philumena has delivered is Pamphilus'.[2]

But until this is surprisingly revealed in the final scene of *Hecyra*, we witness a complicated series of conflicts and confusions arising from Pamphilus' unwillingness to resume his relationship with his wife for *his* honor's sake (403) and his inability to tell others the real reason for his choosing this course (he has in fact pledged to Myrrina not to reveal the rape [402]). These include repeated attempts by Laches and Phidippus to patch things up for their children and Pamphilus' mother's self-effacing offer to leave the city altogether for the sake of her son's marital harmony. More rash accusations are leveled at a mother-in-law (Scene 11), this time Myrrina, once Phidippus discovers Philumena's pregnancy has been kept secret from him, although he knows nothing of the rape and assumes that the child is the legitimate progeny of his daughter and her husband. The old men's frustration reaches its peak when Pamphilus refuses to resume his marriage even after his mother agrees to move to the country (Scene 14). Laches then incorrectly assumes that Pamphilus is sabotaging his marriage so that he can renew his relationship with Bacchis (692ff.), an important misconception for the play in that it prompts the old men to summon Bacchis, whose arrival in turn leads to the final resolution. In the play's finale (Scene 18), an ebullient Pamphilus praises Bacchis as his "savior" (856) for clearing the way for an ostensibly happy ending. But in a departure from more typical happy comic endings, Pamphilus and Bacchis agree (856–872) to keep the entire truth a secret from those who do not already know it, especially Laches.

An expository prologue or a more informative opening scene between characters (as might have been the case in the Greek

2. The audience is given a hint, with Myrrina's mention of the ring taken from Philumena by her rapist (574), that an identification of the rapist is imminent—and so also a marriage, in accordance with the norms of New Comedy (cf. *Samia*, note 20), but at that point they possess no compelling evidence to believe it is Pamphilus.

source play by Apollodorus of Carystus) would have placed less of a burden on Terence's audience. They instead are bombarded with a complicated, sometimes confounding, and largely unfamiliar network of events. In contrast to a more typical plot of New Comedy, the young man or *adulescens* is already married and unusually expresses genuine affection for his wife, but because of his ignorance of *his* being her rapist, seeks to dissolve the marriage, which is in fact the only socially and legally acceptable solution to his crime! He also operates in opposition to his father, who in this unusual case is trying to preserve, not dissolve, his son's relationship with his beloved. In both its plotting and presentation, *Hecyra* thus offers up a jumble of misinformation, misconceptions, and deceptions, along with the potential for serious consequences (esp. divorce). This is a lot for modern readers to sort through and probably was no less vexing for an audience taking in the live theatrical spectacle. While there is no shortage of emotional intensity in *Hecyra,* both for its characters and audience, there is little action and little that can be called comic, as least in terms of the conventions and expectations of New Comedy at Rome.[3] The play perhaps was unsuccessful for all these reasons.

The chief interest of the play lies in its characters and their interactions with other members of their households. There is very little to recommend the male cast of characters, especially the patriarchs Laches and Phidippus. Laches' first entrance, in which he berates his wife, Sostrata, and women in general, immediately reveals him to be an irascible comic father:

> In the name of gods and men, what creatures they are,
> always conspiring and in cahoots
> With each other! I mean women! Always wanting and *not*
> *wanting* the same things!

3. Knorr in Augoustakis and Traill (2013) emphasizes the comic elements in *Hecyra.*

> Search if you like, but you won't find one any of them who thinks differently from the rest.
> And so it is that all mothers-in-law universally despise their daughters-in-law.
> And they share the same zeal and dogged determination to oppose their husbands.
> It's as if they all earned their doctorates in depravity at the same school!
> And if such a school exists, its president definitely is my wife. (198–204)

The audience quickly learns just how wrong his assessment of Sostrata's role—based as it is on stereotypes associated with mothers-in-law—in the current situation is, and this error of judgment calls into his question his broader misogynistic views here as well. Laches, who seems to have abandoned his urban home to female control by moving to the country, cares only about its inner workings insofar as these threaten his public image ("my reputation *outside this house* depends on what you all do *in it*," 218) and asserts that he would have divorced his wife to avoid the current turmoil with the neighbors (221–222). Even after he realizes that he has grossly misrepresented his wife's behavior (777–779), he expresses no remorse and never apologizes to her. His inability to see individuals in any other terms than stereotypes extends to his son as well, as when he mistakenly concludes that Pamphilus must still be seeing his courtesan lover (689ff.). Phidippus' anger toward his wife, Myrrina, is perhaps more understandable, since she has concealed their daughter's pregnancy from him, though not for the reason he assumes. Like his neighbor, Phidippus ascribes a stereotypical mother-in-law's contempt for her daughter's husband to his wife (536–539, 625–632) and makes the same rash cognitive leap as Laches in concluding that all women are naturally malicious (709–710).

Pamphilus, ultimately the play's main character, has provoked considerable negative reaction among modern readers.[4] His first words, "Has love ever placed more pain in anyone's way than it has in mine?" (281), reveal his penchant for self-absorption and self-pity. Pamphilus' portrayal of himself as torn between duty to his mother and his affection for his wife becomes increasingly hollow and self-serving as he invokes his mother's cause to disguise his real motive for rejecting Philumena, namely the offense to *his* honor as the result of her being raped by another man, as he mistakenly thinks:

> As for taking her back, I don't think that's an honorable solution at all,
> And I simply won't do it, however strong our love and intimacy are.
> I can only cry when I think of the sort of life that's in store for me,
> And all the loneliness. Oh Fortune, why are you never in it for the long term? (403–406)

He sticks to this course, even though Myrrina has assured him that the baby will be exposed, and no one else will learn of its existence and the rape.

We obviously run the risk of misapplying modern, more progressive attitudes toward the crime of rape here, but Terence's play departs significantly from the usual New Comedy rape scenario. Pamphilus is drunk when he rapes Philumena (regarded as a mitigating factor in pre-play rapes committed by the reckless young men of New Comedy), but this rape does not happen in the usual festival context, with its relaxed social norms. Bacchis reports that Pamphilus appeared at her house nine months before

4. The case against Pamphilus is made most strongly by Penwill (2004).

the time of the play in an anxious state and after some delay confessed that he raped "a girl he didn't recognize in the street" (828). Further, Pamphilus took Philumena's ring as she fought against her attacker (829). In more typical comedies, some token of identification is required to identify the rapist and effect a marriage between him and his victim (i.e., the stock "happy ending"), but this item usually is something carelessly left behind by the rapist, not a piece of criminal memorabilia.[5] The struggle during which the ring is violently taken also emphasizes the absence of consent by Philumena.

What are all the psychological implications of having Pamphilus bestow the ring in question upon his mistress immediately after his crime? Did all members of an ancient audience share in Pamphilus' and Bacchis' joy at the revelation of the details of the rape (Scenes 17 and 18) or were some disturbed by the extraordinary irony of having a husband who formerly rejected his wife because he believed another man had raped her now happily embrace her owing to the discovery that he in fact was her rapist? In the midst of the ostensibly happy ending of *Hecyra*, there also is something disconcerting about Pamphilus' flirting with Bacchis and the final conspiracy of silence the two characters forge not to divulge the whole story to others, Laches in particular (865–872). What are the pair's motivations for not disclosing the details to all concerned? While there may be pragmatic advantages to this decision, it further highlights Pamphilus' consistently deceptive character, his immaturity, as well as his complete lack of remorse over the rape and its consequences. It also leaves a lingering sense that the play's comic society is not fully repaired. Nor does it seem anachronistic to contemplate the prospects for a comically ideal happy (post-play) marriage between Pamphilus and Philumena.

5. Terence presents another disturbingly atypical (i.e., for New Comedy) rape in his *Eunuchus*: see Christenson, D.M., "*Eunuchus*," pp. 262–280 in Augoustakis and Traill (2013).

The play's single male slave, Parmeno, by his own admission (874ff.) proves to be an inept bungler, of absolutely no use to his younger master Pamphilus, in stark contrast to the more usual role of the clever slave of New Comedy. Because he is such an untrustworthy gossip, Parmeno uncharacteristically must be kept out of the loop by his young master, and for this reason is sent off on a wild-goose chase to the Acropolis by Pamphilus (413–414). He too makes unreasonable assumptions about the apparent rift between Sostrata and Philumena:

> Think of how children argue over the most trivial stuff.
> Why do they do that? Because they're governed by a weak mind.
> And those fickle-minded women are pretty much like children.
> Probably just one single word stirred up all this trouble between them. (310–313)

In the mouth of an utterly failed character who has entirely misconstrued the situation, Parmeno's broad-brush infantilization of women as intellectually frail, child-like others is obviously undermined as well.

Hecyra's female characters are given extensive speaking parts (i.e., for New Comedy), and their words and deeds collectively defy the men's typecasting of mothers-in-law and women in general. The opening conversation between the prostitutes Philotis and Syra pointedly introduces the theme of unfair stereotyping, when the less experienced of the pair, Philotis, poses the question of the brothel's customers, "But isn't it wrong to treat them all the same?" (71). This suggestion that johns might not all be alike is neatly bookended by Bacchis' demonstration at the end of the play that not all prostitutes follow the same code of conduct (see pp. 233–234 below).

The two mother-in-laws, Sostrata and Myrrina, demonstrate profound patience and self-control as their husbands repeatedly misjudge them. Sostrata has no idea why Philumena has left her house and knows that she has done nothing to provoke her departure. She early on makes herself entirely sympathetic to the audience by articulating the injustice of Laches' wild accusations:

> Good lord, it's really not right that a few bad eggs among us
> Stir up such righteous indignation in all our husbands!
> I swear by the gods above I'm innocent of my husband's
> accusations!
> How can I clear myself when men are convinced all of us
> mothers-in-law
> Are evil? That's just not me! I don't understand why this is
> happening:
> I've always treated her exactly as if she were my own
> daughter. (274–279)

Far from being the malicious harpy she is presumed to be, Sostrata scrupulously follows prescribed codes of behavior for the Roman *matrona,* as is seen above all by her devotion to preserving her son's marriage and family harmony, even when this means indulging her foolish husband. She shows her willingness to make the ultimate self-sacrifice for family in deciding to leave the city and her social life there, as she tells her dissembling son directly:

> Your father just now told me how you put me above
> Your love. I'm now determined to return the favor,
> So you can know for sure how much your sense of duty
> means to me.
> I think this is the best course for the two of you, and best for
> my reputation:
> I've decided to go live on our farm with your father,
> So my being here or anything else won't stand in the way
> Of your Philumena coming back to you. (582–588)

Myrrina's behavior is similarly motivated by what she believes to be in her daughter's (and family's) best interests. She no less than Sostrata apparently lives in constant fear of her husband's irrational assumptions (see her frightened entrance at 516–521; cf. 566–569) and is willing to quietly accept Phidippus' unkind and inaccurate depiction of her as a typical mother-in-law opposed to her daughter's husband (536–539) in order to shield Philumena's plight from her husband: "I'd just as soon he'd suspect any reason rather than the true one" (540).

The courtesan Bacchis has been described as a veritable *dea ex machina* (cf. Introduction 6), owing to the role she plays in suddenly resolving all conflict at the play's end. In doing so she completely overturns stereotypes associated with comic prostitutes—especially that they all are only brash, pitiless, and manipulative mercenaries bent on separating men from their money and property. To exonerate Pamphilus of the suspicion that he is still involved with her, she even is willing to meet with her "natural" enemies, married women. Terence has Bacchis do this with full awareness that she is shattering convention and prejudice:

> I'm very happy it was on account of me that all these joys are now his,
> Even if my fellow prostitutes wouldn't like this—and of course it's not
> In our best interests for our lovers to be happily married. But I swear I won't
> Devote myself to evil purposes just for the sake of professional standards.
> He was generous, charming, and good to me while I could be with him.
> I must admit that his marriage was not an opportune moment for me,
> But I know I didn't do anything wrong to make me deserve the marriage.

> It's fair that you put up with the bad from someone who's showered you with good. (833–840; cf. 734–735, 756–757, 788–789)

And in stark contrast to the mothers-in-law, Bacchis actively defends herself and retains her independence of mind in the face of the groundless accusations leveled at her by Laches and Phidippus (Scenes 15 and 16) with an assertiveness that would of course be inappropriate for Roman *matronae.* Most unexpectedly, it is Pamphilus' former mistress who saves his marriage. As Slater aptly comments, "the curious ending of this play leaves us with an ironic but remarkably sensitive appreciation of the position of women within the patriarchal city-state" (1988: 251).

Finally, the female figure about whom much of the play swirls, Philumena, is entirely absent from the stage. Her father shouts back at her as he exits his house (243–245), from where she is soon heard crying out in the throes of labor (316–318). She thus remains a silent and passive vessel in this domestic drama, first as a victim of rape and then as a bearer of the baby that either will destroy or legitimize the marriage, as well as the relationship between the two families. Nor does the absent Philumena escape unfair male censure, as Parmeno includes her in his characterization of women as wanton and whimsical creatures (see p. 231 above). Philumena's identity in the play is constituted solely by views and actions of the male characters.

On the whole, *Hecyra* is a nuanced and emotionally complex play—perhaps too complex for some of Terence's contemporaries who came to the theater expecting more regular comic fare. A central concern of *Hecyra* is the tendency of men, in the absence of clear facts, to make rash judgments about women based on their own preconceptions and prejudices.[6] The play challenges conventions of the highly circumscribed genre of New Comedy

6. For Terence's generally critical attitude on gender and class privilege in Rome, see James (2013).

as well as Roman social norms. The final product may constitute a fairly accurate representation of the emotional lives of two Roman households. We are also granted a sympathetic look into the world of marginalized women, from Syra's hard-edged response to Philotis' concerns about broad-brushing the brothel's customers ("If only I had your youth and beauty—/Or you had my smarts!", 74–75) to Bacchis' exceptional magnanimity in tying up the play's loose ends. Perhaps the enduring success of Terence's *Hecyra* lies in its capacity to push audiences out of their comfort zones.

HECYRA (THE MOTHER-IN-LAW)

CAST OF CHARACTERS (WITH SPEAKING PARTS)

PHILOTIS: a young prostitute

SYRA: an older prostitute

PARMENO: slave of Laches

LACHES: an old man, head of the household

SOSTRATA: wife of Laches

PHIDIPPUS: an old man, neighbor of Laches, father of Philumena

PAMPHILUS: a young man, son of Laches and Myrrina

SOSIA: slave of Laches

MYRRINA: wife of Phidippus, mother of Philumena

BACCHIS: a prostitute and lover of Pamphilus

(*Setting: A street in Athens. The stage backdrop represents the houses of Laches and Phidippus, and the brothel of Bacchis, each of which is accessible through a door.*)

PROLOGUE I[7]

This name of this play is *The Mother-in-Law*. When it
Premièred, one primo of a catastrophe struck,
And no one got to see it or give it a fair hearing.
Why? The crowd was utterly dazed and dazzled

7. This is the prologue of the second (failed) performance of *Hecyra* at the funeral games in honor of Aemilius Paullus in 160 BCE (cf. Introductory Essay 223–224). It probably was delivered by a member of the acting troupe.

By a tightrope walker![8] Today's show is totally new, 5
And its author's not putting on a repeat performance
Only so he can receive a repeat payment.
You've lent his other plays your ears—please do the same
for this one.

PROLOGUE II[9]

Despite my prologist's get-up, I'm here on official business.
Now that I'm an old man, please grant me the same
privileges 10
You did when I was just a young fellow, back when
I took pains to see that instant flops became favorites
Before a play vanished along with its playwright.
Take, for example, the first plays of Caecilus:[10] in the case
of some,
I was booed offstage, while for others I just barely held
my place. 15
Since I knew success on the stage was a risky business,
I made it my business to be all business despite the risks,
And so I persisted in putting on those same panned plays,
So our playwright might be energized into writing some
more.
I succeeded in getting them performed, and those who
saw them 20
Liked them. That's how I took a playwright practically
Driven into retirement by the attacks of his critics
And restored him to his passion, his craft, and to the theater.

8. Roman drama was performed at religious festivals, at which various entertainments might be taking place simultaneously.

9. This prologue belongs to the third (successful) performance of *Hecyra* in 160 BCE: see Introductory Essay 223–224. It probably was delivered by Ambivius Turpio, an actor-impresario known to have produced all of Terence's plays.

10. Popular Roman comic playwright (died 168 BCE) and contemporary of Terence, whose works survive only in fragments and the names of titles.

What if at the time I'd trashed his scripts
25 And directed all my efforts toward discouraging him
And advising him to retire, rather than reviving his career?
Would we have ever seen any more plays out of him?
So now, hear what I'm here for with an open mind:
It's a revival of *The Mother-in-Law*, a catastrophe-plagued
30 Play that never got a fair chance for a full hearing.
I'm relying on your refinement to turn the tide,
And I assume you'll give your blessings to our hard work.
To review: the first time I tried to première it, there were
Reports of boxers (not to mention a tightrope walker too),[11]
35 Flocks of fans, a general uproar, women screaming—
All of which led to my early exit from the stage.
I decided to play it again in my usual manner,
And to test the waters once more: *The Mother-in-Law*,
Take Two.
The first scene's a winner, but then rumors
40 Of gladiator shows start to fly,[12] crowds flock together,
There's a huge hubbub, shouting everywhere, people
fighting for seats.
In the middle of all that, I barely got away with just my skin.
As for today: there's no noise, just peace and quiet.
I've got the opportunity to perform, and you've been
granted
45 The chance to give a dramatic festival its props.
Don't let it be *your* fault that theater becomes the property
Of a privileged few. Instead, use *your* influence
To promote and push for *mine*.
You know I've never been greedy in valuing my art,
50 And have always believed the greatest benefit for me

11. For the various entertainments of Roman festivals, see note 8 above.

12. The second performance of *Hecyra* was held in connection with funeral games for the renowned general Aemilius Paullus in 160 BCE. Gladiator contests were often a feature of funeral games.

Lies in serving your best interests.
And seeing that our playwright has placed his career
In my hands, and put all his trust in yours, join me
In keeping his unjust and carping critics from unjustly cheating him.
And respect his case out of respect for me by giving his play a hearing, 55
So that other authors will take pleasure in writing,
And it'll pay for me to produce any new plays I purchase in the future.[13]

SCENE 1

(*Philotis and Syra enter from Bacchis' house.*)

Philotis[14] Oh my, Syra! There are very few regulars out there
Who end up being faithful to women like us!
Take this neighbor of ours, Pamphilus. He'd swear over and over again 60
To Bacchis—and so sincerely that everyone automatically believed him—
That he'd never marry anyone as long as she was alive.
And—voilà!—he's married. **Syra**[15] Yes, that's exactly why
I keep telling you over and over again not to have feelings for any of them.
Once you have one in your sights, grab him, stab him, and rob him![16] 65

13. The details of production here are not entirely understood: for the general situation, see Manuwald, G., *Roman Republican Theatre* (Cambridge, 2011): 41–125.

14. The root meaning of her name in Greek is "Love," appropriate for a prostitute.

15. Her name ("Syrian") suggests that she is a slave with eastern origins (see further Starks, J., "*servitus, sudor, sitis*: Syra and Syrian Slave Stereotyping in Plautus' *Mercator*." *New England Classical Journal* (Special Issue) 37: 51–64. The conversation between Syra and Philotis here takes the place of an expository prologue (which Terence in fact never delivers in any of his six extant plays), though their exchange still leaves much in suspense (see Introductory Essay 224–225).

16. Syra here advocates the stereotypical behavior associated with comic prostitutes.

PHILOTIS And I shouldn't make a single exception for anyone?
SYRA No one!
Make no mistake about it, not one of them comes here
Who isn't planning to use all his charms
So he can leave happy at the lowest possible price! Really,
70 You *do* have a counter-measure against them, don't you?

PHILOTIS But isn't it wrong to treat them all the same?

SYRA Oh, really? Is it wrong to avenge your enemies,
Or to try to trap them the way they're always trying to trap you?
Poor little old me! If only I had your youth and beauty—
75 Or you had my smarts![17]

SCENE 2

(*Parmeno enters from Laches' house.*)

PARMENO[18] (*calling back into the house*) If the old man's looking for me, just tell him I've gone
Down to the harbor to inquire about Pamphilus' arrival.
Got it straight, Scirtus?[19] If he's looking for me,
That's what you tell him. If he's not, don't say anything,
80 So I can keep this excuse fresh for another occasion.
Is that Philotis I see there? Where's she coming from?
Philotis, very good to see you! PHILOTIS Oh, Parmeno—good to see you too.

SYRA Oh my! Good to see you, Parmeno! PARMENO And the same to you, Syra.
Tell me now, Philotis, how's tricks been with you all this time?

17. For Terentian comedy's unusual interest in the personal lives and psychology of prostitutes, cf. Introduction 19–20.

18. His name means "Trusty" in Greek (cf. *Samia*, note 24), a conventional comic name for a slave who stays at his master's side (*paramenein*), but ironic given Parmeno's overall failures and general absence in the play.

19. A fellow slave in the household.

Philotis Tricks? Hardly! Not since I left here for Corinth[20] 85
With that half-savage soldier.[21] Pure misery,
Having to put up with him for two years non-stop there!

Parmeno My goodness, poor, poor little Philotis!
I'm sure you must have been missing Athens and regretting
Your decision to leave terribly. **Philotis** I can't possibly put into words 90
How much I wanted to get away from the soldier and come back here,
So I could see you all, and enjoy
Dinner parties with you like we always did.
There I could only say what he wanted to hear,
And it all had to be pre-approved. **Parmeno** Not exactly pleasant— 95
The soldier's censoring everything you say.

Philotis But what's up here? That was quite a story Bacchis
Just told me inside! The one thing I never imagined
Would happen—that he'd decide to get married
While she was still breathing! **Parmeno** Get married?
Philotis What? He did get married, right? 100

Parmeno Yes, he did, but I'm afraid the marriage is on shaky ground.

Philotis May the gods and goddesses make it so! Assuming that's in Bacchis' best interests.
But convince me that's really the case, Parmeno.

Parmeno There's no need for it to be public knowledge.
Stop interrogating me about it. **Philotis** Just because you want to keep it quiet? 105
As the gods are my witness, I'm not questioning you about it
So I can publicize it. I just want to know for my own personal pleasure.

20. An important city-state and trade center near the Isthmus, the neck of land that connects mainland Greece and the Peloponnese.

21. A typical long-term client of prostitutes in Roman comedy, consistently portrayed as an obnoxious braggart.

PARMENO Well, my heinie's on the line here, and no matter how much you chat me up,
I'm not putting it in your hands. PHILOTIS Please don't be that way, Parmeno.
110 You know you want to tell me the story a whole lot more
Than I want to have my questions answered.
PARMENO (*aside*) She's got that right—
Gossiping is my number one flaw. (*to Philotis*) I'll tell you
If you promise not to tell anyone. PHILOTIS Now that's your old self again!
I promise. Tell me. PARMENO Then listen.
PHILOTIS I'm all ears. PARMENO Pamphilus
115 Was just as much in love with Bacchis as he ever was.
Then his father started to beg him to get married,
And was really pulling out all the stops, as fathers always do:
"I'm not getting any younger," "You're my single solitary son,"
"I just want some security for my old age."
120 At first he said no, but then his father pressed him
Harder and harder, until he couldn't make up his mind
Whether he was more obligated to family or more to his love.
The old man kept pushing, and finally got his way by wearing him down.
He arranged for a marriage with the next-door neighbor's daughter.
125 Pamphilus didn't take the matter too seriously
Until the wedding day's right upon him and he realizes
Everything's ready, and there's no way to stop it now—
Then he got so sick that I do believe
Even Bacchis would have felt sorry for him if she'd been there.
Whenever he found himself alone and there was a chance
130 to talk,
He'd take me aside and say: "Parmeno,
What've I done? Could I have made things any worse for myself?
I can't do this, Parmeno! I am one sorry, dead man."

PHILOTIS I hope the gods and goddesses blast you for all your meddling, Laches!

PARMENO To make a long story short, he married her. 135
On the first night, he didn't touch the girl.
Next night, same thing—nothing.

PHILOTIS What are trying to tell me? A young man had more than enough[22]
To drink, shares a bed with a virgin, and manages to keep his hands off her?
That's not even remotely plausible. You're lying. 140

PARMENO I'm not surprised you see it that way: no one comes here
Unless he's all hot for you. He was forced to marry her.

PHILOTIS Then what happened? PARMENO Just a few days later,
Pamphilus takes me outside. It's just him and me,
And he tells me that so far as he's concerned she's still a virgin, 145
And that before he actually married her,
He had every expectation that he could deal with the marriage:
"But since I've decided I can no longer keep her,
Parmeno, it's disrespectful for me to treat her like she's a joke.
That's not in her best interests. So what else can I do but 150
Return her to her family just the way I got her—as a virgin?"[23]

PHILOTIS The Pamphilus of your story is certainly tried-and-true.

PARMENO He continued, "I don't think it's in my best interests to make this public,
And it's arrogant to return her to her father when you can't
Find any fault in her. Maybe when she finally realizes 155
She can't be with me, she'll go away on her own."

22. I.e., at the wedding feast, where, Philotis reasonably presumes, wine would have been abundantly available.

23. In light of his rape of Philumena (see further Introductory Essay 229–230), Pamphilus' reported respect for virginity here is darkly ironic, though the audience of course does not yet know of the pertinent events prior to the play.

PHILOTIS What happened in the meantime? Would he go and see Bacchis? PARMENO Every day.[24]
But you know what happens: once *she* realized he's somebody else's,
She got a whole lot meaner and bitchy real fast.[25]
PHILOTIS Small wonder. PARMENO And what really
160 caused the separation,
Was after he got to know himself and Bacchis,
He also came to know the girl in his house better
And took a close inventory of her qualities and Bacchis'.
The girl, as is to be expected of someone who's brought up properly,
Was modest and reserved, and put up with her husband's
165 inconsideration
And mistreatment of her, and hid all his insults from people.
At this point, his heart was overcome by pity
For his wife, and because of Bacchis' poor treatment of him,
He gradually eased away from Bacchis and shifted his affection
170 To the girl once he realized how like-minded he and she were.
Meanwhile, an elderly family relative died on Imbros.[26]
By law, his estate went to the family here, and so
Pamphilus' father forced him (reluctant as he was) to go there.
He left his wife with his mother here. The old man retreated
175 To his country estate, and hardly ever comes back to the city.
PHILOTIS So bring me up to date on the current state of the shaky marriage.
PARMENO I'm getting to that. For the first several days, the two women
Got along well together. But since then,
The girl very strangely has come to despise Sostrata. There wasn't ever
180 A single quarrel between them, no accusations—

24. Cf. Bacchis' claim to the contrary at 751–752.

25. I.e., Bacchis (according to Parmeno) began behaving like a stereotypically mercenary comic prostitute: cf. note 16 above.

26. An island in the northeast Aegean.

Philotis What happened then? **Parmeno** Whenever Sostrata came to chat with the girl,
She'd vanish from sight immediately,
And refuse to see her. Finally, when the girl couldn't put up with it anymore,
She pretends her mother needs her to attend a sacrifice.
After several days of that, Sostrata asked to have the girl sent to her. 185
They came up with some excuse. She has her sent for again.
No response. She sends for her again several times,
And they pretend the girl is sick. Our mistress immediately
Went to visit her, but no one would let her in. Yesterday the old man
Found out about this, and so he's come back from the country. 190
He met with Philumena's father immediately.
I still have no idea what went on between the two of them,
But I'm terribly worried about how things will turn out.
That's the whole story. I'd better be back on my way.

Philotis Me too. I've made an appointment to meet somebody 195
Visiting from out of town. **Parmeno** I hope the gods are with you in that!

Philotis Goodbye and good luck. **Parmeno** Same to you, my dear Philotis. (*they exit*)

SCENE 3

(*Laches and Sostrata enter from their house.*)

Laches[27] In the name of gods and men, what creatures they are, always conspiring and in cahoots
With each other! I mean women! Always wanting and *not wanting* the same things!

27. A common name for old men in comedy, whose etymology may be related to a Greek verb meaning "obtain by lot," and so perhaps suggesting the tendency to get one's way.

Search if you like, but you won't find one any of them who
200 thinks differently from the rest.
And so it is that all mothers-in-law universally despise their daughters-in-law.
And they share the same zeal and dogged determination to oppose their husbands.[28]
It's as if they all earned their doctorates in depravity at the same school!
And if such a school exists, its president definitely is my wife.

Sostrata[29] Oh my, I don't even know what I'm being accused
205 of now. **Laches** Really?
You have no idea? **Sostrata** No, Laches dear, and may heaven help us both!
I just want us to be able to live together with each other. **Laches** Heaven forbid that!

Sostrata You'll soon realize that you've accused me unfairly.

Laches Right, accused you unfairly! Can words even describe what you've done?
You've disgraced yourself and our family, and are bringing
210 your son grief.
And if that wasn't enough, you've turned his in-laws into our enemies instead of our friends.
And after they decided he was good enough to entrust with their daughter!
You're so shameless—you've come here to single-handedly make a mess of everything!

Sostrata Me? **Laches** Yes you, woman! Do you think I'm sub-human and only have rocks in my head?
Just because I prefer to spend my time in the country doesn't
215 mean I don't know
Exactly how each and every one of you behaves here?

28. For the character of Laches and his perspectives on women, see Introductory Essay 227–228.

29. The meaning of her name is "Savior of the Army" (cf. *Lysistrata*, note 9 and *Casina*, note 25).

I have a much better idea what goes on here than where I'm mostly at
For the simple reason that my reputation *outside this house* depends on what you all do *in it.*
I'd been hearing for some time now that Philumena has had enough of you.
That's no surprise, and it would have been more of a surprise if she hadn't. 220
But I had no idea that she'd come to hate our entire family too.
If I'd known that, she'd still be here and you'd be the one booted out.[30]
Sostrata! Just stop and take a look at all the grief *you're* causing me.
I decided to live in the country to oblige you and to manage our estate,
So our income could support all your shopping and "downtime."[31] 225
I've kept working far beyond what's reasonable for someone my age—
And for all that, you couldn't have made a little effort to spare me some grief!

SOSTRATA But it's not my fault! I'm not behind any of this.
LACHES Oh, yes it is!
You were the only one here, and so *you* are the one to blame, Sostrata!
This is the only thing I asked you to take care of. I relieved you of all your other duties. 230
And getting into a fight with a young girl at your age! Aren't you ashamed?
Are you're claiming it's her fault? SOSTRATA No, no! I'm not saying that, Laches!

30. Divorce in ancient Rome was a formulaic speech act (essentially, "keep your property, return mine"); cf. *Casina*, note 33.

31. Laches' rant on women's spending reflects longstanding Roman debates: see further *Casina*, Introductory Essay 166–167.

LACHES Glory be to the gods, for our son's sake! But where you're concerned,
What's to lose? Your shining reputation? You can behave as badly as you like.

235 SOSTRATA How do you know she didn't just pretend she hated me,
So she could spend more time with her mother?
LACHES Really? How much more proof do you need—
Yesterday, no one let you in when you went to visit her.

SOSTRATA No! The reason they said they wouldn't let me see her was that she was really tired.

LACHES My guess is it's your behavior more than anything else that makes her sick.

240 Small wonder, when every one of you women wants your son
To get married, *and* you get to choose who:
You force them to get married,[32] and then you force them to get divorced.

SCENE 4

(*Phidippus enters from his house.*)

PHIDIPPUS[33] (*shouting back into his house*) Philumena, I know I have the right to make you do
Whatever I want, but my paternal feelings are forcing me
245 To cave in and grant you your wish.

LACHES Hey, there's Phidippus! Perfect! He'll tell me what's up.
Phidippus, while it may be the case that I indulge my family too much,
I'm not so laid-back that I'll allow their character to be corrupted.
It's in your best interests and mine to follow my lead—

32. Cf. 116ff. and 686–687 (Laches' own words), where the *paterfamilias* is said to have forced his son to marry.

33. A curious name, with its two Greek parts ("Sparing"/"Horses") paradoxically suggesting both parsimoniousness and aristocratic wealth and extravagance.

As things are, the women in your house have got all the power.[34]
PHIDIPPUS Oh, they do now? 250

LACHES I came to you yesterday about your daughter, but left none the wiser for it.
If you want this marriage arrangement to last, you shouldn't hide your anger.
If we've done anything wrong, don't keep it to yourself.
Either we'll show your information's wrong or we'll clear things up. You can be
The judge of how we straighten things out. But if the reason you're keeping her at home 255
Is that she's sick, and you're afraid she won't get the care she needs at my house,
Then in my opinion you're doing me a major disservice.
And damn it, even if you are her father, I wouldn't assume
You want her safe and sound any more than I do. And then there's my son—
As I can attest, he thinks as much of her as he does of himself. 260
And it's clear to me that my son will take it quite badly
If he finds out about all this. That's why I want her back home before he returns.

PHIDIPPUS Laches, I know how responsible and well-meaning you are,
And that everything is just as you say it is,
But please believe me when I say *I* want her back in your house— 265
If there's some way to do that. LACHES What's stopping you?
Hey, she's not saying her husband's at fault, is she?
PHIDIPPUS Absolutely not! You see,
Once I got serious and started to force her to return, she solemnly swore that
She couldn't stand staying at your house without Pamphilus there.

34. For Laches' attitudes toward women, see Introductory Essay 227–228.

270 Everybody has some defect or another: mine is being so lenient
That I can't say no to my loved ones. **Laches** See, there you are, Sostrata. **Sostrata** No, this is awful!
Laches So that's how it stands? **Phidippus** For now at least, I suppose. Is that it?
There's something I've got to do in the forum now. **Laches** I'm coming with you. (*they exit*)

SCENE 5

(*Sostrata is left alone onstage.*)

Sostrata Good lord, it's really not right that a few bad eggs among us
275 Stir up such righteous indignation in all our husbands!
I swear by the gods above I'm innocent of my husband's accusations!
How can I clear myself when men are convinced all of us mothers-in-law
Are evil? That's just not me! I don't understand why this is happening:
I've always treated her exactly as if she were my own daughter.
280 And my son—I *so* want him to come home now! (*exits*)

SCENE 6

(*Pamphilus and Parmeno enter from the harbor wing.*)

Pamphilus[35] Has love ever placed more pain in anyone's way than it has in mine?
Damn my luck! So this is the life I struggled to save?
This is the reason I wanted to come home so much? Damn!
It would have been so much better to spend the rest of my life anywhere else
285 Than to come back here and find out how awful things are.
When some sort of trouble has been tossed your way,
Every moment before it hits you is precious.

35. His name means "Loved by All."

PARMENO But this way you can find a way to get yourself out of this mess faster.
If you hadn't come back, this quarrel would have been all the more serious.
I'm sure both of them will be respectful of the fact that you've returned. 290
You'll figure out the truth, settle their quarrel, and get them back on good terms.
You've convinced yourself that something trivial is quite serious.

PAMPHILUS Why even try to console me? I must be the most miserable person on earth.
Before I married *her*, I was totally in love with someone else,
But I didn't have the courage to reject the woman my father forced on me. 295
It goes without saying that I was completely miserable then.
I'd *barely* gotten out of that situation and sorted out my feelings about Bacchis,
And *barely* shifted those to *her*, when something happens and I'm yanked away.
Ultimately I suppose I'll find my mother or my wife is to blame—
And once that's done, what can I look forward to except complete misery? 300
My duty to my mother requires me to accept anything she's done wrong, Parmeno.
But I also owe my wife, since she put up with me so graciously then,
And at no point did she ever tell a soul about the things I did wrong to her.[36]
Something big must have happened between them, Parmeno,
To cause such a quarrel that just won't go away. 305

PARMENO Heavens, no! It's trivial. And the truth of the matter is,
The worst quarrels don't always arise from the worst wrongdoing.
It's often the case that one person doesn't even get angry in exactly

36. For the tension between familial duty (here *pietas*, 301) and love, see Introductory Essay 229.

The same sort of situation in which an anger-prone person will become your biggest enemy.

310 Think of how children argue over the most trivial stuff.
Why do they do that? Because they're governed by a weak mind.
And those fickle-minded women are pretty much like children.[37]
Probably just one single word stirred up all this trouble between them.

Pamphilus Go inside and tell them I'm here, Parmeno.
Parmeno Hey, what's that? **Pamphilus** Quiet!
I hear commotion and people running around.
315 **Parmeno** Come on, I'll get closer
To the door. There! Did you hear it? **Pamphilus** Don't say a word!
So help me Jupiter[38] I heard a scream![39] **Parmeno** So it's okay for you to talk but I'm not allowed?

Myrrina[40] (*from inside the house*) Please be quiet, my dear daughter! **Pamphilus** That sounded like Philumena's mother.
I'm dead! **Parmeno** Why? **Pamphilus** I'm so dead! **Parmeno** Why's that? **Pamphilus** There's got to be some
Huge disaster they're keeping from me.
320 **Parmeno** They're saying your wife
Is terribly upset about something. Maybe that's it—I'm not sure.

Pamphilus I'm totally dead! Why didn't you tell me?
Parmeno Because I couldn't tell you all at once.

Pamphilus What's she got? **Parmeno** I don't know.
Pamphilus You mean no one's sent for a doctor?
Parmeno I don't know.

37. For the infantilization of women in the play, see further Introductory Essay 231.

38. For the god Jupiter, see Appendix.

39. Philumena is never seen, but only heard in the throes of childbirth offstage, a stock situation a seasoned audience will immediately recognize.

40. A common name for women in comedy (= "Myrtle"): cf. *Lysistrata*, note 28.

PAMPHILUS I'd better go inside and find out for certain what's up right now.
Oh, my dear Philumena, what affliction am I going to find you in? 325
If you're in danger, I'm just as good as dead too. (*goes inside Phidippus' house*)

PARMENO No point in my following inside after him.
I have the sense they're not well disposed to us:
Yesterday, no one there would even let Sostrata in.
If her illness does get worse— 330
And for my master's sake I certainly hope it doesn't—
They'll say Sostrata's slave was in there,
And tell some tale of how he brought in something nasty
To endanger the life and limb of everyone in the house and make her sicker.
My mistress will get the blame, and I'll get all the pain! 335

SCENE 7

(*Sostrata enters from Laches' house.*)

SOSTRATA (*aside*) Dear me! I've been hearing a commotion in there for quite some time.
I'm terribly afraid Philumena's sickness is getting worse.
I pray to you, Aesculapius[41] and Safety,[42] to keep this from happening!
I'll go see her now. PARMENO Hey, Sostrata! SOSTRATA Who's there? PARMENO You know they won't let you in again.

SOSTRATA Huh? Parmeno? Oh, that was you. I'm a mess. Dear me! What should I do? 340
Can't I even visit Pamphilus' wife when she's sick right next door here?

41. I.e., *Asklepios*, a Greek god of healing.

42. *Salus*, a personified abstraction worshipped in Rome (her temple was on the Quirinal), sometimes identified with Greek *Hygieia* ("Health").

PARMENO *Visit* her? Don't even send someone to visit for you!
In my opinion, loving someone who hates you is stupider than stupid:
You're just wasting your energy and creating more aggravation for that person.
Anyway, right when your son got here, he went in to see how
345 she's doing.

SOSTRATA What? You mean Pamphilus is back?
PARMENO Yes. SOSTRATA Thank the gods for that!
Wow, that lifts my spirits—and what a load off my mind!

PARMENO That's exactly why I don't want you to go inside there now.
If Philumena's pain eases up some, I'm pretty sure
That once the two of them are alone together, she'll tell him
350 the whole story,
Including what's come between you two and how it all started.
But look, there he is coming out now. He looks glum.
SOSTRATA My son!

PARMENO Mom, hello! SOSTRATA I'm so glad you're back safe! Is Philumena
Okay too? PAMPHILUS She's a little better.
SOSTRATA If only the gods would grant it!
355 But why are you crying? Why so gloomy?
PAMPHILUS I'm fine, mom.

SOSTRATA What was all the commotion? Was it a pain that came on all of a sudden?

PAMPHILUS That's what it was. SOSTRATA Any diagnosis?
PAMPHILUS Fever. SOSTRATA A recurring one?
PAMPHILUS That's what they're saying.
Please go inside now. I'll be right behind you, mom.
SOSTRATA All right. (*exits*)

PAMPHILUS Go find the slaves, Parmeno, and help them with the luggage.

PARMENO Huh? They can't find their way home by themselves?
360 PAMPHILUS GO!

SCENE 8

(*Pamphilus is left alone onstage.*)

PAMPHILUS There isn't really any right way to begin my story,
And tell you all the things I didn't expect that've happened to me.
Some of these I actually saw with my very own eyes, others I just heard about,
But together they all drove me out of the house and into this terrible state.
Just now I rushed inside nervously, expecting to see my wife afflicted 365
With some other illness than what I saw—damn!
The instant the slave girls saw I was home, they all shouted out
"He's here!", presumably because they hadn't expected me at all.
But then I noticed a very different look on their faces,
Since my timing obviously was inconvenient. 370
Then one of them quickly ran ahead to report
I'd come. I follow right behind her because I'm eager to see my wife.
The minute I got inside, I saw what her "sickness" was.
The circumstances made it impossible for things to be covered up,
And the only sounds she could make were involuntary ones. 375
After I saw this, I shouted out how shameful it was and rushed out of there,
Crying and shocked by this awful and unbelievable scene.
Her mother followed me out. When I'd reached the door, the poor woman
Fell to her knees in tears. I pitied her. I think I'm definitely right about this:
We're all as high or low as our current circumstances dictate. 380
She then began to plead with me like this:
"O Pamphilus dear, you see why she's left you.
Some degenerate raped her a while back before she got married.[43]

43. Nine months ago: see note 85 below.

She's staying here now to hide the birth from you and
everybody else."
Damn! I can't keep from crying when I think of her begging
385 me like that.
She goes on: "By the goddess Fortuna,[44] who delivered you
to us today—
If justice and the gods' laws are with us—we both beg you
To keep quiet about her misfortunes and hide them from
everyone.
Pamphilus, if you truly ever felt her affection for you,
390 She begs you to grant her this one painless favor in return now.
As for taking her back, you should do what is best for you.
You alone know she's giving birth and that she's not pregnant
by you.
They say[45] she slept with you after two months passed.[46]
And this now is the seventh month since she was married
to you.
395 You obviously know all this. Pamphilus, if you can do it now,
What I want the most and am working hard on is keeping her
father in the dark,
And everyone else too. But if it's not possible to keep them
from finding out,
I'll say there was a miscarriage. I'm sure no one will become
suspicious,
But they'll all think you were its father, which is plausible.
It'll be exposed immediately.[47] This way, there's no inconve-
400 nience for you,

44. Fortuna (= "(good) Fortune") was one of Roman religion's oldest and most august deities; personal and collective prosperity were thought to depend on her goodwill.

45. Pamphilus has told only Parmeno (see 410–411) of the timetable here, and so "they" here perhaps points to the slaves of either household, in whom Philumena might have confided.

46. For the time frame of the pregnancy and the wedding, see note 43 above and Introductory Essay 224–226.

47. For the (common) exposure of babies in antiquity, see the *Oxford Classical Dictionary* (4th ed., 2012) entry for "infanticide".

And, for her sake, you'll also conceal a crime the poor girl didn't deserve."
I gave her my word to keep quiet, and I'm determined to stick to that.
As for taking her back, I don't think that's an honorable solution at all,
And I simply won't do it, however strong our love and intimacy are.[48]
I can only cry when I think of the sort of life that's in store for me, 405
And all the loneliness. Oh Fortune,[49] why are you never in it for the long term?
But at least my last affair[50] trained me for what's happening now.
I reasoned my way through that one. I'll try to do the same in this case.
Parmeno's here with the slaves. He's the last person I need
To be here right now. He's the one person I told back then 410
That I had nothing to do with her at the beginning of our marriage.
If he hears her screaming over and over again,
I'm afraid he'll know she's giving birth. I've got to give him
A job to do somewhere else until she's delivered the baby.[51]

48. There is an underlying assumption here that if the exposure of the child can be kept secret, Philumena is still eligible for marriage with someone else. For Greeks at least, Philumena's physical virginity seems less an issue than her raising an illegitimate child: see further Konstan, D., "Premarital Sex, Illegitimacy, and Male Anxiety in Menander and Athens," pp. 217–235 in A.L. Boegehold and A.C. Scafuro (eds.), *Athenian Identity and Civic Ideology* (Baltimore and London, 1994).

49. See note 44 above.

50. I.e., with Bacchis, which he here indirectly equates with marriage.

51. Pamphilus has told only Parmeno that he and Philumena did not have sex during the first two months of their marriage (410–411), and thus fears the slave will discover that the baby cannot be his. Here Pamphilus unusually plots to send his trusty slave on a wild-goose chase; more often, especially in Plautine comedy, the clever slave tricks the father of the family (*senex*) in this way.

SCENE 9

(*Parmeno, Sosia, and baggage-carriers enter via the harbor wing.*)

415 PARMENO You said the trip was uncomfortable for you?

SOSIA[52] Good god, Parmeno, I couldn't find the words to express
How unpleasant it actually was to travel by sea.[53]

PARMENO That bad? SOSIA Consider yourself blessed to be ignorant of all the misery
You've avoided by never having been at sea!
420 On top of all the other hardships, consider this one:
I was on a ship for thirty days, maybe more, damn it,
And I expected my death every single minute I was there—
Our weather was that bad the entire time.

PARMENO That's horrible. SOSIA Duh? If I knew I had to go back there,
425 I'd just run away rather than return to that ship.

PARMENO Back in the day it took a lot less than that to make you
Do what you're now threatening to do, Sosia.[54]
But look—there's Pamphilus himself standing in front of the door.
Go inside. (*Sosia and the slaves exit*) I'll go see if he wants me to do anything.
Master, are you still here? PAMPHILUS I certainly am and
430 it's you I want to see. PARMENO What's up?

PAMPHILUS I need someone to run to the Acropolis,[55] as in *already*. PARMENO Who? PAMPHILUS You.

PARMENO Me to the Acropolis? Why there?
PAMPHILUS To meet Callidemides,
My host on Mykonos,[56] and my traveling companion.

52. A stock name of slaves in comedy.

53. Cf. note 57 below.

54. For runaway slaves, see *Samia*, note 63 and *Casina*, note 47.

55. The citadel of Athens (cf. the setting of *Lysistrata*).

56. One of a string of islands (= the Cyclades) in the southern Aegean, near Delos.

PARMENO (*aside*) I'm dead! I'm guessing he made a vow that if he made it home safely
He'd bust my hump with running all over the place! [57] 435

PAMPHILUS What's the delay? PARMENO What do you want me to tell him? Or do I just meet him?

PAMPHILUS No, tell him I can't make my appointment to meet him today,
As we'd arranged. I don't want him to wait for me there for nothing. Now disappear.

PARMENO But I don't even know what the man looks like.
PAMPHILUS Here's what he looks like:
Tall, rosy complexion, curly-haired, chunky, gray eyes— 440
Looks like a cadaver. PARMENO (*aside*) May the gods blast him!
(*to Pamphilus*) What if he doesn't show? Do I have to stay there until dark?

PAMPHILUS Yes, wait for him. Now go! PARMENO I can't. I'm so exhausted. (*exits*)

PAMPHILUS He's gone! I'm screwed! What can I do? I have no idea
How to keep quiet about what Myrrina begged me to! 445
Her daughter's having a baby! I feel so sorry for the woman.
I'll do what I can, without compromising my duty to my own parents.
The proper thing's to put my parent before my personal passion.[58]
Yikes! Oh, look, there's Phidippus and my father!
They're coming this way. I have no idea what to say to them. 450

57. A comic twist on the practice of travelers, especially those by sea (a treacherous endeavor in antiquity), who vowed to "pay back" a god upon their safe arrival home, for instance with a sacrificial offering or the construction of a shrine.

58. Cf. note 36 above.

SCENE 10

(*Laches and Phidippus enter via the forum wing.*)

LACHES Didn't you just say she said she was waiting for my son?

PHIDIPPUS Yes. LACHES They tell me he's back. She should come back. PAMPHILUS (*aside*) I have no idea
What reason to give my father for not letting her come back.
LACHES Who's talking there?

PAMPHILUS (*aside*) I'm determined to stay the course I've decided on.

LACHES Oh, it's just the man we were talking about.
455 PAMPHILUS Hello, dad.

LACHES Hello, son. PHIDIPPUS It's good you're back, Pamphilus,
And on top of that, it's great to see you safe and sound!
PAMPHILUS Yes, thanks.

LACHES Are you back just now? PAMPHILUS Just this minute. LACHES Well? How much did our cousin
Phania[59] leave behind? PAMPHILUS Well, turns out he
460 was quite the slave to pleasure
His entire life. Men like that generally don't make their heirs happy,
And usually only leave this epitaph for themselves: "While he lived, he lived well."[60]

LACHES In other words, you've only brought back this one clever saying?

PAMPHILUS Whatever he did leave is profit. LACHES No, it's a loss.
I'd prefer to have him alive and well. PHIDIPPUS There's no risk in your wishing for that:
He's never coming back from the dead. But I do know your
465 preference there!

59. "Little Torch" in Greek, apparently reflecting his lifestyle.

60. Actual Roman epitaphs often record this sentiment and assert that the dead take only what they enjoyed in life with them to the underworld.

Laches (*to Pamphilus*) Yesterday *he* had Philumena brought over to his house. (*to Phidippus*). Say you did.

Phidippus (*to Laches*) Don't jab me. Yes I did.

Laches But he's sending her back soon.

Phidippus Absolutely.

Pamphilus I know all about what happened. I just heard.

Laches Damn those hateful people who take pleasure in publicizing these things!

Pamphilus I'm confident I haven't given your family a reason to find fault with me. 470
Right now I could very truthfully tell you how faithful
And kind and forgiving I've been to her,
But I'd much prefer you to hear all that from her in person.
When she—being the one who's in the wrong now—does right by me,
That'll be the best way for me to gain credibility in your eyes. 475
As the gods are my witness, this breakup was not my fault.
But since she considers herself above either giving in to my mother
Or showing some restraint by putting up with her behavior,
And there's no way they can come to a mutual agreement,
My relationship with either my mother or Philumena has to go, Phidippus. 480
My sense of duty tells me to take my mother's side now.

Laches I'm not unreceptive to what you've said, Pamphilus,
Now that I see you're putting your mother first in all this.
But be careful your anger doesn't lead you astray.

Pamphilus How could my anger lead me to be unfair to her now, 485
Seeing that she's never done me wrong,
Or acted against my wishes, but has always done just what I wanted?
I love her and respect her and miss her terribly.
I know firsthand how amazing she's been to me.
I only hope she can spend the rest of her life 490

With a husband who has much better luck than I do,[61]
Especially now that fate has ripped her away from me.

Phidippus You can keep that from happening.

Laches You're not in your right mind
If you don't tell her to come back immediately.

Pamphilus That's not my intention, father.
I'm committed to mom's best interests. **Laches** Where

495 are you going? Stop!
I said *stop*! Where are you going? (*Pamphilus exits*)

Phidippus Where's this stubbornness coming from?

Laches Didn't I tell you he wouldn't take this well, Phidippus?
That's the reason I begged you to send your daughter back.

Phidippus I most certainly didn't expect he'd be so inhuman about it!
He thinks I'm going to get down on my knees and beg
500 him now?
If he actually wants to take his wife back, that's fine.
But if he has other ideas, he needs to give me the dowry back[62] and get lost.

Laches Come, come now—you're the one being snippy and mean-spirited.

Phidippus (*yelling toward Laches' house*) You've come back here to us with a very stubborn attitude, Pamphilus!

505 **Laches** His anger will let up, even if it's justifiable.

Phidippus You've all gotten high and mighty, now that
A little bit of money's come your way. **Laches** Picking a fight with me now too?

Phidippus He needs to think it through and tell me today
Whether or not he wants her, so that someone else can have her if it's a no.

61. See note 48 above.

62. In Roman practice, this had to be returned in the event of a divorce. Cf. *Casina*, Introductory Essay 166–167.

Laches Come here and listen for just a bit, Phidippus—
he's gone! Whatever! 510
Let the two of them sort it out however they want.
Seeing as neither he nor my son listens to me at all,
Or considers what I say to be the least bit important,
I'm handing this mess
Over to my wife: *she's* behind everything that's happened.
I'll toss everything that ails me right back at her. (*exits*) 515

SCENE 11

(*Myrrina enters from her house, extremely agitated.*)

Myrrina I'm dead! What can I do? Where can I turn?
What will I tell my husband?
Poor me! I think he heard the baby crying:
He rushed off so suddenly to our daughter without saying
a word!
But if he finds out she's given birth, I have absolutely no idea
How I can explain why I kept this a secret. 520
But that's the door creaking. I think he's coming for me.
I'm a wreck!

Phidippus As soon as my wife saw me going into my daughter's
room, she bolted for the door.
Look, there she is. What do you have to say, Myrrina?
Hey, I'm talking to you! **Myrrina** To me, my
husband?

Phidippus Oh, I'm your husband? So you consider me your
husband or a human being at least?
If you'd ever considered me either of these two things, woman, 525
You wouldn't have made a mockery of me by your behavior.
Myrrina What did I do? **Phidippus** You dare ask?
Our daughter's given birth. What, nothing to say?
Whose is it? **Myrrina** Is that an appropriate thing for
a father to ask?
You're killing me, please! Who else's except the man she
married?

PHIDIPPUS Okay, and as her father I shouldn't suppose otherwise. But I'm clueless
As to why you wanted to keep us all in the dark about the birth, 530
Especially when she gave birth on time and the baby was healthy.
Are you so depraved you'd prefer for it to die,[63]
Even when you knew it would strengthen the bond between our families,
Just so she wouldn't have to stay in a marriage with someone you don't like?
I mistakenly believed it was their fault, when it's obviously all yours! 535

MYRRINA I'm so miserable! PHIDIPPUS I wish that were the truth![64] But it just occurred to me
What you said about this when we first accepted him as a son-in-law.
Yes, you said you couldn't tolerate having your daughter married
To someone who was in love with a prostitute and spent his nights with her.

MYRRINA (*aside*) I'd just as soon he'd suspect any reason rather than the true one! 540

PHIDIPPUS I was aware he had a mistress long before you were, Myrrina,
But I've never considered this to be a problem for young men.[65]
It's normal. And he damn well might even come to hate himself for it.
But from the moment you showed your feelings, you never budged an inch!

63. Because she has concealed the baby's birth from him, Phidippus assumes that she plans to expose it (cf. note 47 above).

64. I.e., that she is miserable because she has been falsely accused.

65. Conventional Roman (male) thinking about men's extramarital affairs: see note 66 below.

You wanted to separate your daughter from him and thwart my efforts. 545
The present circumstances prove that's what you wanted.

Myrrina Do you really think that I—her mother!—would be so depraved
As to behave that way, if I knew the marriage was to our family's advantage?

Phidippus Are you capable of looking into the future and determining what's good for us?
Suppose someone told you he was seen going to 550
Or coming from his mistress' house? So what?
As long as he did this infrequently and sensibly,[66] wasn't it smarter
For us to look the other way rather than making him hate us?
If he could just instantly dump a woman
He'd been with for so many years for our daughter's sake, 555
I'd have questions about his humanity and stability.

Myrrina Please forget about his character
And the mistakes you say I've made. Go speak with him alone.
Ask him if he wants his wife or not, and if he says yes,
Return her to him. But if he says no, then I know I've done what's best for her.

Phidippus Even if he doesn't want her and you felt he was to blame, Myrrina, 560
I was here, and the decision to take care of this baby was mine to make.[67]
That's why I'm so angry that you dared to do this without my permission.
I forbid you to take the child so much as one step outside the house!

66. Even the most conservative Roman moral tradition did not disapprove of men frequenting brothels, provided their financial expenditures did not become excessive. Sex with prostitutes was in fact promoted as a much-preferred alternative to committing adultery with another citizen's wife (cf. *Casina*, Introductory Essay 167–168).

67. I.e., as the *paterfamilias*.

But I'd be an idiot to believe she'll follow my instructions:
I'm going inside to order the slaves not to let it be taken out of
565 the house. (*exits*)

Myrrina I swear! Could there be a woman alive who's worse off than I am?
I'm certainly not clueless as to how he's going to take this,
When he's gotten so angry about something much less serious.
And I have no idea how to change his mind.
570 It would only top off a mountain of miseries for me,
If he forces me to raise a child whose father is unknown to us.
As for my daughter's rape: she didn't get a glimpse of him in the dark,
And she didn't take anything from him that could be used for identification.
But he did run off with a ring he snatched off the girl's finger.[68]
At the same time, I worry Pamphilus won't be able to keep
575 what I asked
Him a secret any longer, once he learns we're raising someone else's child. (*exits*)

SCENE 12

(*Sostrata and Pamphilus enter from their house.*)

Sostrata I'm not clueless, son, that you suspect your wife
Has left our house because of my behavior, as much as you try to hide it.
But, as I pray the gods will bless me and all my hopes for you,
I never did anything—at least not on purpose—to deserve
580 her hatred.
I've always believed you loved me, and things are confirming my trust in you now.
Your father just now told me how you put me above
Your love. I'm now determined to return the favor,

68. Such a "token" of the rape will prove instrumental in sorting matters out; in New Comedy, however, it usually is taken from the rapist, not his victim: see Introductory Essay 229–230.

So you can know for sure how much your sense of duty means
to me.
I think this is the best course for the two of you, and best for
my reputation: 585
I've decided to go live on our farm with your father,
So my being here or anything else won't stand in the way
Of your Philumena coming back to you.
PAMPHILUS What sort of plan is that?
You should leave the city and move to the country because of
her foolishness?
I won't let you do it, mother, and I won't tolerate gossipers 590
Claiming it was because of my stubbornness and not because
of your own decency.
I don't want you to give up your friends, relatives, and your
festivals[69]
On my account. SOSTRATA Goodness! Those don't
mean much to me anymore.
I did my share of it all when I was in my prime, and I've had
enough
Of those sorts of things. My main purpose now is not to have
my old age 595
Be a bother to people, or to make them look forward to
my dying.
I see I'm hated here, though it's hardly my fault. It's time for
me to go.
To my thinking, it's best to shield myself from everyone's
hatred.
That way I'll free myself of all suspicion and comply with their
wishes.
Please, I beg you to allow me to avoid the typical prejudice
against women.[70] 600

69. No small sacrifice, as religious festivals, some of which were for women only in both Athens and Rome, were important civic and social occasions. Cf. Introduction 23–24 and 30.

70. I.e., claims of the proverbial wickedness of mothers-in-law, in this instance toward their sons' wives. See further Introductory Essay 227–228.

PAMPHILUS I'd be the luckiest man in every way, were it not for this one thing:[71]
I have such a great mother as you, but a wife like that!
SOSTRATA Please, Pamphilus,
Can't you get it into your head to put up with whatever exactly the problem is?
If things are otherwise than as you want them (and I can see that's so),
Grant me the favor of taking her back, son.
605 PAMPHILUS Oh, I'm so miserable!
SOSTRATA Me too! I'm just as much in the thick of all this as you are, dear.

SCENE 13

(*Laches, who has secretly come onstage during the last scene, now addresses his wife.*)

LACHES I've been taking in your conversation, wife, while standing off in the distance.
It's wise to be flexibly minded whenever that's needed,
And to do what probably will have to be done in the future right now.
SOSTRATA Goodness, I hope so! LACHES So off to the
610 farm. Once you're there, we'll put up with each other.
SOSTRATA I really hope so! LACHES Go inside and gather up what you need to take.
Those are my wishes. SOSTRATA I'll follow your instructions. PAMPHILUS Father!
LACHES Yes, Pamphilus? PAMPHILUS Is mother really going away from here? Please, no! LACHES What do you mean?

71. I.e., the birth of the child.

Pamphilus Because I still don't know what to do about my wife.
Laches What's the problem?
You have no other plan besides taking her back, right?
Pamphilus (*aside*) No, I don't and I'm about to burst out— 615
But I won't change my plan. I'll follow the course that's best.
(*to Laches*)
If I don't take her back, that's what will bring the two of them back together.

Laches You can't be sure. But it won't make any difference if it does or not
Once your mother's gone. Young people find the elderly bothersome.
It's right for your mother to leave. In the end, Pamphilus, 620
We're just "The old man and old lady" in that famous story.[72]
But here's Phidippus coming, and just at the right time. Let's catch him.

SCENE 14

(*Phidippus enters from his house.*)

Phidippus (*shouting back inside*) I most certainly am mad at you too, Philumena—
Extremely mad! By Hercules,[73] your behavior has been disgraceful,
Though you at least have an excuse insofar as your mother egged you on. 625
She has no excuse whatsoever! **Laches** It's nice that you've shown up
At just the right time, Phidippus. **Phidippus** Why's that?

Pamphilus (*aside*) What should I tell them? How can I explain my situation here?

72. The story, whose title may be "The Old Man and Old Lady" (*Senex atque Anus*) is unknown to us.

73. For the god Hercules, sworn to by men, see Appendix.

LACHES Tell your daughter that Sostrata is moving away from here to the country,
So there's no longer any need for her to be afraid of coming
630 home. PHIDIPPUS No!
Your wife doesn't deserve any of the blame for this.
My wife Myrrina's the source of all the trouble!

PAMPHILUS (*aside*) That's fresh. PHIDIPPUS She was the one who created all our problems, Laches.

PAMPHILUS (*aside*) They can stir up all the trouble they want, as long as I don't have to take her back.

635 LACHES Pamphilus, if it's at all possible, my wish is for
This family connection of ours to be truly long-term.
But if that goes against your thinking,
You must take the child.[74] PAMPHILUS (*aside*) He's knows she's given birth. I'm dead!

LACHES Child? What child? PHIDIPPUS We're both grandfathers.
640 Our daughter left your house pregnant,
Though I knew absolutely nothing about it until this very day.

LACHES May the gods bless me, that's excellent news, and I'm glad to know
A child's been born and your daughter's healthy! But what sort of creature
Is your wife? What's with her behavior?
645 The idea that we've been kept in the dark all this time! I can't
Find words to express how wrong what she's done seems to me![75]

PHIDIPPUS I don't like it any more than you do, Laches.

PAMPHILUS (*aside*) I had some doubt about taking her back a while ago,
But there's none now that I see she comes with another man's child!

74. As was his legal right as the child's father.

75. Phidippus, as Laches earlier (532), immediately assumes that Myrrina wanted to expose the child.

LACHES There's no need for any more discussion then,
Pamphilus. 650

PAMPHILUS (*aside*) I'm dead! LACHES We've long awaited
the arrival of the day
When you'd have a child to call you father!
It's happened, and I thank the gods!
PAMPHILUS (*aside*) I'm completely ruined.

LACHES Don't fight against me—take back your wife.

PAMPHILUS If she wanted to be the mother of my children,
father, 655
Or to be married to me, I'm pretty well certain
She wouldn't have kept secret from me what she has.
Seeing that her heart is no longer mine,
And that I don't suppose we can live together after this,
Why should I take her back? LACHES Because this is a
case where 660
A young woman did what her mother urged her to do. Is that
shocking?
Do you think you can find a woman anywhere
Who is faultless? Or do you think men have no
shortcomings?

PHIDIPPUS It's your call now, Laches, and yours, Pamphilus,
as to whether
You think she should be sent back to us or sent home. 665
My wife's behavior is beyond my control,
But in either scenario, I won't cause any trouble.
But what should we do with the child? LACHES That's a
silly question.
Regardless of what happens, you obviously have to give
Pamphilus his child,
So we can raise it. PAMPHILUS A child whose own father
rejected it? 670
Me, raise it? LACHES *What* did you say? We aren't going
to raise it, Pamphilus? Huh?
Really! You'd prefer to abandon it? Why all this crazy talk?
No, I won't keep quiet about this any longer!

You're forcing me to say exactly what I don't want to in his presence.
675 Do you think I'm unaware of your tears
Or what's bothering you so much?
You originally claimed that the reason
You couldn't keep your wife at home was your mother.
Your mother then agreed to leave the house.
680 And now when you have this excuse taken away from you,
You seize on another one: that the child was born without your knowledge.
You're mistaken if you believe I don't know what you're thinking.
After I allowed you to love your mistress for such a long time,
So that you would at long last finally wrap your head around this marriage!
685 The bills I paid for that affair![76] The patience I showed you!
I begged and pleaded with you to get married,
I said it was time. You got married at my insistence.
You acted properly then in obeying me.
But now all your attention is back on your mistress,
690 And by obeying her, you're mistreating your wife!
It's clear to me you've slipped right back into
Your old lifestyle again. **Pamphilus** Me?
Laches Yes, you! And you're mistreating her!
You're cooking up excuses to sabotage the relationship
So you can live it up with her once you've taken your wife out of the picture.
Your wife caught wind of it—what other possible reason
695 could there be
For her leaving your house? **Phidippus** (*aside*) This man obviously is a psychic! He's nailed it!

Pamphilus I'll swear an oath that nothing you say is true.
Laches Then
Take your wife back or say why you won't.

76. Roman children remained under the control of the *paterfamilias* until his death or he relinquished his power (e.g., as the result of marriage), and he rigorously controlled their finances.

PAMPHILUS Now's not the time. LACHES You should take the baby—this certainly
Isn't his fault. I'll see to the mother later. 700

PAMPHILUS (*aside*) I'm as miserable as I possibly could be, and have no idea what to do!
Poor, poor me! My father has got me cornered in with all these considerations.
I'm making very little progress here, and so I'm taking off.
I don't think they'll raise the child without my permission,
Especially when my mother-in-law's on my side in this. (*exits*) 705

LACHES So you're taking off? Hey, how about giving me a straight answer?
Does he seem to be in his right mind to you, Phidippus? So much for him.
Give me the baby, Phidippus—I'll raise it.
PHIDIPPUS Absolutely.
Little wonder my wife has taken this so poorly.
Women are ill natured: they don't take these things well. 710
That's why there's all this conflict—she told me so herself.[77]
I didn't want to tell you that in his presence,
And I didn't even believe her at first. The truth's out now,
And I can see his heart is utterly closed to marriage.

LACHES What should I do then, Phidippus? What do you advise? 715

PHIDIPPUS What should you do? My thought is that we go find the mistress first.
We present her with the evidence, we make an appeal to her, and finally,
We talk tough to her if she has any intention of hooking up with him again in the future.

LACHES I'm right with you there. Hey, slave-boy! Run over to our neighbor
Bacchis' house here. Have her come here at my request. 720
And I can't beg you enough to keep working with me on this.
PHIDIPPUS Well,

77. See 536ff.

As I've been telling you forever and I'll tell once again, Laches:
I want this alliance between our families to last,
If that's at all possible, and I hope it still is.
725 Do you want me there when you speak with her?

LACHES No, you go off while I look for someone to nurse the child. (*Phidippus exits*)

SCENE 15

(*Bacchis enters from her house, along with two of her slave-maids.*)

BACCHIS[78] (*to the audience*) Laches hasn't sent for me without a good reason.
And I have a pretty good idea what he wants.

LACHES (*aside*) I've got to watch out that I don't get less than I might because I'm angry,
730 Or push her too far and regret it afterwards.
I'll go over to her. Bacchis, hello! BACCHIS Hello, Laches. LACHES You must be wondering
Why I sent my slave to bring you out here.

BACCHIS I'm certainly a bit afraid, when I recall who and what I am,
And how my profession creates prejudice. But I can easily
735 defend my own behavior.[79]

LACHES If you tell the truth, I'm no danger to you, woman,
As I'm now of an age that I can't expect people to excuse my mistakes.
That's why I'm on guard against acting rashly in everything I do.
If you're behaving like a good woman should, and plan to keep doing so,
It's senseless and unfair of me to insult you when you don't
740 deserve it.

78. Her name associates her with the god Bacchus and ecstatic Bacchic revels (cf. *Lysistrata*, note 10 and *Casina*, note 92), and partying in general, ironically so in that she plays a pivotal role in restoring order at the play's end.

79. For Bacchis' unusual character, see Introductory Essay 233–235.

BACCHIS My goodness! I should be *so* grateful to you for that!
If you apologized after the insult, what would I get out of it?
What's this all about? LACHES You're entertaining my son Pamphilus in your house. BACCHIS *I am*?

LACHES Let me talk. Before he got married, I tolerated your love affair.
Hold on, I haven't finished saying what I wanted to. He's married now. 745
Look for a longer-term lover while you have the opportunity to think it through.
He won't have the same feelings for you forever, and you won't be young forever.

BACCHIS Who's saying this? LACHES His mother-in-law. BACCHIS About me? LACHES Yes, and she's taken her daughter back in,
And for this reason, she's decided to secretly kill the baby that was born.

BACCHIS If I knew of something stronger in your eyes than my personal oath 750
To convince you of my honesty, Laches, I'd swear by it
That I've had no contact with Pamphilus since he got married.[80]

LACHES That's lovely. But do you know what I'd really like you to do?
BACCHIS Please tell me.

LACHES I want you to go inside to the women and deliver that same guarantee
To them. That will take a load off their minds and clear your name up. 755

BACCHIS That calls for something I don't think anyone else in my profession would do:
Presenting herself to a married woman concerning a matter of this sort!

80. Parmeno claims otherwise at 157–159.

But I'd prefer your son not be under suspicion because of a false rumor,
Or that you consider him too flakey, as that would be extremely unfair
And he doesn't deserve it. He deserves all the help I can
760 possibly give him.

LACHES What you say makes me lenient and well-disposed towards you.
It wasn't just the women that believed this—I did too.
Now that I've determined you're not the person I expected,
Stay the same in the future and you'll benefit much from our relationship.
Behave differently and—I'll stop myself right there so you
765 don't have to hear something ugly.
I'll leave you with this piece of advice: find out what sort of friend I can be for you,
And what I can do *for you*, rather than what I'm capable of as an enemy.

SCENE 16

(*Phidippus enters with a wet-nurse for the baby.*)

PHIDIPPUS (*to nurse*) You'll have everything you need at my house—it'll be generously provided for you.
But once you're stuffed and tipsy,[81] don't forget to feed the baby.

LACHES Look, there's my fellow father-in-law. He's got a
770 wet-nurse for the baby.
Phidippus, Bacchis has most solemnly sworn—
PHIDIPPUS Is that her? LACHES Yes.

PHIDIPPUS Really! Those types don't respect the gods and are not looked after by them!

81. For the stock comic charge of women's bibulousness, see *Lysistrata* Introductory Essay 43 and note 10.

Bacchis Here are my maids: you can interrogate them with the torture-device of your choice.[82]
Here's what's at stake: it's right for me to see that Pamphilus' wife
Comes back to him. If I can achieve that, I'll be perfectly happy 775
To be the only prostitute to have done what all my colleagues don't even dare.

Laches Phidippus, since we've found out that we wrongly accused our wives
In this matter, let's go ahead and put Bacchis here to the test.
If your wife discovers she's believed an unfair allegation,
She'll let go of her anger. And if my son is upset because his wife 780
Kept her pregnancy secret, it's no big deal. His anger will soon pass.
There's definitely no wrongdoing that calls for a divorce here.

Phidippus I certainly don't want one! **Laches** Ask her yourself: she should be able to satisfy you.

Phidippus Why are you telling me this? Or didn't you hear me just now saying
What my thoughts were on this?[83] It's only the women's minds you need to put at ease. 785

Laches And for heaven's sake, Bacchis, please keep your promise to me.

Bacchis That's why you want me to go inside?
Laches Yes, go in and put them at ease. Make them believe you.

Bacchis I'm going in, even though I know the very sight of me today will be hateful to them.
A prostitute's a bride's worst enemy when a husband and wife are separated.[84]

82. A casual reference to the harsh fact that in the Greco-Roman world the testimony of slaves was binding only if extracted under torture.

83. See 722–724.

84. For Bacchis' surprising role here and the theme of women's solidarity, see Introduction 1–3 and Introductory Essay 233–235.

LACHES Once they know why you're there, they'll become
790 friendly.
You'll straighten them out and at the same time clear up
your name.

BACCHIS (*aside*) I'm dead! I'm so ashamed about Philumena.
(*to maids*) You two, follow me inside here.

LACHES I can't think of anything I'd rather see happening to her
than this—
795 She's helping me and storing up favors for free.
If she and Pamphilus really have broken up now,
She knows this is the start of fame, fortune, and renown for her!
In one fell swoop, she'll return his kindness and make some
new friends. (*exits*)

SCENE 17

(*Parmeno enters from the forum wing.*)

PARMENO There's no doubt my master doesn't think much of
my service to him,
800 Seeing as he sent me on a bogus mission! I spent the whole day
Waiting for his friend Callidemides on the Acropolis.
So I sit there all day like an idiot, approaching everyone
who came by
And saying "Young man, can you tell me if you're from
Mykonos?"
"I'm not." "Is your name Callidemides?" "No." "Do you have
a friend named
Pamphilus here?" They all said no, to the point where I doubt
805 he even exists.
Damn, I finally got so embarrassed that I left. But why do I see
Bacchis coming out of our in-laws' house? What business
does she have there?

BACCHIS Parmeno, you're here just in time. Run off to
Pamphilus' house this instant.

PARMENO What for? BACCHIS Tell him that I asked for
him to come. PARMENO To you? BACCHIS No,
to Philumena.

PARMENO What's up? BACCHIS Stop asking questions about what's none of your business. 810

PARMENO Is that all I say? BACCHIS No. Also tell him that Myrrina recognized
Her daughter's ring—it's one he gave to me a while back. PARMENO Got it.
Anything else? BACCHIS That's all of it. He'll come instantly when he hears this from you.
Why are you dawdling? PARMENO I'm not. There's been no chance of that today,
As I've wasted all of it running and walking around for nothing. (*exits*) 815

BACCHIS (*to audience*) Oh, the joy I've brought Pamphilus by coming here today!
I've brought him so many blessings, and eliminated so many worries!
I'm reuniting him with his child, who almost died because of his and the women's doing.
Same for his wife, who he never thought would be with him again!
I've cleared up all his father's and father-in-law's suspicions about him. 820
The discovery of the truth started right here with this ring.
I remember him running to my house completely out of breath one evening
About ten months ago,[85] all by himself[86] and very drunk, and holding
This ring. I was instantly terrified, and said, "My dear Pamphilus, please
Tell me why you're out of breath. And where did you get that ring?" 825
He pretended nothing was wrong, and when I saw that,

85. Ten lunar months = nine calendar months.

86. An indication of his panic, as a free person would normally be accompanied by at least one slave at night.

I began to suspect something big was up and pressed him
to tell me.
The guy confesses he'd raped a girl he didn't recognize
in the street,
And said he grabbed the ring from her while she fought
back.[87]
Myrrina here just now recognized the ring, which I was
830 wearing on my finger.
She asked me where I got it, and I told her everything.
Then we realized
It was Philumena he had raped and the child was the result
of that.
I'm very happy it was on account of me that all these joys
are now his,
Even if my fellow prostitutes wouldn't like this—and of
course it's not
In our best interests for our lovers to be happily married.
835 But I swear I won't
Devote myself to evil purposes just for the sake of professional
standards.[88]
He was generous, charming, and good to me while I could be
with him.
I must admit that his marriage was not an opportune moment
for me,
But I know I didn't do anything wrong to make me deserve
the marriage.
It's fair that you put up with the bad from someone who's
840 showered you with good.

SCENE 18

(*Pamphilus enters, along with Parmeno.*)

PAMPHILUS Parmeno, my friend, please confirm your message is
accurate and un-garbled!
Don't mislead me into pointlessly celebrating a short-lived joy!

87. Cf. Introductory Essay 230.

88. For Bacchis' atypically magnanimous character, see Introductory Essay 233–235.

PARMENO It's been confirmed. PAMPHILUS For sure?
PARMENO For sure. PAMPHILUS I'm a god if it's true!
PARMENO Oh, it's true.

PAMPHILUS Now hold on just a minute, please. I have a suspicion you're telling me one thing and I'm hearing another.

PARMENO I'm waiting. PAMPHILUS Did I correctly hear you say that Myrrina found out 845
Bacchis was wearing her ring? PARMENO You did.
PAMPHILUS The one I gave her a while back?
PARMENO That's so.

PAMPHILUS Who's luckier than me, or so full of Venus'[89] favor?
How can I reward you for this news? How? How possibly? I don't know.

PARMENO I have an idea. PAMPHILUS What's that?
PARMENO Oh, nothing really. 850
I don't see how either I or my news benefitted you.

PAMPHILUS What? The very idea that I'd let you go off without any reward after you
Resurrected me from my hell and restored me to light? Do you think I'm a bum?
But look, there's Bacchis standing in front of our house.
I presume she's waiting for me. I'm going over to her.
BACCHIS Hello, Pamphilus. 855

PAMPHILUS Oh Bacchis, my dear Bacchis, my savior!

BACCHIS Well said, and the pleasure is mine.
PAMPHILUS What you've done makes me trust you.
And you haven't lost any of your old charms.
What a delight running into you, talking with you, meeting you will always be,
Wherever that happens! BACCHIS And I swear you haven't lost any of your old style. 860
There's not a single man in the world who's as slick as you are.

89. For the goddess, see Appendix.

PAMPHILUS Ha, ha! You're saying that about me?
BACCHIS You were right to fall in love with your wife.
I don't think I'd ever seen her in person before today.
She seems like a good person. PAMPHILUS Tell me the truth. BACCHIS I swear by the gods I am, Pamphilus

PAMPHILUS Have you said a word about these things to my father?
865 BACCHIS No. PAMPHILUS And you shouldn't,
Not even so much as a whisper. I'd prefer not to have one of those typical comic endings—[90]
You know, everyone learns everything. In this instance, those who should know know,
But those who shouldn't know won't find out or ever know.

BACCHIS On top of that, I'll tell you how our secret can easily
870 be kept quiet:
Myrrina told Phidippus that she trusted my oath,
And as a result you were exonerated in her eyes.
PAMPHILUS Excellent!
And I hope this matter turns out exactly to our liking!

PARMENO Master, can I possibly be informed of what good deed it was I did today?
Or what it was that you two were talking about just now?
PAMPHILUS No, you can't. PARMENO I'm still suspicious.
(*aside*) Just how did I resurrect this guy from hell?
875 PAMPHILUS You have no idea
How much you did for me today, Parmeno, and the trouble you saved me from.

PARMENO Well, actually I do—I had complete knowledge of what I was doing. PAMPHILUS Oh, *of course* you did.
PARMENO Now
Would Parmeno be so foolishly out of the loop when a job needed to be done?

90. An unusual, but clever metacomic twist on the usual tying up of loose ends: see Introductory Essay 230.

PAMPHILUS Follow me in, Parmeno. PARMENO Right
behind you. To be honest, I've done more good
By accident today than I ever did before on purpose![91]
Now *applaud*![92]

91. Parmeno acknowledges his utter ineptitude in helping out his master, in contrast to the clever slave of Roman comedy (best known from notorious examples in Plautus [e.g., Pseudolus]); cf. Introductory Essay 231.

92. Terence ends his plays with this formal call for applause (*plaudite*) from the audience, though it is not clear if it is delivered by the last actor to speak, all the actors onstage, or a representative of the entire company. Cf. *Casina*, note 98.

Appendix: Olympian Deities

Aphrodite/Venus: goddess of sex and love, incongruously and unfaithfully married to Hephaestus/Vulcan.

Apollo: god of medicine, prophecy, poetry, music, and other "civilized" arts. His chief oracle was at Delphi in Greece, to which individuals and representatives of city-states flocked for centuries to get a glimpse into the god's will by consulting the Pythia, the god's inspired priestess.

Ares/Mars: destructive god of war. In Roman myth, Mars raped Rhea Silvia, a Vestal Virgin, who gave birth to Romulus, Rome's founder, and his twin brother Remus.

Artemis/Diana: a virgin goddess associated with the wilderness and hunting. Artemis played an important role in Greek rituals marking the transition to marriage. Diana in origin was an Italian goddess of the moon, and retained that association for the Romans.

Athena/Minerva: a fierce virgin warrior goddess, but also a patron of crafts and generally associated with skill and intelligence. Athena was the great city goddess and protector of Athens, while Minerva with Jupiter and Juno formed the venerable Capitoline Triad in Rome.

Demeter/Ceres: a goddess of corn, long associated with fertility (the Indo-European root **mā-*, "mother," can be glimpsed in Demeter's name). Ceres similarly in origin was an ancient Italian goddess of growth in general and grain in particular, and so, by metonymy, she often stands for food. In myth, Demeter/Ceres is best known from the story of Hades' abduction of her daughter Persephone.

Dionysus/Bacchus: a god of fertility, wine, and intoxication. In Athens, he was the god who presided over theater, both tragic and comic. The ecstatic cult followers of Dionysus/Bacchus, mostly females called maenads, were believed to be liberated by a madness inspired by the god, who induced unpredictable and irrational behavior in them.

Hephaestus/Vulcan: a god of fire, for which he often stands by metonymy, portrayed as a handicapped blacksmith. He oddly is married to the alluring Aphrodite/Venus.

Hera/Juno: wife of Jupiter and a goddess of marriage; in myth she must constantly deal with her husband's constant infidelity.

Herakles/Hercules: hero and son of Jupiter by Alcmena, to whom Jupiter appeared disguised as her husband Amphitryon. He was promoted to the status of Olympian god following the completion of his many labors.

Hermes/Mercury: god of boundaries, commerce, prosperity, and messengers; he moves swiftly and freely between men and gods, as also the worlds of the living and dead.

Hestia/Vesta: goddess of the hearth-fire. In Rome the cult of Vesta, administered by Vestal Virgins, was considered to be essential to the city's prosperity.

Poseidon/Neptune: a god of the sea, also associated with horses, bulls, and earthquakes. In Athenian myth, he lost the competition for the patronage of the city to Athena.

Zeus/Jupiter: chief god in the pantheon, originally the powerful Indo-European sky and weather deity, husband of Juno and a notorious philanderer.

CPSIA information can be obtained
at www.ICGtesting.com
Printed in the USA
BVHW072118301118
534480BV00001B/6/P

9 780199 797448